Dear Reader,

I'm delighted to welcome you to a very special Bestselling Author Collection for 2024! In celebration of Harlequin's 75 years in publishing, this collection features fan-favorite stories from some of our readers' most cherished authors. Each book also includes a free full-length story by an exciting writer from one of our current programs.

Our company has grown and changed since its inception 75 years ago. Today, Harlequin publishes more than 100 titles a month in 30 countries and 15 languages, with stories for a diverse readership across a range of genres and formats, including hardcover, trade paperback, mass-market paperback, ebook and audiobook.

But our commitment to you, our romance reader, remains the same: in every Harlequin romance, a guaranteed happily-ever-after!

Thank you for coming on this journey with us. And happy reading as we embark on the next 75 years of bringing joy to readers around the world!

Dianne Moggy

Vice President, Editorial

Harlequin

New York Times and *USA TODAY* bestselling author **Heather Graham** has written more than two hundred novels. She is pleased to have been published in over twenty-five languages, with sixty million books in print. Heather is a proud recipient of the Silver Bullet from Thriller Writers and was awarded the prestigious Thriller Master Award in 2016. She is also a recipient of Lifetime Achievement Awards from RWA and *The Strand* and is the founder of The Slush Pile Players, an author band and theatrical group. An avid scuba diver, ballroom dancer and mother of five, she still enjoys her South Florida home but also loves to travel. Heather is grateful every day for a career she loves so very much.

For more information, check out her website, theoriginalheathergraham.com, or find Heather on Facebook.

Jessica R. Patch lives in the Mid-South, where she pens inspirational contemporary romance and romantic suspense novels. When she's not hunched over her laptop or going on adventurous trips with willing friends in the name of research, you can find her watching way too much Netflix with her family and collecting recipes for amazing dishes she'll probably never cook. To learn more about Jessica, please visit her at jessicarpatch.com.

TOUCH OF DOUBT

NEW YORK TIMES BESTSELLING AUTHOR
HEATHER GRAHAM

Previously published as *An Angel for Christmas*

BESTSELLING AUTHOR COLLECTION

Harlequin®
BESTSELLING
AUTHOR
COLLECTION

Recycling programs
for this product may
not exist in your area.

ISBN-13: 978-1-335-46276-3

Touch of Doubt
First published as An Angel for Christmas in 2011.
This edition published in 2024.
Copyright © 2011 by Heather Graham Pozzessere

Yuletide Cold Case Cover-Up
First published as 2021.
This edition published in 2024.
Copyright © 2021 by Jessica R. Patch

Harlequin Enterprises ULC
22 Adelaide St. West, 41st Floor
Toronto, Ontario M5H 4E3, Canada
www.Harlequin.com

Printed in U.S.A.

CONTENTS

TOUCH OF DOUBT   7
Heather Graham

YULETIDE COLD CASE COVER-UP   217
Jessica R. Patch

Also by Heather Graham

MIRA

The Blackbird Trilogy

Cursed at Dawn
Secrets in the Dark
Whispers at Dusk

New York Confidential

The Final Deception
A Lethal Legacy
A Dangerous Game
A Perfect Obsession
Flawless

Harlequin Intrigue

Undercover Connection
Out of the Darkness
Shadows in the Night
Law and Disorder
Tangled Threat
A Murderer Among Us

Visit her Author Profile page
at Harlequin.com for more titles!

TOUCH OF DOUBT

Heather Graham

To Eric Curtis

Certainly one of the world's finest photographers

Prologue

Gabe Lange's quarry was right in front of him.

The chase had begun in vehicles, his a police cruiser. The perp had quickly taken the lead in a stolen Maserati. Still, Gabe had discovered that the police car was well equipped to handle such a race, and he'd been right behind him all the way. In fact, while the con had eventually crashed into a snowbank, he'd managed to swerve to a stop, without even spinning in the snow and ice as he might have done.

Luke had surely faced some injury in the crash; sore muscles, if nothing else. Gabe had come out unscathed. But Luke appeared to be good at disappearing, even amidst a crash, and for a moment—when Gabe had followed him up the first steep hill that led to the road up the mountain—he'd lost him.

He could not lose him; it was Christmas Eve. He

couldn't let Luke loose on some unsuspecting family about to settle down to a Christmas Eve dinner. He could already picture the kind of home where Luke might try to find entry; a couple placing the last of the presents under the tree, perhaps. There might be a crèche set up on a coffee table, a tree with brilliant lights facing the parlor or living room with a multi-paned window allowing the lights to shine upon the snow. Little ones would be put to bed; the father might be doing the last work, scratching his head as he tried to follow the "simple" instructions for finishing a bike or a video system that would be there, big and beautiful, beneath the tree. Here, especially here, in the mountains of Virginia, people had a habit of being welcoming. The houses and old cabins were few and far between, and the neighbors, even those who only came for the summer and holidays, learned to be welcoming and giving. Usually, of course.

Maybe Luke would happen upon the one family who was more than wary of strangers, and ready with a shotgun.

But Gabe hadn't lost Luke; when he came around a copse of trees, he saw him again, limping, but continuing upward once again. The roads here were poorly plowed, but even with snowdrifts swirling through the air and the few feet of accumulation, the path that led to the sparse population here was apparent; it was an indentation in the banks of snow.

And Luke was heading toward it.

Gabe quickened his pace, grateful that he had the kind of body that had been kept in shape; powerful arms and legs, and good lungs. That seemed especially important now. Breathing was good one minute—the air being so crisp, smogless, empty of diesel fuel, the fumes of buses and trucks—and then hard the next; the snow was still coming.

He heard his own breathing as he surged on upward. Luke had a body that was honed as well; young, muscled and lithe. Had he been a gymnast or a sprinter at some time? He was moving just like—just like a bat out of hell.

Huffing and puffing, Gabe kept climbing. When he reached the road, Luke had once again disappeared.

He held very still, trying to listen.

But the snow kept the dried branches of the naked, skeletal trees snapping and the wind that hurried the snow flurries along seemed to whistle and moan; he couldn't hear any other sound.

He turned, searching out the trees, and then he looked to his feet, hoping that the flurries weren't falling fast enough to erase all signs of footprints.

He could barely make them out. Luke had escaped across the road into the trees to the northwest, but it seemed that he'd somehow doubled back....

That realization dawned just in time for Gabe to turn around halfway and almost ward off the blow that came his way when the perp, Luke, cracked him hard over the head with a massive oak branch. The wood was dry and brittle, and he could almost hear it cry out at the abuse as his own head began to spin, and the jarring pain took hold.

Gabe fell to his knees. Luke let out the sound of delighted laughter. "Gotcha!" he said.

No. It wasn't ending here. Gabe wasn't dying in a pile of snow while Luke went on to torment a family on Christmas Eve.

Or worse.

He reached out, glad of his strength as he snaked a firm grip around his opponent's ankle, jerking him off his feet. Luke crashed down beside him. He tried to seize the advantage and jump on his quarry, but Luke rolled, and Gabe was left to stagger to his feet. There was something trickling down his forehead, blinding him.

Blood.

He let out a cry of determination and flew at Luke, tackling him down into the snow. Luke fell once again. Gabe landed a good hook to Luke's left cheek, but he had no time for satisfaction. Luke, bellowing in pain, still managed to catch hold of something in the snow.

A rock.

"Oh, my old friend! The night is mine now. I'm ahead of you at every step!" Luke said with pleasure.

Go figure. Luke found a rock on the road beneath the snow. As proud as a crow, he held it for a fraction of a second above Gabe.

"The challenge is on—and you've lost already!" he said.

He brought the rock down hard against Gabe's skull, and Gabe went down....

He saw the flurries in the sky, and couldn't help but think, *How beautiful. So much on God's earth, even in winter, was stunningly beautiful...*

He slumped down, stars spinning before his eyes, and then fading away to the blackness of a moonless night...

Gabe came to; he didn't know how much later. He blinked away the pain, and pressed cold snow against his face, hoping that would help clear his head. It did.

He tried to stagger to his feet. His first attempt failed; he tried again.

When he stood, he realized that his vision was fine. The world seemed to be a strange shade of gray because dusk was falling. Somewhere, people were watching the extraordinary show of the sun sinking in the west; here, the day was just going from opaque and overcast to the murky gray that promised a very dark night very soon.

Which way had Luke gone?

He brought his gloved fingers to his face, and noted that something was off. He stretched out his arms and looked down at his legs, and groaned.

Luke had stolen his clothing—his Virginia Department of Law Enforcement uniform.

God help him. The challenge was really on now.

Chapter 1

The landscape was crystal, dusted in a fresh fall of snow that seemed to make tree branches shimmer, as if they were dotted with jewels.

Of course, the same new snow that made everything so beautiful could also become treacherous, Morwenna thought, trying to adjust her defroster as the car climbed up the mountainside.

With her initial reaction of, "How beautiful," barely out of her mind, she wondered why her parents hadn't decided to buy a retreat in the Bahamas, Arizona or Florida instead of forever maintaining the centuries-old, difficult-to-heat rustic old cabin in the Blue Ridge Mountains. If the snow started up again—which fore-casters were predicting—the beauty would definitely become dangerous.

"Other people opt for warmth," she muttered aloud.

"Birds do it—they fly south for the winter!" If the snow had started up a bit earlier, she might have had a great excuse not to come.

That thought immediately made her feel guilty. She loved her parents. She even loved her siblings—with whom she'd been fighting all her life. But this was going to be a rough Christmas. She winced; Shayne was going to be miserable. *His own fault.* She'd tried to tell her brother many times that he needed to start working harder at communicating if he was going to save his marriage. Shayne always thought that he was doing the right thing, and, of course, if it was the *right* thing in his head, everyone knew it was the wrong thing. Then, of course, there was Bobby. Baby brother Bobby, hardly a baby anymore; he was on his third college, having come home midsemester twice. Bobby was brilliant, which made her all the more angry with him, but so far, he'd majored in political science, education and biology. Now, he was once again searching for himself.

She was about to stop the car; the flurries were growing stronger, and even in her nice little Audi, the defrosting system was beginning to wear out in the woods on the mountaintop. Her mother had grown up there, but Morwenna and her siblings had not. When Stacy Byrne had met the rising young attorney from Philadelphia, Michael MacDougal, she had fallen head over heels in love, and had left home behind to follow him, wherever he might lead. But she'd lost her parents at a young age, and the house had become hers. By then, of course, it had needed extensive repairs and just about a new everything to remain standing. Her father might have joined a zillion private firms as a criminal defense attorney and made oodles of money, but he liked working in the D.A.'s office, and that was where he had stayed. They had never wanted for anything, but she often felt sorry for her dad—maintaining the cottage in the mountains had precluded any possibility of him buying one of those nice little time-shares in the islands or a warmer climate.

They were all grown up now—well, more or less. Bobby was twenty-one. But every time Morwenna thought about a brilliant excuse *not* to join her family for Christmas and accept one of the invitations she so often received to head to Jamaica or Grand Cayman for the holiday, she always chickened out at the last minute. Was that actually chickening out? No! Honestly, it was doing the right thing. Maybe she was feeling an edge—even an edge of bitterness—because Alex Hampton had urged her to join him for a jaunt to Cancún for an eight-day hiatus, a lovely bout of warmth from Christmas Eve until January 2. Of course, she'd asked Alex to join her in the mountains, but others from their office were going to Cancún, and, he'd explained, he had to go since he was the one who had instigated the trip.

Sure, he'd had to go. Why? He couldn't have just explained that the two of them were dating—no, more than dating. They were together. They should have been together at Christmas.

Well, he hadn't. And—perhaps because he'd been so stubborn, she'd been stubborn as well. And maybe she had hoped until the last minute that Alex would realize he was in love with her, and he had to come with her on a family holiday.

But he hadn't.

So Alex was on his way to Cancún, and she was…

nearly blinded in the snow on top of a frigid mountain in Virginia.

She should have given in, she thought.

But he should have wanted to be with her; Christmas was a time for family!

For a moment, the cabin looked like a shack in the wilderness. Then it seemed that the snow miraculously cleared. She saw the porches, and the extensions of the wings. And from inside, the lights from a Christmas tree. Red and blue, green and yellow, festive and glittering out onto the snow. Her mother's home was reputed to have once been the property of Thomas Jefferson, or at least the property of a Jefferson-family relative. It had been a tavern way back when, and had eighteenth-century pocket doors that slid across the parlor; at night, when the family had finished with the business of the day, children had been sent upstairs to bed while the doors had been opened, and all in the vicinity came to drink—and, she'd heard, plot against the British. During the Civil War, the MacDougals had been what would have been referred to today as "closet" Abolitionists, which had made the place part of the Underground Railroad. It did have history, she thought. She was amused to think as well that, since the area was known a bit for the Hatfield-and-McCoy kind of feuding, it had even survived the aftermath of the war, when grown men had dressed up in sheets as the Klan and come around burning down those who had aided the North in any way.

"So, it's still ours!" she murmured.

She had arrived.

Morwenna wasn't sure if her other siblings had arrived yet, or how they had come, but the garage door was open despite the snow. Her mother wouldn't have wanted them to have to stop to open the doors, and the kids no longer had automatic openers for the door.

She wished that, in all their great wisdom, they'd managed a garage that connected directly to the house. But they hadn't.

She grabbed her bag and, huffing and grunting, dislodged it from her small car. She slipped out the side door and headed for the house.

Once again, she stared at it.

"You're a white elephant!" she said aloud to the structure.

Naturally, it didn't reply.

She began the trudge to the porch. "Home, yep. Oh, yeah, home for the holidays."

Bobby MacDougal added another ornament to the tree, wincing as he heard what had been the low murmur of his parents' voices grow to a pitch that was far louder.

They were fighting about him, of course. They'd fought about him many times in his twenty-one years of life; he was the misfit of the family.

He didn't want them fighting about him. Then again, while his mother had a tendency to view the world through Pollyanna eyes, and his father was more on the doom-and-gloom side and was always practical. But, then, of course, he worked with the worst of humanity at times, and Bobby had to figure that swayed his thinking now and then. On the other side, his mother liked to believe that everything was going to be all right when there wasn't a snowball's chance in hell that it would be.

Still, he didn't want to be the cause of their argument. He'd tried—good God, he'd tried, really—but he hated the law. His father always thought it would be great if he got a degree in anything that was academic, and he had always understood facts and figures, and he honestly loved the different sciences. But he only loved exploration as a hobby, he didn't want to dissect frogs or other cold-blooded creatures that the powers that be had decided were fine to take apart. He now knew what he wanted; he just knew that his parents would be horrified, and so, since he had arrived at the mountaintop a few days ago, he'd tried to keep silent and listen to the lectures.

And those lectures were endless.

He understood that his father was a superachiever, but his father of all people should have understood. Mike MacDougal made a decent living; he might have swept the world away. He had chosen not to, which would make people think that he'd be understanding of the fact that his son wasn't looking to dominate the stock market, just something to do for a living that would suffice—as long as he was happy. Bobby had tried once to explain that he didn't need to make a fortune; he wanted to get along fine. He'd made the argument that when the economy went down, even computer scientists were struggling for a living, and that nurses might be in high demand, but hospitals couldn't pay them. His father always just stared at him blankly.

Bobby looked at the little ornament he held. He hadn't realized that he'd picked it up, or what it was— one of his mom's cherished antiques. It was a little angel with a trumpet. He assumed that the angel was trumpeting the birth of Christ.

"Ah, but maybe you're just a naked little cherub— advertising!" he told the ornament.

He could really hear the voices from the kitchen now. His father's voice was growing aggravated. "Look, Stacy, you're missing the point. He's going to wind up being a bum on the streets of New York, drinking out of a paper bag and asking for handouts. And for what? Because he 'can't find himself'?"

"Shh! He'll hear you," his mother whispered!

"He should hear me—he knows how I feel. You've got Morwenna, working more than sixty hours a week at that ad firm, and you've got Shayne, who works all day *as a doctor,* and comes home to take care of the kids."

"Shayne only takes care of the kids on his day," Stacy MacDougal reminded her husband.

Mike was silent for a minute. "The point is," he said. "He works hard."

"Too hard," Stacy said more quietly.

"If that bitch of a wife of his had just appreciated the time he was putting in for her and the kids, she'd still be with him—and she and the kids would have been here, too," Mike said.

"I am going to miss the children terribly!" Stacy said.

At least they'd stopped talking about him! Bobby thought. *Still, he was sad. He'd cared about his sister-in-law. She had her eccentricities like everyone alive; she had probably just been fed up. Shayne was so seldom home; she had little help and no social life.*

"The thing is this—no matter what, Shayne and Morwenna are going to be all right," Mike said. "They know how to *work.* They'll survive. You know, Stacy, life isn't one big Christmas holiday. It's reality. You have to work to make a living. You have to make a living to have food and shelter!"

Back to him!

He set the angel or cherub or antique-whatever on the tree. As he did so, he heard the purr of an engine and hurried over to the window—the Audi. Morwenna had arrived.

Morwenna would jump right into the lectures with their father. Great. At least Shayne was just depressed beyond all measure, so tangled up in his own misery over his divorce that he wasn't about to pick on anyone else. He'd be able to let Shayne bemoan the loss of his wife as soon as he arrived. Better than listening to the same lecture over and over again.

"Hey!" he cried loudly. "Morwenna's here!"

Bobby hurried to the door, rushing out to help his sister with her bag. He grinned as he saw her; Morwenna was always the height of fashion. She'd grown into a stunning woman, tall and leggy, with eyes so deep a blue they were the kind referred to as violet. Her hair was their dad's pitch-black, although now, Mike Mac-Dougal's hair was definitely showing more than minor touches of distinguished gray. Morwenna's hair, however, was the old MacDougal hair, as lustrous as a raven's wing. And stylish, of course. Perfectly coiffed. She was in advertising and marketing, and he knew that in her mind, people trusted you to make them look good when *you* looked good.

"Baby bro!" she said, dropping the suitcase to give him a fierce hug.

That's the way it always started out; hugs and kisses and warmth and happiness.

Then...drumroll...the sniping began!

"Hey, big sis," he said. He frowned, looking around. "Where's the boy toy?"

She looked at him with irritation. "*Alex* is in Cancún. He couldn't get out of it. I guess he planned it before he knew that I had to come home. He kept trying to get me to go, but…"

"Ah, poor girl! Cancún. Hmm. And he went without you," Bobby said.

"It's business, Bobby. He had others in the firm going with him."

"Sure," Bobby said.

"Let's get this inside. I can do the carrying. Was it bad getting up?"

"Horrible."

"I hope that Shayne is close behind," Bobby said.

"Hey, I'm just glad that Shayne is coming! I've talked to him, and he is just about the most depressed man in the world right now," Morwenna said, her voice troubled. "I hope he doesn't back out and work hundred-hour emergency shifts just to have something to do."

"Shayne is coming. He said he might not have the ex or his kids, but we'd be the best place a depressed lonely guy could be for Christmas," Bobby assured her.

"*Our* family is the best group to be with when you're depressed?" She laughed.

He grinned. "Family—the only people you can rip to shreds in the name of love! Naw, we'll make him feel better."

"Good. At least, I think so!" Morwenna said. She glanced at him. "Well, how's it going for you?"

"Fine."

She looked at him skeptically. "Honestly, though, Bobby, you dropped out again?"

He sighed. "I didn't drop out, Morwenna. I finished the semester."

"But you're not going back?"

Lord, save me! Maybe God heard; before Bobby could answer, he heard the crunch of a car's tires on the snow. "Hey, it's Shayne!"

He should feel guilty; his manically depressed brother had arrived. Now, they could all worry about Shayne's problems!

"Yeah, it's Shayne," Morwenna said. She shaded her eyes against the glare on the snow. "He's not alone. Who is that?"

"Think he picked up a hot babe for Christmas?" Bobby asked.

Morwenna elbowed him. "Shayne...with someone he met in the last few days?"

"No, no, too small. It's the kids," Bobby said. "Looks like Connor is in the front, and that's Genevieve in the back."

Shayne stopped the car in the driveway. Bobby thought that the kids were so excited that they had to get out. Connor had just turned nine, and Bobby was sure that the divorce was hard on him. Though Genevieve was just six, it seemed that she actually comprehended the change with the flexibility young children seemed to have.

She jumped out of the car. "Uncle Bobby!" And rushed him like a guard about to tackle. For a moment he caught his sister's expression. She seemed a little hurt, and a little jealous.

But, then, he'd taken a lot more trouble to make sure that he'd seen his nephew and niece over the years; he knew that Morwenna always meant to.

She was just busy.

"Hey, little one!" Bobby said. He hiked her up on

his hip. "Give Aunt Wenna a nice smooch right on the cheek there!"

Genevieve did; and she reached out with a cherubic smile. Morwenna took her, giving her a good hug and a kiss back. She looked at Bobby. Was there even a bit of gratitude in that glance?

Then Connor came flying out of the front, racing to them. He just gave Bobby a hug; Bobby opted not to pick him up. It might be against the boy's dignity. Besides, at nine, Connor was tall and solid.

The car moved on into the garage.

"Didn't know you were coming, munchkins," Bobby said.

"We weren't—then Mommy said we might have a better time with Daddy. And she said that we might really hurt Gram and Gramps if we didn't come," Connor said.

"Yep, she said that Connor and I were lucky to be loved by so many people," Genevieve said.

Yes, Bobby thought, *his sister-in-law—or ex-sister-in-law—would have said just such a thing, and meant it. She'd never known her own grandparents, and her parents had died the year before she'd met Shayne.*

Shayne had emerged from the car by then and was walking toward them. "Hey, family," he said. He was trying to smile.

"You got the kids!" Morwenna said.

"Yeah. Yeah," Shayne said reflectively. Shayne, Bobby thought, was just as pretty as Morwenna—in a manly sort of way, of course. His brother was a good six foot three with the same dark hair and deep blue eyes. He was fit, and his posture was as straight as an iron girder. He had embraced being a physician, and lived well. Bobby had smoked on and off, over the years; he'd given it up last time because his brother had tortured him so much that the withdrawal was easier than listening to Shayne's speeches.

"That's great," Morwenna said. "That was kind of Cindy."

Shayne sniffed. "Yeah. Kind. She's heading to Europe with the new love of her life. She decided that the kids might be a hindrance."

"Hey!" Morwenna said, frowning. Shayne had the grace to wince, realizing that both his children were there, listening.

Shayne hunkered down by Genevieve. "Hey, guys, remember the rules at Gram's house—you don't come outside without someone here. What's the other rule—do you remember, Connor?"

Connor nodded gravely. "Never take the side path out to the garage or shed in winter. Never. Never, never, never. The snow hides the slope and we could fall and get hurt."

"Good," Shayne said. "Now, Genevieve?"

Genevieve giggled. "Oh, Daddy! We know where the path is!"

"Genevieve, don't come outside without an adult ever," Shayne said. His voice had taken on an angry tone. "I'm serious."

Connor came closer to his sister. "She knows, Dad. She just likes to argue lately. It's a kid thing."

Shayne nodded, looking at his son with gratitude.

Genevieve hugged him. "I'm sorry, Daddy. I wish Mommy was here, too. She makes good snowmen."

Shayne nodded. "Yes, she makes good snowmen, but she is off on a trip, so we'll have to make do with whatever Uncle Bobby and the rest of us can come up with. Now, run in and give big smooches and hugs to Gram and Gramps, okay? You're going to be the best surprise for them!" Shayne said.

"Shayne," Bobby said quietly. "You've got to be careful."

"I know, I know. Sometimes I can't help it," Shayne said.

"Shayne, damn it. Bobby is right!" Morwenna said firmly. "Cindy is *not* a bad human being, and she was never a bad mother. I told you, she needed more time from you. She held down the fort when the kids were babies—I doubt if you ever changed a diaper—and—"

"Stop it, Morwenna! I changed plenty of diapers," Shayne said. "You weren't around much, so how the hell are you going to tell me what I did and didn't do! I was working—"

"Come on, Wenna," Bobby said. "Shayne was a good dad—you really do work a lot—"

"Better than you, who can't even get the hell through school?" Morwenna interrupted angrily.

Before he could answer, they all froze in silence.

They'd heard...*something*.

"What was that?" Morwenna asked. She frowned, turning around. "We're the only shack up here!"

"House," Bobby said.

"Whatever. You have to head down to the lower peak just to get to the tavern," Morwenna said.

"Maybe it was nothing," Shayne said. "Or," he added, giving her a rueful smile, "the voice of God, warning us not to go inside like squabbling children."

"And lay off each other," Bobby added softly. "We are supposed to be adults."

"No…toward the trees," Morwenna said, frowning.

The sound came again. It was definitely a groan.

"There is someone up here," Shayne said. He started walking.

Morwenna ran after him, leaping like a rabbit through the snow. "Shayne, stop. Let me get Dad, and his gun."

"Morwenna, let's see what it is," Bobby said.

"It's a man—I can hear human groans," Shayne said.

Bobby rushed past Morwenna and grabbed her hand. "Come on—he wouldn't be groaning if he was dangerous!"

"It could be a criminal," Morwenna warned.

"Up here? A criminal came all the way up here to groan by our shack? Please!" Bobby said.

Shayne was in the lead, striding through the snow, with Bobby—dragging Morwenna along—following.

Right at the copse that bordered the snow-driven path, there was a man half buried in the drifts. As Shayne hunkered down by him, reaching for a pulse, Bobby studied him.

He appeared to be about thirty, with tawny blood-matted hair and a face with aesthetic contours, although they were half concealed, since he was on his side in the snow.

"He's alive," Shayne said. "Steady enough pulse, though it's slow."

"We've got to get him in," Bobby said.

"In! He *could* be a criminal," Morwenna insisted.

"Wenna!" Shayne looked across the fallen body at his sister. "What should I do? Leave him out here to freeze to death? I'm a *doctor*. I can't do that."

"Well, of course, we can't let him freeze to death," Morwenna said. "It's just that…he's a total stranger."

"So what other choice do we have?" Shayne asked.

"Morwenna, it will be okay," Bobby assured her. "Hey, there's a pack of us, and one of him. It's going to be all right. And Dad does have his shotgun."

"Can he actually shoot?" Morwenna asked.

"Well, I've seen him go skeet shooting," Bobby said, grinning. "I think he hit a few plates."

"What? When?" Morwenna asked.

"When we were kids, remember? We were in Memphis. The parental units brought us all on a canoeing vacation, and we went to see Graceland. It was great, if I recall."

"Yeah," Morwenna said, lowering her eyes. "It was great, wasn't it?" she said softly.

"Doesn't matter right now whether Dad can hit the eye of a needle or miss the side of a barn, it's freezing out here," Shayne said. He had deftly run his hands over the stranger, checking for broken bones or other injuries. "Seems like just his head is bleeding. Maybe he got stranded, got out of his car and fell. God knows, this place has lots of rocks, for certain. Wenna, back up. Bobby, get around over there."

"I'm not puny—I can help," Morwenna said.

"I know that you're the queen of Pilates, Morwenna, but let Bobby help me right now," Shayne said.

"All right, all right, I'll get the door. Be careful, you two. Maybe he's faking it."

"One, two, three…lift beneath the shoulders," Shayne said.

"Your children are inside that house," Morwenna said worriedly.

"You know he could sue you if we injure him more, Shayne," Bobby said, still not having moved.

"That can't be helped—he'll freeze. He might be in shock…he might well be on the way to hypothermia," Shayne said. "Look, we have to move him, or he'll die."

"I guess that we really have no choice. We can't—"

"No, but…we can't let him just stay here. I guess we can't ask questions or get to know him," Morwenna said.

"I just hope we don't hurt him worse," Bobby said.

Bobby did as his brother instructed, dipping low, and sliding his arm beneath the stranger's back while Shayne carefully did the same from his angle. The stranger groaned again as they managed to get him to his feet.

"It's all right, it's all right!" Shayne said quickly. "We're bringing you in. We're trying to help you."

The man had green eyes, Bobby noted. Strange green eyes. They were actually a greener color than he'd *ever* seen before, and also weirdly translucent.

He noted that Morwenna was staring at the man, looking into his eyes.

And the man was staring back at her.

He managed a single whisper. "Thank you."

She turned and hurried to the house while they followed more slowly with the injured man.

Morwenna opened the door and stood back. Shayne and Bobby staggered toward it, and paused in the doorway, catching their balance.

She looked at Bobby. "Well, this will be different," she said softly. "I can't help but wonder just *who* in the hell we've invited in for Christmas?"

Chapter 2

"What in the name of—" Mike MacDougal began, hurrying into the parlor as his sons stumbled in with the bleeding stranger.

Morwenna looked at her father; she was worried about what they were doing, herself, but to avoid a family argument over Shayne's absolute determination to be a physician at all times, she waved a hand in the air.

"This guy was out there hurt, Dad," she said. "We have to help him."

Stacy, drying her hands on a dish towel, came hurrying into the parlor as well.

"Oh, no! The poor man. Get him onto the sofa, Shayne. Oh, he's bleeding! I'll get a clean washcloth and warm water. I'll—" Stacy began.

"Hey!" Mike protested. "Bleeding, in the snow, in the middle of nowhere? How the hell did he get here?

How do we know he's not an escaped convict or mass murderer?"

"That's what I said, Dad," Morwenna replied, setting a hand firmly on his chest. "But your son, the physician, refused to allow anyone to bleed to death. Now, Dad—move, please!"

Mike groaned, staring at the man on the sofa. "If you saw everything that I saw, you'd be more careful," he said.

"Dad?" Shayne said.

Genevieve and Connor appeared in the kitchen doorway—just their little heads popping out.

Morwenna hurried toward them. "Hey, little ones. Want to do me a favor? Run upstairs to my bedroom and bring me one of the pillows off my bed. And a blanket, huh? Can you do that?"

They both nodded at her gravely. "Don't worry," Connor told her. "My father will help that man."

"Of course he will," Morwenna said.

She went into the kitchen. Her mother was already filling a basin with warm water; she walked to the pantry and found a stack of fresh linens. "Mom, can I take these?"

Her mother glanced at her. "Of course! You can take anything. The guy's bleeding!"

Stacy was ready with the basin. Morwenna grabbed the towels and they returned to the parlor. Shayne nodded his gratitude and took the basin and the towels. "Looks like he took a good wallop to the side of his head…and there, on his temple. I'm going to need my bag. It's still in the car."

"I'm on it," Bobby said. He turned and exited by the front door.

"Don't just hover!" Shayne said, looking up at Morwenna and his parents as he began to dab carefully at the stranger's wounds. "I think he needs to breathe, too, you know?"

They all stared blankly at him for a minute, and then took a step back.

The kids came clunking down the stairway, bearing a blanket and pillow.

"Good, good, let's get his head propped up," Shayne said. He glanced at his sister, perhaps surprised she'd asked that one of *her* pillows be used for the cause.

She shrugged and watched her older brother as he moved the stranger's head carefully. "His vital signs are growing stronger. I think the blow weakened him and the cold did the rest," he told them. "Of course, I can't make sure he hasn't suffered any serious head trauma until we get him to a hospital."

The stranger stirred. By now, Shayne had washed away the little trails of blood that had streaked down his face.

It was a good face, Morwenna thought. *Nicely chiseled, a bit like the statues she'd seen of Greek and Roman gods. Except, of course, he had a slightly more rugged appeal. Actually, he was a very nice-looking stranger.*

And still a stranger! she warned herself.

They needed him out of their house.

His eyes flew open as she entertained that thought. He was looking straight at her.

She was surprised when she knelt down and touched his cheek. "Hey, it's all right. *You're* all right. We're the MacDougal family. We found you outside in the snow.

Do you know who you are? Do you know what you're doing up here? You're hurt."

"Morwenna," Shayne said. "One question at a time for the poor man."

The stranger struggled to sit up and winced. Shayne pressed him back down by the shoulders. "Don't try to get up yet. Let's see how you do. Someone hit you good."

He eased back for a minute, closing his eyes again. "Yeah, someone hit me good. Um…my name is Gabe."

They all looked around at one another. "I'm Gabe," he repeated. "Gabe Lange." He winced, and opened his eyes again. "Could I possibly have some water, please?"

"Water, of course," Stacy said, and turned toward the kitchen.

"Move slowly, and when the water comes, take your first drink slowly," Shayne instructed.

Stacy returned quickly with the water. Morwenna thought that actually, it must have been pretty scary for him to open his eyes, to find all of them looking down at him as if he were an unknown wounded creature they had dragged in.

But, then again, he was.

She glanced at Bobby, who seemed to be a step ahead of her. "Hey, urchins!" he said to Connor and Genevieve. "Let's give your dad the doc some space. I need some help upstairs with presents."

"But…is that guy going to be okay?" Connor asked.

Genevieve's little lips were trembling. Morwenna turned toward her niece. "Yes, of course, my darling. Go on up with Uncle Bobby. The nice man just needs some rest." She glanced at Shayne. Was that all he needed?

"Come on, Lady Niece, Lord Nephew!" Bobby said.

The kids followed him up the stairs.

Morwenna suddenly found herself thinking all kinds of horrible thoughts. He wasn't all right; he was bleeding internally, and he was going to die on her mother's sofa on Christmas.

She lowered her head quickly. What a horrible concept! A man's life could be in the balance, and she was thinking that his death might affect their Christmas!

The stranger's gaze was on her when she raised her head again. A small smile tugged at his lips as if he had read her thoughts. "I'm strong, really. I'm feeling better already."

"Well, lie still until I've gotten that wound cleaned up," Shayne said firmly.

Gabe winced when Shayne laced the wound with disinfectant, but he didn't let out a sound. "The thing is, you probably do have a concussion," Shayne told him. "You'll need to be careful."

"One of us can stay with him and keep an eye on him," Stacy said.

"I'm going to call an ambulance," Mike told her, speaking up. "Any objections?" he asked. He wasn't speaking to the stranger; he was looking at his wife, daughter and son.

"Not to an ambulance," Shayne assured his father. "What the heck happened to you?"

"Obviously, he got into a fight!" Mike jumped in, his voice harsh.

"I'm with the Virginia State Police," Gabe said. "I was after a man. He eluded me."

"Gabe Lange, with the Virginia State Police?" Mike demanded. Her father sounded as if he was interrogating a prisoner of war. Maybe, in his mind, he was.

"There's nothing to worry about," Gabe assured them. He looked at Morwenna and grimaced. "I was an idiot. I let him get away. But I crawled up here before I passed out. I'm afraid he's long gone."

"I'll call that ambulance," Mike said, reaching into his pocket for his cell phone. He stared at Gabe while he dialed. Nothing happened, and he frowned at his phone: "3G, 4G—10G! I don't care how many *Gs* you have, the damned things never work in some places. They're all full of it. Wenna, you're on a different carrier—try your phone."

"Okay, Dad, let me just see where I dropped my purse," she said. She had dropped it inside, hadn't she? Maybe not.

"I think it's outside," she said.

"Morwenna Alysse MacDougal!" her father said. "What have I taught you about—"

"Hurt guy on the sofa, Dad," Morwenna said. "You always told me that human life was worth more than anything I could possibly own, remember?"

He scowled at her. She hurried outside. She had dropped her purse somewhere out there. It took her a few minutes, but she found it and walked back in the house, pulling her cell phone from it as she did so.

"What number do you want me calling?" she asked.

Mike MacDougal looked at their uninvited guest. "Nine-one-one, of course."

She dialed. She looked at the phone—it, too, said that she was out of range. "Sorry," she told him.

"Well, what the hell is going on?" Mike demanded. "We always have decent satellite coverage up here."

"Dad, calm down—it might be the storm," Shayne told his father.

"Try your phone, Shayne," Mike insisted.

Shayne sighed. She was standing again; he'd patched up Gabe Lange's head nicely, and there was color returning to the man's cheeks. He did look well enough to sit up. He might be entrenched on the couch with her blanket warming him, but she did think then that he must be wet and freezing beneath the covers.

"No bars, Dad. No coverage. It's one hell of a storm brewing up," Shayne said.

Mike snapped his fingers. "Let me see if I can get them out here online!"

He headed for the computer in his office, just down the hall from the stairway.

"Thank you," Gabe told Shayne. "Thank you for patching me up—a stranger on your doorstep."

"Hippocratic oath," Shayne said, grinning. "We're not supposed to trip over the injured and ignore them."

"If I hadn't fallen where I had…if you all hadn't seen me…" Gabe said.

Mike came storming back in from the office. "The goddamn cable is down!" he said irritably.

"Mike! It's Christmas. For the love of *God*—watch your language!" Stacy said.

"Mom, Dad, *please,* both of you!" Morwenna murmured.

"Dad, you don't need the cops anyway—he *is* a cop," Shayne said.

"Likely story!" Mike said.

"Mike!" Stacy gasped.

"Dad!" Shayne and Morwenna said in unison.

They didn't deter their father at all. He turned on Gabe Lange. "I have a shotgun in this house, and I know how to use it. I'm a district attorney in Philadelphia, young man, and I know my way around crooks. And if you're a cop, where's your gun? Eh? Where's your uniform?"

"My gun was lost quickly—I try never to use firearms. Innocent people get hurt as often as the bad guys, so it seems. But, yeah, I carry a weapon. Now it's gone, somewhere in a bush halfway up the mountainside," Gabe said. "Look, sir, I'm not here to hurt anyone, I swear it!"

"And so the devil swears!" Mike muttered, and walked away.

"Sorry, the lawyer side of my husband is always angry. But he's a really good man," Stacy told Gabe. Then, she suddenly thrust her hand forward. "I'm Stacy, my husband is Mike. Your real live doctor is Shayne, and this is our daughter, Morwenna. She's an artist and advertising exec. She took business as well as art. Don't you think that was incredibly smart? She is able to use her talent *and* keep a job, and—"

"Mom!" Morwenna said, interrupting her quickly. She glared at her mother, meaning, *Let's not just air the family laundry.*

"He doesn't need a dossier on all of us!" she added and laughed to soften the statement. "To finish the introductions in the family, my little brother is Bobby, and Shayne's kids are named Connor and Genevieve. Welcome to our home for Christmas. I'm so sorry about what happened to you. Won't your family be worried?"

Gabe looked away from her for a moment. "I have a huge extended family, but my immediate family wasn't expecting me. They'll be fine without me—there's a lot of work that goes on tonight. I'm grateful that you've taken me in."

Shayne squeezed his shoulder. "I would be happier if you were in a hospital," he said.

Gabe pushed back the blanket and sat up, despite Shayne's protests. "I'm not even dizzy anymore. I swear," he said. "I'm not sure I'd want to hit the ring for a few bouts or anything, but I'm doing fine."

"Then sit."

"I'm sitting," Gabe said.

His teeth began to chatter.

Shayne brought out his little light, and told Gabe to follow the beam. He inspected their guest's eyes with a serious expression, then let out a sigh and shrugged. "Your pupils are showing no signs of a possible problem."

"He's fine, but he's freezing," Morwenna said. "He must be soaked."

"Oh, how very rude of us," Stacy said. She looked at her oldest son. "Shayne, there must still be jeans and T's and flannel shirts up in your room. Can you loan something to Mr. Lange?"

"Gabe, please," their visitor insisted. "I *am* on your sofa."

"Of course." Shayne seemed troubled, but he shook his head. "We'll head up to my old room. You can get out of those wet clothes, take a shower and then put on something dry and warm."

"That would be great. My most sincere gratitude to you all," Gabe said.

"I'll give you a hand getting up," Shayne said. "Use the banister—I'll support you on the other side."

Morwenna hovered, watching as they started up the stairs. "Great kids," Gabe told Shayne.

He didn't ask about their mother; somehow, Shayne volunteered information.

"Yes, they're great kids. They've stayed that way through the divorce," Shayne said.

"Most important thing to remember in a divorce—your children still have you both as parents, the people they love most in the world. I'm glad to hear that you and your ex are respecting one another. You should be proud."

Morwenna didn't get to hear her brother's answer; they were already up the stairs.

Her father emerged from the kitchen, a glass in his hand.

"What the hell is going on?" he demanded.

"Honestly, Mike, it's Christmas!" Stacy said.

"Shayne is giving him something to wear that isn't soaked with snow," Morwenna said.

"I'm getting the shotgun," Mike said. "I just don't trust that guy. I'm going to have it on hand at all times."

Genevieve, unsurprisingly for her age, was not an ace at wrapping packages. In a few instances when he didn't cut the paper quickly enough, she cut pieces that were too small. Small items, stocking stuffers, were wrapped in enough paper to conceal a small elephant.

"Wow, there's a lot of stuff here!" Connor told Bobby, his eyes wide. Then they clouded. "I guess we won't get much here," he added.

"We won't get presents?" Genevieve asked.

"Of course you'll get presents," Bobby told him.

But Connor shook his head knowingly. "We did get presents, Genevieve. Remember? Daddy and Gram and all sent them before, and we opened them at home." He looked at his uncle apologetically. "We got good presents, Uncle Bobby. Gram likes to give presents, huh—is that why there are so many here?"

"Gram has always loved to make everyone a stocking," Bobby said, "including Gramps. But I wouldn't worry—you'll get presents."

"Yes!" Genevieve said. She had a little lisp. Her front tooth was loose. "Santa Claus will come here, right?"

Shayne knew that Connor didn't believe in Santa Claus, so he brought a finger to his lips and winked.

"That's right. And Santa Claus can find any house," he assured Genevieve.

Connor rolled his eyes. "Yeah, sure."

Shayne poked his head in the doorway. "Hey, Bobby, thanks. Want to take over in my room for a minute?"

"Sure. Take over what?"

"Watching our—guest. The guy we picked up—Gabe—is freezing. The snow soaked through his clothing. I've got him in my room, but I need you to stand by the door while I dig in my closet for something for him to wear."

"I can find him something—" Bobby said.

"No, that's cool, I still have you by an inch or so in the shoulder and chest region, and the guy looks like he's about my size. I just don't want to leave him standing there. Connor, you can watch your sister for a minute, huh?"

"Yeah, sure, Dad," Connor said. He made a face. "Bobby still has scissors from when he was in grade school. Can you believe that Gram keeps stuff that long?" he asked with a laugh. "I'll watch her, but I don't think Genevieve can hurt herself."

"I can cut paper!" Genevieve announced proudly.

Shayne walked over to ruffle his son's hair. "Thanks," he said. "And, of course you know how to cut paper, Genevieve. You're a very bright little girl."

"Mommy taught me," she said.

"Yell if you need me," Bobby said, rising quickly to follow his brother out to the hall and to Shayne's room. *Shayne's room. None of them lived there anymore; actually, they'd never lived there. Well, Mom had, and they had often spent summer months and spring and Christmas breaks there. This place evoked a lot of good memories. His parents were in Philadelphia, Shayne was in Pittsburgh and Morwenna was in New York. Not that far, as the world went. But this was where they had always gathered.*

Where it seemed their mother had created a memorial to the past, when they'd actually been a family.

Bobby was suddenly ashamed of his thoughts. They *were* a family.

The bathroom door was ajar.

"He took a serious crack on the head," Shayne said when Bobby crooked a brow at him. "He could fall—he could need help. Look, none of us are in high school football anymore. Just hang around outside the door and be ready to rush in if you hear him slip or scream or rip out the shower curtain, huh?"

"Fine, I'll be ready," Bobby said. He leaned against the wall by the door that was an inch or so open. The water started to spray.

He heard his brother fumbling around in the closet. Shayne emerged. "I'm just going down to toss this stuff in the dryer—freshen it up. I'll be right back."

"Big bro, you're the M.D. Don't be gone long," Bobby said.

"Two minutes. Just going to toss the stuff around because it's been in a closet," Shayne said. Two minutes? Hell! What if something happened? What if the guy did fall? Shayne was right—they weren't accustomed to showering in a mass steam room of sweat anymore.

Awkward.

He could hear the shower spray, and nothing else.

He tapped lightly on the door. "You all right in there?" he asked.

"Yep, fine, thanks."

"Yell, if—"

"Thanks!"

Bobby was startled when the shower stopped. He backed into the foot of his brother's bed and sat with a plop.

Gabe Lange came out from the bathroom, one towel tied around his waist as he used a second to dry his hair.

"I can't tell you how good it feels to be warm," Gabe said.

"Ah, great. Yeah. I can imagine."

"Are you from here? Winter can be pretty brutal, huh?"

"My mom is actually from here. I was born in Philadelphia. We were all born in Philadelphia. I mean, Shayne, Morwenna and I," Bobby said. "What about you?"

"Down in the city," Gabe said. "Richmond."

"Nice. So—how did you come to be out here in the mountains?" Bobby asked.

"State police—we go wherever. Within the state, of course. So, are you a college student?" Gabe asked him.

Bobby couldn't help but roll his eyes. "Yes, and no.

I've just applied again. I've been to Columbia and North-western."

"Those are good schools. Where are you trying to go now?"

The question was entirely innocent, and a natural get-to-know-you question. Bobby looked at the door; he didn't want Shayne to hear him.

"They don't know it—none of them know it—I applied to Juilliard."

"Ah. For—"

"I'm a guitarist, and I want to write my own music," Bobby said, warmth entering his voice; he was speaking quickly. "My family—they're all superachievers. My dad could write his ticket anywhere, though he's stayed with the D.A.'s office. Maybe he'll run for something someday, who knows? My brother is, as you know, an M.D., and my sister, bless her heart, is an executive with one of Manhattan's finest ad agencies. All respectable moneymakers."

"And are they happy?" Gabe asked him.

"Well, yeah, I think. Shayne loves medicine. I know—through the years—that my folks have talked about his work every time he got an offer to go into private practice. And Morwenna…"

"Yeah?"

"She was an artist once. A really good artist."

"Doesn't she get to use that talent at the ad agency?"

"I think that was the idea. But I think it got lost in one of the executive meetings," Bobby said wryly. "I loved it when I was a kid. She was always drawing fantasy creatures for me. Being snowed in up here isn't really anything all that new. It's happened before. God forbid they sell this place and head south!"

"Would you want them to?" Gabe asked him.

Bobby thought about that for a minute. "Palm Springs, Daytona Beach…snowbound mountains!" He laughed. "No, I don't suppose I would want them to sell. The house is historic—really historic. You can tell by the horrible plumbing and the really bad electricity. But the place really means something to my mom. And, in all honesty, I guess it means something to me, too."

"That's nice to hear. But, what's the story with your music?" Gabe asked.

"According to my father, music is a hobby. Not a career. You go to school for a career." Bobby looked at the door again. "I'm an adult. If I really want it, I can just stop taking parental financial aid and go it on my own. It will be much harder, but I'm willing to give it go. The thing is…" Bobby trailed off.

"Yeah?" Gabe pressed.

He laughed suddenly. "I guess it's a good thing. We fight like cats and dogs, and it's hard to plan a family dinner with a pack of overachievers…but, still, my parents always loved us. It's the way that they look at me that kills me. It's the disappointment." Bobby shut up, wondering why the hell he had just kind of spilled out so much to a stranger. Maybe, he thought, because he'd needed to tell someone, but he didn't want to tell them until he knew what might happen. He knew the odds were against him; getting into Juilliard was a numbers game, and there could only be so many people who got into the school. There were other music schools—if he didn't make it, he'd try again.

But he didn't want to tell anyone in the house that he'd auditioned. He didn't want them to see his hope, or, his disappointment if he didn't make it. Even though it meant they were sure to lecture him through the holiday, he was sticking with the story that he'd gotten a job working in New York City for the coming semester, until he figured out just what he did want. It wasn't a lie; he did have a job offer working with a group of musical waiters at a place called Napoli. They waited on tables, stopped, picked up their instruments and did quick numbers in between.

Even if he made it into Juilliard, Mario, the head of the group and a great vocalist, had assured him they'd be happy to work with his schedule.

It was all okay, really. But he could just hear his father's voice: "A singing waiter? What kind of life is that, Bobby? What if you want a family, kids? There's no advancement, Bobby. Nowhere to go."

"Sounds to me like you know how to get where you want to go—just have to hang in and take those first steps. So," Gabe said loudly, "Christmas here every year, huh?"

Bobby realized that Shayne was coming back with clothing for their guest.

He'd told a stranger, and not his brother, what he was hoping to do with his life.

"Yep, every year," he said.

As Shayne walked in, Bobby walked out. "Patient seems to be fine," he said.

Back in his own room, he found Genevieve and Connor sitting in the midst of a massive pile of wrapping-paper scraps. Rudolph was dancing here and there, and little blue snowflakes lay in strips across the floor.

"Nice job," he said cheerfully. He looked around at the mess. "I think I hear Gram calling you from the kitchen!"

He led them back past his brother's door, and could hear the drone of Shayne's voice. No surprise. Shayne was willing to talk about the difficulty of the divorce at the drop of a hat.

Except that Shayne didn't seem to be doing all the talking. He stopped speaking now and then, and Bobby could hear the stranger's voice.

That he was speaking wasn't odd at all.

That Shayne apparently stopped speaking to actually listen was odd indeed.

Chapter 3

"Dinner's ready!" Morwenna called up the stairs.

Her father had been in his study and he emerged, slipping an arm around her shoulders. "So, kid, what happened? I thought we were going to get to meet Mr. Perfect this year."

"He couldn't come, Dad, and he isn't Mr. Perfect."

"But he's a major presence in your life, right?" her father asked her.

"Dad, we've been seeing each other about six months. He still has his apartment, I still have mine. I—"

"I should hope so!" Mike said, disgruntled.

Morwenna chuckled softly. "Dad! You'd be surprised at the mismatched couples that jump in together in New York. The cost of living is staggering. But we're both doing well, and he's really a nice guy."

"So nice that he isn't here with you at Christmas," her

father said. He shook his head, crossing his arms over his chest. She had seen him in the courtroom, standing in just that position, when he was arguing the guilt of an accused.

He was good at the stance.

"Dad, an entire group from our agency was going to Cancún. Alex put the trip together before he knew that I was coming home."

"And a bunch of adults couldn't go to Cancún without him?"

"Hey! I'm an adult, too. I could have gone with them."

Mike MacDougal shook his head sadly and sagely.

"No, because you know that you would break your mother's heart if you did something like that."

"When people are together—married, cohabiting, etcetera—they often go to one family one year, and another family the next. And children of divorced parents sometimes wind up so confused they don't know where to go anymore—so they head to Cancún."

Mike was silent, shaking his head for a minute, and then said, "Here's the only truth I know—we're all going to die. You can even get out of the 'taxes' part of death and taxes. And when we die, there's only one thing we take with us."

"What's that?"

"Love," Mike said, tapping his heart. "You and your siblings will talk about your mother and me when we're gone, and that way, we'll still be alive. Love lives on—not trips to Cancún, fruity drinks imbibed on a beach, or expensive clothing, or even a hotshot job. Your family loves you…you deserve a guy who knows about family, and love."

Morwenna stared at her father, stunned. She'd never heard such a speech from him before.

"You were the one who pushed me through school," she reminded him. "Then it was, 'We all have to be independent, make our mark in life! There's no one you can depend on but yourself.' I went to school. I learned how to negotiate, engage a client, play all the business games. I even own stock, for God's sake."

She was surprised when he didn't laugh, or at least crack a smile.

"Christmas," he said softly, "always makes me kind of sentimental."

He walked past her. Bobby came down the stairs, followed by Shayne, the kids and their strange guest, Gabe Lange.

"What's up? What's with that look?" Bobby asked her.

"Dad. Our father has gotten all weird," she whispered, looking past him with a careful smile. "Christmas Eve dinner is on, Mr. Lange."

He looked even better. Despite looking a bit worse for wear, the guy really did have a great face, all the right bone structure in place, but a face that wasn't too pretty, and the structure didn't take away from the strength of his jawline. In Shayne's flannel shirt and old jeans, he looked like a sandy-haired woodsman. He could have done a commercial for some kind of rugged men's cologne.

She reminded herself that many a serial killer had offered the world a pleasant face. She still didn't trust him. He was a stranger in their midst.

"Thank you," he told her. "Thank you for having me in your home like this. Christmas is a special time. I didn't really mean to intrude," he told her.

"Well, I guess you didn't collapse by our house on purpose," Morwenna said dryly. "Come along."

She led the way from the parlor along the hall to the dining room, attached to the kitchen. Her mom was directing their extra guests to take their seats.

They hadn't expected Shayne's kids, and they certainly hadn't expected Gabe Lange, but her mother could always manage to make a meal stretch. Turkey would be the main course tomorrow. For Christmas Eve, Stacy always cooked a strange conglomeration of food—linguini with clam sauce, and potatoes and rice, a roast, broccoli with hollandaise sauce, green beans with slivered almonds, a massive "kitchen sink" salad and bread pudding. Perhaps the meal stretched so well because there were so many items to be had.

Morwenna looked at her mother. "What else? What can I get? What can I do?"

"Drinks," her mother said, setting the bowl with the linguini on the table. "Take a tally. Kids, are you having juice? What would you like?"

They were all startled when Genevieve answered with a little sniff. "I would like Mommy to be here," she said.

The adults froze. Connor placed his arm around his sister. "She's on a trip. We'll see her again soon," he said.

Morwenna dived in quickly, not wanting Shayne to say anything. She knew he couldn't understand what had happened to his marriage, and that he didn't intend to hurt the kids. He also couldn't help but be bitter.

"I'll bet she'll come back with great and wonderful gifts!" Morwenna said, walking around to hug Genevieve. "So, until then, what will you have to drink?"

"Can we have soda, Dad?" Connor asked.

"It's Christmas Eve, why not?" Shayne told his son. Morwenna caught her brother's eyes. He smiled at her; he was not going to make a disparaging remark about his ex-wife. Something about him seemed to have changed, just since he'd gotten to the house. Maybe he'd had a long talk with Bobby upstairs.

"Two sodas... Bobby? Soda, beer, wine?"

"Hey, it's my first 'legal' Christmas. Please serve me a lovely glass of Cabernet," Bobby said. "And Dad can't even get arrested because I'm legal these days!"

"I'd have myself arrested?" Mike asked.

"Yeah, you would, Dad. In the name of justice for all!" He laughed. "My dad may be the best assistant D.A. in the country. I think he'd have himself arrested under the innkeeper law," he told Gabe.

Mike groaned. "You were underage—you and your friends. It's illegal for an adult to aid a young person in securing alcoholic beverages. Now you are twenty-one. Go for it."

"Tough to grow up in such a household," Shayne told Gabe.

"Not so bad. We just decided to smoke pot, since everything was illegal for us," Bobby said cheerfully.

Mike looked as if he would explode.

"Chill, Dad, chill, just kidding!" Bobby said.

"An honest man. Rare to find," Gabe said. He had a curious expression. "I think I'd like a beer, if I may. Sounds intriguing—um, good, sorry. Sounds good."

The seeds of mistrust settled more deeply into Morwenna's soul. *Intriguing? Beer? Where the hell had this guy been? Locked up somewhere?*

"Mom, Dad, Shayne?" Morwenna asked.

In the end, she had two caffeine-free sodas, four glasses of wine and two bottles of beer. She moved into the kitchen to get the drinks, and found herself pausing to look around.

And feel guilty.

Stacy even cleaned while she cooked. With all that she had prepared, her mother had kept up with pots and other utensils as well. She had done so much; every year she did so much. She'd always been an at-home mom. Morwenna wondered if she had ever had her own set of dreams, and if their father's career had changed Stacy's life. She'd always cooked breakfast, made lunches, driven the children to Girl Scouts, Boy Scouts and Little League, sewn costumes, bought the candy, gone trick-or-treating and done everything imaginable.

Stacy followed her into the kitchen. "I'll get the sodas," she said. "If you pour the wine."

"Mom, why don't you just sit, and let me do this."

"Are you kidding? I'm in my element, sweetheart. And we don't get days like these often anymore—you know, when I have all of you!"

Morwenna walked to the counter where her mother was pouring the sodas. She slipped her arms around her waist. "Mom, did you ever want to really do anything? I mean, you know, have a career—do something else besides wait on Dad and all of us?"

Stacy turned to stare at her, her eyes wide. "Morwenna, *this* is my career, my life."

"But, did Dad stop you from having any other dreams? Now would be the time to fulfill a dream. It's never too late, you know."

She was surprised; she was trying to stand up for her mother, and her mother was angry. "You get it out of

your head that your father stopped me from doing anything. Because of your father, I could live my dream, I
could have *this* career."

"But we're gone now, Mom. We're all gone, out of
the house, grown up."

"And that means you're not my children anymore?"

"But Dad pushed me so hard to make sure that I had
a career—" Morwenna began.

Stacy quickly cut her off. "Your father pushed *you*,
yes, because you needed more. And because the world
is changing. Now two people have to work sometimes in
order to afford to raise a family. I guess you don't understand. You have all your sleek, chic clothing, designer
briefcases and all-important meetings. And I concen-
trate on making sure a roast is edible. But, Morwenna,
don't try to fix me. I like what I am, and I like what I
do, and there are ups and downs in life all the time, but
I'm *happy.* Maybe your ex-sister-in-law is the only one
who really knows that, since she made sure that the kids
came here for Christmas. The only one who appreciates
family, it seems, is the one no longer in the family!"

Morwenna didn't have a chance to respond; Stacy
expertly balanced the four wineglasses and seemed to
sail out of the kitchen, her head held regally high.

"I wanted to draw!" she said, aware that her mother
couldn't hear her. "I wanted to draw, and paint, and
create things!"

She hesitated, aware that, supposedly, the job she
had taken would allow her to do just that. But she had
become a stereotype of corporate America instead.

"I like my clothes!" she told the swinging door.

She tucked two bottles of beer under her arm, picked

up the sodas and followed Stacy back to the dinner table.

"Ah, Morwenna is here now. We can say grace," Stacy said.

Mike stood and looked around the table. "Thank you, Lord, for the food we are about to eat. Thank you for the safety and lives of our family. Amen."

"Nice," Gabe commented.

"Better than the old joke, eh, of just saying *'Grace'!*" Bobby teased.

"We know better than to give the task to you, son," Mike said, but he was grinning.

"Wait!" Genevieve said. "Wait, Gram, please! Can we do that thing that Mommy's family does?"

They all looked at her. Genevieve grinned and stood up. She took Bobby's hand and reached for her brother's.

"Ah, Genevieve, what are you doing?" Connor demanded.

"Give me your hand, Connor. I don't have any cooties!" Genevieve said.

Connor shrugged and gave her his hand. "This is just silly. Mom isn't here."

"Hey, your sister wants to have your mom here— in spirit," Shayne said. "And let's all try to make each other happy, huh?"

Genevieve grinned happily. "Okay, everybody, now, *shake a lot of love!*"

Around the table, they held hands, and on Genevieve's command, they all shook their hands up and down.

"Now," Genevieve said complacently, "it's almost kind of Christmas!"

"They don't even really know what day Christmas

Day is supposed to be," Connor said. "Some popes or priests somewhere got together to pick a day."

"That's right, Connor," Gabe said. "But it doesn't take away from the fact that the day was chosen, and it's the day when Christians celebrate the birth of Jesus. So, it's the chosen day, and your sister is right—it's almost here."

"So it might have been any day," Morwenna murmured. Except that she was heard. She looked at Gabe, who was staring at her with amusement.

"What? It's a day for miracles or the like?" she asked him softly.

"Miracles are what we make ourselves," he said. He looked upward. "Maybe the Lord can lend a hand, but we have to create magic ourselves."

She groaned softly. "A do-gooder cop. Great."

He just grinned. She did, too.

And, somehow, the meal went along with the conversation pleasant instead of strained, with the family asking questions instead of throwing out accusations, and her father actually asked Bobby to bring out his guitar when they got to the bread pudding.

He played Christmas carols and the family chimed in, except for Morwenna.

Gabe looked at her. "Are you really that 'bah, humbug'?" he asked her.

"No. I sound like a wounded hyena when I sing," she told him.

"But these are Christmas carols. Everyone sings Christmas carols." He looked upward again. "He doesn't care what you sound like."

Morwenna laughed. "I think I'll pick up the plates."

She was surprised when he caught her hand. "'O Lit-

tle Town of Bethlehem,'" he said. "I know you know it.
I'll help with the plates. One song, huh?"

With an exaggerated sigh, she sat again. She sang
along with the family, watching Gabe. "See?"

"I thought you were great."

She drew back, looking at him suspiciously. "Do you
actually have a family?" she asked him.

"I do. I have a wonderful family," he assured her.

"Why aren't you going crazy, trying to find a working phone?" she demanded. "You're not with them."

"Because I'm not the kind to beat my head against
the wall when something can't work," he told her.

She wanted to argue the point, but she really couldn't.
The storm had done nothing but grow stronger in the
hours since she had arrived, and it did seem that they
had lost all phone connections. Were the satellites all
snowbound as well?

"No television for the kiddies," she murmured. "No
computer games."

"Bobby, play 'Silent Night' for me, please?" Stacy
asked.

Bobby looked over at his mother. "Sure, Mom. I
thought you didn't care for the song on a guitar that
much. You always like it on piano."

"And one of these days, I'm going to get one here,"
she assured him. "But, please, play it for me."

"Nothing like a rock version of 'Silent Night,'" Mike
said.

Of course, Bobby heard him.

"I'd love to hear it, too," Morwenna said. "Scrooge
can go into the kitchen!"

They all managed to laugh at that, even Mike. And
Bobby played. Gabe sang the song alone this time with

a clear, smooth, fluid tenor voice that was absolutely beautiful. When the song was over, everyone at the table just stared at him.

"Wow," Bobby said.

"That was all you. You can really play," Gabe said.

Fearful that a fight would begin over Bobby's music versus his college education, Morwenna quickly rose. "Let's get the plates into the kitchen," she said.

"Really, kids, I'm fine," Stacy said.

Morwenna looked at her mother. "Mom, please let us help. Remember, you don't get all of us that often and we want to be with you—if we help, we're with you."

Stacy nodded, but looked at Connor and Genevieve. "Shayne, maybe you could read the kids a story. I'm afraid that we have no internet and we're not getting television reception, either."

"No cable?" Connor asked, horrified.

"Yes, but that's okay. We can do other things to have fun!" Stacy said.

Shayne looked blankly back at his mother. Morwenna felt her heart contract. Shayne was too much like her; they both worked so much they didn't really know how to have fun.

Just as that thought struck her, Bobby piped up. "I know what we'll do! Auntie Morwenna will draw up a Christmas creature, and we'll make up a story about it as we go along."

"Doesn't anyone have an iPad?" Connor asked hopefully.

Yes, actually, she did, Morwenna thought.

But Bobby was looking at her hopefully. She smiled. She really loved her little brother. He might be the ne'er-do-well of the group, but he had heart. She winced inwardly. *And he did have talent. But Dad was overprotective and mistrustful of everyone. He'd worked with too many crooks. In his mind, too, he'd let too many go free. So had they fallen back on their father's words too many times because they were afraid of taking chances? Afraid of having faith in their own abilities?*

"Plates in the kitchen!" Morwenna said. "We all help Mom, and then we'll do a whole Christmas story of our own in the parlor!"

As she passed Shayne with plates, he caught her arm. "You really don't have your iPad?" he asked hopefully.

"Shayne MacDougal, believe it or not, the artist in me loves a pencil and paper, and we're going to play," she said. "Difficult, I know. But your kids will love it, and you don't have to be embarrassed. Hey, you can play a monster."

She hurried by her brother. *Shayne loved his job. He just needed to realize that his loved ones needed healing as much as his patients.*

With everyone helping, it was quick work getting the table cleared. Luckily, the dishwasher and electricity were still functioning, so within twenty minutes, food was stowed, plates and glasses and serving pieces rinsed and set to wash and the kitchen squeaky clean.

Mike asked his sons for help with the logs; they rebuilt the fire in the parlor. They managed to do so, only jokingly taunting one another as they shared the labor.

But, before they could start, Stacy turned back to the kitchen. "We have to have hot cocoa for the performance."

Bobby groaned. "You'd think we were starving, Ma."

"She likes to have the fire—and her kids drinking cocoa," Morwenna said.

"Spike mine, Ma," Bobby called.

When cocoa was finished—spiked for the adults, plain old cocoa for the kids—Bobby ushered his mother back to the sofa. He hiked Genevieve over his head, and then set her on his mother's lap.

Morwenna hurried to her room and found one of her old sketchbooks and quickly looked up something she had created years before—Magala, the Christmas elf. She ran back downstairs with the sketchbook. "Bobby, you get to be Wager, the traveling troubadour." She frowned, and then looked at Gabe, who was waiting expectantly. "Gabe, you can play Magala, the Christmas elf," she said, and showed him the picture. "And, Shayne, you get to be Mr. Mean, the Abominable Snowman who lives by the workshop at the North Pole."

"Great!" Shayne said.

But Connor giggled, and Shayne flashed his son a smile. He lifted his arms in a huge Abominable Snowman pose.

"Who are you, Aunt Morwenna?" Genevieve asked, cuddling her teddy bear as she sat on her grandmother's lap.

"The narrator," Morwenna said. "Hang on just one minute." Glancing at her pictures, she scurried first to the kitchen. She found a new mop head and came back to put it on Shayne's head, which delighted the kids further. But Shayne wasn't complete until she had whitened his face with cold cream. The more Shayne groaned, the more his kids laughed, and she was happy when she saw him smile—despite the goop on his face.

Bobby had secured one of his old Robin Hood hats from a long-gone Renaissance festival, and for Gabe,

Morwenna found an old pair of Halloween ears. They were ready.

"Intro!" Morwenna told Bobby. He strummed a light tune that grew dark.

"Once upon a time, up at the North Pole, there lived a good elf named Magala," Morwenna said.

Gabe got into the action, leaping up, smiling and bowing. It was good; he didn't seem to have suffered any real damage from his fight in the snow.

"He worked all day at creating toys for children," Morwenna continued.

Gabe pantomimed the creation of a bicycle, and everyone laughed as he kept turning the invisible instruction sheet around and around.

"But, nearby, in the darkest, dankest cave, lived Mr. Mean, the Abominable Snowman," Morwenna said.

Bobby played a few dark and threatening chords as Shayne stood up, lifted his arms and shoulders in a huge display of strength.

"I'm mean!" Shayne said. He looked at Morwenna. "How am I mean? What do I do?"

"While Magala works day and night, trying to make a wonderful Christmas for children everywhere, Mr. Mean plans to destroy all the toys!" Morwenna said.

Bobby played even darker music.

Shayne walked over to Gabe, stared at him and picked up the imaginary bike. He threw it to the ground and then hopped up and down on it.

"That's what I always felt like doing with those instruction sheets," Mike said softly, drawing laughter from all of them.

"Daddy, you're so mean!" Genevieve said, delighted.

"And I just stare at him while he ruins Christmas?" Gabe asked.

"No! Here's the thing—Mr. Mean goes away all proud of himself for having taken care of Christmas. But, you see, Magala is a magic elf, and as soon as Mr. Mean is gone, he just puts the bicycle back together again, and he does it double time," Morwenna said.

The children were delighted as Gabe tried to perform all his actions again in double time.

"So, all the toys were ready to go, to be placed in Santa's sleigh," Morwenna said.

Gabe put his hands on his hips and nodded proudly.

"But!" Morwenna said, and Bobby strummed out a dire musical warning.

"Mr. Mean came in and stomped on the toys again!"

Big-armed and growling, Shayne grabbed the imaginary bike, tossed it to the floor and hopped up and down, his dramatic antics growing with each jump.

"And then what happened?" Connor demanded, clearly drawn in.

"Magala didn't have any presents for Santa's sleigh!" Genevieve said.

"Ah, but you see, he did," Gabe told her.

"But the bike is smashed to bits," Connor protested.

"Smashed, yeah, broken. But all the pieces were there," Gabe said, flashing Morwenna a quick smile.

"So," Morwenna said, "Magala the elf picked up all the pieces, and when the children awoke in the morning, they realized that they hadn't just gotten a present—they'd gotten a puzzle, too. They just had to work together and connect the pieces."

Genevieve, with wide and innocent eyes, leaped up and ran over to stand by the imaginary bike.

"My dad could put it back together. Especially when he's not being Mr. Mean!" Genevieve said.

"Ah, yes. And there's the magic to the Christmas story," Morwenna said. "When Mr. Mean realized that he couldn't break something that can't be seen or touched—like the love shared at Christmas—he gave up being Mr. Mean, and he became Mr. Nice, and he went about the country, finding children who didn't have fathers, and helping them put all their toys back together again!"

Bobby strummed the guitar. "The end!" he announced.

"The end, and time for little people to go to bed," Shayne said. "Morwenna—"

"Absolutely, my beautiful little niece is in with me," Morwenna said.

"And I'll take Connor, and—"

"Gabe can have the lower bunk in my room," Bobby said.

"But for now…young'uns, to bed! Santa can't come if you don't go to bed," Shayne said firmly.

"I'm not that young," Connor protested, standing tall to prove his point.

"Hey—Uncle Bobby worked hard on that tree. And your grandmother baked cookies for Santa. You're going to go to bed, and Santa is going to come," Morwenna said. She was surprised when Connor looked at her, blushed, lowered his head and smiled.

"Alrighty, Auntie Wenna," Connor said. "I like playing your games. I'll think of it that way."

"That's wonderfully mature, Connor," she told him.

"Kiss Gramps and Gram, and let's go on up," Morwenna suggested.

Connor kissed his family, and Genevieve followed him around. When he reached Gabe, Connor somberly shook his hand.

"And a good night to you, young man," Gabe said.

Genevieve impulsively gave Gabe a kiss on the cheek. He smiled. "Thank you. And good night, Genevieve. I have a feeling you'll go through life fixing the things that need to be fixed, young lady. You have a good night's sleep."

"It works when we all fix stuff, huh?" Genevieve asked.

Gabe grinned. "Just like magic," he agreed.

"Come on, come on up," Morwenna urged the two. Shayne probably had the kids' presents out in the car, in the garage, and the storm was still pounding them. It was going to be a trick to get everything in. She was worried, too, about what they'd find in the house to give the children so that they had something to wake up to; they'd sent the family presents on ahead to Cindy a few weeks ago, since she was going to have the children for Christmas and Shayne would have them for the New Year's weekend.

"I'm good, Auntie Wenna," Connor said at the door to Bobby's room. "I'm cool. I can put myself to bed."

She hesitated. He reminded her of a brave little warrior standing there.

"Both your parents love you very much, Connor," she told him.

He nodded. "Yeah, well, I just need to learn to handle things on my own. I've got Genevieve to think about."

Morwenna smiled and ruffled his hair. "Good night, Connor. Love you."

"Love you, too, Auntie Wenna," he said.

She brought Genevieve into her room, stood with her while she washed her face and brushed her teeth, helped her into an old flannel gown of her own that was far too big, but which Genevieve wanted to wear, and sat at the foot of the bed.

"Say prayers with me, Auntie Wenna?" she asked.

"Um, sure," Morwenna said a little awkwardly. She smiled; as a child, she had gotten down on her knees at night and told God all her problems. As an adult, she'd figured out that he was busy with more serious issues, such as war, starvation and disease.

When had she gotten to a point where she believed that she had to fight alone against the world? When she'd figured out hers was just a little life, a grain in the sands of time.

She knelt down next to her niece and folded her hands prayer fashion.

"Dear God. Happy birthday to baby Jesus—whatever his birthday might be. We love him, no matter when it is. Please keep my mommy and daddy safe, and Auntie Wenna, Uncle Bobby, Gram and Gramps. And don't worry about toys for me this Christmas. Honest." She opened her eyes for a moment to take a sideways glance at Morwenna. "Auntie Morwenna will let me play with some of her stuff, so I'm really good. Oh, thank you for the bread pudding. It was especially yummy. Amen."

"Nice prayer, young lady. Good night."

"Aren't you going to say your prayers?" Genevieve asked her.

She looked at her niece for a moment. In her head, thoughts she couldn't say out loud in front of the child—or anyone—swirled into a prayer. *Dear God, please don't make it that I am an idiot; that Alex really wants to be with me 'cause he believes I'm on the top rungs of the professional ladder, and that he isn't in Cancún, chasing after Double-D Debbie from Accounting on the beach...*

She gave herself a mental shake and folded her hands again. "Dear God, thank you for my brothers, my mom and dad, and especially my nephew, Connor, and my niece, Genevieve. Guard them for me, please, through whatever life offers." She hesitated a minute. "Help me be a better, more understanding me."

Genevieve nudged her. "And happy birthday to baby Jesus."

"Yes, of course. Happy birthday to baby Jesus."

"And may we all get back together again. My mom and dad," Genevieve said, looking upward again.

Morwenna rose and lifted Genevieve, hugging her. "Sometimes, honey, that just can't happen. What you need to know is how much they both love you and Connor."

"How can they love anybody when they hate each other so much?" Genevieve asked her.

"They don't hate each other."

"They sure act like it sometimes," Genevieve said.

"They—they're just angry because they...they..."

"They didn't know how to fix things," Genevieve said. "That's why I really prayed that we could learn to fix things."

"Praying for miracles," Morwenna murmured.

Genevieve smiled sadly at her. "Well, fixing things is like a miracle."

"Yes, it is, sweetie, yes, it is," Morwenna agreed. She tucked Genevieve into her bed, pulling the covers close. "I'll leave the bathroom light on, okay, kid? And the door ajar."

"Good night," Genevieve said. "Don't let the bedbugs bite."

"Let's hope not. We'll have the same bedbugs," Morwenna said. Genevieve giggled. Morwenna kissed her once again and left her, cuddling her teddy bear.

She hesitated and looked out the window from the upstairs hallway. She could see that Shayne had bundled up and was headed to the garage. About ten feet behind him, someone else was walking. Too broad shouldered to be Bobby; it was Gabe. Gabe Lange was going out to help him.

Something stirred inside her.

Distrust. Sadly, she had a lot of her father inside her. She didn't naturally trust anyone. And they found him in the snow. He claimed to be a cop, but he hadn't been wearing any kind of uniform, and they'd found him with no identification. Was he who he said he was?

All she knew at that moment was that the guy was following her brother. On a dark, snow-swept night. They were heading into the garage.

She tore down the stairs, pausing at the hooks by the door for her coat and scarf. Her brother was likely lost in his own thoughts as he always was, unable to feel the first hint of danger.

Luke DeFeo shivered, staring at a cottage that sat on the side of the mountain. It was dark, but everything was dark. Still, he had the feeling that there was no one there.

He swore aloud in the night. The air was bitterly cold, and he could feel it. He wanted to be off the damn frigid mountains, but there seemed to be no traffic anywhere in the area, and he had yet to stumble onto any signs that life actually existed in the frozen wasteland. He cursed Gabe in his mind; this was one hell of a way to spend the night.

He'd thought he'd killed him; he'd thought that he'd killed Gabe, but he hadn't. The deadly game between them was still on. Luke could somehow sense that Gabe was still out there.

Well, he didn't have to sense it, not really. Stumbling around in the snow and ice-covered wilderness, he had come upon the place where they had fought—and Gabe had been gone. So he was still out there, somewhere in the night.

Luke made his way to the little wooden cottage on the mountain. It was dark and he couldn't hear any signs of life. He rapped at the door and received no answer. After a moment, he threw his shoulder against the door, and then kicked it in. He stepped into the house, but as he did so, he knew that it was empty. The inhabitants were apparently smart—they'd gone somewhere for the holiday.

He looked around, and wondered if he wanted something from the cottage. But there wasn't anything there; it was empty and it was cold. It was a shelter against the cold and the snow and the wretchedness of the night, of course.

But he couldn't stay.

He hadn't killed Gabe.

He left the door to the cottage swinging and started out, feeling the bitter cold again. He could take it.

He was going to find Gabe, and end the game between them.

Chapter 4

"I'm going to head out and help Shayne," Bobby told his mother. He'd come from the kitchen, having insisted he clean up the hot-cocoa cups. Stacy had been straightening out the apron around the Christmas tree to ready it for Shayne's packages.

"You don't need to help, Bobby—Gabe went out behind him, and Morwenna went running out after him." She was staring at the tree as she spoke, but turned to smile at him. "You did a beautiful job with the ornaments, Bobby."

"It was easy. Dad did the lights. That's the pain in the ass, Mom."

She rolled her eyes. "Butt, Bobby. Pain in the butt. It's a nicer word." She stepped closer to the tree, studying one of the ornaments. It was the little angel or cherub he had pondered himself earlier.

He walked over to his mother, setting a hand on her shoulder. "That's pretty," he told her.

She smiled. "I think I told you the story that goes with this ornament, years ago."

"Did you?"

"It belonged to my great-great-grandmother."

"Mom, the house is almost two hundred years old. And half the stuff in it belonged to your great-great-grandmother."

"Ah, but this one was special! During the winter of 1864, a wounded Union soldier found himself running through the mountains, terrified, of course, about what might happen to him if he was captured by a Confederate guerrilla band. The commanders of the armies, both sides, were fairly honorable men, but sometimes the militiamen and the guerrillas combing the mountains were fanatics—not so much on the eastern front, but in the west the men were often little more than common murderers. Anyway, my great-great-grandmother found him trying to seek shelter in the barn—the garage now. And she couldn't let any wounded man suffer, and took him in to nurse him. When the menfolk in the family wanted to turn him in, she said she just didn't give a damn about the war, she cared about people. He got a fever, and he was delirious, and when he woke up, he said that she was his angel. His angel of mercy. He had this little ornament to bring home as a gift for his mother, but when he left, he said that his mother would want the angel who had saved his life to have the figure. He said that he prayed the angel would look after her all her days. She lived to be ninety-nine, so I guess the angel was looking after her."

"Great story, Mom," Bobby said. She smiled. And

for that minute, Stacy looked almost like a young girl
again. She was his mother, but it seemed that he could
take a step back for a moment and take a look at her
as a human being. He smiled inwardly, thinking she
must have really been something at one time. He'd always known that his big sister was beautiful. And now
he could recognize the fact that Morwenna had gotten
her looks from their mother.

Kids seldom saw such things, but it was nice to realize—Stacy was still a pretty woman.

"The story gets better," she told him. "The Union soldier she saved went on to become a congressman from
Massachusetts—and he helped fight to stop the puni-
tive measures toward the postwar South." She touched
the ornament tenderly. "When I was little, her daughter, my great-grandmother, used to tell me that angels
did influence our lives, and that they helped us sometimes, when we didn't even know they were there. I like
to believe that, Bobby."

"Sure, Mom." He gave her a hug. He marveled at his
mother, and he had to wonder if people did come together for a reason. His mom was the ray of hope and
light. His father was the doomsayer. They could both
be right; Mike MacDougal had seen all the worst that
man had to offer his fellow man. Stacy believed in the
goodness that she felt prevailed among most people.

"They've been out there a while," Bobby said. "I think
I'll help. Maybe there's a bicycle out there and those mis-
fits are dropping all the pieces!" With a quick kiss on the
cheek, he left her, striding to the door for his heavy coat.

The snow kept falling in huge, wet flakes and the
wind blew hard. Morwenna felt as if she was battling a

storm in the Antarctic as she made her way to the garage.
When she reached the side door, it was a fight against
the wind to open it. But she suddenly felt desperate; she
could see through the four-paned little window that Gabe
was standing close to her brother by the trunk of his car.

The door flew open, slamming against the wooden
wall of the garage.

Both men looked toward her; Gabe hurried over,
drawing her in and closing the door.

"Hey!" Shayne said. "What are you doing out here?
It's freezing!"

"I, um, you were taking some time. I thought you
might need help," Morwenna said. She felt a little ridiculous, and then not. They didn't know Gabe Lange.

"Oh, we were just talking," Shayne told her. "I was
showing Gabe some of the things for the kids."

"And we were discussing the merits of live action
versus video games," Gabe said. "Shayne's right—this
one electronic thingy he got for Connor is great—it's
a word game, teaches you how to spell, and what the
definitions for the words are once they're found. And
you win funny little cars with each correct answer—
virtual cars."

"Will it work—does it have to be downloaded?"
Morwenna asked. "I'm surprised we still have electricity. The cable is down, and none of the phones work."

"It's battery operated, and doesn't need any down-
loads, so Connor will be able to play with it no matter, tomorrow," Shayne said. "I have to admit, I think
the kids had a great time tonight—without electronic
devices."

"Who knew you'd make such a great Mr. Mean?"
Morwenna said lightly.

Shayne half smiled. "It was fun. I really had fun."

"Do you write children's books?" Gabe asked her.

"No! Oh, Lord, no," Morwenna said. "I'm an executive at an ad agency in Manhattan."

"Yeah, I heard that. But, people may do one thing for a living, and another on the side. I thought that maybe you wrote for children on the side. And I take it that you draw a lot?" Gabe asked.

"Sure. Sometimes. I always loved to draw."

"Once upon a time you spent a lot more time just doodling," Shayne said.

"I can't. I mean, I don't really have the time. Not anymore. Now I spend a lot of time in meetings," Morwenna said.

"You should illustrate," Gabe said.

She hesitated. She could have explained that she had intended to, things hadn't quite gone in the direction she had intended. "I don't really have the time," she said simply. "I can come up with the creatures, but I'm not sure what they should be doing. A story needs a beginning, a middle and an end."

"But you could work with someone else, right?" Gabe asked her.

"Sure," she murmured. "Maybe in my retirement."

"I guess we all do what we need to do in life," Gabe said. "You're good. And it's obvious that you love it. Maybe take a sketch pad on your next vacation."

"This *is* my vacation," she said.

"Morwenna is mourning the fact that she's not in Cancún," Shayne told him.

"I am not! I chose to be here," Morwenna said.

Shayne laughed and brushed her cheek with his knuckles, teasing her as he had when they'd been in high school. "Sense of duty, right, sis? Her lover boy is off in Cancún, and she must be dying to know what he's up to."

"Shayne, please, it's a mature relationship," Morwenna said.

"Ah," Gabe said knowingly. "Like an open relationship?"

"No! Oh, for God's sake, please. It's possible to have a relationship in which people remain monogamous when they're apart," Morwenna said.

"Sure," Shayne said, turning away.

"It is!" Morwenna insisted.

"I was agreeing with you, Morwenna. I'm sorry— I didn't mean to hurt you. I was just teasing, really," Shayne said.

"You didn't hurt me," she protested. *A lie! She was worried; if it had been a really good relationship, wouldn't he have told the others just to be adults and have a good time on their own because he wanted to be with the woman he loved at Christmas?*

Or were their values simply different? she wondered. It was hard to admit; she had come because of a sense of duty. But she had also wanted to come—Christmas to her had always been this house on top of the mountain. New Year's might be right for a wild jaunt, but Christmas meant being with the ones she loved. That didn't negate other values, she assured herself. It was just what it meant to her.

"I'm not a family member, but I'm glad that you're here," Gabe told her. "It's been nice to meet you."

She gave him a weak smile. *Really? I'd have thought about leaving you in the snow; I'm my father's daughter, braving the trenches of Manhattan in a state of continual suspicion.*

She wasn't sure what to reply.

"Well, you made a great Christmas elf," she told him.

"I'm going to haul in the first bag of stuff," Shayne said. He grimaced. "We were talking about putting the bicycle together out here...keep all the packing and stuff out of the house," he said.

"We were just about to start, and I'm afraid the reality may be as hard as the imagery we were playing with before," Gabe said.

"I'm good with directions. I'll help," Morwenna said.

"Okay, you two get started. I'll be right back. Or as soon as the wind will let me," Shayne told them.

Gabe got the door so Shayne could head out with a large canvas bag. She saw that the box with the bike parts was already on the floor, opened. "Where are the directions?" she asked Gabe.

"Right here," he said, handing her a sheet from the top of the box.

"Easy. A1 goes to A2, as soon as you have B1 connected to C1, and then, somehow, D2 has been thrown into the lot. Ah, there's E3!"

Gabe groaned, and started pulling all the pieces out of the box. They knelt down together to study the diagram.

Morwenna couldn't help but be aware of him as a man, and she found herself wondering how she would have felt about him if they'd met under different circumstances. But, of course, this *was* a strange circumstance, and she was committed.

She had never been able to date casually. Of course, she'd dated Alex before they'd become a couple, and she'd found it awkward and difficult. Her friends in Manhattan had tried hard to teach her that every dinner didn't have to lead to sex, and that she wasn't obligated to have sex, but then again, didn't she want it now and then? In college, she'd had one relationship, and they had both been honest and committed, and then, at graduation, they had realized the bond wasn't strong enough for either of them to change their goals in life, and they had parted as friends. And eventually, of course, their calls had grown infrequent, and time had gone by.

Then, Alex had come into the firm, and the first time they'd gone out, she'd been smitten. She'd still held back until they'd been seeing each other for a few months, and the time had been right, and she'd believed that they both really cared about each other. She had to admit to herself, though, that they hadn't used the all-important four-letter word yet—love.

"Hand over Al there, will you?" Gabe asked. "The body of the beast!"

She did so.

"Your brothers are really good guys," he told her.

"Love them to pieces," she said. "I just wish that…"

He looked up at her. "What?"

She laughed suddenly. "You're reminding me of how it was when we were kids. I could be ready to throttle Shayne or Bobby, but if anyone else said something about them, I'd be ready to throttle that person."

Gabe grinned. "I guess that's the way it should be."

"I think that Shayne's current situation is just terribly painful. He really loved Cindy. I don't think he was a great husband. I mean, he's so dedicated to his patients. Oh, he adores his kids, but Cindy was the one who was with them most, and I think he's as happy as can be that he does have them for Christmas, but without Mom and Dad or Cindy, I don't think he remembers how to do Christmas."

Gabe found the "screwdriver included!" bag and nodded as he divided his attention between her and his task. "The most intelligent people in the world can usually look around and figure out what would fix things for someone else, and yet struggle with their own situation," he said.

"Genevieve broke my heart tonight. In her prayers, she basically asked God to put her parents back together."

"That's natural."

"And probably impossible. Cindy, I'm sure, thought long and hard before she left my brother."

"Nothing is impossible while we're drawing breath, kid," he said lightly.

"Then you believe in miracles, huh?" Morwenna asked him.

"If you think about it, life itself is a miracle. Sure, I believe in miracles." He grinned at her, pausing for a moment. "Just like your little play—miracles are out there. We have to make them happen."

"Well, you're just like Little Miss Sunshine, Pollyanna and a ray of light, all rolled into one," Morwenna said. "Life isn't like that. It's all messy, and complicated, and I'm sure that Shayne tried to fix things. Sometimes, when things are broken, they're shattered, and that's that."

He laughed and sat back for a moment, staring at her. "Wow! From what I can see, you all have a really good life going here. The three of you grew up with parents who really love you. They have their personalities and their opinions, but they love you, and it's obvious that every move they've ever made was with your best interests at heart. Shayne is doing what he loves for a living. You have a good job, even if it's not what you planned, and if you had any balls, you would do what you really wanted. Your problem with the fellow your brother referred to as lover boy or boy toy is probably the fact that you decided you needed *someone,* even if he wasn't the right one, and you're really not happy with yourself, so you're playing the game of trying to assemble the right pieces. Bobby—"

"Yeah, go on, pick on Bobby, the dropout!" Morwenna said, angry and about to get to her feet and leave.

"I was about to say that Bobby is the one on the right track. He knows what he wants—and he's going to go after it. His biggest fear is hurting those who love him while he's on the way. All that he needs is a little faith."

Morwenna frowned. "What are you talking about?"

"Your brother really is a brilliant musician. Have you ever really listened to him play? He's amazing. He wants to pursue it. But in your family music is a hobby. Bobby can make more out of it, he just feels he has to prove to all of you that he can do it before he really gives it his whole heart. But he's moving in the right direction."

"Well, thank you, Mr. Cop-without-a-badge-or-uniform!" Morwenna said. "And how do I fix my life?"

"Oh, Morwenna, that's so easy. Quit playing the game. Stop trying to fix other people, and support them, in whatever they need. Don't try to play any roles in life, and stop and think about what you really want," he told her.

"So simple!" she told him with heat. "So simple— and maybe you might want to think about life that way yourself! You're just great at pointing out problems.

Surely you have something in your life that you're not dealing with. Maybe you should worry about yourself."

"I didn't mean to be intrusive," he said. "You're just good people—you should be happy."

"What is happy? I mean, who is happy every single minute?"

"Content, then. Happiness is going through life with problems, and yet knowing where you're going, and enjoying the moments that are filled with laughter and love."

I am happy! she thought defensively.

Was she?

She turned away from him. This time of year, getting together—it *could* be one of those times when they were just happy, and appreciating one another.

"Hey," he said softly, and she looked up at him. For a moment, she felt as if the fleeting seconds of time they shared, on the floor in the cold of the garage, were some of the most intimate she had ever known. His eyes were a green like the grass in summer. They seemed to speak in a whisper to her soul. She wanted to touch his face, and marvel that anything with such rugged appeal could be so tender and knowing.

She almost moved back. She liked him. And she was in a relationship, and she wasn't going to have any dreams about a stranger suddenly cast on their doorstep.

"I'm sorry," he said. "I can see that you all wind up in tangles because you do love one another so much. But here's the good—whether or not there is a miracle and Cindy and Shayne wind up back together or not, they're on their way to being the best they can possibly be. Cindy sent those kids here, right? Likely because she decided that they should have a real family Christmas, even if that meant it was one without her."

Morwenna sighed. "Shayne thinks she wanted quality time with the new love of her life."

"Well, of course he does. Someday he'll step back and rethink that."

"What's this about Bobby? He's my brother—what do you think you know about him that I don't?" Morwenna demanded.

"You should ask Bobby," he told her. "Hand me part D3a, will you, please?"

She did so. For a moment, she didn't really see him. She rose awkwardly, thinking about the things Gabe had told her. It was true; Shayne was hurting. And Bobby…

She wanted to talk to her brother. Alone.

"There we go!" Gabe said.

Startled, she looked back to him. He had risen as well; the bike was completely assembled.

"Wow," she said.

He grinned. "Not bad, eh?"

"Not bad at all. Now, all we have to do is get it to the house in this storm."

As she spoke, the garage door opened with a thud. Bobby, bracing himself, stood in the doorway.

"Thank the Lord! It's done, and I don't have to help," he said, eyeing the bike.

"That's the ticket," Morwenna said. She smiled at her younger brother. "Get here as soon as it's done. But you can help. We have to get the bike up to the house. Where is Shayne? I thought he was coming right back?"

"Connor called him from upstairs—he wanted a glass of water. And maybe he still believes in Santa, just a little, because he didn't want to come down the stairs—maybe jinx the possibility," Bobby said. "Shayne's with him now."

"Good for them both," Morwenna said, her voice a little husky. She realized that she was fighting the desire to cry. They did have their health. They had each other. People, good people, were out of work, starving in America and around the world.

She walked over to her brother and gave him a fierce hug. "I love you, Bobby." Then she hurried out of the garage and headed for the house.

Despite the cold and the wind, she paused. The bright lights of the Christmas tree shone out on the crystal-white glitter of the snow. It was beautiful. The warmth inside beckoned to her.

Life itself was a miracle.

And the beauty of the night, even in the wind and snow, was astounding. She smiled to herself, thoughts swirling in a real prayer.

Happy birthday, Jesus. And thank you.

"Easier said than done!" Bobby laughed. He had the back half of the bike; Gabe had the front. It wasn't even that big a bike; it was just awkward making their way through the snowdrifts to the house. When they reached the door, though, Morwenna was waiting, and they were able to walk right in, shedding snowflakes as they did so. Bobby stared at Morwenna, feeling awkward for a moment. He smiled at her.

She smiled back.

Shayne came down the stairs just as they entered.

"Hey! Great. That's amazing! It's already together!"

"Your sister reads directions well," Gabe said.

"Let's put that right here, to the left of the tree," Stacy

suggested. "Shayne, you did a great job getting stuff here at the last minute for the children."

"Thanks," he said huskily. "Too bad I can't give them the one thing they really want."

"No, not Cindy," Morwenna said, walking over to Shayne. She stood on her toes and gave him a kiss on the cheek. "But they've got their dad, and you're a great dad, Shayne."

"I suck," Shayne admitted.

"But you're already working on not sucking," Bobby said. "So all is good! Mom, the tree looks great. Absolutely great."

"I just have to sneak up to my room when I'm sure Genevieve is deep asleep to get a few more things," Morwenna said. "I have a little dress-up set I'd bought for Alex's niece and a comic-book creature one of our clients gave me. My real gifts for the kids went through Cindy, of course, but they'll have something from me."

"I scrounged together a few old pieces, too," Stacy said. "They'll be good."

"Well, I didn't scrounge anything, but I have a Christmas-morning present for them, too," Bobby told them. He grimaced. "I wrote them a song."

"Their own song. Cool, really cool," Gabe said.

Mike MacDougal studied his son. "That will be great, Bobby. We'll all look forward to hearing it."

Bobby thought that his father sounded a little awkward; words of praise had always been hard for him. He smiled.

Stacy stretched and yawned. "Well, I'm to bed," she said. "It's been a wonderful Christmas Eve. Thank you all. Thank you all for being here with us."

Stacy walked over and kissed Morwenna, then

Shayne, and then came to Bobby. There was something glittering in his mother's eyes.

Happiness, he thought.

He hugged her warmly in return. "Good night, Mom," he told her. "Thank you. It was a great Christmas Eve dinner."

"Glad you liked it," she told him. She turned, and paused, seeing Gabe. Stacy smiled warmly and gave him a hug as well. "Welcome to our home for Christmas. You're all set, right?"

"Your family has been great. I have more than I would have had anywhere," he assured her.

"Well, good night, kids," Mike said. He repeated Stacy's actions, giving each of his children a hug, and pausing in front of Gabe. He offered him a handshake. "Merry almost Christmas, Mr. Lange."

"And to you, sir," Gabe said.

Mike stared at him. "Aren't you worried? Your, uh, your prisoner is still out there—at large nearby."

"I will be vigilant," Gabe said. "I won't let any harm come to your family."

Mike wagged a finger at Gabe. "Trust me. *I* won't let any harm come to my family."

As his parents walked up the stairs, Bobby heard his father whispering to his mother. "What do we know? The guy could be a crook! We could wake up to find out that he's robbed the entire place. Or worse, we could *not* get to wake up at all!"

"Hush!" Stacy said.

But Mike raised his voice, intending to be heard.

"You know I always sleep with that shotgun by my bed. You never know when a starving bear is going to wake up."

"Bears hibernate, Mike, you know that," Stacy said.

Then they were upstairs and out of earshot. The three MacDougal children looked awkwardly at Gabe.

"Dad's been a prosecutor for a really long time," Bobby said.

Gabe laughed. "Hey, he's a bright man, and he's seen the worst. That's okay. It's not a bad thing to be prepared for—bad things."

"Yes, despite all the miracles in the world," Morwenna said, "they do happen!"

"So do good things," Gabe countered. As he spoke, the old grandfather clock in the parlor chimed midnight.

They all stood still, listening.

"Merry Christmas, bros!" Morwenna said then, and kissed Shayne and Bobby. She studied her brothers' expressions. "Merry Christmas," she said again softly. "And I hope that your present is the future, and that it brings you all that you want—and deserve," she said. She moved quickly away, and walked over to Gabe.

She hesitated a minute, and then gave him a hug. "And you'd better not prove to be a lowlife thief or anything of the like," she told him.

She turned around to look at them all. "I'm going to grab those little gifts for the kids. And, then, I'm cuddling up with my niece to get some sleep. See you all in the morning."

She ran up the stairs. Shayne, Gabe and Bobby called after her, "Merry Christmas!"

They looked at one another. "I'm going to go on up and cuddle with my son, myself," Shayne said. "Guess I need to grab those chances when I get them," he said.

"'Night, Shayne," Bobby said.

Shayne paused in front of Gabe. "Merry Christmas. And thanks."

"Hey, I need to thank you all," Gabe told him.

Shayne nodded and headed on up.

"Top bunk or bottom?" Bobby asked Gabe.

"Whichever one you don't sleep in," Gabe said. "I could be dying of hypothermia right now. Or resting on a slab at the morgue. I'm delighted just to be indoors."

"Actually, we're lucky we found you. It's been a helluva good Christmas Eve with you around, stranger. Glad to have you," Bobby told him.

And it was true. What might have been tedious had been fun; what could have been arguments had turned to camaraderie and laughter.

He found himself turning to the tree. One of the golden glowing lights was touching the face of the little angel ornament.

An injured cop had turned out to be their Christmas angel, in his way.

"Want some water or anything before I turn out the lights down here? It won't be completely dark. We leave the tree lights on through the night. My mom used to say they were a beacon for Santa. And, of course, since we burned logs in the fireplace, she convinced us that Santa had a key."

Gabe laughed. "Nope, I'm good. Thanks. I'll head on up. Which did you prefer? The upper bunk, or the lower?"

"Top—but I really don't care."

"I'll crawl into the lower," Gabe said.

Bobby started around the house to check the doors and turn off the lights. When he returned to the parlor, he saw that Morwenna had set her extra gifts under the tree for the kids.

She was just walking back up the stairs.

"'Night, sis!"

"'Night!" she called back.

As she reached the upper landing, Gabe was just coming out of Shayne's room. Shayne must have supplied him with the flannel night trousers he was wearing.

Gabe and Morwenna almost ran into each other. Gabe was still shirtless, carrying the pajama top in his hands.

Morwenna seemed to have frozen there.

As had Gabe.

Bobby grinned.

Two such beautiful people; Morwenna in a long white flannel gown, raven hair flowing down her back; Gabe, appearing to have such strength.

"'Night!" Morwenna said, the sound almost desperate. She turned and fled into her own room.

"Good night," Gabe called after her.

Bobby grinned as he walked up the stairs. He thought that Morwenna had a bit of a crush on their visitor—and that the feelings were returned.

Gabe had already turned into the room. When Bobby entered, their visitor was in the lower bunk.

"Merry Christmas," Bobby said, crawling up.

"Yes," Gabe said thoughtfully. "Merry Christmas."

Bobby yawned. For a moment, he thought that if their visitor was a maniacal killer, he'd be the first to go.

But the guy wasn't a killer of any kind. He was certain. He didn't know how he was certain.

But, as the stranger seemed to be teaching them, sometimes, you just had to have faith.

Chapter 5

Morwenna woke up with a start. She could actually hear bells; church bells coming from the little village that was around the bend and down the mountain about a mile.

She started to move and realized that something warm was next to her, and she raised her arms quickly, hoping that she hadn't batted her niece in the head. She looked down at Genevieve, still sleeping soundly, little cheeks rosy and flushed.

She looked like an angel.

It had been nice sleeping with her; nice to wake up with a trusting little bundle of a child next to her. She rose carefully, trying not to awaken Genevieve, moved to gather fresh clothing as silently as she could and then headed into her bathroom to shower. As she turned on the water, she thought back to early yesterday morning, when she and Alex had stood in the shower together. They had teased and played, and it had been nice, and of course, he'd reminded her that she could still get on the plane with him—no matter what it cost, they could buy a ticket. She'd reminded him that he could forget Cancún and come with her.

But they'd parted anyway. He hadn't let her drive him to the airport; they were all going on one plane out of Kennedy, he told her, and Kennedy would be in the opposite direction. He wished her a wonderful Christmas, and sounded sincere when he said that she should enjoy her family.

She hoped she had sounded equally sincere when she had told him to enjoy Cancún.

Just a little more than twenty-four hours ago now and yet it seemed like forever.

As she stood under the warm spray of the shower, she wondered how her life in Manhattan could seem so far away. There had actually been moments when she hadn't really thought about Alex in Cancún, or really worried half as much as she might have. Well, that was probably thanks to the stranger, too; he seemed to be keeping them all on their good behavior.

And, apparently, he *wasn't* a maniacal serial killer, since she was pretty sure they'd all wakened that morning in their beds.

Dressed and ready for the day, she stepped back into her room. Genevieve was still sleeping.

Morwenna hesitated, and then quietly opened her bag. There was a wrapped gift there in her luggage, one she had forgotten to give Alex. She'd planned it as part of his Christmas stocking if he'd come home with her, since at the MacDougal house, everyone got a stocking.

It was a little box of her favorite men's cologne. She studied the prettily wrapped little package. She honestly didn't even know if Alex liked it or not. He'd said he did when they'd started dating. But then, at that time, if she liked something, he liked it.

It was cologne, she could replace it easily. She found a new tag and put Gabe's name on it, and the words *From Santa*.

Morwenna left the room and hurried downstairs.

There was no one in the parlor as she dropped the little gift under the tree, or in the dining room. Her mother, she knew, was up. But as she headed for the kitchen, she paused. She could hear her mother speaking to Gabe.

"It's my favorite day. My favorite day of the year. It always has been. I like my birthday just fine, mind you. Thanksgiving is wonderful, and so is Easter. But Christmas... I don't know. I always believe just a little in magic when it's Christmas Day," Stacy said.

"It's a lovely day," Gabe replied.

She started to move on in, but then hesitated; her mother spoke again, bringing up her name.

"I wish I could give that magic to my children," she said. "Morwenna..."

Morwenna tensed.

Eavesdropping was not at all nice! she reminded herself.

But she felt frozen in place.

"My daughter," Stacy continued, "I love her so much. And I don't know what happened. I think she forgot how to be happy. I think she even thinks she *is* happy most of the time, but...take a look at my husband. He's a rather suspicious fellow. Well, his father wanted him to be an attorney. I don't think he even liked the law at first—he went into the law because that's what the sons in the family did. Then, along the way, he discovered that he did have a passion for seeing that *victims* received what was right, and that those who hurt others must be put away. He did what people thought he should, but somehow he made it work on his terms. He seems gruff and hard sometimes, but when he wins a case and comes home having put away the bad guy, he's so happy! You're in law enforcement—you must understand some of the feelings he has, and how he can be up and down and frustrated. And when he doesn't win, I'm there to help him through the struggle. But with Morwenna... I fear sometimes that we hurt her. She's like a little hamster on a wheel, running and running. I worry that she's not going where she wants to be. Last night really brought it home to me. She's forgotten—and I think that most of the world forgets— that it's nice sometimes just to wake up and be happy for what we do have, and remember that *happy* isn't a constant state for anyone."

"Well, Mrs. MacDougal, I think you are wise beyond measure," Gabe told her. "And, to be truthful, I think that your daughter is very smart, and a very good person, and that she will find her way."

"Wenna!"

She turned, her cheeks reddening as she heard the whisper from the dining room doorway.

Bobby was there. He had pure mischief in his eyes and he shook his finger in a "no-no" gesture. He tiptoed up to her. "Eavesdropping? On your mother?"

She elbowed him in the ribs. "I wasn't eavesdropping!" she protested. "I just got here."

"Yeah, and you always walk around with your ear glued to the wall," Bobby said.

She elbowed him again. "Hey! Lay off the ribs, will you? There could be a hot girl in my future somewhere," he told her.

"Your future here? In this house?" she asked skeptically.

"No. But, my dear, just because the weather *was* so wretched we couldn't get out of the house and our little area, things always change! If the weather holds, we'll go down to the village. Gabe can get ahold of his headquarters and tell them that a con is running around somewhere, and we'll have a wassail drink at the old tavern later on. I think Mom wants to go to the cemetery and do her prayer thing there, and, of course, there's church tonight," Bobby reminded her.

"Ah, yes! Drive-in Mass."

"Gotta love Father Donaldson. He says that if he can get his parishioners into the church for twenty minutes and a quickie mass, it's better than no mass at all."

"Which works for Dad," Morwenna agreed. "I think Mom would like a service with more singing, and a sermon that's longer than 'Please, Lord, help team X win the Super Bowl!'"

"I think that Mom is just glad Dad goes to church, and agrees to her little MacDougal prayer service at the cemetery," Bobby said.

"You're probably right," Morwenna said.

Stacy came through the swinging door, smiling. "I thought I heard you two out here. Good morning. Good—beautiful—Christmas morning!"

Gabe followed her out of the kitchen, smiling to see them. Morwenna caught his smile—Lord, but it was a good smile. But he wasn't just a stranger, she reminded herself, there was something about him that made the odd little sensual twinges she was feeling seem just not right somehow.

Didn't matter! Soon she'd be back in Manhattan, running the rat race and spending time with Alex.

"Merry Christmas," he said.

"And likewise!" she returned. "You slept well?"

"Like a baby."

As Gabe replied, Morwenna's father came into the dining room. "Merry Christmas, all. The little ones up yet?"

"Genevieve was still sleeping when I got up," Morwenna said.

"Well," Mike said, "I imagine they'll be up soon enough. Is coffee on in the kitchen?"

"Yes, dear, I'll get you a cup," Stacy said.

But Mike MacDougal set his hands on his wife's shoulders and kissed the top of her head. "Thank you, Stacy. I can get coffee. You spoil us all."

"I'll take some, too, Dad," Bobby said.

"You can come in and fix your own coffee. I don't know what you take with it these days," Mike said.

As Mike disappeared into the kitchen, they heard a loud screech of delight from the parlor.

"Kids are up!" Stacy said happily, hurrying out.

Morwenna followed her mother. She paused though, in the doorway, her smile deepening, something tugging at her heart.

Connor and little Genevieve were in front of the tree, hand in hand, staring at the ornaments and the packages beneath. Connor had let out the whoop, having seen his new bicycle.

"Santa came—I told you he would come," Genevieve said.

Shayne had followed his children down the stairs and stood behind them, silent. Connor turned around and hurried over to him, throwing his arms around his father. "Thanks, Dad," he said huskily. "It was the only... like, *thing* that I wanted and kind of needed."

Morwenna felt her heart would break as she watched her brother put his hand gently on his son's head. "I'm afraid you won't be able to use it much for a while. I'm pretty sure the snow is piled high in Pittsburgh, too. And don't worry—you don't have to keep it at my apartment. You can keep it at your mom's house. You go back and forth from school there most of the time."

Connor nodded. "Thanks," he said again.

"Daddy, can I open something, please?" Genevieve asked. "Connor can see his bike! My stuff is all wrapped," she said.

"Ask your grandmother. She's our mistress of ceremonies," Shayne said.

Genevieve looked hopefully to her grandmother. "Go for it, Genevieve. In fact, why don't you and Connor hand out the presents. Hand them all to everyone first, and then we'll open in order of our ages, youngest to oldest."

Genevieve giggled. "That means me first!"

"And Connor second."

"Anyone else for coffee or cocoa?" Morwenna asked. "I can make it while Genevieve is handing out the gifts."

"I'll help you," Gabe said. He shrugged. "I'm not a family member—I can give out coffee and keep the kitchen going, and I'll enjoy watching all of you in between."

"You may be surprised," she told him. "But sure, help me hand out coffee."

Genevieve and Connor were already out by the tree, looking for names on tags.

Morwenna smiled as Gabe followed her into the kitchen. As she poured coffee into mugs, Gabe got the milk from the refrigerator and found a copper-bottomed pan hanging from the wooden overhead above the work-station in the center of the kitchen.

"Why don't I heat up the milk for the cocoa?" he said.

Morwenna went for the sugar, and looked over at Gabe. "This fellow that you were chasing—what had he done?" she asked.

"Luke DeFeo? He's been sentenced before—petty larceny. This time he stole the funds for the homeless from a church just outside Richmond."

"A thief, but not a murderer?" Morwenna asked. "Well, that's good to know, if this guy is running around the mountain somewhere."

"Not a murderer; but still a very dangerous man," Gabe said. He hesitated, adding the chocolate squares Morwenna provided to the heating milk. "Sometime this evening, thanks to your brother's kind medical care, I'll be able to head out and try to track him again. I really need to find him before the day is done."

"Why? What difference will it make when you catch him?" Morwenna asked.

Gabe looked at the milk and chocolate he was stirring. "Because he's especially dangerous on a day like today, that's why." He looked at her.

There was something about his words that seemed strange.

"Yes, I guess, what with all the presents. But I'm not sure you should head back out into the snow today," she said. "You seem to be absolutely fine, but you did take a nasty beating yesterday."

"I'll be fine," he assured her.

She realized that she didn't want their uninvited guest to leave.

"Gabe, we are the citizens you're supposed to be protecting, no matter the actual jurisdiction. If you're looking for someone who might be interested in stealing, you should hang with us most of the day."

"I will protect you from him," Gabe said, his tone almost fierce.

"I believe you will," Morwenna said. She felt awkward for a moment. "Mom likes to do a little service at the cemetery, and then we're heading down to the village tavern for a drink. And hey, we need some outside company, to divert us from ripping on each other," she said. "Kind of sad, isn't it? Most of us really love our families so much, and yet, we're cruel to one another in a way we wouldn't be with others. I guess that's because others would just walk away."

"That's one way to look at it," he told her. "Maybe, sometimes, we're mean to our families because they're the people who see what we don't want to admit to ourselves, and will love us no matter what."

"I think I'm just going to call you Mr. Sunshine from now on," Morwenna told him.

He laughed, stirring the hot chocolate mixture a last time. "Doesn't that have to do with the fact that you can see the glass as half-empty—or half-full?"

"Come along, Mr. Sunshine. The gifts are surely divided by now," Morwenna said.

They made two trips with the cups of hot chocolate and coffee, and then took seats on the sofa where their presents had been left. Morwenna quickly saw that she wasn't the only one who had found something for Gabe; he had a stack of four gifts.

He looked around the room. "You didn't need to do this! You gave me everything—by taking me in," he said.

Genevieve came to him and with her little hands pushed him down into his chair. "Santa knew you were here, Gabe. But I get to go first!"

Morwenna noted that her mother had done a good job whipping up stockings for the children at the last minute. Genevieve received Fruit Roll-ups, quarters for the games at the tavern and a pretty little set of silver earrings—probably something her mom had bought for herself, since she was always losing one earring. She was delighted. Her present from her father was a real working kids' stove and an electronic game. Stacy had wrapped up one of her collectible Cabbage Patch dolls, and the little girl was in awe of it, playing with it as Connor opened the rest of his gifts.

Then Bobby told them that his gift was a song, and he pulled out his guitar and sang to them:

Christmas morning, what a thrill, for Gen and Connor are here,
Pretty girl, handsome lad,
Giving us the best Christmas ever had!
Christmas Day, what a thrill, for Gen and Connor here!
Clever girl, brilliant lad,
When they're around, nothing can be bad,

Oh, it's a Gen and Connor Christmas,
How we love it, ever so dear,
Connor and Genevieve,
Ring the bells!
Light the lights!
When Gen smiles, all the world is bright!
Ring the bells!
Light the lights!
When Connor is with us,
The world is all right!
Oh, it's a Gen and Connor Christmas,
A Gen and Connor Christmas,
And Christmas Day
Burns so bright!

The kids, giggling all the while, pounced on Bobby, hugging him.

"Hey," Bobby cried. "Munchkins! Watch the guitar."

"Come on, Uncle Bobby. You're up next!" Genevieve told him.

"Okay, okay. Pummel the flesh, but not the guitar, eh?" Bobby teased. "Gen, you help me with that one. I don't wrap well, and I open even worse."

"You can't open a present badly," Genevieve told him, but she began tearing at the wrapping paper for him.

Bobby was also delighted with his gifts. His stocking had been filled with Pez animals, beef jerky, turkey jerky and more. His parents had gotten him a new, down-lined coat. Shayne had gotten him an electronic reader with a special music application, and Morwenna had gone out of her way wrapping up a gift certificate to a national-chain music store, nestled in a bed of guitar picks, strings and a tuner.

"Now you, Auntie Wenna!" Genevieve said. "Are you really bad at unwrapping, too?"

"Well, of course I am," Morwenna said, sitting her niece on her lap. "Go for it, girl."

First, the stocking. Morwenna's had sugar substitute, lip gloss guaranteed to prevent chapping in cold weather, nail polish and emery boards. Genevieve happily tore apart Morwenna's gifts for her. Morwenna oohed and aahed over her presents—a computer bag with just the right number of pockets, a beautiful black cocktail dress, a snow hat with matching gloves and a tiny little box.

"What's this?" Genevieve asked.

"I don't know. Open it."

Genevieve opened the little box. It held a delicate gold chain that held an angel or cherub, almost like the one on her mother's tree. It was a beautiful piece.

Morwenna looked around the room; there was no signature on the box.

"Mom, where did you find this?" Morwenna asked.

"I didn't. Mike?" Stacy asked.

"No, I didn't buy it, I'm sorry to say," Mike said.

"Not me—I'm the hat and gloves," Bobby said.

"I'm the computer bag," Shayne said.

"Santa Claus!" Genevieve announced.

"How curious," Morwenna said. She took out the chain and little medallion, and Bobby offered to fasten it around her neck. She felt it as it lay against her flesh, and touched it gently. "I'll figure out my secret Santa, guys. But thank you one and all."

"So who is next—Shayne or Gabe?" Connor asked.

"Gabe—I believe I'm older," Shayne said.

Gabe seemed humbled and appreciative as he opened

his gifts. When he got to Morwenna's present, he smiled at her. "Uncanny! It's my favorite. But—"

"Hey!" Stacy said. "You're our guest. Please enjoy what little we have to offer. And, now, Shayne, it's to you!"

Shayne feigned excitement over his gifts and Morwenna wanted to make it all better for her older brother.

It was his first Christmas as a divorced man.

The kids went on to help Mike and Stacy open their presents, and then Stacy announced that it was time for a quick breakfast.

"But not too many people in the kitchen, please, or I can't get anything done," Stacy said. "Morwenna, you and Gabe can come with me. Bobby, you and Dad set the table. Shayne, gather up all the wrappings and get them into the garbage—all right, everyone?"

It was agreed. Stacy had her crowd well in hand; she turned on a Christmas CD, and everyone went about their tasks.

On egg duty with Gabe in the kitchen, Morwenna realized that he had put on a spray of the men's cologne she had given him.

She smiled. "Nice," she told him. She hesitated, staring at him. "Was the angel from you?"

"Angels are from above," he teased in return.

"But, seriously, was it? Was it meant for someone else in your life?" she asked.

"Was the cologne?"

"Cologne is easy—it's in every department store," she said.

He laughed. "Maybe angels are easy, too, if you just look."

She turned away, humming to the song on the CD, "O Little Town of Bethlehem."

"You don't sound at all like a sick hyena," Gabe told her.

"Anyone can hum," she assured him.

"Watch the eggs!" Stacy commanded.

They both laughed. Once Stacy pulled the toast out and Morwenna's father and brothers wound up in the kitchen and they all bumped into each other as they brought the food out to the table.

In a few minutes breakfast was all set up, and they gathered around the table, and there were several minutes of "Pass the toast, please," or "Can you hand me that plate of hash browns?" until all their plates were filled. Coffee and drinks were poured and passed, and everyone praised Stacy for a delicious breakfast, and then Bobby told the kids to go up and get their snow-suits on, threatening them with a snowball fight.

When the kids had gone with Shayne to get dressed for the snow, Stacy sat back with her coffee and said, "Bobby, play us something. Something Christmasy and magical."

When Bobby returned with his guitar, he perched on a kitchen stool and strummed a few notes.

"'O Holy Night,'" Gabe suggested.

Bobby nodded and played and sang. When he finished, Stacy stood and came over and kissed him on the cheek, tears brimming in her eyes. "That was really beautiful," she said.

"I've applied to Juilliard," Bobby said, wincing slightly as he looked at his father. "I may well not make it. I don't know how many incredibly talented people apply every year. But I know how you feel, Dad, and you won't be responsible for helping me. I've found a way to work through school."

"Juilliard!" Stacy said.

"Juilliard," Mike repeated, frowning slightly, clearly taken off guard.

"Juilliard is one of the most prestigious schools in the country, Bobby. I hope you make it!" Morwenna said, surprising herself with her readiness to step in for her brother.

"I'll know in the next few days," Bobby said, sounding amazed by her enthusiasm. "I missed the usual auditions, and had to get a special audience with the music school, but somehow, believe it or not, they were chockfull of pianists and violinists, and a little light on those auditioning for guitar this year. So... I'll know right after New Year's."

"Juilliard," Mike said again. He blinked. "Bobby, do you know how hard it is to make a living with a guitar? Every kid out there has one. Every kid dreams of being a rock star."

"Might as well dream big," Bobby said. He glanced at his sister, silently thanking her for the support she had offered him.

"It's not just a 'rock star' thing, Dad," Morwenna said. "You just heard him play a Christmas carol that was so beautiful, it made tears spring to the eyes."

"It's a hard, hard living, son," Mike said.

"I don't mind working hard," Bobby said.

Morwenna glanced at Gabe; of course, he wasn't a member of their family, and he hadn't said a word. As she looked at him, though, she realized that he had known. Bobby had told him.

Mike stood. "We can talk about this later," he said.

Bobby stood as well. "We can talk all you want, Dad, but my mind is made up. I know you want the best for me, and I respect that. But if I don't make it into Juilliard, I'll find another music academy or institute. I'm going for what I want. I'm not going to be Morwenna, brilliant—and languishing in business meetings!"

"What?" Morwenna gasped. "Bobby, I have a great job—"

"Yes, you have a great job, and it should have given you a wonderful outlet for your work. But it didn't. It turned you into corporate America, which would be just fine, if what you really wanted was corporate America. You're not that old, Morwenna. Actually, that wouldn't even matter. You can start over at any time in life— you can start over and start drawing again. Anyway, sorry. I didn't want to ruin Christmas for anyone. I'm going to head out and have a snowball fight with the kids like I promised."

Indignant, Morwenna watched him go. She blinked hard; she had a great job. She might know herself that corporate America hadn't been her dream, but to the outside world, she had an enviable job. She had a great guy, Alex. This—this being home for the holidays— this was out of context.

She looked at her parents. They still seemed to be in shock.

Gabe stood up. "I think I'll join in the snowball fight," he said. He looked down at Morwenna and offered her a hand. "Are you coming?"

"Yes, I'm going to whack the sh—the stuffing out of Bobby," she said. She headed out quickly, and Gabe followed her. At the door she slipped into her heavy parka and gloves, and burst outside, gathering up a handful of snow before she reached the yard. Connor and Genevieve had been using one of the high-growing pines as shelter against Bobby's attacks. Morwenna headed straight for her brother with a big, wet, sloppy snowball.

She creamed him.

The kids, laughing delightedly, came from around the pines. Bobby was down in the snow, howling in protest and laughter, when Shayne came running out and pelted Morwenna. She stood, aimed back at him and hit Gabe in the chest.

In a few minutes, they were rolling in the snow, all soaked and still tossing snow and laughing.

Morwenna was vaguely aware of the crunch of footsteps on the snow; she was still startled when a deep, loud angry voice called out.

"Hey!"

They all paused, rolled and looked down the slope. A tall man in a Virginia State Police uniform and parka was heading up toward them.

"Hey!" he shouted again. "Stop right there, all of you. Don't move. You're harboring a *murderer!*"

Chapter 6

Stunned, half-frozen in the snow, Morwenna stared at the newcomer.

He was a tall, well-muscled man of about thirty, or thirty-five, dark-haired, with fierce dark eyes and a rugged-looking face.

He could have been a cop...

He was in uniform...

"Get up, Gabe!" he said, striding over to stand above Gabe, Morwenna and the kids where they were tangled together in their snow brawl.

Gabe stood, staring at the newcomer. "He isn't a cop," he said evenly. "He has the clothes because he stole them off me. He isn't a cop, and I'm not a murderer, and *he* isn't even a murderer."

Morwenna was vaguely aware that the door to their house had opened and closed.

Genevieve was clinging to her pants. Connor was just staring wide-eyed.

Shayne walked the few feet to the men. "All right, let's sort this out here," he said. "May I see your credentials? Are you armed?"

The man's eyes flickered for a minute, and then seemed to gleam with an angry fire. "My sidearm was lost when I grappled with this escaped convict. Trust me, he's dangerous. I need to take custody of him now."

"He's lying," Gabe said. "He's the convict. The thief."

The door to the house burst open and Mike, followed by Bobby, came bursting out of the house.

Mike had his shotgun, and it was aimed at the two strangers in their midst.

"All right, what the hell is going on here?" Mike demanded.

"I'm Officer Luke DeFeo of the Virginia State Police," the newcomer said, his voice filled with authority. "You've been deceived by a criminal, a convicted killer."

"That's a lie. He's the con. You found me half dead in the snow because we wrestled when I was trying to bring him back to justice. He stole my clothing, and gave me his," Gabe said. "You have to believe me. This man isn't a murderer, but he could prove to be the most dangerous man who ever walked into your lives."

"Don't be ridiculous! Put that gun down. You can see that I'm the cop!" Luke DeFeo said. He started walking toward Mike angrily.

But Assistant District Attorney Michael MacDougal was no man's fool. Morwenna was proud when her father cocked the shotgun and said, "I have damn good aim. You stay right where you are. Now, can either of you prove what you're saying? Let's see some ID."

"Look at what I'm wearing!" DeFeo snapped.

"I can see what you're wearing," Mike said. "And you may well be a cop, but this fellow has been with us for a lot of hours now, and we're all alive and well, and it seems that things are appearing in our house rather than disappearing."

Morwenna felt the little angel against her neck. It wasn't studded with gems, but it was still a nice piece. He had given it to her.

Suspicion crept into her mind. Had he taken it off someone else? Maybe someone now lying dead in the snow.

"You leave him alone!" Genevieve said, leaping up with the agility of a child and running to DeFeo. She gave him a hard kick in the shin.

DeFeo let out an angry yell, and almost reached for Genevieve.

"My sister!" Connor cried.

"You touch my daughter, and I'll kill you, cop or no!" Shayne announced. "Genevieve, get over here."

Genevieve obeyed without a murmur.

"Connor, you, too," Shayne said.

Gabe and Morwenna stood, dusting snow from their bodies, staring, and watching and waiting.

"You're going to find yourself under arrest for aiding and abetting a criminal," DeFeo said.

"Let's see your credentials," Mike said firmly.

"Hey, you can see I have a badge."

"And I'll see some ID, too," Mike said firmly.

DeFeo scowled. "I don't have my wallet—I lost it in the tussle with the con you're protecting!"

"If you have no real ID, I have no real proof. No one is going to intimidate me," Mike announced. "If I know one thing, I know the law. And I know that we don't have any way of knowing which of you is telling the truth. So—you. Yeah, you, Virginia State policeman. Raise your arms. Bobby, see if he has cuffs. And if he does, put them on him."

"Yes, sir! Yes, sir, Dad!" Bobby said, and sprang into action.

Morwenna had never seen her brother Bobby as the tough-guy type, and then again, she'd never seen lifesaving Shayne threaten someone's life. But then, his children had been threatened, and now Bobby was ready to spring to the fore.

"If your son touches me, I'll see that he does jail time, too," DeFeo warned.

"And if you touch my son, I'll blow your head off," Mike promised.

Bobby walked straight for DeFeo. "Listen, buddy, if you're legit, and we all wind up at a police station looking like fools, we'll take our chances in court," he said.

"You're risking your lives!" DeFeo said, standing still as Bobby found the cuffs he did have hooked to his belt and slipped them around DeFeo's wrists. "I'm telling you, he's the criminal. If you hold me against my will, he'll find a way to kill me, and slaughter you and your whole family in your beds!"

"We're not taking any chances," Mike said. "We're not taking chances—with anyone. I'm going to disbelieve both of you—until we learn the truth. Morwenna, get in the house. I have good nylon rope in the pantry. I want Gabe tied up, too."

Morwenna stared back at her father, blinking.

"Morwenna!"

She looked down at Gabe, stunned to realize that

they really didn't know. If Gabe was a crook, he could be damn good at deceiving people. It felt as if the cold suddenly swept through her. *Why wouldn't he have killed them last night?*

Because he'd wanted his turkey, that's why.

Gabe looked up and said calmly, "Get the rope, like your father says. Keep us both tied up, and away from the house. Keep your family safe."

"But, Daddy," Genevieve began.

"Hush," Shayne said softly.

"Connor, Genevieve, come with me, please," Morwenna said, and hurried into the house. Stacy was standing in the parlor, looking out the window, her face knit in a worried frown.

"Morwenna?"

"That guy showed up, saying Gabe is a crook, and that he himself is a cop," Morwenna explained briefly.

"I was so worried when I saw your father get the shotgun. I tried the phone again, but that and the computer are still down, too. We've got electricity, but the television is all static. Morwenna, what are we going to do?"

"Keep them both tied up until we can get help," Morwenna said.

"We're on a mountaintop!" Stacy said.

"Mom, Dad has it covered. Besides, we have cars," Morwenna assured her.

Morwenna hurried back out, disturbed to see that her mother had come out to the front without even bothering to put on her coat. Though she had locked the door behind her, with the children inside.

She rushed by her, though. Gabe was standing a distance from Luke DeFeo. He offered his hands to her as she approached him.

"Behind his back!" DeFeo said. "Like you did me!"

"Wait!" Stacy said. She walked forward into the group. "One of these men is a criminal, and we really don't know what kind of criminal. But one of them isn't. And we're not breaking any arms or starving either of them. Tie their hands in front. We have the shotgun, and there are five of us adults here—we can watch them."

Shayne walked over to their mother. "Mom, we can't know how long until the phone and computer are back up, and it looks like we might have more bad weather coming in. We have to make sure that these guys are secure."

He pointed to the sky; it had been so blue.

Now, gray clouds were hovering. Strange gray clouds. Morwenna couldn't tell if they were coming from east or west, north or south. But they seemed to be converging over their house.

"We'll take turns watching them," Stacy insisted.

Gabe lifted his hands.

"Secure, Morwenna!" her father called.

"Yes, sir."

Gabe didn't move. She was close to him. The subtle scent of the cologne she had given him seemed to sweep around her. She looked at him. His eyes remained steady, green and open.

She looked down and tied his hand securely in a clove hitch. Her father, still keeping an eye on Luke DeFeo as Bobby recinched the metal cuffs, walked over to see that she had tied the knot correctly. He nodded his approval.

"Now what?" DeFeo asked. He let out a sigh. His voice changed to something that was just weary. "This is ridiculous, honestly. You all need to help me. You seem like a nice family. I don't want you running into trouble. If you don't see what's going on here soon, you will face jail time, and you've just afforded yourselves a miserable day. You're going to spend your Christmas staring at the two of us. I would have taken this wretch back to justice!"

"And how were you going to do that?" Mike Mac-Dougal asked him, his words barking. Morwenna imagined him in a courtroom. Her father, she knew, often managed to get people to say things they had surely never intended to say. "You came by foot."

"I'd have walked the bastard down the mountain," DeFeo said, his tone angry again. Then he seemed to gain control. "Look, you've all been fooled. You don't know what you're dealing with here."

"That's right," Shayne said quietly. "We don't know what we're dealing with here."

"And there's no way in hell anyone is walking anyone down the mountain," Stacy said. "It's a hard trip at best—hours walking in spring. There is weather coming in again."

"That's right, and you should let me handle it. We'll be out of your way in a moment," DeFeo pleaded.

"So…what now?" Morwenna asked.

Mike looked at the sky. "It may clear up soon enough," he said. "I can't tell right now exactly what the weather is going to do, but I think it would be foolhardy to try to reach even the village right now. Looks like we'll have to hold tight for a while."

"The garage and the shed," Stacy said. "You've got to keep them separated, and out of the wind. As soon as the weather clears, we'll get them both down to the tavern. They must have a way to reach some kind of help there."

"Bobby, you're on watch with Gabe. Shayne, you

take DeFeo. The toolshed is empty. I brought the shovel and anything else anyone could use as a weapon into the house once we had a guest in the house," Mike said, glancing toward Gabe. "Shayne, you keep the shotgun. God knows what someone could find in the garage. I'll spell you in thirty minutes. Morwenna, you'll take over for Bobby."

Morwenna nodded. Neither of the men offered resistance as they were brought, handcuffed, to their respective places, Mike behind them both.

Morwenna looked up. The sky was darkening, and it couldn't have been later than ten in the morning.

As her father walked back to the house, he said, "I guess we'll have turkey later, Stacy. As soon as we can, we'll head down to Scott's Tavern with these two men."

Stacy started to walk into the house, and then she paused, looking at her husband. "The cemetery is on the way," she said.

"Stacy, we've got a criminal on our hands, and— depending on which man you believe—one of them might be a murderer."

Stacy straightened her shoulders. "The weather is going to be iffy all day. The cemetery is on the way to the village. It will only take a minute or two."

"Stacy," Mike said, "we could walk all the way and get rid of these two guys—"

"Mike! There's no guarantee that we'll have any communication when we reach the village, and no guarantee that there will be someone there who can watch them. This may remain our burden until we can get help up the mountain. The cemetery is on the way— we're going to stop briefly. We can keep the shotgun on them for one minute while we say a prayer. I'm still saying my Christmas prayers over my family's graves!"

With that, Stacy walked firmly into the house. Mike followed, but the door slammed in his face. He turned and looked at Morwenna and the kids. "All right, so the cemetery is on the way. How ridiculous is all this? One of us will stand with the shotgun trained on the two of them, and we'll say a prayer—in a graveyard. Christmas!"

He didn't say it, but Morwenna could almost imagine that he did.

Christmas! Bah, humbug!

"Look, I'm really sorry about this," Bobby said. And then, a little edge of doubt crept in. How often had he seen his father exhausted when a judge had ruled out key evidence and the jury was being swayed because the con could speak so persuasively?

Did he want to believe in this guy because this guy wanted him to believe in him?

"At least, I think I'm sorry," he muttered.

"It's all right. Man is a creature who must see something, hold it, find it tangible, before he really believes," Gabe said.

"He is wearing the uniform," Bobby pointed out.

"So he is."

Gabe walked ahead of Bobby into the shed.

There were two little windows in the small building, so light could come in. When there was light. Right now, the sky was darkening. Bobby ushered Gabe in; even out of the growing wind, though, the shed was cold. The garage, he figured, was just as cold. But there were lights in the garage; several of them. The shed had one overhanging bulb. Bobby turned it on. It provided some light. A concrete floor had been poured years before, but the concrete emanated cold.

Bobby sat down against the back wall. There were wooden shelves and brackets, but, as his dad had said, the few tools they usually kept there had been brought into the house. His father, he realized, was a smart man.

"Bobby, there's nothing in this shed I could use to hurt anyone, if I had that in mind," Gabe said. "You don't have to stay out here—it's freezing."

"Yeah, it's cold," Bobby said briefly. "When Morwenna comes, I'll see to it that you get some blankets out here. And, hopefully, this won't last long. We'll get you both down to the tavern, or we'll get law enforcement up here one way or the other."

Gabe nodded. "Hard to tell. If a bad storm comes in…" He grinned. "Too bad you didn't bring your guitar. I'd be entertained. Honored, actually. And, at least you've said what you needed to say to your family now. You've got it in you."

Bobby laughed. "You want to know the funniest thing? I had confidence, and I had hope. But now that I've spit it all out, I'm suddenly afraid."

Gabe thought about that for a minute. "Well, before, if you failed, you were just failing yourself. Now, in your mind, if you were to fail, you'd be failing them instead."

"Failing everyone," Bobby murmured.

"Personally, I think the only way you fail is if you never try," Gabe said lightly.

Gabe seemed comfortable enough—he was shivering a little—but he seemed relaxed. *Resigned,* maybe. They might have been having a conversation in a warm kitchen over a cup of coffee.

But, Bobby thought, if he'd wanted to, Gabe could suddenly...

Head butt him?

"I'm telling you the truth," Gabe said, as if reading his mind. "I'm the cop—he's the bad guy."

"And I want to believe you," Bobby said.

"I'm glad."

"But I can't let you go."

"I know that. I understand."

"My mother, my sister...my niece and nephew...they are all vulnerable here," Bobby said.

"I know. I told you... I understand."

Bobby walked away from the door, looking up at the sky.

It seemed the darkness was closing in all around them, but in the center of it all, there was light. Maybe the weather would break.

He prayed heartily that it would do so...and soon.

Shayne leaned against his car, the shotgun in his hand as he stared at the man in the Virginia State Police uniform.

The guy wasn't fighting with him. He was just leaning against the garage, staring at him with a hard look that made his features severe.

"I wish you'd listen to me," DeFeo said at last. "You look like an intelligent guy. You can *see* that I'm a cop, no matter what kind of story that guy gave you. Look, he's got that green-eyed thing going for him. He knows how to say all the right things. That's how he managed to break out. He was being transferred from one facility to another, talked the guard into letting him have a cigarette—then bashed the poor fellow's head halfway in. You should be worried—that's your sister, I take it—and your mom. And your children. You've got a lot at stake here. Think about it. He's been using you."

"He could have killed us in our sleep last night or robbed the place blind," Shayne said. "He didn't."

DeFeo sighed. "Ted Bundy."

"What?"

"Ted Bundy. The serial killer. You know he actually babysat for his neighbor, right? John Wayne Gacy—he was a clown. Hey, kids love clowns. Don't you get it— the good-guy thing is an act."

"He's been acting well enough to win an Oscar," Shayne said. His voice was even. His pulse was racing. What if they were wrong? This guy did look and sound like a cop. And he had a badge—but he didn't have an ID.

Shayne felt a cold sweat break out.

His children... What if they had entertained some kind of real crook, a killer? What if Gabe Lange was just what this guy said he was, and DeFeo had come upon them just in time to save them?

"Officer DeFeo," he said, "you may be all that you say you are, but we don't know that any more than we know that he *isn't* who he claims to be. Just wait it out. When we can, we'll get to the authorities, and if we've wronged you, I'll apologize a thousand times over."

DeFeo shook his head, disgusted. "And what if he breaks out? Who is watching him next? Your sister, right? What if she falls for his act?"

"My sister isn't stupid."

"Not unless he talks her into being stupid. I'm sure he's given her all kinds of speeches on how wonderful she is at something, at how she needs to trust her instincts and have belief in herself and all that. That's his game. I know this guy—trust me," DeFeo said.

"She's not going to fall for any lines. She's in a relationship."

DeFeo laughed. "Sure. And he's making her doubt that relationship."

"This conversation is going nowhere," Shayne said. "I'm not letting you go."

"Just because your father is a fo—just because your father is misguided is no reason for you to wind up caught in the trap. You're taking a chance with your children. That's damn dangerous, my friend. I'm telling you, he's been using you. When he was done playing his game, when your mother had cooked everything up for a great turkey dinner, your family would have been done for. You really want to thank your lucky stars that I found this old house when I did."

"My father isn't a fool, DeFeo. He's done the one really smart thing—he's refused to take either of you at face value."

"Sure, that would be smart. If it weren't possible that Gabe would escape—and bring us all down, because I'm handcuffed and can't help you. Let's pray he doesn't get his hands on that shotgun, that's all I have to say."

Shayne didn't answer him. He couldn't help but listen to him, and he couldn't help but wonder if he was right.

DeFeo was silent for a while. "Cute kids," he said finally, as if he felt the need to talk about something.

"Yep."

"You here with them alone? Where's the wife? Oh, sorry, you're divorced, I take it."

"Yep."

"I've been down that path," DeFeo said. "I guess she

was good to let you have them for Christmas. Usually, after a divorce, the mother has the power. Fathers are screwed. They pay all the bills, and the wives either hound them for more support, or play games, not even letting the dads see the kids."

"You're divorced?"

DeFeo nodded. "I spent hours working. She spent them at a gym. Took off with a personal trainer, and still got the kids. And I still pay the bills."

"I'm sorry to hear that. Hope you get them for a while around the holidays."

"She claimed she wanted the holiday, and then, turns out the trainer dude she was seeing didn't want kids at the holidays. But, this year, I had to work, so it was too bad." He smiled. "Sorry, I guess I shouldn't be happy, but he took off for San Diego without her. So, she has the kids for Christmas."

"How many?"

"I have the same thing as you—my boy is ten, and my little girl is five."

"Mine are nine and six."

"Just about the same."

Shayne shifted, pulling his scarf higher around his face; it was really cold in the garage.

"What's the weather doing? Can you see from there?"

"It's still dark and gray, but no snow."

"I'm just saying, I hope your dad can carry through his plan to get us somewhere before Gabe Lange makes his break. Because, if not, well, it's going to be one hell of a Christmas."

"This is just ridiculous," Morwenna said.

Her father was pacing in the parlor; Stacy was trying

to distract Connor and Genevieve with their new toys, but the children had picked up on the tension in the air.

Mike walked to the window. "The snow is deep. If it starts up again and we're walking down to the tavern, someone could really get hurt. I wish it would just do something, one way or the other."

"Well, it's like an ice age out there," Morwenna said. "I'm going to get blankets, and we'll go and spell Bobby and Shayne. They have to be half-frozen, and we've got to do something for both those men, since we've no idea which man is the good one."

"Gabe is really nice," Genevieve said. "How could he be a bad man?"

Mike looked at his granddaughter. He walked over to her, hunkered down and pulled her to him, hugging her tenderly. "Sometimes, it's just hard to tell. And sometimes, we have to really listen and weigh everything that's going on. Sometimes, wolves wear sheep's clothing," he said.

"I'll get the blankets, Dad," Morwenna said.

"There are plenty extra in the hall closet," Stacy said. "And there are some of those little hot packets that you all use when you go out sometimes. They're in a box in the closet, too. Hang on. I'll fix a couple of thermoses with coffee," Stacy said.

"We don't have to baby either of them, Stacy," Mike said.

"Keeping someone alive is hardly babying them!" she said indignantly.

"We're not killing anyone," Mike said wearily.

"I just have a bad time myself not believing Gabe," Stacy said.

Mike stood and looked at his wife. "We're not disbelieving him, Stacy. We're being safe."

He indicated the children. Stacy nodded. "But coffee won't be a bad thing."

"No, Stacy," Mike said. "You fix those thermoses."

Ten minutes later, Morwenna and her father started out of the house, each holding a thermos, a blanket and a handful of heat packs.

As they neared the garage, Mike warned, "Morwenna, take care. Please. I don't think that guy could possibly find anything in the storage shed to hurt anyone with, but…remember, words can be a dangerous weapon. *Kind* words can be dangerous. That man was a guest in our house…he made us all laugh. But it could have all been a lie. Don't fall for anything, please?"

"I'm not going to fall for a man I don't know. Come on—you know that I'm involved with someone else."

He was silent as they walked for a minute; she could hear the loud crunching sound their feet made in the snow.

"And I know that even while you've cheerfully explained to us why this 'someone else' isn't here, you're trying to sell yourself on the same explanation. Just be careful. I can see that Gabe Lange could be a very attractive man."

"Dad! I was raised by a prosecutor, and I live in Manhattan. I'm nearly as suspicious of all humanity as you." She kissed his cheek, and turned, heading for the shed.

Bobby hadn't closed the door; he was standing in the door frame, hugging himself, and looking as if he was nearly shriveled with cold.

"Go back to the house," she told him. "My turn to take over."

He nodded to her gratefully. "That blanket for me?"

"No, you're heading to the house. It's for Gabe."

"Oh, yeah, makes sense. You going to be okay? You're sure?"

"Fine. Go," she said.

She gave him a little shove and looked into the shed. Gabe was seated on the floor against the wall, and like Bobby, he was curled in on himself as much as was humanly possible.

"Here," she said, tossing down the blanket. He tried to catch it awkwardly with his tied hands. She came close enough to drape it over him, and then carefully stretched out her arm to give him the heat packs. "I have coffee for you, too, but you can put those down your shirt. They'll warm you up for a good hour or so, maybe even two hours."

He nodded, apparently familiar with the little bean-baglike sacks. Morwenna could appreciate her mother's wisdom in seeing that the men were handcuffed with their hands at the front of their bodies rather than behind; she wasn't sure she would have wanted the task of trying to slip the heat packs down into his clothing. It was disconcerting to come even this close.

He managed to get the packs beneath his clothing. Keeping her distance, she handed him the thermos.

"Thanks," he told her. He opened the thermos and took a long swallow of coffee.

"Makes a man feel like he might thaw out again one day," he told her.

"Sure," she said.

"That's better. May be the best coffee I've ever had," he said.

"I'm sure my mother would be glad."

"How's she doing?" he asked.

"My mother? She's fine, of course. We're all going to be fine. We'll watch both of you until we can get you down to the tavern," Morwenna said.

"Thank God," he murmured.

She stared at him.

"I've been telling you the truth. And when we reach the tavern, you'll know that. Is the weather clearing?"

Morwenna hesitated. It had grown quite dark earlier, but it did seem now that it was beginning to lighten.

"I think so," she said.

"Then we'll be able to leave soon... How about you?" he asked. "How are you holding up?"

"I'm fine."

"And I'm sorry. This is a tough Christmas for you."

"No, it's not."

"Sorry, I just meant—"

"You meant the fact that 'boy toy,' as my brothers call him, didn't bother to come with me," Morwenna said irritably.

"Look, I'm sorry."

"I know, sure. And maybe he's just not the right one for me. And maybe he's enjoying beach bunnies in Cancún."

Gabe grinned. "If he is, he's a fool."

"Your lips to God's ear!" she said.

He laughed. "Something like that. Honestly, I'm just anxious that we move before...well, he's a tricky devil, that one. DeFeo. I'm grateful that your family didn't just believe him. I'm afraid that he'll pull something, and everyone will be in danger."

"I thought he was just a thief."

"You can never trust a cornered thief."

Morwenna stepped away from the door for a moment, studying the sky again. It did seem to be clearing, but not in the ordinary way. It appeared almost as if the light was breaking right above the house, like a giant golden ball, and rays of darkness ebbed into it, and then curled back, ebbing away again.

"We should be able to go soon," she said curtly.

She frowned. The front door to the house had opened. Genevieve, cradling her precious teddy bear, was stepping out of the house alone.

"What the heck is she doing?" Morwenna wondered.

Gabe stumbled to his feet, coming to the doorway.

"No!" Morwenna called suddenly.

Genevieve was trying to come out, to see for herself what they were doing. Whatever distraction her mother had been employing with them, it wasn't working.

The little girl was sneaking out—and trying to make sure that she wasn't being seen.

Morwenna could see that her niece meant to approach the shed from the cliff side. Since she was trying not to be seen, she was running around in a wide fashion; she knew that she wasn't allowed to go too far around the house, and yet it suddenly seemed as if she didn't remember. She was a child—a curious child. Morwenna wasn't half as angry as she was afraid.

If she went too far, which she could easily do in the snow, she'd be on uneven ground, and could tumble down a hundred feet or so.

"No!" Morwenna cried.

Too late.

Genevieve let out a shrill scream as she stepped into the snow...and hit nothing beneath it. As Morwenna bolted across the yard, Genevieve began to fall.

Chapter 7

"We can go out soon," Shayne heard his mother say. She'd been sitting beneath the tree with Genevieve, polishing her nails with a pink color from the package Morwenna had given her, when Shayne had first come in. He thanked God for his mother; she loved his children and she was good with them.

But now, coming back to the parlor from the kitchen, Shayne saw that Stacy was looking out the window. He knew that she was anxious. The kids were growing increasingly restless. Of course, if it was storming, they knew they had to stay in. But they'd been anxious to help with the turkey dinner, and now, Stacy wasn't cooking, and Christmas Day had taken a drastic turn.

"The clouds—or whatever!—are just sitting up there," Stacy said, staring out at the sky. "It's just gray and… actually clearing, maybe."

She turned around suddenly.

"Genevieve?"

Connor was playing with the electronic game he'd gotten. He didn't look up.

"Connor, where did Genevieve go?" Stacy asked.

Connor looked up. "She was right here," he said, frowning.

Stacy looked back to the window and gasped.

"Oh, my God! She's on the side path!" Stacy cried.

Shayne bolted for the door and threw it open, unaware of the blast of frigid air that hit him. Genevieve had disappeared beyond the snow.

"My God!" he cried, and raced to the side path that was so pretty in summer, so treacherous in winter.

"Genevieve!" His daughter's name tore from his throat.

In an instant, a fraction of a second in time, he realized that he'd been a bitter fool; that even with the pain of the divorce, he'd been the luckiest man in the world. He had two beautiful, healthy children, and they were worth everything in the world.

And now...

As he ran, he could see his sister coming from the opposite direction. And someone was behind her, and then, overtaking her.

Gabe Lange.

Hands still tied, he was moving like cannon shot, a blur in the snow and the gray. Then, he cleanly disappeared.

He had pitched himself down the ledge, toward Genevieve. Morwenna screamed and followed him.

Shayne heard his heart thundering, heard the gasp of

his breath as he reached the path and beyond; the ledge.
And he stopped himself in time.

Gabe had managed to get himself down the slope
and wedged next to some kind of brush; he'd prevented
Genevieve from tumbling farther with the length of his
body. He was struggling to keep his grasp on whatever bush or outcrop of rock was beneath the snow.
And Morwenna was just above the two; he could see
the branch she held—naked and thin, stripped bare of
green, as if it were a skeletal hand reaching for her instead of the other way around.

"Hold still! I'll get rope!" Shayne shouted.

He turned to head back to the house; his mother
was behind him, terror in her eyes. She was ready to
pitch herself down the mountain, but Shayne grabbed
her shoulders.

"Mom! The rope, the cord of nylon rope in the
kitchen—go get the whole thing, quickly, please!"

"Oh, Shayne!" she cried.

"Mom, go!"

She turned and fled back to the house; he'd never
seen her move so fast.

"Hang on!" he called down the slope.

"Hanging on!" Gabe called up.

Bobby and Connor came running out behind Stacy,
who now had the rope. Shayne looked around; there
was nothing close enough that was steady and stable to
work the rope. Bobby hurried to him, seeing the problem. "You and me, bro. You and me!" he said.

He nodded. "I'm bigger. I'll be the anchor, you the
control."

Bobby didn't argue with him; they had perhaps seconds before something down the slope began to give.

He expertly knotted the nylon around himself while Bobby made a loop with the other end.

Bobby stood at the precipice, testing his footing. He called down to Gabe. "I've got a loop—coming your way."

Shayne angled himself down on the ground, using his weight as an anchor as Bobby tossed the rope down. It fell almost to Genevieve on the first try, and Bobby cursed beneath his breath. Shayne lowered his head, praying. He heard his sister cry up. "Bobby, I've got it. It's good. I'm getting it to Gabe and Genevieve."

"Got it!" Gabe called.

Shayne heard Genevieve's terrified tears then, and he winced, gritting his teeth, digging in farther. The ground was so slick, with patches of ice beneath the snow. He felt something on his legs; his mother had thrown herself down into the snow, too. They looked at one another, and despite his terror, he offered her a weak smile. "Thanks, Mom. We're going to do this."

She nodded grimly.

"I can't! I can't!" Genevieve cried. "Auntie Wenna, I'm so scared."

"Let Gabe get the rope around you. Your daddy is up there. He's going to get you."

"Bobby?" Shayne asked.

His brother was hunkered down, trying to guide the rope, but Bobby glanced at him. "Gabe is getting the loop around her. Morwenna is talking to her, assuring her."

Shayne was aware of the soft sound of sniffles near him. He looked around. Connor was just standing there, frozen as he watched, too little to help, too big not to know what was going on.

And he was surely blaming himself that his sister had slipped out.

"Okay!" Morwenna called up. "She's secure!"

Bobby started to pull on the rope. Shayne heard Genevieve sniffling and crying again. As Bobby secured the rope, Shayne began to inch backward.

Bobby swore suddenly; Shayne saw Connor make a dive.

"What?" he cried hoarsely.

"It was stuck—Connor slipped it. We're good. Keep moving."

His daughter wasn't even heavy; she was a little thing. And yet he felt as if he strained as he never had before, as if each millisecond was years in the making.

"I've got her!" Bobby cried, and Shayne dared look up again. Bobby was falling back from the ledge, Genevieve in his arms. Shayne lowered his head, trying to stop the shaking that had seized hold of his body.

Thank God, thank God, thank God, thank God...

His instinct was to rise and grab his daughter; he knew he couldn't do so. He called out to his mother. "Mom, get Gen. Get her inside, please. Connor, get Gramps. Get him out of the garage—now, please, Connor."

He heard the footsteps in the snow. Morwenna wasn't heavy—maybe a hundred and twenty pounds. But the snow was slick, and the hauling was hard. "Bobby?"

"I've got it back down. Morwenna has the rope... it's around her. Now, Shayne, now, I'm hauling it up."

Again, Shayne began his backward crawl in the snow. He kept fit; being a physician had made him do so, but he felt every muscle, and it seemed every speck of blood and bone in him, ache with the effort.

As he thought he might not make it, his father came

running across the snow; he reached Bobby's side and took on some of the weight, and Shayne inched backward again.

He heard his sister cry out. "I'm here—I've caught the ledge. Just…your hand, Dad."

Shayne looked up again. Mike MacDougal had Morwenna in his arms. The two of them fell backward in the snow, Morwenna half laughing and half crying in their father's arms.

"We've still got Gabe down there!" Bobby reminded them all.

"If you were smart, you'd leave him there."

Shayne twisted to see who was talking. Of course, Mike had left his post at the garage door; Luke DeFeo had followed him out.

"If you're really law enforcement," Mike said, "you'll remember that you catch the criminals, and the justice system sees to punishment."

"And if you're an ADA," DeFeo countered, "you know that half the scum of the earth winds up in court—and then walking."

"Shayne, you ready?" Bobby asked. "Rope is going down again. Can you handle it?"

"Yes," Shayne said.

And yes, he would.

"Go! You've got Dad to help you lever the weight."

This time, it was going to be really hard; Gabe Lange was at least six-two, and had to weigh a well-muscled two hundred–plus pounds.

"Damn!" Bobby swore. He'd not gotten the rope down far enough.

As he pulled it up to toss it down again, they all heard

the cracking of a branch, as loud as thunder in the crisp and silent air of the tension-filled winter morning.

"Hurry!" Morwenna breathed.

"Got it, got it," Bobby assured her.

He tossed the rope again.

They heard Gabe shouting from below. "I have it!"

Just as the echo of his words died, they heard a crack like a gunshot; it was the end of the bush that had broken Gabe's fall down the slope.

Shayne felt himself jerked forward as Gabe's weight fell fully on the rope.

Morwenna screamed, throwing herself on Shayne to further anchor him; Mike lunged forward, catching the rope with Bobby, and they both leaned back, trying to brace their boots against the slick white snow.

"Wenna, back...inch back little by little," Shayne said.

She obeyed him; she wasn't much on size, but the fact that she was there with him, clinging to him as if he were salvation itself, gave him strength. She braced his legs, moving as slowly as a snail, adding weight to his anchor as he painfully wormed his way back, feeling as if his shoulders would break and his spine would snap if they didn't make it soon.

But then, just when he thought he wouldn't make it, the pressure eased up. He and Morwenna had been trying so hard to keep moving that they actually slid backward a foot when the tension on the rope eased.

Again, he dared to look up. Mike had dragged Gabe up the last few feet. And now he, Bobby and Gabe were lying halfway entangled with one another by the slope, gasping for breath, laughing with relief and congratulating one another.

Shayne rolled to his back and looked up at the sky. It had cleared; the dark clouds were gone.

He glanced to the side. Still handcuffed, Luke DeFeo was looking on.

"He's a damn good actor," he said quietly to Shayne.

"I don't give a damn if it was an act or not," Shayne said. "My daughter and my sister are alive."

Morwenna, showered, changed and headed downstairs. She could hear her father speaking to her brother Bobby, and she stopped before reaching the parlor.

"He showered, got into dry warm clothes and let me put the ropes right back on him," Bobby said. "Dad, I just can't see how the man could be any kind of killer."

"I have to admit, Bobby, I just don't see it either. But the thing is, we still don't *know*. What if DeFeo is right?"

"Dad, Gabe pitched himself over a cliff to save Genevieve," Bobby said.

"So did your sister," Mike said huskily.

"Morwenna is my hero, Dad. But she's Genevieve's aunt. Gabe was ready to give his life for a little girl he just met."

She heard her father sigh deeply. "I know that, Bobby. But the sky has cleared. We're getting these guys down to the tavern. Someone there will have some way to communicate with the rest of the world. And if we're right, and Gabe is a good guy, we'll know it then."

Morwenna hurried down the stairs.

"Where are our—prisoners now?" she asked.

"In the kitchen," her father told her.

"With Shayne?"

"Shayne is trying to make Genevieve and Connor

understand that they still have to learn to listen to what they're told," Bobby said.

"Then who is watching the prisoners?" she asked.

"Your mother," Mike said.

"Mom?"

Mike grinned. "Don't underestimate the power of a mother and grandmother, Morwenna," he told her. "She's grateful to Gabe, but she's hard as nails when she wants to be. She knows we're all going to start down to the tavern."

Morwenna stared at her father and Bobby with surprise, and then hurried into the kitchen.

Both men were seated on stools by the island workstation with steaming cups in front of them. It wasn't coffee; Morwenna smelled the aroma of chicken soup.

Stacy was seated away from them at the far end, the shotgun in her hand.

She glanced at Morwenna as she entered. "Make sure you're dressed good and warm," she told her daughter. "We're going to leave as soon as everyone is ready."

"We're walking down, I take it?" she asked her mother, eyeing the two men. They were at opposite sides of the table, but Stacy had seen to it that neither could possibly reach out and grab her—or the shotgun.

"We have to. There isn't a plausible path a car could make anywhere on the mountain right now," her mother said. "Yesterday was dangerous, and there's been more snow since then. Last night, late in the night, I woke up, and I saw that it was snowing again."

Morwenna couldn't help but look across the table at Gabe. He looked at her with a grin and a shrug.

"On this walk, you'd better keep a close eye on Gabe Lange," DeFeo warned. "Don't you people see? He figured that once he'd saved the little girl, you'd be so grateful, you'd untie him."

"He could have died," Morwenna pointed out.

"Yes, but he's facing life in prison or a death sentence if you get him down the mountain," DeFeo said. "The Commonwealth of Virginia still carries out the death penalty when the judge determines that it's appropriate. And you people still don't know the half of what he's capable of."

"We've established that," Morwenna said.

"Fine—take your chances walking down to the tavern," DeFeo said.

"That's what we're doing," Stacy said firmly.

"Stacy!"

Mike's voice sounded from the parlor.

"Yes, Mike?"

"We're ready. Head them on out," he called.

"You heard my husband," Stacy said. "Rise slowly and carefully, gentlemen, one at a time, please, and keep your distance from each other as we head out."

The men rose. Gabe stared at Luke. "After you."

"No, no. I wouldn't be so rude. After you," DeFeo said.

"DeFeo, you first!" Morwenna said. "And I'll be behind you with a frying pan, and trust me, I actually know how to use one on someone's head!"

"Careful not to get in my line of fire," Stacy said lightly.

DeFeo started out. For a moment, Morwenna thought he was going to make a lunge for the knives in the wooden holder on the counter; she quickly made good on her threat and reached for the copper-bottomed frying pan above her head, but it appeared he had just stumbled; he righted himself, balancing against the counter as he headed out.

In the parlor, Stacy handed the shotgun over to Mike. Shayne had brought the children down, dressed in dry snowsuits for the walk down to the tavern. Genevieve was clinging to Connor; Connor had an arm around his sister. She was still white-faced and silent.

Morwenna knew that Shayne had to have done something to discipline her, no matter how grateful he was that she was alive. What she had done was against what she'd been told, and she had certainly been terrified by her misdeed.

Still, she offered her niece a smile. Genevieve looked up at her brother, and then ran to Morwenna, burying her face against Morwenna's thigh.

"Sweetie, we're all right," Morwenna said gently. She lifted the little girl, and looked at Shayne. She didn't think that her brother had been too hard on his daughter.

"Head on out," Mike said grimly.

Bobby led the way; Morwenna followed, Genevieve in her arms, Connor close behind. Ahead of the others a little, Morwenna asked Genevieve, "What made you run out like that? Daddy told you never to go near the path in winter."

Genevieve didn't answer. She laid her head against Morwenna's neck.

"Sweetie?"

"I had to make sure you didn't hurt him."

"Hurt—Gabe?"

Genevieve nodded.

"What made you think someone was hurting him?" Morwenna asked.

Genevieve looked up at her without speaking.

"She decided to look at the angel, and she dropped it, and she was all freaked out for some reason," Connor said, shaking his head with the wisdom of his older-brother years.

"Honey, the angel on the tree is just an ornament," Morwenna said. "And no ornament in the world is worth risking one pretty little hair on your head."

"It didn't break," Genevieve whispered.

"Well, that's good. But it doesn't matter."

"It did matter. I almost broke it," Genevieve said. "We should never hurt our angels. Angels are there to protect us."

"She's just not going to make any sense," Connor said sagely.

"I understand," Morwenna said, smiling. "But the ornament didn't break, and it is an ornament, Genevieve, a pretty ornament that makes us think of angels. But it's all really all right."

"Follow me—I know the road best," Bobby said. He looked back at her and grinned. "I am the baby, you know. Adult baby now, of course, but I've spent the most time with the folks around here lately. I'll keep you from sinking into the snow." He frowned, arching a brow to Morwenna. "How long do you think you can carry her?"

Morwenna wondered that herself. The snow was deep, at least two feet, and every step they took was something of an effort.

"I think the snow may be taller than she is," Morwenna said.

"We can trade off," Bobby assured her.

Morwenna turned back. Shayne had positioned himself between DeFeo and Morwenna and his children;

Gabe followed DeFeo, and her mother walked by her father's side at the rear.

She shifted Genevieve's weight. It was true; Genevieve might be a little bit of a girl, but she got heavy quickly as they floundered in the snow. The path, even with Bobby leading, was rough; there were patches of ice, and he warned her about them as he slipped and slid his way in the lead. They were going downward, and though, beneath the snow, the road was decent, it was bound to be difficult going.

Her arms began to ache, but she was determined to make it another ten minutes; Bobby was the lead, testing the ground. She was afraid that Shayne would wind up with muscle spasms, after all that he'd been through, dragging everyone back up the slope. Her father had the shotgun, and she was afraid that her mother would snap somewhere along the line. Stacy could be so strong— but how strong?

"We are idiots, you know," Bobby said.

She looked at him, smiling. "I'm certain we often are—on many levels. But why are you saying that?"

"We have little sleds! Why didn't we bring one of the sleds—we could have pulled the children."

"Because we weren't thinking. Because we don't know who is a convict and who is a good guy."

"All right…but we should have thought of the sled," Bobby said.

Morwenna hugged Genevieve more tightly.

She winced, thinking of the horrible minutes she'd been caught on the ledge. First, trying to get Genevieve up. She'd never imagined what it could be like to be so terrified for her own life, and even more afraid for the life of the little girl. Terrified, and frozen.

Gabe can't be bad! she told herself. *She could recall his words; she could almost hear his voice aloud as she remembered the way he had assured her: "It's all right. I've got a hold here that's solid enough for a few minutes. I've got Genevieve. Just get the rope... there, you can do it. Have faith in yourself, Morwenna, you can do it."*

And still, when DeFeo spoke, warning them that people could appear to be so many things that they weren't, doubt crept in.

He could have let Genevieve go; he could have even reached for her, and killed her on the ledge.

Ah, but then what would he have done? As DeFeo said, he was securely "handcuffed" by the rope. He would have died himself on the ledge, with no one to haul him back up.

He'd never *had* to go over the ledge; he'd risked his life to do it.

But if there was the possibility he was facing a death sentence...

Doubt!

Why was doubt so much easier than faith? Or, could doubt and care be associated with simple intelligence. And where the hell did instinct fit into it all? Her instinct was to trust Gabe, but could it be that people were too easily led?

"The cemetery is ahead on the left!" she heard her mother call out to Bobby.

"The cemetery?" she asked incredulously.

Bobby turned to her.

"Mom still intends to say her Christmas prayers at the family grave site and tomb, come heaven or hell!" Bobby told her.

"There's too much snow! We won't even see the graves," Morwenna protested.

"You try to tell her that!"

The old stone wall of the little cemetery in the mountains was, at least, still above the snow. They reached it in about a minute, and Morwenna realized that Bobby had kept them on a straight-and-narrow path, following the line of the road. There was a curve in the wall ahead—the entry, which could be accessed by cars when cars could get on the road.

With any luck, she thought, *the gate would be locked!*

But the gate wasn't locked.

Bobby looked at her. "Not our lucky day," he said lightly.

Despite the fact that the gray clouds that had hovered earlier had moved on, the cemetery seemed shadowed and eerie. It lay beneath the naked and fragmented branches of trees, with only an evergreen here and there to remind the living that spring would come again.

The snow lay heavy over many of the graves, and they were clearly the first ones to brave the road into the graveyard that day. The tips of a few stones just peeked over the snow in some areas.

Bobby was careful to keep them on the roadway through the graveyard—that way, at least, no one would trip over any of the stones, markers or memorials that lay beneath the blanket of white.

"Just ahead," Connor murmured.

Morwenna was glad; she was going to have to trade off with someone. The world was icy cold; she could see her breath coming from her in a fog, but her arm burned like a fiery rod, the muscles giving in after the long walk.

She paused for a minute, staring ahead. Her mother's maiden name was Byrne; the name, she had been told, meant raven, and a large raven stood guard on the wrought-iron fence that led to the little vault and the graves that surrounded it.

High atop the vault, there was a beautiful marble angel. The angel wasn't lowered upon one knee in sorrow, but rather seemed to stand tall against the wind, robes and wings flying behind it as it proudly faced the world. She'd always liked the angel. She wished, in fact, that she'd at least draw something so beautiful at some time in her life.

Bobby pushed hard at the wrought-iron gate; it creaked and squealed, fighting against the snow as it scraped open. Morwenna entered the enclosed area, and set Genevieve up on one of the steps to the vault that was still higher than the snow.

She heard the others pile in behind her, and she thought of the incongruity of their group there; the kids, her mom, determined to say her Christmas prayers at the family grave site, and her father, ready to pray with her mother while still keeping a sharp eye on their prisoners, his shotgun at the ready.

"Mom?" Morwenna said.

Stacy moved forward to the steps, hugging Genevieve to her side, and looking out at them. "Christmas Day, again, and we're all together, and I'm so grateful. I want to thank God for the family that came before me. I want to tell my folks that I loved them very much. And I want, most of all, to say thank-you for the family that I have now. Guide us, be with us. Keep us safe."

"You're definitely not safe yet," DeFeo said quietly.

"Will you stop—this is a sacred time for my mother!" Shayne snapped angrily.

As he spoke, they were startled as a large black bird suddenly shot through the trees, letting out an eerie shriek. Morwenna ducked as it flew by them.

Stacy watched the bird without flinching. "It's a raven!" she said, and laughed. "Mike, I think that the family is grateful that we're here."

"All right, all right, it's a great and wonderful family day," Luke DeFeo said. "Let me help. Bow your heads in prayer!"

Startled, Morwenna watched him, but slowly, one by one, the other members of her family did so.

"Praise be to the God and Father of our Lord Jesus Christ," DeFeo said, his voice ringing clearly, "who has blessed us in the heavenly realms with every spiritual blessing in Christ. For he chose us in him before the creation of the world to be holy and blameless in his sight. In love he predestined us to be adopted as his sons through Jesus Christ, in accordance with his pleasure and will to the praise of his glorious grace, which he has freely given us in the One he loves. In him we have redemption through his blood, the forgiveness of sins, in accordance with the riches of God's grace that he lavished on us with all wisdom and understanding. And he made known to us the mystery of his will according to his good pleasure, which he purposed in Christ, to be put into effect when the times will have reached their fulfillment to bring all things in heaven and on earth together under one head, even Christ."

He finished speaking.

"Very nice," Gabe said. "Ephesians, I:3-10."

DeFeo arched a brow to him, a look of satisfaction on his face.

Stacy didn't notice either of them. "Amen!" she said happily.

Morwenna found that she was studying the two men; Gabe didn't seem disturbed, but he was watching DeFeo curiously. DeFeo looked very proud of himself, as if he had proven a point.

"Thank you, Father," Gabe said then, smiling as he looked up at the angel. "Thank you for this family, for the pride and courage and love to be found among them, even here, among those who have passed over to your realm. May you bless the lives of those who have proven to be so kind, and who value human life, even among those they know not as friends or enemies."

"Amen," Stacy said again, and this time, her family followed suit. "Anyone else?" she asked.

"Dear God and Jesus," Genevieve said. "Happy birthday again. Also, could you please make it just a little bit warmer?"

"Amen!" Bobby said, laughing. And he added, "This was lovely, Mom. But maybe we should move on."

Morwenna heard a slight rumbling. She looked up. It seemed that the clouds were coming back again. And again, strangely, light remained among them. The angel on the tomb stood proud in a fierce ray of light, the sun, somehow, shooting down upon it through all the turbulence in the atmosphere.

Shayne came to her side. "I'll take Gen," he said quietly. "I can't believe you made it this far."

She smiled at him, and touched his cheek. She found herself thinking of the way they had fought like cats and dogs as children, and she was suddenly aware that he would have killed himself, not just to get his daughter back, but her, too.

"She's not so heavy. Okay, I'm lying. My arms are killing me. But you must still be feeling some muscle pain of your own, huh?"

"Yeah, but it's all over," he said, grinning. "My arms can take a little more."

He bent down to pick up his daughter.

"It's cold, Daddy," Genevieve said.

"Actually, sweetheart," Stacy said, "I think you prayed it a tiny bit warmer."

"We're almost down to the tavern, baby," Shayne said. "We'll get some nice hot cocoa there—hey, and I'll bet they have turkey on the menu, too."

"It won't be as good as Gram's turkey," Genevieve said.

"No, it won't be, but it will be warm."

"Move 'em out!" Bobby said, taking the lead again.

Morwenna paused, looking up at the angel that rode so beautifully over the tomb.

She smiled suddenly. She barely remembered her mother's parents now, but they had been good people. Hardy mountain stock, very independent—and very loving at the same time. They hadn't built the tomb, of course. The tomb dated back to the early eighteen hundreds.

And yet, someone, way back in her family, had known what a tomb should offer; not sorrow and pain, but pride and hope.

"Morwenna!"

She started; her father was waiting for her, and nervously watching the procession that had gone ahead of him at the same time.

"Coming, Dad!" she said.

But as he started away, she said her own prayer.

"Thanks," she murmured huskily, adding quickly, "Thank you for Genevieve, and thank you for me, and for us all…and help us! Please help us do what's right."

She almost expected the angel to move.

It didn't.

She turned and hurried out after her family. It was still another twenty to thirty minutes down the slippery road until they reached the little tavern nestled in the mountains among the pines.

Chapter 8

Breaking onto the last stretch, Bobby was glad to see that the lights were on at Scott's Tavern, or, as a neon subtitle below the main sign stated, Scott's Ye Olde Tavern and Grill.

There were even two cars parked in the lot, but Bobby didn't think they'd be going anywhere soon; there would have to be some major digging done before the roads were navigable. He wondered if people from the tavern had held off on the digging because, like his family, they'd expected snow to begin falling in earnest again at any point.

He turned back. Now, DeFeo was heading along behind him, Gabe behind Defeo, and behind Gabe, Shayne was walking with Connor's hand in his. His father had Genevieve and walked alongside his mother, and following behind, ever aware she was carrying a loaded shotgun, came Morwenna.

"Yes, we've made it," Gabe said, coming up so that he stood next to Luke DeFeo, and giving him a smile.

"Not really, not yet," DeFeo said.

Then Bobby wasn't really sure what happened. He didn't know if DeFeo went after Gabe, or if Gabe went after DeFeo, or even if one of them had slipped on a patch of black ice, which knocked them over the embankment together.

Either way, they were sliding away fast.

"Hey!" he shouted to the others.

Shayne, of course, had seen what had happened and was already racing up to Bobby; Bobby started down through the snow and brush for the men. They were still rolling, snapping branches and twigs off dead brush as they sped along. He began to run, leaping over obstacles, aware that Shayne was right behind him.

"Hey, stop!" he yelled at the two men.

They were fighting in desperate, awkward moves, since they both had their hands cuffed or tied. DeFeo got his arms around Gabe's neck, and Bobby shouted again, seeing the man's face begin to turn red. But Gabe was surprisingly agile and strong, throwing himself forward so that DeFeo was thrown over his head and sent into the brush again. When DeFeo would have risen and charged, he was stopped by the loud sound of a bullet blasting into the air.

"Stop it! Now!" Morwenna, as fierce as a lioness, was standing up on the embankment, the shotgun in her hand. But even as she spoke, Gabe was at DeFeo's side; he wasn't attacking him. He was giving him a hand to get to his feet.

As he neared the two of them, he heard them talking.

"Great! Give me a hand, huh? Oh, how *saintly* of you," DeFeo said.

"You've got on borrowed togs," Gabe said. "You want to be careful with them."

That sounded odd. Maybe he'd heard him wrong. Maybe he was just speaking lightly. But why get into a fight with a guy that might have killed one of them and worry about *togs. Clothing?*

"Come on, you two," Bobby said, determined to sound as fierce as his sister looked, standing on the embankment. "Let's go. The tavern is just ahead."

To his amazement, they both listened to him. Gabe led the way. Luke DeFeo followed.

"Still need the cops," DeFeo murmured.

Gabe ignored him. Bobby waited, following as the two men headed back up to the road.

"What the hell was that?" Morwenna demanded when everyone reached the road.

"Hey, we fell," DeFeo said. He looked at Gabe.

"But you, you…"

"That's the tavern, right in front of us?" he said.

Morwenna looked at him. "That's the tavern."

"They still have electricity. Maybe they'll have internet service, or working phones," Gabe said.

"Maybe they will, and maybe they won't," DeFeo said. "You haven't won anything yet, you know."

"Ah," Gabe said, "but my glass is always half-full."

Morwenna could have kissed the ground when they finally walked into the tavern. Whether she was right or not, she didn't know—but the responsibility for deciding which man was telling the truth had, at the least, been expanded. Once they walked through the door, she saw her parents' old friend, Mac Scott, behind the bar.

As long as she could remember, Mac had been behind the bar. He owned Scott's, which was a small legend, in a way. To anyone who lived in the area, or visited the remote mountain area with any frequency, Mac Scott's place was *the* place.

It was the *only* place.

Nestled in a little valley in the heights, it lay on the outskirts of what might optimistically be called a village. It was next to a shop that sold cold-weather gear and hiking and climbing equipment, and down and across the single street from the church, and across from the gas station–slash–convenience store that accommodated the area. A rangers' station was down another level, and the little area served all those who kept homes, part-time or year-round, in the mid area of the Virginia Blue Ridge peaks.

"Morwenna! Morwenna MacDougal!" Mac called from behind the bar. He was a big, tall man, a mountain man whose ancestors had been in the region for years.

He still looked like a massive highlander.

"Mac, hey," she said.

"Is the family with you?" Mac asked.

"Right behind me."

"You're early. What, did Stacy cook turkey for breakfast?" Mac asked.

Stacy shook her head, hurrying over to the bar as the others filed in behind her. "Mac, we have a problem. Do you have a working phone, or internet—or any way to contact anyone? We had a stranger hurt out by us—"

"Wow. Was Shayne there then? Thank God that boy is a doctor," Mac said. He frowned, and she realized that he was looking over her shoulder and seeing Gabe and Luke DeFeo being ushered in—the one with his hands tied, and the other in cuffs.

He looked back at Stacy, arching a black shaggy brow. "Shayne's got some bedside manner," he said quietly.

"Very funny. The first guy, Gabe, the lighter-haired one, said that he was a cop, and he'd gone down in a skirmish with a con. The second guy came and said that *he* was the cop, and the first guy was the con, and we have no way of knowing who is telling the truth," Morwenna explained. "Neither has ID."

"Well, hell," Mac said.

"You—that booth," her father told Gabe. "And you, DeFeo—you in that booth over there."

Mac looked at Morwenna again. "You've got to be kidding me."

"Mac, does it look like I'm joking?" Morwenna asked.

Genevieve ran over to join her at the bar, crawling up on a stood to smile at Mac and reach out for him. In Genevieve's six-year-old world, she realized, nothing precluded a hug from an old friend.

Mac reached over the bar, and Genevieve hugged him. Mac was her "big bear," she always said.

"Hey, there, little missy," Mac said. "Merry Christmas."

Frowning, he looked at Morwenna.

"So, can you help?" she asked.

"Morwenna, I'm sorry—my cable has been out forever. I've still got electricity, and I was counting my blessings for that! But I can't get anything on television except for the local channels. And I haven't been able to call out on the bar phone or on my cell since yesterday morning. Once that snow started coming in yesterday, everything went wacko."

Morwenna frowned, looking toward the back booth. "Who else is here?" She craned her neck, trying to see who might be sitting in the high-backed booths.

"The Williamsons and their two boys—do you know them? Brian Williamson's folks owned his house, just like your mom's folks owned your house on up the mountain," Mac said. He was talking to Morwenna again, but looking over at the booths—and Mike Mac-Dougal, with his shotgun.

"Have they been stuck here?" Morwenna asked. "Snowbound, I mean?"

"No," Mac said. "They walked up, the same way you all came down."

As they spoke, of course, the Williamson family noted that there were newcomers at the tavern; Brian Williamson, plumber by day, banjo player upon occasion, rose and walked across the tavern to the booths, frowning as he saw Mike MacDougal with a shotgun.

"Mike, Merry Christmas, and what the hell?" he demanded.

Morwenna watched as her father went through the explanation. "You don't happen to have a working phone on you, do you?" Mike asked Brian.

"No, Mary and I were just talking about that— phones and internet, kaput! The boys were playing pool until a few minutes ago." He looked from one stranger to the next as he spoke. He added firmly, "But you've done well to bring them down here. Now you've got Mac and me and the boys—they're fifteen and seventeen—to make sure that neither of these fellows causes any mischief."

"I'm an officer," Luke said, "an officer of the law, and if anyone in this place had any sense, you'd all realize it. If you help these people keep me incarcerated and that con gets away, I promise you that you'll have hell to pay as well!"

Gabe lowered his head, shaking it, and then looked up at Brian Williamson, and across the pool table and the bar at Mac. "He's a liar. And the MacDougal family knows that I'm not out to hurt any of them."

Mac leaned across the bar. "Who the hell knows which one of you is a liar? Mike, what can I get you to drink? Don't you worry none. You have help around you now to keep an eye on those men."

Morwenna frowned, realizing that the TV was running.

"Mac—you have television. So...how?"

"Yeah, the cable is down, but I jimmied the old antenna. We're getting some local stuff," Mac said. "It comes and goes. Some static, some show. Well, now, you had a long walk down here in the cold. What can I get everyone?"

"Hot chocolate!" Genevieve said, not in the least shy about asking her "big bear" for anything.

"Yeah, sure, thanks," Connor said.

"I'd love a beer," Mike said, still watching both men as he approached the bar.

"Yeah," Shayne said huskily.

"Not me. I'll have a nice Irish coffee," Stacy said, approaching the bar as well.

"Mac, do you have any turkey? My tummy is rumbling," Genevieve said.

"Mac, you're getting a lot of orders here. If I may, I'll come on back and help," Morwenna told him.

He was well equipped for the clientele he got during the winter season; he had a steamer that made hot chocolate, and it was easy to use. Morwenna figured all the kids were going to want hot chocolate, so she went ahead and made cups for the Williamson boys, too. When she set them on the counter, Bobby was there to take them out for her. Mac was pouring draft beers, and her father was seated on a bar stool then, watching the two men in the booths. Stacy sat by her husband, pulling her granddaughter onto her lap.

"Think Mac does have turkey?" she asked hopefully.

"Mac, got turkey?" Morwenna asked.

"Yes, I got turkey," Mac said. "And I'll just get you situated with drinks, and go on back and get you some food, too," he assured her.

"What about them?" Morwenna asked, looking at her father and indicating the men in the booths. Brian Williamson and his wife, Mary, were watching the two strangers.

"I could go for a beer," Gabe said.

"Give them both a beer. What the hell. Looks like we're all in a fix here," Mike said.

Morwenna poured the drafts for their prisoners, and then walked around to the tables. She set one down in front of Luke DeFeo first, and then one in front of Gabe. As she did so, DeFeo said, "Look! The picture's back on the television. Turn it up, please, someone. Maybe the news will come on and show that Gabe Lange is a wanted man."

He was right; the TV set suddenly went from static to a picture.

They had just missed a news report, but the picture was suddenly clear, and an attractive young anchorwoman was seated at a desk with a similarly attractive young man.

"Happy holidays to our viewers across the world," the woman said.

Morwenna found herself slipping in to sit at the booth across from Gabe, staring up at the screen.

She was startled when Gabe's hand fell on hers. "Remember what I told you before," he said quietly.

"What? Told me about what?"

"About *you*," he said. "You should never just settle. You should never spend your life living out someone else's love, career or goals. The best is out there—the best of everything that will really make you happy. And you will find the way, and the right people in the world. Don't become a hamster on a wheel."

She shook her head, irritated. There was actually something on the television, and she wanted to see the familiar sight of people far away moving across a big flat-screen television. It was sad to realize, but TV was a *norm* in the average life, even when one wasn't exactly watching it.

And maybe the powers that be would break in with a news bulletin!

"People of all faiths and creeds now partake in our American holiday season, which, to everyone, becomes a time of spending their days in either family bonding—"

"Or not!" the man at her side interrupted jokingly.

His co-anchor laughed as she looked at him.

"Yes, and some take off for exotic locations," the woman said. "With that in mind, we've had our reporters around the globe bring us a short video on Christmas—around the globe!" she said.

The screen flashed to a scene at the Vatican where throngs, in their Christmas best, stood in Saint Peter's Square as the pope spoke. The anchorman narrated over the visual clips.

"Isn't it beautiful at the Vatican? For some, it's the holiest of holy days! The scene is familiar at Westminster Abbey in London." The scene switched to England; there was snow on the ground outside the abbey, and it looked like a postcard. Christmas lights fell upon gargoyles and angels, and Morwenna could almost hear Big Ben chiming in the background.

"In areas of the South, we have a different kind of music going on," the young anchorwoman said, and the television screen portrayed a church with far more simple decor; plain pews and a minister directing a choir; for a moment, the music was beautiful and a chorus sang gospel renditions of very old carols.

"Now, it's fun time, too," the anchorwoman said, and they switched to a scene of a couple at a ski resort, the man laughing as the woman nearly fell, uneasy on her skis; she grabbed on to him, and they exchanged a long kiss.

"And, if cold isn't your thing, there are the beaches of Mexico!"

Morwenna looked over at Gabe. His head was down, as if he knew what she was going to see before she saw it.

He seemed to be concentrating.

She frowned, and glanced back at the television.

For a moment, static broke up the picture.

Then the screen straightened.

What was the size and population of Mexico? Morwenna wondered. *The country was certainly fairly large, and the population was well over a hundred million. There must have been hundreds of thousands of tourists besides, and yet...*

There he was on the screen. Alex. Tall, handsome, perfect corporate-America Alex, tanned and well-muscled, looking like a cover model. He was running down the beach in bathing trunks, chasing after...

Yes. Yes, it was Double-D Debbie Richards from Accounting.

And the camera stayed focused on the pair as the sparkling water of the Gulf of Mexico flew up around them in a crystal spray, as Alex caught up with a laughing Debbie, encircled her waist with his arms and crashed with her into the surf.

The screen changed as the newscasters brought their audience to Australia, and then onward to Jerusalem.

Morwenna didn't really see any more of the pictures dancing before her eyes.

She felt Gabe's hand on hers again. She met his eyes.

"You're not surprised," he told her quietly. "And more than that, you're not brokenhearted. You've known that you've been playing a role, and it came to you fairly easily. Morwenna, don't let what you saw eat at you. You're due to have much more in life. Much more that is *real*."

She heard his words; they were nice words. She still felt frozen, as she hadn't once in all the fierce cold that had surrounded them in winter's white chill.

She was barely aware of Gabe's hand on hers.

No matter what he said, it hurt. Seeing Alex up

there... She had just said goodbye to him yesterday morning.

Bobby slid into the booth next to her. She was suddenly aware of the world around her again. She could see her mother, still entertaining Genevieve at the bar. Her father was sitting at the bar having a conversation with Brian and Mary Williamson while keeping an eagle eye on the two booths. Shayne had walked back to where Sam and Adam Williamson were playing an electronic game with Connor.

"What's the matter?" he asked her.

"What?" she asked, looking at him.

"You've turned white." He stared at Gabe, his eyes narrowing, as if he suspected that Gabe had said something that had disturbed his sister.

Yes, that's exactly what he thought.

"What did you do?" he demanded of Gabe.

Somehow, those fierce, protective words from her cheerful, guitar-playing baby brother brought a flush of warmth into her system again.

"He didn't do or say anything," Morwenna said.

"Then...are you sick? Are you all right?" He set the back of his hand on her forehead.

"I'm fine," she assured him.

He glanced at the television.

"Oh!" he said softly. "You're wishing you were in Mexico." He squeezed her arm. "I'm sorry, sis. I guess it's hard to think that you could be lying out on the beach, or splashing in the water—instead of trying to figure out if we have a cop and thief or a cop and a homicidal murderer on our hands."

"I wasn't after a murderer," Gabe said quietly.

"And I wasn't wishing that I was anywhere else,"

Morwenna said. She looked at her brother, and a smile came to her lips. "Really," she said, and she realized it was the truth. In their day-to-day lives, her brothers were so far away. And they were busy. And it was easy to forget that while she worried about her brothers and their lives, she forgot sometimes just what they meant to her.

And what she meant to them.

"It's okay. *I'm* okay, really. It was just the TV."

Bobby's eyes widened suddenly as he stared at her. "Oh!" he said.

"What?"

"Mexico, oh, my God! We haven't had a television, and we have it for two minutes…was that *Alex* on the screen? With that girl?"

Double-D Debbie from Accounting.

She didn't say it out loud.

"Oh, Wenna, I'm so sorry," Bobby said.

"It's okay, really. It's okay," she said.

He looked at Gabe. "You *knew.* How the hell did you know?"

Before Gabe could answer, they were all startled by a different voice coming through the speakers. "We are interrupting your local programming for a news bulletin. Be on the lookout for—"

The screen suddenly turned back to snow; no words issued through the speakers, only a fizzing sound that went with the snow.

"Lost it again!" Mac said, walking back from the kitchen area into the bar. "It's been like that all day, on one minute, and gone the next. Little Miss MacDougal, I will have your turkey out in just a matter of minutes."

"Turkey," Mike echoed, staring at the snow-covered

television screen, and then lowering his head as he shook it.

"Can you believe the TV went out right when it did?" Bobby asked rhetorically.

"Yes, I can," Gabe said. His eyes were downcast. He was talking to himself, really, Morwenna thought, and he sounded a little bitter, and somewhat resigned.

"Bobby, dear baby brother, let me out," Morwenna said. "I'm going to go and help Mac with the dinner plates. He's all alone here, and nine of us just plopped into his bar. He definitely needs a hand."

"Sure. I can help, too," Bobby said.

"No, no—two can handle it. You stay here—and keep an eye on him," she said, looking at Gabe.

His eyes met hers. Still that clear green, and so seemingly without guile.

He didn't smile; he didn't say a word. He just looked at her, and when she turned to walk away, she knew that his eyes were following her.

He may not be the con, she thought. But there was something odd going on. It was as if he knew far more about them and their situations than they did.

She turned and stared at Luke DeFeo. He was looking back at her. "We'd love turkey, too, you know. Please," he said politely.

She nodded. "We don't intend to starve anyone."

He smiled.

And it was strange; she thought that he, too, knew something that she didn't.

A chilling thought struck her: What if they were both cons, just playing a game with the family? And what if...?

What if they were both just depending on the de-

*cency of the family, waiting for a chance to rob them
all blind or—or worse?*

She squared her shoulders. There was nothing she
could do that they weren't already doing.

Waiting.

Hoping.

Praying.

Shayne finally left his position at the bar and walked
over to the booths; Bobby was across from Gabe, keeping an eye on him.

He slid in across from Luke DeFeo.

"You would have seen it. You would have seen that
he was the homicidal escaped con if the television
hadn't gone out."

"Maybe," Shayne said, reminding himself to main-
tain a poker face, no matter what the man had to say
to him. "And maybe we would have seen that you're a
lying scumbag."

DeFeo took a swallow of his beer. His handcuffs
clinked together as he did so.

Despite the hindrance, he seemed to really enjoy
the beer.

He lifted his glass. "I'm grateful...grateful to your
family. At least, you're not treating us like animals. At
least, not too much so."

"You're not animals. And, frankly, around my family, animals are treated like people. My mother is a
sucker for any lost puppy or kitten that comes her way."

"And what about you—and yours?" DeFeo asked.

"What do you mean?"

"Oh, yeah, I forgot—you're divorced. I guess it
would be the wife who wanted to take in every stray."

Shayne blinked, not speaking for a minute. Yes, of course, over the years, they'd had many a visitor. When a dog or cat made it into their yard without a tag, they kept it, and Cindy spent endless hours walking the streets, putting up flyers and heading to every animal shelter in the area to see that a flyer went up. She raged against those who didn't neuter or spay their pets; she cried over the fate of ill-treated creatures. And, to her credit, any time Cindy hadn't found the rightful owner, she had found someone in need of a stray.

"Sorry, didn't mean to cause you any pain, I know what it can be like. I've gone the route," DeFeo said.

"We're all doing all right," Shayne said.

"Sure, sure, of course."

"Turkey!"

Shayne heard the excited cry come from the bar; it was Genevieve, of course. Mac had decided to bring the first plates out to Shayne's mom and daughter.

But Genevieve squirmed off her grandmother's lap and reached for the plate. "I think they're hungry," she told Stacy, inclining her head toward the booths. "They looked like they were fighting before. Maybe 'cause they were hungry. Daddy told me that people do bad things sometimes 'cause they don't have anything, and they're hungry. So I'll give that man my plate, and maybe he won't look like he's snarling all the time."

Shayne smiled, and he reminded himself that whatever agony and loss he felt over his marriage, Cindy was a good person, and a good mother, and between them, they'd created a couple of really good children.

Genevieve, the plate wobbling a little precariously in her hands, walked over and set it in front of Luke DeFeo.

He studied her for a long moment.

"Thanks, kid," he said.

The television screen flashed back into working order; local news was on.

"We expect snow at this time of year," a weatherman was saying, "but the intensity of the drifts that reached the mountains was higher than predicted. Plows are busy, and police and rescue agencies are out on the roads searching for those who started out for homes in the Blue Ridge area and didn't quite make it home for Christmas."

A cameraman was focused on a car that had slid into an embankment, precariously near the guardrail. From that area, if a car had gone over...

Shayne leaned forward, feeling as if his heart were caught in his throat.

It couldn't be. It couldn't be Cindy's Subaru! Cindy was on her way to Paris; she'd started seeing a travel agent when the divorce had been final and he'd been offered a freebie at a chalet in France. She'd been due to leave on Christmas Eve.

Of course, it couldn't be Cindy's car. There were thousands of Subaru Foresters in the area. They were good cars for harsh winters.

It was a moss-green Forester, just like his wife's car. Ex-wife's car! he reminded himself.

Shayne glanced around quickly, wondering if the children were watching the screen; they weren't. Genevieve was still staring at Luke DeFeo, smiling, as if she admired him a great deal, and Connor was involved in his game.

He stared back at the television screen.

If there was a cameraman there, the driver and passengers, assuming there were any, had to be all right.

"It's an overhead shot," DeFeo said.

"What?"

"Look, it's an overhead shot. Must be a helicopter... Look how the shot shakes, zooming in and out."

He was right.

Shayne felt every muscle in his body tighten; he studied everything he could for the seconds that the waving shot remained on the screen. He searched for a sign of some kind that would tell him exactly where in the mountains the car was stranded.

He found it, right before the screen switched to a traffic pileup in Charlottesburg.

Dead Man's Curve.

It wasn't an official designation, and he wasn't sure just what mile marker it was in the Blue Ridge. It was about five miles down from them. He knew it from the overlook at the apron of the curve and the flat-face rock just to the side of it.

He stood, heedless of DeFeo. He walked over to the bar. Mac had paused to exchange a few words with his father.

"I don't know, and I don't know why, but I think that Cindy is stranded on the mountain, maybe freezing to death. Dad, I'm going down there."

Chapter 9

There would be no arguing with Shayne; Morwenna knew that.

Stacy, of course, was upset. Shayne might be a working physician in his mid-thirties and a father himself; he was still *her* child. Stacy was disturbed already—of course they all were—and now this new danger to her family seemed to be making her even more anxious. "But, Shayne, really—Cindy is supposed to be in Europe by now," Stacy said.

"There's no way you could know that you saw *Cindy's* car," Mike said.

"Look, I know exactly where the car was stuck," Shayne said. "You don't understand. I have a feeling. A gut feeling. And I know Cindy, and I know that she never knew these mountains like we do. She's probably in that car—maybe even injured. I have to go. I have to."

"I'll go with you," Morwenna said.

Both her parents gasped.

"No, Morwenna, let me go with Shayne," Bobby said.

She turned to look at her brother. "Look, Wenna, I'm not saying you're out of shape or anything. You're in great shape. But I do way more in the snow than you do. I'm a far better skier, I am much better with a snowboard and I'm even a better hiker."

"You can't take skis out there," Stacy said. "The snow is covering too many ruts...you won't always see the ledges—with the sun out, the snow can be blinding."

"And if you walked again, it could take forever," Mike said.

"I've got a snowmobile out back," Mac said. "She's not the newest model, but she's a workhorse. If you follow close to the road, you'll be safe enough in it."

"You have any survival kits?" Shayne asked him. "Bobby, don't make Mom and Dad worry for two. If Mac can lend me the snowmobile, I'll be there and back in no time."

"Hell, no," Bobby said. "I know the roads better than any of you. I'm the one who still spends the most time here."

"Kid!" Luke DeFeo called from the booth. "Your brother doesn't know that his wife is in any car stuck anywhere. She's in Europe. That car could belong to anyone. I understand how you feel, but you need to be sensible."

Morwenna looked at him. Could the man really be worried about her family?

Genevieve had been standing there, looking from

adult to adult. She suddenly cried out and ran to her father. "Daddy, is Mommy out in the snow?"

Shayne shot Luke DeFeo a murderous stare. "No, darling, probably not. I'm just kind of a worrywart, you know that. I saw a car stuck that looks kind of like Mommy's."

Morwenna hadn't even seen Connor come over to stand behind his grandfather.

"It could be Mommy," he said. "She was crying before you came to get us yesterday morning, Dad. She wanted us to be with you, but she didn't want to be away from us."

Morwenna felt something behind her back and she turned around, startled. Gabe Lange had left his booth, and stood just behind her.

They were getting too lax! They needed to be watching him.

"Connor, I don't think that you have to worry. Your dad is a doctor, and I think he would have thought about getting to that car whether it's actually your mom in it or not. Whoever is stranded probably needs help," he said.

"I have to go," Shayne said quietly.

Stacy looked at her son for a long moment. "Yes, of course you do," she said.

"You realize," Luke DeFeo called from his booth. "Gabe wants two of the able-bodied men out of here because he's planning something. This could be a fool's errand; that car could have been stranded since last night, and whoever is in it is probably dead."

Genevieve started to sob. Stacy picked her up. "Honey, it could be someone else's car, and your mommy may be safe in a nice warm chalet somewhere," she said.

"And there are two able-bodied men and a few strong

boys here as well," Mac protested in a growl. "Shayne, there's a rescue kit on the back wall of the kitchen— take that. The snowmobile keys are right by it. You and Bobby get going. You'll be back here in no time, and you're going to want to be back before dark."

"We'll be here—Mac and my family and I," Brian Williamson said firmly. "Everything will be status quo."

"We'll be fine, won't we, Mom?" Morwenna said, setting an arm around her mother's shoulders.

"At least grab a piece of turkey before you leave," Stacy said, forcing a smile.

"All right, we're going," Shayne said. Genevieve came running over to hug his legs; Shayne picked her up and gave her a kiss on the cheek. "Don't you worry, munchkin. And Connor, you watch out for your sister for me, right?"

Connor nodded gravely.

The two grabbed their coats and headed around the bar to go out through the kitchen. Mike was staring worriedly after his sons; he held the shotgun in a lax position.

Morwenna turned to Gabe. "You! Back to the table," she told him.

"This worries me sick!" DeFeo said from his position in his booth. "They're on a fool's errand. The snow is blanketing all kinds of hazards. And," he said, looking directly at Morwenna, "your brother hates his ex-wife."

Genevieve gasped.

"You shut up, and shut up right now," Morwenna said, approaching the table. "One more word, and you may be the ghost of J. Edgar Hoover, but I'll knock you out flat with my rifle butt and not feel a twitch of guilt as I do it!" she warned.

There was an uncomfortable silence.

And they all heard the motor of the snowmobile start up and rev.

Morwenna looked from DeFeo to Gabe Lange, who had taken his seat again. He was watching her. He smiled when their eyes met. "They're going to be fine," he told her with assurance.

"Maybe," DeFeo said, sounding weary. He groaned. "I really wish you could see what's happening here. This man is being as nice as he can be. He's trying to make you all like him. He's pretending to be good and kind, and worried about you rather than himself. That's his act. He's seducing you all with his gentle personality. And then he'll strike."

They were all silent for a minute.

"Eat your turkey!" Stacy told him. "Before we lock you in the outhouse!"

DeFeo smiled. "There's an outhouse?"

"We can arrange for one," Mike assured him.

"I wish you'd let me help you," DeFeo said. "You're good people. I wish I could make you see what you're doing, and that you're being used, which puts you into a greater realm of danger."

Bobby was glad that Mac Scott was a real mountain man; his survival kit contained rope, carabiners, pulleys, water, bandages, water and medical supplies. His snowmobile had three compartments, and one held a heavy windbreaker and blanket, while another held flashlights and emergency flares.

He convinced his brother to sit behind him and let him do the steering; Shayne was feeling desperate, he knew, but his brother was never stupid. Bobby did know the mountain best.

Still, it was rough going. The snow was deep, and all discernible lines between the road itself, the embankment on the right and the guardrails on the left had all but disappeared.

Bobby kept the speed in check. At the best of times, in a car with the world's finest tires, mountain roads could be treacherous. No one in their right mind would have been on the roads late yesterday; only those who really knew the mountain could have foreseen just how bad it was going to be.

Were they crazy? Was Cindy in Europe? Were they really on a fool's errand, whose only possible end would be to come across a corpse frozen in place behind the wheel?

And yet it was true; Shayne had panicked because of his ex-wife. But, if he had realized that he could reach the car and that it might be occupied, he would have come out anyway. No physician had ever taken his oath more seriously.

He was jarred from his thoughts as the snowmobile suddenly bounced high and slammed back down—he'd hit a rock or obstruction on the road. He heard Shayne swear, and felt his brother's arms tighten around him. When they landed, he cut his speed, slowing almost to a stop and shouting back at Shayne, "You okay?"

"Yeah, yeah, slow her down more, I guess," Shayne said.

"Can't save anyone if we're dead or broken," Bobby agreed.

He'd almost come to a stop; he revved the motor again, making sure to keep it alive as well. The snowy air hit his face with a fierce blast—stinging. He hugged the mountain as closely as he dared. They were on a road, damn it, but they might as well have been on a field of snow. Only the towering heights of the pines and evergreens on the mountainside gave him any sense of direction.

He should have grabbed a ski mask. He felt as if his nose was so cold, it was burning off.

He rounded bend after bend, and slowed as the slope became greater.

He blinked hard as his eyes watered at the cold air. He didn't dare look too far to the left; they could see the towns in the valley below, so far down that they looked like little houses in a Christmas display.

He focused on driving, and again, they curved down another bend.

And there they saw the moss-green Subaru, slammed against the overhead, and the embankment, and far too close to the ledge.

If Morwenna had been feeling fraught with tension before, it was nothing compared to the way she was feeling now. Shayne and Bobby were gone, and from the time they left, she discovered that she was looking up at the big, carved bear-framed clock over the bar.

Seconds ticked by so slowly.

Brian and Mary Williamson and their boys had been a godsend; Brian had gotten it into his head to teach Conner how to play pool, and so he and Mary—an excellent player herself—were distracting him to the best of their ability. Stacy was keeping Genevieve as busy as possible, having her help out, putting down and picking up plates and refilling beverage glasses.

Mac and Morwenna had gotten the rest of the turkey dinners out, only everyone had seemed to have lost their appetite. The boys ate a few bites between shots; Morwenna played with her fork, herself, pushing her food around on her plate.

Only their two prisoners seemed to clean up their turkey and stuffing, mashed potatoes and gravy, green beans and cranberry sauce.

They, too, seemed to be watching the clock.

It had seemed like forever before the day had begun—it was only four in the afternoon. Morwenna prayed that her brothers would return before the sun fell in earnest.

The TV had given nothing but static since it had last gone out.

"Hey!" Gabe called to her softly.

She narrowed her eyes, looking at him. It was best, she'd decided, to keep away from both the men. Gabe had thought immediately that Shayne and Bobby should risk their own lives. DeFeo had openly voiced the thought that if it was Cindy in the stranded car, she might well be dead.

"Is that a jukebox? A working one?" he asked her.

She looked down past the pool tables.

"Yes, it still works."

"Maybe it has some Christmas carols," he said. "May I go look?"

Morwenna looked at her father. Mike now maintained an iron grasp around the shotgun.

Her father shrugged. Stacy looked up; Genevieve was on her lap and they were drawing pictures on a cocktail napkin.

"Go ahead. And, remember, Dad *will* shoot you if you make a wrong move," Morwenna said.

Gabe eased himself out of the booth and headed down past the pool players. For a moment, Morwenna feared that she had been an idiot; Gabe could have stopped by one of the boys, slipped his bound wrists over the head of one of them and threatened to strangle him. He could have then threatened a life...using a child as a hostage to escape.

She pictured the scene in her mind's eye, and she almost cried out in fear and warning. But she saw that her father had no intention of risking the children. He had risen, and though Gabe couldn't see him, Mike had kept himself in a position to shoot if Gabe had made so much as a move in the wrong direction.

Gabe walked right by the pool players and down to the jukebox.

He looked back at her with a rueful smile. "It works off of quarters."

"Here!" Mac spoke up from behind the bar and opened the cash register to find a handful of coins; he handed them to Morwenna. She met his eyes, and he nodded. "Lord knows, we could use something in here beyond the sound of that TV static," he said.

Morwenna walked down to the jukebox with the coins in her hand. When she reached it, she began to feed them into the machine.

"You all have to be careful," DeFeo said.

"I am careful—always," Mike told him.

Gabe was able to hit the button that changed the pages.

"A17. Nice, Bing Crosby and David Bowie singing together, 'Little Drummer Boy' and 'Peace on Earth,'" he said.

"You're letting him run the show!" DeFeo warned.

"He's choosing a few Christmas tunes. A nice idea, really," Morwenna said.

"So, I'm stuck here in cuffs with a group that is going to be in big trouble when the real law arrives. But we all get to play Christmas tunes. Great!"

She opted to ignore DeFeo.

"Play what you choose," Morwenna said.

Gabe hit A17 without answering DeFeo. He flipped more pages. Morwenna was startled when Genevieve called out "Do they have 'Rudolph the Red-Nosed Reindeer'?"

"Well, I'll just bet they do," Gabe told her. "And there it is! D22!"

"I'd like 'Do You Hear What I Hear?'" Stacy called.

"And there's the ever-popular 'Rockin' Around the Christmas Tree'!" Mike called from the bar.

He was still clutching the shotgun. What a contrast to Genevieve, who wasn't questioning what she believed in any way. She simply liked Gabe.

The faith of a child...

Gabe began to push buttons. As he did so, Morwenna stepped back to join the boys gathered around the pool table. Connor grinned up at her; she realized that although he was still worried about his parents and aware of the tense situation in which the family found itself, he was doing all right.

Friends had made that so—learning pool tricks from the Williamson family was easing the day for him.

She smiled back at him. "A budding pool shark, eh?" she teased affectionately.

He smiled back at her. "My dad...my dad is going to be okay, right, Auntie Wenna?" he asked.

She saw that Gabe was still listening and obeying

as the group in the tavern vied for selections on the old jukebox. His eyes were alight.

She had been suspicious of the man from the beginning. Then she had begun to believe in him. Then she had found her way back to mistrust. And why? Because someone else spoke against him.

She winced. Well, that hadn't stood history very well. Proof was needed. Well, proof was what they awaited.

"You dad is going to be just fine, Connor," Morwenna said. "And so are we."

But just as the words left her mouth, the electricity went.

And the tavern was pitched into shadow.

Bobby braked the snowmobile just off the point where he *thought* the road made way for the lookout point. Shayne dismounted and instantly started for the car.

"Bro! We have to be careful. That car is right on the ledge," Bobby told him.

Shayne froze in his tracks, as if at his statement, and Bobby saw that his face was white. And then he knew why. He couldn't see that it was indeed Cindy in the car, but he could see the driver.

And the driver was in a hooded parka, head down on the steering wheel. Frost and snow covered most of the windshield.

There was no way to tell, until they touched the driver, whether the person was alive or dead.

"All right, come on, Shayne, I want to bring you both—and me!—back alive. Let's take it slow." He reached into the side compartments on the snowmobile. He got out the rope and the pulley chair, and followed

Shayne as his brother more cautiously approached the car. He saw one of the huge light poles by the side of the road. It wouldn't carry the weight of a car if something happened, but it would carry the weight of a man—and a woman.

"Approach the car, and carefully open that front door just in case the ground by the back tires is—is gone. Grab the person out of the car, and screw whatever the hell else is in it, okay?" Bobby said. "I'll tie us together with the rope."

Shayne nodded. "Let's hurry," he said.

Bobby took the rope to the massive light stand and quickly tied it around, securing it with double loops. He hurried back to where his brother stood, already securing himself. He looked at Bobby. "Thanks," he told him.

"I'll be right here, but not coming close. Until she's out of the car, and you need me," Bobby said.

His brother moved toward the car then, taking every step carefully.

Bobby looked back at the rope attached to the giant light pole, and then frowned as he looked up at the light. Dusk was settling on them more heavily now with each minute that passed.

And the streetlight hadn't kicked on.

Strange, the lights usually came on automatically as dusk moved in.

Unless, of course, the electricity had finally gone in the mountaintops here.

And, if so, back at the tavern, his family was locked in darkness.

Bobby forced himself to remain still, to watch his brother, and to wait. He couldn't go screaming like a terrified child, and rush back to the snowmobile and leave Shayne and the driver.

What if the woman was Cindy, and she had skidded and lost control last night, and she had frozen to death already?

He didn't dare think it.

What about his family, back in the tavern, suddenly pitched into darkness?

His father was a smart man; he'd have his shotgun at the ready.

But could he aim in the dark?

"Almost there," Shayne called to him. "And the ground feels steady thus far…don't know about the back, and I'm not going to test it."

Shayne stood then by the driver's-side door. He reached for it slowly, and opened it more slowly. He let out a cry as the driver slumped to the side, and into his arms. He fell to his knees, cradling the woman in his arms.

Bobby heard a strange sound; it was like a rumble, but it was a quiet rumbling. He looked at the Subaru, and the back end of it seemed to be sinking.

"Shayne, get her out of there!" Bobby shouted. He went for the rope, ready to drag his brother if it went taut against the pole.

But Shayne stood, cradling his ex-wife to his chest, and he started a stumbling run through the snow toward Bobby. And as he did, Bobby heard a creaking sound, once and again, and then growing louder, and he saw that the Subaru was slipping, slipping…

There was a loud smashing sound as it hit the guardrail, and then a rumble as it burst through the railing and went tumbling down the mountain.

"Brace yourself!" Bobby said, hunkering down.

And Shayne dropped to a knee, covering Cindy's body with his own. They both waited for an explosion.

None came.

Bobby stood slowly and walked as close as he dared to the ledge. He looked over, and he was glad to see that the Subaru had not exploded, or hurt anything other than a number of scraggly, half-dead winter trees and brush. It had landed—right side up—on a narrow ledge about fifty feet down.

He looked at Shayne. His brother had gotten Cindy to the snowmobile; he had her wrapped in the blanket, and he was trying to urge some brandy through her lips. Bobby hurried over to them, falling to his knees in the snow, and looking down at his sister-in-law's face. She was such a beautiful woman, but right now, he felt a burst of cold fear sweep through him. She was so white; her eyes were closed, and her lips appeared to be a strange shade of blue.

"She's—she's—" Bobby began.

Shayne smiled grimly at him. "She's alive," he assured her. "She's...she's a fighter. She's going to make it. Her pulse is weak, but steady. She's going to come around. We just have to get her back as soon as possible, and get her warm...and I can find out if any damage was done. She should get to a hospital, but the tavern will do. I need her to come around...to sip some of this."

Bobby felt words coming in a repetitious prayer.

Let her live, let her live, please, God, let her live.

"Come on, come on, come on...please, God!" Shayne breathed.

Cindy suddenly choked, coughed and stuttered.

Her eyes flew open in panic, and she strained at the arms that held her: Shayne's.

A weak scream escaped her lips, and then died as her eyes focused on Shayne's face.

"Shayne!" she said.

"Hey," Shayne said, his voice tremulous. "You're all right. You're all right."

Was she? Bobby wondered. God knew, she might be suffering from some kind of frostbite.

She saw Bobby then. "Bobby!" she whispered. "My God, you two found me…how on earth did you find me? You couldn't have known that I was coming. I didn't know that I was coming until it was time to leave for the airport, and then I knew I—I knew I couldn't leave for the whole week, and I tried to call you all, but no one was answering and I just took a chance, and, oh, Lord, please forgive me, Shayne… I meant to get here and beg that you all forgive me for showing up so rudely, and let me spend the holidays with the kids, too, and—"

"Cindy, you may be suffering some real effects from this," Shayne said gently. "Drink a bit more of this, and let me get you some water, too. We'll wrap you up really tightly in the parka, because it's even colder when we're on the snowmobile. It will be slow going…the thing is only meant for two, but I know that we'll manage. The tavern is warm, and once we're there, we'll talk."

"But, Shayne, I asked you to take the children, and I came here, and then… I thought I was going to die. I was terrified to move in the car." She stopped speaking and stared at Bobby. "The car, I was in the car…"

Shayne looked at him. "Um, well, it's standing. But I have a feeling the insurance company might consider it to be totaled," Bobby said.

"Oh! Oh, God! It did go over! I was terrified when the car spun out and stalled, and then when the wheels wouldn't catch. There was nothing for them to catch on!"

"It's okay, Cindy, you're safe," Shayne said.

"Shayne, you risked your life for me," Cindy said, her eyes filled with wonder as she looked at him. "After everything…but, it's what you do, isn't it?" Her eyes filled with tears.

Shayne drew her to him.

"Cindy, don't cry. Please, don't cry."

"But you forgive me?" she whispered.

"Forgive you? For loving our children? Don't be silly, Cindy, there is nothing to forgive. And you will always be a part of the family, and always welcome," Shayne said.

"And we'll all freeze if we don't get back," Bobby interjected.

He glanced at the light pole, and far up—at the light that wasn't lit.

Cindy was alive.

And now, the worry that something had gone wrong at the tavern began to eat into him again.

"We need to hurry, as much as we safely can," Shayne said.

Screw safely!

Bobby's urge to get back to the tavern was almost overwhelming. He began hurriedly gathering the equipment they had used, stuffing it into the compartments. He crawled back onto the snowmobile and felt Shayne doing his best to get on with his ex-wife in his arms.

"What is it? What's wrong?" Cindy asked.

Where in the hell did they begin to explain?

He'd leave that to Shayne, Bobby decided.

He turned on the snowmobile's lights—a contrast to the darkness now settling heavy on the mountains.

The cold hit Bobby's face as he revved the snowmobile into gear; going back would be even more treacherous.

He kept seeing the pool of light before him.

And all he could think was *dark, dark, dark*.

His family was trapped in the dark, with strangers whose intentions were still unknown.

Chapter 10

The sudden darkness seemed complete at first; the sun was almost down outside the tavern walls, and the shadowy world of the outside was now inside, compounded by the walls surrounding them.

But it wasn't completely dark.

There was that moment when it was just suddenly dead silent, smoke gray, and dead still, and yet shapes and shadows seemed to run amok.

They were frightened, of course; man's fear of the dark was an instinct left over from prehistory when darkness meant the coming of fearsome beasts of prey.

Morwenna wasn't sure at all why such stark terror came to her. It wasn't unusual that they should lose the electricity. Mac had a generator, and it would kick in soon. But she had the strangest feeling that *this* sudden darkness was worse than any other, and that something evil was moving about the room. Light couldn't come back to them fast enough.

Something almost touched her, and for a moment, she felt as if her skin was literally crawling, as if a horrible scent of death, decay and sulfur filled the air.

She reached for Genevieve, terrified that the little girl was in some kind of danger. She groped blindly, watching shadows move.

"Hey, folks, it's okay, everything's all right now. We've got an emergency generator," Mac said.

As if on cue, low light returned to the tavern, and the jukebox spun into action. Bing Crosby and David Bowie came on together.

Morwenna looked instantly for her niece; she was standing beside and slightly behind Gabe, almost wedged against the jukebox. She had a wide-eyed look of fear on her face.

"Baby, it's okay," Morwenna said. "It's all right, see, the light is back on."

"Auntie Wenna, I was scared!" Genevieve said.

Morwenna quickly hunkered down by her side.

"It's all right. It was just dark," Morwenna said.

But Genevieve shook her head. "No, didn't you feel it…someone was here, someone very, very bad!"

"Genevieve, no one else is here. It was just a matter of moments before the lights came back on."

Genevieve looked up at her. "No! No, Gabe saved me. He saved me from the bad thing, the evil thing that was here."

"Hey!" Mike said suddenly.

Morwenna quickly glanced to her father. He had jumped up first, apparently to look for his family members, and to assure himself that they were all right.

"What?" Mac asked.

"He's gone!" Mike said.

Morwenna looked to the booth where Luke DeFeo had been sitting.

It was empty.

She quickly looked around the room. DeFeo wasn't anywhere to be seen.

She had the uneasy feeling that he had been near; that he had nearly touched her.

And Genevieve.

"Well, hell, maybe that's just good riddance!" Mac said.

"I didn't hear or see the door open," Connor noted, frowning.

"Well, he is gone," Stacy said. "Maybe—maybe it is just as well."

Gabe spoke up suddenly. "No, no, it's not just as well. He's still out there somewhere. And he's dangerous."

"Dangerous? But," Morwenna said, turning to him, "*you* said that he was a white-collar criminal. He said that *you* were the dangerous one."

He shook his head. "You don't understand…you can't understand. He's—all right, he's on the run. And he may want to bring a few down with him. You have to let me go after him."

He walked around the pool table, toward Mike. As he did so, Morwenna noticed the distance from the booths and around the pool table to where she was standing.

Luke DeFeo couldn't have come around the whole place so quickly. Could he? And yet she had the uncomfortable, uncanny feeling that he had.

"But—he's out there, alone in the snow. He won't be coming back here," Mac said.

"He's out there, and he's thinking of something, and he will come back," Gabe said firmly.

"My sons are out there," Stacy said. "My sons are out there, somewhere on the mountain."

"I can find him. I can stop him," Gabe said. "Look, please. I was with you for a long time, and no harm came to you. Trust me. Let me go after him, before he finds a way to hurt anyone. Please."

A silence followed his words. Thoughts raced through Morwenna's mind.

There was simply no way to know the truth; maybe Luke DeFeo had escaped because he was desperate to find a way to communicate with the law. Maybe he had escaped because he was a cop, and he was going to come back.

And maybe every word that Gabe was saying was the truth. He'd done nothing but show them gratitude and kindness since he'd been with him.

She stepped forward, coming to stand behind him. "I think we need to believe in Gabe. He's been nothing but level and kind—he risked his life for Genevieve, and I don't care what DeFeo said—Gabe risked his life, and you don't do that unless there is something really decent in you. He wants to set out to find Luke DeFeo. I say we let him go, and I say that I go with him."

"What?" Stacy said incredulously, sliding off her bar stool to stare at her daughter.

"Mom, I'm well over twenty-one," she said quietly.

"No, I should go," Mike said.

Morwenna shook her head. "No, Dad. You and Mom need to stay. You need to be here, because you're really great parents." She paused, looking at Genevieve and

Connor, not wanting to scare the children, but hoping her parents would understand.

If something had happened to Shayne, Bobby or Cindy—and something was to happen to her, God forbid!—the kids would need stable, loving parents.

And that, she realized, *they were.*

She smiled suddenly. "Gabe will never hurt me. I know it. I know it just as I know the sun will rise in the morning. And I'm going to untie his hands, and we're going to go out together. When we reach Shayne and Bobby, I'll come back with them. But they have to know that DeFeo is out there, and he could be very dangerous. We can't accomplish that with one person—I'll need to come back, and Gabe will need to find DeFeo."

"Now, wait, I can go out with this man," Brian Williamson said.

"Or me," Mac volunteered.

"I'll be able to find my brothers. I *know* I'll be able to find my brothers," Morwenna said.

"This is crazy!" Mike said, still studying her.

"It's what we need to do, Dad. Mr. Williamson, you need to stay with your kids. And Mac, well, you just need to watch out for everyone here. And I need to find my brothers, and Gabe needs to stop DeFeo," Morwenna said firmly.

"And my mommy!" Genevieve said. "You need to find my mommy!"

"If she's with them," Morwenna said.

"She is," Connor said. "She is. My father went to find her. He *knew* that she was out there, and he went to find her. And I know that he did."

"Morwenna!" Her father lowered his head. "Morwenna, we just don't *know!*"

But Genevieve came to stand next to Morwenna and Connor. "I know!" she said. "I know that Gabe is good, and that he can find my daddy. Gramps, please, let him go, and let Auntie Morwenna go with him to bring my mommy and daddy and Uncle Bobby back."

Her father stared at her. She didn't know if he was thinking that he couldn't really stop her, or if he was feeling the same way; *they had to be right about Gabe Lange.* He nodded slowly. "You're taking my only daughter out there," he said to Gabe.

"I'll be careful with her," Gabe promised. "I swear to you, I would lay down my life for her."

Genevieve tugged on Morwenna's shirt, and Morwenna hunkered down to her. Genevieve looked at her with a child's wide eyes and then reached out to touch the little gold angel she was wearing around her neck.

"You'll be protected. You have your angel."

Morwenna smiled.

Faith, again.

Children could be so amazing. And it could be argued that faith could lead to stupidity, and that fanatical faith could lead to horrible things, but this wasn't that kind of faith. There was something in Gabe Lange's eyes unlike anything she had ever known before.

He made her believe.

She walked across the tavern, collecting her coat and gloves and scarf.

"We'll be back before you know it!" she assured the room cheerfully.

"Wait!" Mike protested. "You're just walking out with nothing—"

"We'll find Bobby and Shayne and the equipment. Dad, I know this mountain, and the valleys. We'll find them soon—I know it. I'm good, I'm fine. Have faith in me!"

Mike looked into her eyes. He smiled slowly and painfully. "I do have faith in you," he said.

Gabe followed her, and turned back. "You are going to be all right, and so are the others. I will find DeFeo. And I will stop him."

Bobby drove the snowmobile slowly and carefully; even so, the air was biting, and bits and chips of snow and ice flew before them and around them. Shayne's face was numb.

And yet, he felt a sense of wonder as they moved through the snow.

He had never been a violent man in any way, and certainly not with his wife or children. But when he looked back, he could see the danger signs that had led to his divorce. He had been oblivious to the amount of time he was gone—he felt that his days had been full from beginning to end. He *had* changed diapers. In fact, when trying to explain why she was leaving, Cindy had told him that he'd been a wonderful father when the kids had been babies. He was still a wonderful father.

He had tried to understand when she'd told him that she'd rather be alone on her own than always alone with him. That hadn't made sense. Not then. He'd been perplexed; he didn't go to strip bars, he didn't head out on wild nights looking for something new, hoping to get lucky with an exotic stranger.

But she hadn't thought that, apparently.

And he hadn't seen it coming, and when he did, it had been too late. She hadn't been angry; she had told him that she just didn't know him anymore, and he certainly didn't know her. And it was better to be alone, going about life on her own schedule than wondering what his might be, or if and when they were going to see him. Maybe if she wasn't always on the spot, he'd show up for his son's baseball games, or realize that Connor was falling in love with music, much like his uncle Bobby, who would really stop and listen to him at times.

Now, of course, it was all so clear.

He still loved his wife.

He was certain that even if she had fallen out of love with him, she still cared about him.

And his hold on her was firm; he realized at that moment, as long as he had breath in his body there was hope, and if they never made it back together again, he was desperately glad that she was alive. She was a wonderful person, and an exceptional mother, and thank God, no matter what they chose to do themselves in the future, they were lucky—they knew how to be family.

Cindy moved slightly in his arms, wedged between him and Bobby on the snowmobile. She looked up at him, and she smiled.

She didn't try to speak, the snowmobile was making far too much noise.

He wished he could try to explain; he had been indignant, so certain that he had done nothing wrong.

And he hadn't. He just hadn't been there.

But the way that she looked at him then...

He brought his lips as close to her as possible, and whispered against the roar of the motor, "Cindy, I... don't ever feel that you have to...to look at me that way or be too grateful... I mean, I know I wronged you, and I'm just so grateful that you're alive!"

"I *feel* alive right now," she told him. "And I feel that I'm *with* you as I haven't been in forever, Shayne."

He started to lean his head against hers. Then he heard his brother shout over the loud *whir* of the snowmobile. "Almost there! Just one more bend!"

Shayne nodded. He moved his head enough to smile at Cindy.

"The kids will think that you're the best Christmas present ever," he told her.

She smiled.

Then Shayne heard Bobby shout, "What the hell?"

He slowed the snowmobile, but too late.

They hit something again, something buried beneath the white drifts.

And the snowmobile veered to the side—thankfully inward, toward the mountain—but then it careened into the pines, cracked against a tree and overturned.

"You know where you're going, right?" Gabe asked Morwenna.

She looked at him; it was bitterly cold. They'd already made the walk down, and made it through the snow. But it seemed that the going was rougher now. It was difficult to make sure that she was staying on the road, and it seemed that here, even more so than higher, the snow had collected in deeper piles.

She shrugged with a sheepish smile. "Down," she told him. She added anxiously, "They should be getting back up toward us, but I keep thinking we should hear the motor of that snowmobile—it's old, and it's loud."

"We'll catch up with them soon," he said.

"And how do you know that? And aren't you looking for DeFeo—not my family?" she asked him.

He looked ahead, and there was something grim in his expression.

Morwenna gasped. "You think that DeFeo is after my brothers! But, why? Why would he be after my brothers? Why wouldn't he just want to escape?"

"He wants to use them," Gabe said after a minute.

"Use them? As hostages? Gabe, he's unarmed, and my brothers aren't exactly puny!"

"He has his ways." Gabe looked at her then and sighed. "There are many things that you can steal from someone that aren't really tangible."

"That made no sense! What could he steal from my brothers?" she asked.

"Sorry," he said. "He might be after something extremely tangible—like the snowmobile."

She kept looking at him; he had changed his mind—regarding what he might have said to her.

"Gabe, what are you really trying to say?" she asked, and her concentration was so hard on his face as she tried to read what was behind his passive expression that she stumbled and fell into him, bringing them both down into the snow.

"I'm sorry," she breathed, pressing her gloved hands into the biting snow to rise above him, blushing.

He shook his head. "It's fine," he said. He stared up at her for a long moment, and there was something of wonder in his eyes, and then he sighed. "We need to move," he told her.

He laughed, getting his footing, and helping her to find hers once again.

"We've got to keep walking," he told her.

"We'll freeze," she agreed. "And we have to find them."

"We will find them."

"You're so sure!"

"Ah, well, you see," he said lightly, "I believe in Christmas, for all that it means."

"You're not talking about a lit tree and ornaments, are you?" Morwenna said, smiling at him. "You are sunshine and light," she added dryly.

"Ah, well, I know that it's sometimes hard to see, and often impossible to understand, but I do believe in a greater power, and I may be a cop, but I do believe that *most* people are inherently good. We have basic needs, and then we have wants…and then we have desires. We're easily hurt, and when we're hurt, we're defensive, and we lash out. There really are seven sins, you know," he said lightly.

"And we all, in some way or another, fall into them all?" she asked.

"Not all of us into *all* of them," he said, grinning. "And," he added, "Christmas Day is special in many ways. You know—if you're a kid, you wait for Santa. If you're Christian, you believe in celebrating the birth of the man who taught us that we could be saved from all the bad we can fall into because we are human. No matter how people see their faith, the world is really one big family, and they say, too, that it's a family above and below the world as well."

"Heaven and hell?" Morwenna asked him.

He grinned. "Think of it all as one big family. Except there was one child who was very, very bad in his behavior. He envied his sisters and his brothers, and he envied every other creature, certain that everyone and everything was loved more than he was. And so let's say his parent sent him to stand in the corner, and while he was standing in the corner, he plotted a zillion other ways to get into trouble—and to get others to get into trouble with him. Now, as badly as he might be behaving, like any child, he's still loved. But his brothers and sisters have to look after him all the time, and make sure that he doesn't hurt others or get them into trouble with him."

Morwenna stared at him incredulously. She laughed softly. "Okay, so we're all one big family. God and man and—"

"All the angels," he told her. "Those who are well behaved, and, of course, the brother who just can't seem to behave. But, you see, here's the good thing—as bad as things look, and as bad as they are at times, we do have Christmas, when we celebrate the fact that good will outweigh what's bad. Belief is the hardest thing in the world…belief in what's intangible, and belief in ourselves."

Morwenna looked ahead, and she didn't know why, but she was suddenly reminded of the scene she had seen on television. Mexico. Over a hundred million strong—and a country with tons of tourist cities. But Alex had managed to get himself captured—with Double-D Debbie—for a few seconds on camera. She had been hurt, yes. Hurt—or had she felt humiliated? Or was it both? Of course she felt hurt. *But had she known? Had she realized, when they couldn't come to an agreement over the holiday, that there was something that… that just wasn't there?*

And if she was so hurt, why didn't she feel it now?

Because she loved her brothers; her brothers loved her. And they were out there somewhere.

She turned and looked at Gabe and laughed. "You are one crazy policeman, you know?"

He shrugged. "Maybe. But I'm also a very lucky one today."

"Why is that?"

"I happened upon people who prove the point that decency and goodness can so often win out. Miss Mac-Dougal, I do indeed rest my point!"

She shook her head, smiling.

"If we find them," she whispered then.

"We will," he assured her.

"How can you be so certain that everything will be all right?" she demanded.

"Because of you, right now. Because I know that you won't stop until you find them."

She laughed again, with a dry note in her voice. "No, you don't know the mountains. Terrible things happen so easily. There are high ridges that fall straight down a thousand feet. When there's weather, there are horrible potholes that can wreck almost any kind of vehicle. And there's treacherous ice. And the weather is so cold—we can all freeze on the mountain."

He smiled at her again. "Well, then, I will have been privileged to have known you all."

She met his eyes, and she felt oddly warm and certain despite the cold. "No," she said softly. "I think we have been privileged to have known you."

He looked back at her for a long moment.

"Look!" Gabe pointed out. "Look—there are some tracks, and something…"

"Something what?" Morwenna demanded.

"Something heavy was dragged through the snow," Gabe said.

And it had been. There was a flattened path of ground ahead of them.

"Hurry!" Gabe said, and he started ahead of her, somehow making tremendous speed across the slick ground.

And then it seemed that the world around them groaned, as if there was a crack of thunder that had split the sky. The sound echoed and ricocheted through the trees.

"What…?" Morwenna began.

"He's found them," Gabe said grimly. "DeFeo has found your brothers."

Bobby had felt himself lose control; it had been like spinning on black ice…no, he had been spinning, but it's because they had hit something beneath the snow that shouldn't have been there.

The impact of the vehicle had shuddered down the length of him.

And then he'd landed in the snow, and for a moment, he was aware only of the cold, the feel of the air and the pain in his body. There was something on top of him. The world was white…

He was pinned beneath the snowmobile.

"Shayne!" He cried his brother's name. "Cindy!"

"Yeah, yeah…" Shayne said. "Cindy, Cindy…"

He felt his brother trying to scramble around him, pulling his ex-wife from the wreckage.

"Is she all right?" Bobby asked.

"I'm—I'm okay!" Cindy said.

"Bobby?" Shayne asked, rushing to his side.

"I can't—I can't get out," Bobby said.

"Can you feel your legs, can you move them?" Shayne demanded.

His brother was there, down on his knees in the snow, next to him. Bobby tried to wiggle his toes and move his ankles. He didn't think that anything was broken; he was just stuck.

"Yes, yes, I can move everything," Bobby said.

Shayne nodded. "All right, I'm going to try to move the snowmobile. And when I do, you have to wriggle out quickly."

"Gotcha."

"Shayne, what do I do?" Cindy asked.

"You can try to add your weight when I lift," Shayne told her. "Ready?"

Cindy stood by him, ready to lift.

But though Shayne was strong, and had Cindy's help, the weight of the snowmobile was just too much.

"Listen, you two just get back to the tavern," Bobby said, forcing cheerfulness into his voice. "Get help, and get back here."

"I'm not leaving you like this," Shayne told him.

"Hey, Shayne!" Bobby protested. "We can't all just stay here—where will that get us?"

"I'm going to get a pulley system going...we've still got the rope. Cindy, you should probably be in a hospital, but can you take the rope—you remember how to do the knots, right?"

"Of course," Cindy said. "Hey, I didn't spend time with Dad for nothing! I mean, your father," she amended quickly. "I've got it. I'm really all right, Shayne, I can help. Give me the rope."

"All right," Shayne said, pausing and looking around. "There...walk over there. That tree looks good and sturdy and it's at the right angle…take that end of the rope, Cindy, and make sure it's a good knot."

Bobby heard the snow crunching as Cindy hurried off to do as she had been instructed. He watched as Shayne studied the snowmobile and the way it had fallen and then started to loop the heavy nylon rope around the snowmobile. "With the tree helping to create a lever system, we will get this thing up in no time," Shayne promised him.

Bobby was able to grab his brother's ankle. Shayne looked down at him.

"If you don't get this up now," Bobby said sternly, "you're going to take Cindy to the tavern, get Dad and Mac and come back for me."

"I'm going to get it up. What, are you kidding me? Can you imagine Mom if I come back without you? Don't worry—I'm going to manage this!" Shayne told him. "Cindy—"

Shayne went dead still, and quiet. Bobby tried to twist around and see what was going on; he couldn't.

He could only see his brother's face, and his features were knotted in a look of wary dread.

"What?" Bobby whispered.

But Shayne didn't look down at him.

Bobby heard someone else speaking, and he knew the voice.

Luke DeFeo.

"That's right, I have the pretty little ex-missus!" DeFeo said. "And nothing is going to happen to her. As long as you all play it right. I want that snowmobile. You're going to get it up and running, and then everything will be fine."

Bobby strained and twisted, trying to see around the

snowmobile. He managed to wriggle enough to look around the front; Luke DeFeo had Cindy in a choke hold against his body.

"I know what I'm doing," he said quietly. "One wrong move and her neck snaps. And I still get the snowmobile. Are we clear?"

"Perfectly," Shayne said, ice in his words.

Bobby saw DeFeo smile. "Don't worry. I let her get a good knot on that rope before I nabbed her. Dr. Mac-Dougal, now it's all up to you and your brother there. I want the snowmobile up, and I want it running, and when it is, I'll take your ex with me just down the road a hair, and I'll leave her for you gentlemen to find again."

Cindy was staring at Shayne, tears in her eyes. Bobby knew why she hadn't screamed; she was flat against DeFeo's back, and his arm was in a hold that prevented her from uttering so much as a squeak. She looked at Shayne with apology in her eyes, and fear that she couldn't quite hide.

Cindy hadn't even known about DeFeo! She hadn't known anything about the strange night that had passed, or about the stranger day that had followed...

The darkness was beginning to settle around them in earnest.

And with the darkness would come a greater cold.

"I have to get to the tree with the lever," Shayne said. "I'm moving, and I'm going to need to be there. I'm going to get the snowmobile off my brother, and we'll get it up together. Don't do anything. I'll get you the damn snowmobile."

"Fine. Do it," DeFeo said.

Something of a little squeak did escape Cindy as DeFeo jerked her back and away from the tree.

Bobby cursed himself for getting stuck beneath the snowmobile. If he had just realized what could have happened, if he'd have tried to jump clear...

Bobby saw as Shayne moved, delving first into the storage compartment for the lever. He then heard his brother's footsteps crunching through the snow as he headed for the tree.

He could barely see Shayne anymore, and DeFeo was caught in the crazy light that emanated from the headlight of the snowmobile. There was something not quite right about the man.

He could hear Shayne, struggling with the pulley system he was trying to assemble and work with the tree and the rope. His brother, he thought, had it rigged, and he was using all his strength to pull. The snowmobile seemed to ease up on Bobby; he tried to slip out.

His brother let out a grunt, having to stop for a minute.

"Or," DeFeo said quietly, "you could leave me to deal with this. Take the little lady up to the tavern—and leave me here with your brother. What a fix! Desert your baby brother. What should you do, Shayne? You've got about two more minutes to move that snowmobile, or I'll take charge in the way that I see fit."

"I'm not leaving anyone!" Shayne snapped.

"Then you'd better get going, right?" DeFeo warned.

Shayne faced him. "Really? Aren't you a bit of a fool? The minute you release Cindy, we'll all be right on top of you, you lying bastard!"

Bobby winced. He wasn't sure that threatening the man was the way to go. But Shayne wasn't going to leave him, and he wasn't going to let the man hurt

Cindy. He was testing Shayne, trying to make him decide between the mother of his children and his brother.

"What do you care about the woman?" DeFeo asked him. "Didn't she leave you? Didn't she walk out on you, screw around with some other man using the money you worked for? The bitch is only here now because she couldn't stand you having her children."

"If you hurt her," Shayne said, "you will be a dead man."

DeFeo started to laugh. Bobby blinked. He looked so strange in the glow that was cast by the headlight. He seemed bigger than he had been. He seemed to radiate a strange smell so powerful that it even reached Bobby where he lay, caught beneath the heavy snowmobile.

It was something like the scent of...brimstone!

"Boy, where's the Hippocratic oath now?" DeFeo said. "Well, Mr. Moralist, you'll have to figure out something here, won't you? Your brother or your ex-wife, the precious mother of your precocious little brats!"

"I'll get you the snowmobile!" Shayne said.

"Oh, I don't know," DeFeo said. "Maybe I'll just take her with me all the way..."

His hold on Cindy must have eased a fraction.

She cried out, "Shayne, don't let him hurt Bobby, don't—"

The sound strangled as he clenched his arm more tightly around her.

Dear God, Bobby prayed. *What do we do, what can I say, how—*

He was suddenly aware of a rush of sound. And suddenly, Cindy was almost flying toward him in the snow.

DeFeo cried out in surprise.

And Bobby realized that someone had come up behind DeFeo; they had all been so intent on the interaction between them that none of them had heard a thing.

They hadn't seen a thing...

But someone had come.

Gabe Lange.

Morwenna ran as fast behind Gabe as she could. Following him, she had first gone dead still in horror. The snowmobile was on its side...on top of someone!

And then, of course, she had seen DeFeo's back. And she had realized that he was holding someone in a death grip. And she hadn't even had time to think.

Gabe had taken off.

And then he was on DeFeo's back.

She heard a scream, and it came from Cindy, who had been thrust forward, falling into a massive drift. While Gabe attacked DeFeo from behind, DeFeo reached around, shouting out in rage, grabbing at Gabe.

Morwenna raced toward the trees, finding a stick. She ran around in front of the grappling men and began thrashing hard at DeFeo with her haphazard weapon. He lashed out with a fist, and he struck her in the chest. She was stunned at the blow; it sent her flying back hard into the trees. She was aware of Shayne rushing by her, ready to join the attack, and then she was aware of Shayne again, flying by her as if he weighed no more than an Easter bunny.

She heard Bobby, roaring in frustration, unable to help. She saw that Cindy was up, crawling over toward Bobby, and that Shayne was trying to rise, shaking his head, as if he could clear it.

She scrambled to her feet and looked around for a

weapon. There was a huge tree branch by her feet and she went for it, and then charged in again, whacking at DeFeo—trying to make sure that she missed Gabe.

Except that she didn't miss him; she caught him in the arm. He bellowed, but he didn't even seem to notice her, so intent was he on DeFeo.

"Give it up! Give it up!" Gabe raged to DeFeo. "I've won. You're done here, you're done here! Give it up!"

Shayne charged in again, going for DeFeo's legs. He toppled the man, but Gabe went down, too. Morwenna grabbed her branch, trying again to get a good crack in on DeFeo's head.

She aimed well, and this time, she hit him.

She *knew* that she hit him.

But he didn't even notice. Even though the sound seemed like a shot in the cold air, *it didn't even faze him*.

She went to strike again, but to her amazement, both men were up.

"You've lost!" Gabe shouted again. "You've lost!"

But DeFeo didn't want to give up the fight. His face was contorted in a hideous mask of rage, and he stared at Gabe, as if he *knew* somewhere he had been defeated, but he just couldn't accept that it might be so. He was going to lunge at Gabe again, but then another sound seemed to rip apart the crisp air and the icy mountaintop.

A roll of thunder. There was no lightning, there was no sign of a coming storm...

But the sky suddenly lit up as if the earth had spun crazily toward the sun for one bizarre moment; then the sound of thunder roared again.

The night returned to darkness.

DeFeo turned, and started to run. Gabe tore after him.

"No, Gabe!" Morwenna shouted. "Let him go!"

Gabe looked at her briefly. "I can't," he said quietly.

He turned and ran after DeFeo. She saw Gabe catch hold of DeFeo again.

"Stay still—give in and stay still, please!" Gabe begged the other man.

It wasn't to be. DeFeo let out with a punch that landed hard on Gabe's jaw.

"No," DeFeo cried. "You have to win, and you know it. And I just have to escape you."

The man sounded almost gleeful.

Gabe twisted to secure the other man's arms, but DeFeo wasn't willing to give in. In the struggle, they began to roll. They rolled hard and fast, and she shrieked again in horror; they were rolling toward the ledge. She could barely see in the darkness of the night, but she could still hear the two and they kept rolling...

"Gabe!" she cried.

But she couldn't see the two men any longer; she couldn't hear them. There was no crunch of snow. There was no grunting, no sound of blows falling...nothing.

She felt Shayne behind her, setting his hands on her shoulders.

"Oh, my God!" she breathed. "We've got to find him."

"We'll go after him," Shayne promised. "We'll go after him. But we've got to work here first. And fast."

"Shayne—"

"Bobby is caught," Shayne said, and he looked into her eyes. "And... I'm sorry, Morwenna, so sorry, but if Gabe does lose... DeFeo could come back."

"Just get me out!" Bobby cried.

"Come on. Cindy—" Shayne began, spinning around. Cindy was already waiting at the tree. "I don't even know what just happened. But we've got to get Bobby out from under there. And we're going to be all right. Come on!"

Morwenna looked at Shayne, and together they hurried to the tree. Shayne took the front position. Morwenna strained. Her muscles ached to the core. They strained and pulled, and slowly, with Shayne shouting instructions, they brought the snowmobile back to rest on its tracks.

She fell back in the snow, exhausted and amazed that Shayne's system had worked. Her brother walked to the snowmobile, hunkering down to help Bobby up. Bobby winced, trying to stand.

"Nothing broken," he said.

"The tavern is just up ahead. Take Cindy. Get her back to the tavern," Shayne said.

Bobby nodded, realizing that he couldn't help.

"Can you make it without the snowmobile?" he asked Bobby and Cindy.

"We will make it without the snowmobile," Bobby assured them. "You two need it."

Cindy nodded, hurrying to Bobby to lend support to help him limp along.

But, as Morwenna watched, Cindy paused, staring at Shayne with anguish in her eyes. She rushed to him, caught hold of his jacket, rose to her toes and kissed his lips.

And, if only quickly, Shayne kissed her back.

"We've all got to move!" he commanded.

Cindy nodded and ran back to Bobby.

Shayne mounted the snowmobile. The headlight was still on; he turned the key in the ignition and nothing happened. He turned it again.

And the motor sprang back to life. Shayne carefully eased it into Reverse, and the mangled machinery moved.

"Go!" he said to Bobby and Cindy. He looked at Morwenna. "Climb on!" he told her.

She did so quickly, and they moved on into the darkness of the night.

Chapter 11

Bobby's leg was killing him. He was sure that he hadn't broken any bones, but he had done some mean damage to himself.

He leaned hard on Cindy for support, and they moved through the night. He could hear the strain of his breathing; even in the dim light of the moon that shone down upon them, he could see the massive mist of each breath he took.

Cindy labored at his side.

"I'm sorry!" he said.

"Oh, Bobby," she returned. "I'm all right, really. I'm tougher than I look, and I was never really hurt badly. I was frozen…blacked out a bit, but I'm all right. You can lean on me."

"Maybe you should run ahead," he suggested.

"Never," she told him. "Bobby, I don't understand anything about tonight."

"I'm not sure *we* even know what happened," he said.

"That light…" she murmured.

"Strange, huh?"

"Very!" she said. Then she stopped in her tracks. "Bobby!"

"What?"

"I can see it!"

"See what?"

"A star!"

"What?"

She laughed. "I see a star, and it's actually the tavern! The electricity must have just gone back on. Look! It's all lit up, and it seems like a zillion colors are shining out—oh, it's the lights on the tree, Bobby. I can see the tree with the star on top! Look through the pines, and you can see the tree right through the window!"

He paused, and he peered through the trees.

And he smiled, unaware of the pain in his leg.

The star at the top of Mac's tavern tree seemed brilliant. It was a guide, and it was a sign.

They were almost there.

"Cindy, come on. Hot chocolate is so close I can almost taste it!"

They took the beat-up snowmobile around bend after bend.

And there was no sign of either Gabe Lange or Luke DeFeo.

Shayne drew to a stop, revving the motor as he tried to look around.

"Morwenna," he murmured. "We're not going to find them."

"No, no, no!" she said. "They've gone over the ledge. Oh, Shayne…"

"Maybe not, Morwenna. Gabe is a resourceful fellow."

"We can't give up! We can't give up."

"Morwenna, you can't go over the ledge. It's a far drop down."

"We can't give up."

"We have to. It's dark—the light isn't showing us much. They might be down over the ledge, but safe on some kind of outcrop. They might have wound up taking the fight up one of the slopes. They could have wound up in the trees anywhere."

He was right; she felt ill.

"Oh, Shayne!"

He turned and touched her cheek. "We could be heading for frostbite now, Morwenna. We have to go back. We need a helicopter, and we need light. We'll get Dad and Mac, we'll see if anyone has been able to get hold of someone who can really help," he said gently.

She nodded and leaned her head against his back. "Shayne, we tied him up!"

He nodded. "Yep."

"Genevieve never stopped believing in him."

"No," Shayne agreed. He cleared his throat. "DeFeo arrived in a cop's uniform, Morwenna. We had no choice."

"But he saved Genevieve's life. And then…he might have saved all of us."

"He did save all of us," Shayne said.

She nodded against his back. Her heart ached. *This* hurt. This hurt in a way that was far worse than anything she had ever felt. It seemed silly and irrelevant that

she had cared at all that Alex had been on a beach—
chasing Double-D Debbie.

Shayne revved the motor and carefully turned the
snowmobile.

When they finally reached the place where the fight
had begun, Morwenna begged him to stop for a minute.

She crawled off the snowmobile and carefully moved
toward the ledge.

"Wait! Be careful. I'll get a light."

She heard her brother swearing softly as he struggled
to open the bent-up storage compartment on the side
of the snowmobile that had hit the ground. She heard
a wrenching sound as it gave, and then she was aware
that Shayne followed her to where she stood with a
high-powered flashlight.

Silently, they searched the terrain below them. The
moon was casting a decent glow, and they looked and
looked.

"Anything?" she whispered.

"No," he said.

"Try farther down, Shayne. Cast the light down."

He did.

But no one was there.

Shayne set his arm around her shoulders and led her
back to the snowmobile. "It's good that we didn't find
them, you know that, right?" Shayne asked her.

She imagined Gabe at the bottom of the mountain,
crushed, mangled and bleeding.

"Yes," she said huskily. Silently, she crawled on the
snowmobile behind him.

"Hey!" he said.

"Yeah?"

"The lights are back on at the tavern," he said.

"So they are."

* * *

Bobby wasn't sure he'd ever seen anything as beautiful as his mother's look of joy when he and Cindy stumbled into the tavern.

Ah, but maybe there was. It was Genevieve's face as she saw her mother.

"Mommy!" she cried. Delight in her voice. "Oh, Mommy!"

Genevieve threw herself against Cindy, who nearly fell over.

"Careful!" Connor cried. And then he was sobbing, too.

"I knew that Daddy would find you," Genevieve said. "I knew that he would!"

"I don't know how he even knew that I was out there!" Cindy said, accepting hugs from all around.

Bobby found himself crushed in a ferocious bear hug by his mother, and then his father. And he wondered if the way that his father looked at him with such pride and love wasn't one of the best gifts he'd ever received at Christmas.

Then his mother cried out, "Bobby, you're hurt!"

"Just a sore leg. My brother will fix it."

Stacy drew back, concern in her eyes again. "They're not here. Shayne and Morwenna. Where are they?"

Then he and Cindy tried to explain, each interrupting one another to add a detail.

"But—but they went to try to help Gabe. Against DeFeo!" his mother said, fear in her voice.

"They're on the snowmobile. They're fine. It's still working. And, Mom, honestly, I think that Gabe is going to rearrest DeFeo. I don't think there's any question," Bobby said.

Brian Williamson came over to them. "Bobby, get that wet coat off. Come on, everybody. These two need to be warmed up."

Mary jumped to at her husband's words, smiling as she hurried to put her coat on Cindy until she could warm up. Bobby felt himself divested of his wet snow gear and bundled into an oversize coat.

"My God," Stacy said, hurrying to the window. "Where are they? Where are they?"

Cindy walked over to Stacy, touching her gently on the shoulder. "Mom… I mean, Stacy, I'm so sorry. Shayne should never have been out. I don't know how he knew to come looking. I just can't believe that he did…"

Stacy turned to look at her. She reached out and drew her into a big hug.

"It's not your fault! It's not your fault at all for wanting to be with your family at Christmas. And you call me Mom forever, no matter what you two do in the future, do you hear me?" Stacy demanded.

Cindy nodded, tears in her eyes.

Mike walked up behind her, pulling her from his wife and into his arms.

"We are always happy to see you, Cindy," he told her. "Listen to your old dad."

Cindy started to cry.

Bobby felt tears welling in his own eyes.

"Now is the time for Irish coffee!" Mac boomed out. "Stacy MacDougal, come back here and help me. Those children need something warm in their bodies!"

"Yes, yes, of course," Stacy said. "And we'll need to make two extra, because Shayne and Morwenna will be back any minute."

She walked around the bar to busy herself helping Mac.

The Williamson family stood near the window, watching, offering silent support.

Genevieve and Connor clung to their mother.

Bobby sat back in a booth, his leg up. His mother brought him the first steaming Irish coffee. He smiled at her. He sipped it. "They'll be here," he said firmly. He pointed at the star at the top of the Christmas tree. "It will lead them home, you'll see. The electricity miraculously came back on at the right time to see to it that the star leads them back. It brought Cindy and me in."

Stacy nodded. "Yes, yes, it did."

Bobby perked up suddenly. "Listen! Listen, I can hear the motor," he said.

"They're coming!" Adam Williamson said from the window. "They're coming!"

Stacy stood by Bobby, closing her eyes in gratitude. She looked at Bobby. "It's a beautiful sound right now."

Shayne slipped his arm around Morwenna as she crawled off the back of the snowmobile. She hadn't realized it, but her cheeks were frozen on her face—and her "cheeks" were frozen elsewhere, as well. Without Shayne's arm around her, she might have stumbled.

The door to the tavern burst open.

Her mother and father came running out, heedless of the cold, hugging them both and urging them into the warmth.

Morwenna felt like a star, friends and family everywhere, helping her off with the wet and on with dry, a sweater and a scarf someone had once left behind, and held in the tavern's back room in hopes the owner would return for it. Her mother held her hands in her own, rubbing them and warming them. Hot, stiff coffee was set before her, and her father listened while Shayne explained where they had searched, and that they hadn't found anything.

She tried not to cry.

She couldn't believe that Gabe Lange had been in their lives so briefly, and that she felt as bereft as she did. She wanted to pray that he was alive and was so afraid he couldn't possibly be.

She was vaguely aware of everyone talking as she sipped her laced coffee.

"DeFeo could still be out there," Mike said.

"You enjoy your family," Brian Williamson told him. "I've got the shotgun, and I'll be watching the front."

"And no one is coming in the back," Mac assured him. "Windows and doors are bolted."

"He's not coming back," Morwenna said. "Not unless…not unless Gabe is dead," she whispered.

"Gabe isn't dead!" Genevieve announced fiercely.

"Of course not," Morwenna said. She tried to smile at her niece. But Genevieve wasn't worried.

She was trying to reassure her aunt.

"Gabe isn't dead," she repeated. "He's going to find us all again." She pointed at the star. "He'll see it, too!"

"You're absolutely right," she told Genevieve.

She wished she believed it.

She leaned back again, taking a long swallow of the coffee brew. It was good. The alcohol warmed her to the core. It seemed impossible, but she was warm again. She closed her eyes, and she listened to those around her.

She could hear Bobby and her father talking.

"I'm hoping for Juilliard, Dad," Bobby said. "I'm

really hoping. And I will work my way through it. I wouldn't drop out, I swear."

"Son, not that I don't have faith in you—I do," Mike said. "But—here's the thing. If it isn't Juilliard, we'll search. We'll search until we find the right school. There's Ball State University of Music. There's Harvard. And, son, you will get into one of them," he said firmly.

"Thanks, Dad," Bobby said softly.

She opened one eye, and was glad to see them at the next booth, heads together, close.

She turned her head around a little, and there was Shayne.

With his family.

He was seated next to Cindy. They were close. The kids were on top of both of them; Shayne held his son in his lap while Cindy held her daughter. It was such a perfect picture.

She didn't know if they actually would get back together. But whether they did or not, they would always share a very special bond now, she thought. And the fighting would all be over.

She closed her eyes again. She smiled. It was good. And yet...

Her heart ached.

Morwenna looked at the TV to distract herself. The television was still snowy, but a picture was starting to show.

A newscaster stood on a roadway. Morwenna could see the buildings around her and she recognized the little town just at the base of the mountain. The reporter was standing just outside the police station.

"Police have recaptured escaped white-collar criminal Luke DeFeo," she said, her voice cheerful. "DeFeo

managed to escape during a prisoner transfer yesterday, midday. It's Christmas for the cops, too! The con
walked right into the police station, half-delirious, and
gave himself up. One of the state's finest, Detective Ga-
briel Lange, had been in hot pursuit—we have no information as to Lange's whereabouts, but rescue crews are
out now, searching for him. In other news, despite the
snowstorm, electricity is being restored to about five
thousand homes, and in all, it looks like a white and
merry Christmas. Over to you, now, Walter!"

"How the heck did the man get down the mountain
so fast?" Mac asked incredulously.

"Really, that's just about impossible," Mike said.

"You think they got the right man?" Bobby asked.

"Yeah, they flashed his picture up there in the corner, didn't you see it?" Mac asked.

"Maybe he fell down half of it," Stacy suggested.

"Well, they have him, and that's that," Bobby said.
He limped over to Morwenna and slid into the booth
next to her. "Gabe is going to be all right, too, then."

"Sounds odd, doesn't it, Bobby?" she asked.

"What's that?"

"DeFeo handed himself in," Morwenna said. "He
handed himself in. That really doesn't sound like the
guy who was fighting Gabe on the mountain."

"But it was him, Morwenna. And," he said, offering
her a smile, "they will find Gabe. And he'll be all right."

She smiled, squeezed his hand and leaned her head
back again. She fingered the little angel on her chain.

*But it was bitterly cold out. He was on a mountain.
He could have fallen. He could be somewhere with his
leg broken, or worse.*

"Morwenna," Bobby said gently.

She opened her eyes.

"They have helicopters, they have search dogs, they know what they're doing," he said.

She nodded again.

Something seemed to flash before her eyes. She turned. The star on the top of the tavern tree seemed to be glowing more brightly.

Electrical surge! she thought.

"Bobby, let's see that leg. Mac will have something. You've got bruised muscles or torn ligaments, baby bro. I need to get you wrapped up," Shayne said, coming over to assist Bobby.

"Yes, sir," Bobby said.

He kissed his sister's forehead, and went to Shayne to have the damage assessed.

Genevieve came over to her. She looked at Morwenna solemnly. "Gabe is going to be okay. I know it, Auntie Wenna."

She put her arm around the little girl, pulling her closer.

"I'm sure he is. He was telling me a little story about the angels getting feisty at Christmas. And there's a fallen angel, you know."

"Lucifer," Connor said.

Morwenna smiled. Her nephew had come over to try to give her comfort, too.

"Right," Genevieve said. She was very grave. "Except that God loves everyone, even those who are bad."

"Fallen," Connor said, sighing with great patience.

Morwenna smiled. "When you get in trouble, you know your folks still love you, right?"

Genevieve nodded gravely.

Morwenna reached for one of the big white napkins

in the holder at the end of the booth and found a pencil. She started to sketch for the children. "So, here, you see, here's Lucifer, who is like a bad child, trying to instigate trouble. Now, as you said, God loves everyone, no matter what, just like a parent loves a child, even when that child's behavior is not so good. But a parent knows when he or she has a kid who can cause trouble..." She paused, sketching an angel. "So he sends out a friend, or maybe even a sibling or a cousin, an angel who does behave, to try to make the mischief-making angel behave, and not hurt other people. Is that the story, Genevieve?"

"Yes!" Genevieve said. "Gabe was saying that God sometimes has to send out one of his good angels to make sure that trouble doesn't happen." She looked at her aunt in wonder.

"That's a nice thought, Genevieve," Morwenna said.

"It's a nice story! I really like that story!" Genevieve said. She touched the paper Morwenna had been drawing on. "You can draw in people," she said. "You and my dad and Uncle Bobby, Gram and Gramps, Connor and me. And maybe even my mom."

"Definitely, your mom, too," Morwenna agreed, and sketched.

When she finished, Genevieve reached up and touched the little gold angel that hung around Morwenna's neck. "We have angels," she said. "Good angels. Like Gram's little angel on her tree. I held it, and I dropped it, but I never broke it," she said.

"No," Morwenna assured her, hugging her again as she smiled at Connor. "You didn't break it—none of us broke what was really important today," she said. Looking over Genevieve's head, she noted the star on the tree again. It was odd how it seemed to be burning more and more brightly.

"As if it is leading someone home," she murmured.

"What?" Genevieve asked.

"Sweetie, let me get up," Morwenna said. Genevieve obliged, and Morwenna hurried toward the door, heedless of a coat or the cold.

The moon was out, and the glow from the tavern seemed to be lighting up the mountaintop as she burst out into the night. She saw nothing at first, and she felt the cold, and wondered if she was an idiot.

Then she heard a groan. She might have imagined it. But she hadn't.

She raced out into the snow, listening. "Gabe!" She cried his name, and ran along the edge of the trees. "Gabe!"

She heard something…a rustling. And then she saw the heap of a man in the snow.

She raced over to him, falling to her knees.

It was Gabe!

He lay as if he had been walking to the door, and then collapsed.

"Gabe! Gabe! Oh, my God, you're hurt, you're…"

She touched his face, searched for a pulse.

His eyes opened, and he stared at her. He stared at her without a single sign of recognition.

"Gabe, it's Morwenna. You're hurt. We're going to get you in. Oh, thank God, you're alive!" She couldn't help herself. She leaned in and kissed his lips, quickly. She moved away, just an inch, looking into his eyes.

She saw confusion…and yet, a strange sense of recognition. And she wasn't sure if she moved, or if he moved, but she found that she was kissing him again.

Or he was kissing her. And the kiss was good, and sweet, and natural. And if it weren't for the circumstances, she would want it to be much deeper, and far more...

Passionate.

But he had been hurt, and they were out in the snow, and others would be there. She broke away, touching his cheek tenderly. "I..." he began, but fell silent.

"It's all right. Don't try to talk. We're going to get you in, get you warm. Oh, Gabe!" she said. Tears stung her eyes. They were instantly like ice. She didn't care.

"I can't remember," he said. He winced. "My head..."

"Maybe a concussion," Morwenna said. "But it's all right. Shayne will know what to do. You're going to be all right. And I don't know how you did it, Gabe, but Luke DeFeo is in custody and—"

"DeFeo," he said. "Yes, I was chasing him and then... I don't remember."

"You were wonderful," she assured him, worried.

He almost smiled. He touched her cheek. "I know that I have been saved by an angel!" he told her.

She shook her head, clutching his hand. "No, *we* have!" she told him. She thought that she'd never really understand what had happened that Christmas on the mountain, and she couldn't help but wonder just what had been at play. Had she and her family been caught in a strange battle? A battle in which they had actually been given a choice between a fallen angel and a strange force for good that gave them back something special they had been missing as a family, and in life.

And now...

She smiled.

Was it possible? Had the angels taken on the flesh

and blood of the men they had known in the last hours? And was the man she now faced in essence the same— but not the same at all?

She heard Shayne shouting to his father and Mac; her mother was out on the steps. They were all calling out with concern and joy that he'd been found. The church bells began to peal, and she remembered that it was still Christmas night, and the one service for the few people in the little mountaintop area would begin at eight.

It was still Christmas.

She stared down at Gabe, into the green of his eyes, and she realized that something about him was just a little bit different, and yet...

He was Gabe. And so much about him was going to be exactly like the man she had come to know.

Her family rushed around her. She was aware that her mother was scolding her for being out without a coat. Genevieve was hopping up and down, saying she had known that Gabe would come back to them.

Her father and Shayne got him to his feet. They started moving toward the tavern.

Morwenna followed, and paused, looking at the star on top of the Christmas tree through the tavern windows.

She smiled. "Thank you! Thank you so much!" she said, her voice a whisper in the night air. "And as Genevieve would say, happy birthday."

* * * * *

YULETIDE
COLD CASE COVER-UP

Jessica R. Patch

For those who do not feel worth forgiving...you are.

A special thanks to my agent, Rachel Kent; my editor, Shana Asaro; my friend and author Susan L. Tuttle; and my family. I appreciate you all so much and couldn't do this without you. Thank you.

There is therefore now no condemnation
to them which are in Christ Jesus.
—*Romans* 8:1

Chapter 1

The Christmas season would never be the same—not that it had been normal for the past seventeen years, but there had always been a ringing bell of hope. Until a few hours ago, when four words numbed Poppy Holliday's faculties and the bell stopped tolling.

They found her remains.

Those words had resounded through her head as she drove through the misty December night to Gray Creek, Mississippi, less than two hours from the Mississippi Bureau of Investigation in Batesville, where she worked with the cold case unit and now lived. But on that chilly, late night in November when Cora had gone missing, Poppy had lived in Gray Creek. She'd been seventeen—a senior—and Cora had been fifteen, a freshman at Gray Creek High.

Poppy switched on her brights, then gripped the

steering wheel tighter as the lights illuminated the dark road. But nothing illuminated her internal dark void. Tears filmed her eyes, and she blinked in rhythm with her windshield wipers. If only she could turn a switch to swish away the pain like the wiper blades cleared the tiny flecks of sleet from the windshield. Like her lashes swept away the salty tears.

She slowed as she took the sharp turn. Out here on the country back roads, hitting deer was the leading cause of death.

What or who had killed Cora?

Her sister's remains had been found along with her purse and wallet, which held Cora's student identification card.

Another round of tears—of grief mixed with fond memories—slipped down Poppy's cheeks and then she sobered as she approached the Weaverman property, which lay on the outskirts of Gray Creek. The once-thriving farm had been secluded and abandoned for years. The only evidence left was a silo and old pump house—where Cora had been for seventeen years and one month. The original house had been torn down long ago.

Earlier today, a few teenage boys had decided to play Truth or Dare, which landed one of them down the old, dried-up well in the dilapidated pump house with a rope tied around his waist and his friends egging him on. He'd gotten more than he bargained for when he discovered the remains. At least they'd had the brains to call the sheriff's office and report it.

After seventeen years of weather and time, not much would be left to identify, but a DNA test was being done, and with the purse, identification card and a few tattered remains of clothing, Poppy and her family were convinced it was Cora.

She parked at the edge of the road, her headlights spotlighting the yellow crime scene tape rattling in the unusually wintry weather for the South. Forecasters called for a white Christmas, but a lot could change in a week. Already, snow had fallen twice this month—a dusting, really. Enough to close schools but not to build snowmen or forts. Poppy and Cora had constructed a few of those when Dad had been stationed at Fort Myer in Virginia. She'd done it for Cora, who'd loved frigid temperatures. Poppy had never been a fan of weather under sixty-five degrees, but she had been a fan of besting her four older brothers in a competition.

Tack, her oldest brother, had stayed behind in Texas when the family had moved to Gray Creek to care for Grandma. He was living his dream as a Texas Ranger in the unsolved-homicide unit. Poppy was most like him, even professionally. Neither admitted their draw to cold cases had been born from Cora's disappearance. Tack had been the one to inform Poppy of the news earlier today.

Not Dad. Not Mom.

Tack had insisted Dad's reason for not calling was he didn't want to leave Mom's grieving side. But Poppy knew better.

When her family had returned to Texas the year after Cora vanished and Grandma died, Poppy stuck around and attended college at Mississippi State, then went on to the police academy, landing a job after at the Desoto County Sheriff's Office before transferring to the MBI cold case unit in Batesville. She'd loved her time at the SO, but one of her more rotten choices of getting romantically involved with Liam—a sheriff's deputy—had pushed her transfer to the MBI. Moving back to Texas instead would have been too difficult. Her brothers never blamed Poppy for Cora's death, but the accusation that pulsed behind Dad's steely eyes and Mom's cries when Poppy was around let her know fast they did find her at fault.

And Poppy agreed.

Her remains should be at the bottom of the well. Poppy had been the rebellious daughter, jumping into potentially dangerous situations like a kid in a lake on a summer day. Poppy had been the back talker and limit pusher. Cora had been sweet and kind and obedient. The easy child. The good child. The favorite—and rightly so.

Standing in the wind, her thin red sweater doing nothing for warmth, Poppy surveyed the property. Overgrown weeds. Bare trees. The entire place reeked of decay and neglect.

Like Cora's body.

Poppy pushed her bangs from her eyes, and released past hurt and frustration without restraint. No one was here to witness the depth of grief in her sobs or the unending guilt. No matter how hard she'd worked to pay for her sins, nothing she did washed them away. Nothing washed away the shame. Not tears. Not closing other cases—and she closed more cases than anyone on her team. They called her competitive, and to some degree they were right, but with every case she solved, she expected a measure of peace for what had happened to Cora—for the part she'd played in Cora's disappearance and ultimately her death.

But peace never came. Not one ounce.

Gently, she touched the frosty plastic crime scene tape and slipped underneath into the scene that she'd observe with the eyes of a detective when the sun rose in the morning. Tonight, she was here as a broken sister who needed to be where Cora had lain all these years. Tonight, she needed to unleash all the pain, allowing the wind to carry it away before daylight, when she would refrain from shedding tears among her colleagues as they combed the well for possible evidence connected to Cora's demise. By the time officials had made it out here tonight, it had been too dark and manpower too little to station someone to keep guard, though Poppy had pushed the issue with Sheriff Pritchard, who promised drive-bys.

Cora, did you willingly come out here that night? Did someone force you here? Were you alive when you were tossed away like trash?

As she slid down the old cinder-block walls, the smell of earth and must filled her senses. She ignored the cobwebs, spiders and rodents that would surely be inside. She wrapped her arms around her drawn-up knees and rested her chin on them.

When she thought she had no tears left, a fresh wave erupted.

It should have been her at the bottom of this well.

I'm sorry, Cora.

Sorry wasn't even close to a satisfactory response, but she whispered it each time she thought of Cora. And that was every day.

Finally, the cold seeped into her bones and she stood, retrieving her Maglite and flicking it on. She forced herself to shine the slim beam of light down the well, to inspect as much as to keep moving, keep her blood circulating to warm up. Unable to see the bottom, she shivered and spun around as a chill not associated with the temperature launched down her spine. The feeling of eyes invading her private moment raised hairs on her bare neck, and she silently listened for any sound of human movement outside the pump house.

Wind and fallen leaves blowing. Nighttime creatures hunting. But it felt like something else—someone else—was also on the prowl. Or maybe the thought of Cora's end and the terrifying scenarios accompanying the finality of her sister's life had her imagination creating shadows that weren't truly out there in the darkness.

Her phone rang and she startled at the shrill timbre. Glancing at the caller's name, she cringed. Another frigid gust in her crummy day—Rhett Wallace, unit team member and all-around Boy Scout. A stickler for rules, an overthinker and entirely too attractive for his own good—which might be the biggest annoyance to Poppy. At times, his presence was a distraction, so she managed to be careful of letting it happen often.

Answering, she didn't hide her irritation for being attracted to him. "It's almost eleven o'clock. What could you possibly need?"

Rude? Yes, but necessary.

If she lowered her carefully crafted wall of indifference toward Rhett, Poppy was terrified she'd gravitate to places she had no business going. Acting as if he meant nothing to her personally was far easier than allowing herself the possibility of exploring how she could feel about Rhett aside from being her unit partner.

She'd save his bacon, professionally. In a heartbeat. And that's as far as it would go. Besides, Poppy wasn't exactly Rhett's favorite person. The man was a pillar of patience and politeness—except where Poppy was concerned. He'd made it abundantly clear on an almost daily basis that Poppy flared his temper and ate away at his composure.

She was to Rhett what orange juice was to freshly brushed teeth.

That's the way she liked it. The way she needed it. The way it was going to be.

"Well," he said in his put-on patient tone, "I thought you might need a friend."

She wouldn't say they *weren't* friends. They were mostly friendly when they weren't bickering, and they could work well together—when the work was done Poppy's way. "I don't."

"Okay," he said with a strained voice, "the truth is I drew the short end of the stick and get to aid you in the investigation."

That sounded more like truth, but to be honest, she could use a friend. "Colt called you?" Their unit chief didn't love the idea of Poppy investigating her sister's cold case, but he also knew how much it meant to her. Not that long ago he'd reopened and investigated his best friend's unsolved homicide, and she'd reminded him of that more than once until she basically wore him down. Poppy was good at that—wearing people down. It worked to her benefit on most occasions when suspects or witnesses were hiding information.

"Yes, he told me you weren't going to back down. And since I know that stubborn tone and defiant glare—which no doubt you gave him—I get to be present to remind you that you aren't Doc Holliday, you're Poppy Holliday."

"Oh, I'm gonna be somebody's huckleberry, Rhett.

Make no mistake about that," she said, referencing the iconic Wyatt Earp movie *Tombstone*—a beloved film they had in common. "I'm not backing down. No one will investigate this case like me." She wasn't called Bulldog, in an appreciative manner, by her colleagues for nothing. "I'm going to turn over every rock—even the pebbles—and I'm going to squeeze myself into every nook and cranny. When I get done, this case is going to be closed and whoever killed my sister will rot away in a prison cell until kingdom come. No other option."

Rhett sighed. "I'm with you, Poppy." His tone bore compassion and understanding, and—complete agreement. "In every nook and cranny. Under every rock. We'll do everything you've said. With—"

"Within the legal bounds and without kicking up dust like a gun-totin' law dog. I know this. I don't want the perpetrator to get off on a technicality because I didn't go by the book. I'll go by the book." She didn't say which book. But Rhett didn't need to know that.

She could see him now, pinching the bridge of his perfectly straight nose and slowly shaking that dark-haired head of his. "I'm about fifteen minutes out from Gray Creek. I reserved a room at the B&B you're staying in. Found it odd it's not booked up with it being the week before Christmas. Owner seemed nice, though."

"She told me they blocked the week before and of Christmas because they might be traveling, but her plans fell through. When I told her why I needed to reserve a room at least through Christmas, maybe longer, she gave it to me. I can be persuasive."

Rhett snorted. "You mean a nag and whiner."

"Says you. Either way, it works." Poppy stepped outside the pump house. That cold, thorny feeling scraped her nerves again, and she surveyed the surrounding woods as the knee-high grass rustled against her legs.

"Poppy, you there?"

"Yeah," she said absently, "I'm out at the scene."

"You shouldn't be out there alone," he said.

"I'm capable of taking care of myself and not messing with evidence." She bit back a huff as she strained her eyes against the inky atmosphere.

"I didn't mean for those reasons," he murmured.

Rhett had lost a sibling when he'd been a kid too. She didn't know all the details, but he would be able to at least relate to her grief. Understand her pain to some degree. But why did it have to shake the tough foundation she'd taken years to lay? "I appreciate that," she said with less bark. "I needed to, though, you know? Alone." Surely, he'd get that too.

A beat of silence. "I do. I'll be there in less than fifteen minutes. Meet you at the B&B?"

"Sure. I'm wrapping up here anyway." They ended the call and Poppy rubbed her arms. Winter was the worst. She pocketed her cell phone and headed for her car. It was going to take more than its heater to warm her up, though.

She paused one last time and scanned the property. When it came to danger, her gut was usually on point. If someone was out there, they were well hidden in the shadows. Chances were no one was. No one knew she'd be here. But still, Poppy was on edge.

Hurrying to her car, she unlocked it, retrieved her cell from her back pocket—she'd made one too many accidental calls—and tossed it in the drink holder, then grabbed her coat. She barely had one arm inside the sleeve when a powerful force knocked her to the ground. Poppy flipped onto her back as the attacker loomed over her, his dark, heavy coat blurring his build, his knit cap covering his hair and the gray wool scarf hiding the lower half of his face.

She kicked his chest as he bent toward her, knocking him off balance and giving her a second to spring to her feet, then rush back toward her car. His footsteps crunched along the gravel at the edge of the road. As she clutched her door, something hard connected with the back of her head, throwing her vision into a fuzzy spin.

Strong arms gripped and lifted her as dots popped along her eyesight. Completely disoriented and feeling dazed, she couldn't fight. Couldn't get her bearings.

Fragments of sound invaded her ears. A car horn. A door slamming and an engine revving. A wave of nausea rose in her stomach.

Poppy rubbed her throbbing head, wet with sticky blood.

Faint Christmas music floated into the cramped space. "It's the Most Wonderful Time of the Year" reached her stuffy ears. Were they moving or was the world simply spinning?

Gravel crunched, revealing she was in the trunk of a moving car.

Moving!

Poppy's pulse slammed into overdrive. Self-Defense 101—never let an attacker place you into a vehicle. Chances of survival lessened when relocated. Where was he taking her? What was he going to do with her? Acid scorched her throat and panic set in, but she was trained. Poppy reached into her pocket for her phone but it was missing. She'd placed it in the drink holder. If only she hadn't cared about making accidental calls.

Begging her mind to think clearly, Poppy felt around the trunk, searching for a release button, but they would normally glow in the dark. No button. Older-model car. She filed that fact away and changed gears. Without newer technology, she'd have to resort to kicking out a taillight and hoping someone would see her hand waving, but she wasn't stupid. No one was out here this time of night in the middle of nowhere. Why had he been? He was either an opportunist who had seen a lone woman alone on a back road or he was at the scene in connection to Cora's murder. Poppy's gut had been right, and she'd passed it off as the heebie-jeebies.

She finagled her body to direct her foot in the right position as Andy Williams belted out being of good cheer, then geared up to kick out the taillight.

The most wonderful time of the year. Yeah, right.

The song continued with lyrics of friends coming to call. She needed a friend to come calling right now. She reared back, put some muscle into her kick and the light broke free, frigid wind rushing inside the trunk.

Poppy thrust her hand through the opening, waving frantically and hoping for a rescue. Fear skittered underneath her skin, sending a frenzied shiver through her, but she breathed deep and forced herself to gain composure. Allowing fear to run the show meant she'd make fatal mistakes. Instead, she'd use her God-given brain to work herself out of this terrorizing predicament.

Sleet and wind numbed her hands. Plan B. Using her other hand, she searched the trunk for anything she could wield as a weapon. Tire iron! She gripped it and prepared to lie in wait.

The vehicle took too many turns and twists for her to keep up with their direction. All she had to gauge time was the music. Instead of focusing on what might happen to her, she concentrated on seeing her steps to freedom. If she could envision and practice the motions in her mind, she had a better shot of success.

The car turned and slowed onto a bumpy road, which tousled her, but she kept a solid grip on her only weapon. Finally, the vehicle came to a complete stop. "It's the Most Wonderful Time of the Year" ended, informing her that she'd only traveled about two to three minutes away from the Weaverman property, but she had no clue in which direction.

Readjusting her grip due to sweaty palms, she braced herself in preparation for her fight *and* flight. The driver's side door dinged.

It was open, but no sound of footsteps. Likely he was walking on dirt or grass.

A key was inserted into the trunk and a lock clicked. Definitely an older car.

Poppy didn't give the creep time to lift the trunk fully before she sprang up, startling him, and swung the tire iron like a major-league baseball player. She nailed him in the shoulder, and he cried out in a deep voice and stumbled backward, giving her the chance to jackrabbit out of the trunk and down the dirt road filled with ruts.

She swallowed down the nausea and begged the dizziness to subside as she approached the main road. Poppy had always been a long-distance runner and was more familiar with pavement. Not taking chances on tripping and hurting herself in the woods across the highway, she picked up her pace and hauled herself down the winding, empty two-lane road. Thankfully, she had adrenaline on her side. Her only hope was outrunning the guy she'd jacked with the tire iron or some Good Samaritan slowing down to rescue her. She hoped for the latter.

She continued to fight the nausea and dizziness as she pumped her arms, thankful for her long legs and running shoes on her feet.

Footfalls on pavement pounded behind her.

Increasing her stride, Poppy sprinted around the curve, and in the distance, salvation shined.

Rhett Wallace cracked his windows. Hot-blooded and in love with cold temperatures, he welcomed the wintry weather. It was the Southern summers that tempted him to regret choosing the snowy mountains to live and work. According to his navigation system, the old farm property was about five minutes away. He'd told Poppy he'd meet up at the B&B, but she might still be at the old Weaverman property grieving alone, and Rhett knew well that was a terrible way to mourn the loss of a loved one. He'd swing by and wait in his car in case she did need a friend—or coworker—to lean on for support.

A sibling's death was like having thousand-pound cinder blocks laid on your chest one at a time until no breathing room remained. After all these years, that weight continued to rob him of breath. He'd lost Keith two days before Christmas twenty years ago. Rhett would never get over waking up Christmas Day and seeing all of Keith's unopened gifts under the tree, which would remain that way permanently. It was the worst thing he'd ever witnessed, next to watching his big brother drown while attempting to save Rhett's life.

All because of one stupid dare from their cousin to walk across the frozen pond.

He slowed at the curve. Deer would be present and if the sleet stuck, the roads would be slick. Rhett didn't take dangerous chances anymore. No more daring or impulsive behavior.

Poppy called him an overthinker and a stiff shirt—stuffed, but the woman never got her idioms right and it drove him bonkers. But he'd rather be overly cautious and safe than sorry. That was his sole purpose in law enforcement: to save lives, not take them like he'd taken Keith's.

Whether or not she liked it, Poppy needed Rhett on this investigation. She was a wild card who needed to be reined in on occasion, and with this case being personal, Poppy would likely take unnecessary chances and risks. Colt was on vacation in the Smoky Mountains with his wife, Georgia, and his other team member, Mae Vogel-Ryland, was on her honeymoon in the Bahamas. There was no one else to be the voice of reason and caution to Poppy. So he'd suck up her ridicule and snide remarks no matter how much they got under his skin. She pretty much prided herself on the fact she could rile him up; he wasn't sure why he couldn't ignore her and shrug it off.

His phone rang and he answered through his Bluetooth.

"Hi, honey." Mom's voice rang clearly through the car speakers.

"Hey, Mom. How you and Dad doin'?"

"Good."

"Mindy?" His younger sister—by eighteen months—and her family would be settled into Mom and Dad's for the Christmas holiday. Plenty of snow would already have fallen in the East Tennessee mountains.

"Got here an hour ago. I was calling to see if you might be able to make it this year. We miss you, honey."

He missed them too. But he didn't miss the stories about Keith that caused Mom's tears or Dad's blank stare out the window. And he didn't want to be present on the anniversary of Keith's death. Didn't matter if they'd told him a million times he wasn't responsible for Keith's death, that it had been an accident. He *was* responsible. He *was* to blame. He'd been the cause.

"Sorry, Mom. I can't. My colleague is working her sister's cold case and I'm aiding the investigation."

The silence on the line crushed him; he didn't want to intentionally hurt his family, but his being there—a glaring reminder that they no longer had one of their sons—wouldn't benefit anyone.

"I understand. I'll be praying for her and her family. And I'm praying for you. I love you, Rhett."

A knot grew in his throat. "I love you too."

"Come home soon."

He would. Just not during the holidays. Most likely in the spring, when he usually visited. "I will." As he ended the call, something flashed in the road and he slammed on the brakes. He'd been careful to watch for deer.

This wasn't a deer.

A woman! Rhett squealed to a complete stop and bounded from the car as Poppy's voice reached his ears. "Poppy?" he hollered and raced toward her, as a million questions ran through his mind.

She collapsed against him and he braced her from falling, somewhat shocked at her vulnerability. Poppy was the epitome of hard-shelled and hard-nosed.

"Talk to me, Poppy." He touched the side of her hair and noticed the blood. His heart rate kicked up. Had she been in an accident? "What's going on?"

She turned her head, looking back, and he followed her line of sight. Nothing but an empty, deserted road.

"He's gone," she mumbled and slumped against him again, her arms clinging to the back of his leather jacket. The way she melted into him sent a ripple of awareness through him. Poppy was a gorgeous woman in a no-nonsense kind of way. Never one to wear much makeup, she had naturally dark lashes and sharp hazel eyes that bordered on green depending on what she wore—eyes that were cloudy and confused at the moment.

He brushed her midnight-black bangs from her eyes; sometimes she wore them straight across her brow and sometimes to the side, blending with the rest of her hair that hung to the edge of her defined jawline.

He released her and examined her for further injuries—as a colleague and agent, not as a man scared half out of his gourd.

"Who's gone?"

She gave her head a quick shake and blinked herself out of her stupor as her long, lean body went rigid. She straightened her shoulders and put the hard-nosed mask back into place. "I was attacked at the Weaverman property and tossed in an old sedan." She relayed the details as they loaded into Rhett's Maxima and slowly drove along the road in search of her abductor. When they found the nearest access road, Rhett assumed it must be the one Poppy had been taken down. Fresh tire tracks and footprints confirmed it.

"I have a kit in the trunk. I can take an impression," Rhett said.

Poppy snorted. "Of course you do. You have a first aid kit too?"

"Actually, yes." He popped the trunk and shrugged out of his lightweight brown leather jacket, then went to work on obtaining the tire and shoe impressions. Once the casts were completed, he packed away his gear and studied Poppy. Pale and visibly shaken, but doing a moderate job of hiding it.

"Can you drive?"

She nodded.

"I'll take you back to your car, then we can get to the B&B and talk."

Poppy shivered and Rhett turned on the passenger seat warmer. Laying her head against the light leather headrest, she exhaled a long, deep breath. "Opportunist or connected to Cora's case?" she asked.

As ruffled as she was, Poppy wasn't one to not be working at all times. "I was thinking about that while making the impressions. Thing is, there's nothing out here for miles. I put the coordinates in my navigation system, thinking I might catch you. Join you in a look around." Good thing he had.

"It's the scenic way into town, but not the quickest. Why would a creep troll around out here? What normal woman would be out here this late and alone?"

Rhett smirked. "No *normal* woman would. But when have you ever been tagged as normal?"

She actually grinned and he was glad to see it, especially since her eyes were red rimmed and puffy. Evidence of crying. Rhett knew better than to comment. Besides, grief was deeply personal and he had no plans to invade those boundaries. He'd simply wanted to be available if she invited him in.

"Ha. Ha. Rhett Wallace—the stiff shirt—has jokes."

"It's stuffed shirt and you know it. I've corrected you before." He neared a bridge—a small green sign with reflective words let them know it was the Gray Creek bridge they were crossing. "Welcome to Gray Creek," he muttered.

Poppy grunted, then shifted in her seat as if surprised. "Seat warmers? Nice. I need these in my car."

"I never use them. Too hot." He shrugged. "You live in a lot of places growing up?" he asked, aware that when it came to Poppy, he didn't know much about her personal life. Only tidbits here and there from her conversations with Mae or brief conversations at their morning meetings. Nothing deep.

"Yup. Military brat…so…back to the case. Opportunist or—"

"Cora." No point pressing her for any further personal information. When Poppy was done, she was done. No skin off his teeth. "I think he was out here in connection to her case. The question is why."

Rhett had a few dark ideas, but he'd let Poppy do the speculating aloud. It would come easier from her lips than his. Besides, from what he'd read of the case file, there were few leads.

She cleared her throat and after a long moment, she spoke. "He might have been out here to remember. That makes me sick."

Killers often revisited their crime scenes for a myriad of twisted reasons. "I know. Me too."

"Or he didn't expect her to be found. He might have been double-checking to see if he'd left anything behind. The Gray Creek SO will be collecting evidence come daylight."

The crime scene tape blew in the wind as he parked behind her Acura. "Mind if I walk you to your car?"

"No, I don't mind."

They walked in silence; the sleet had stopped. Nothing seemed out of place. She peered inside. "Nothing taken. My phone's still here." She opened her console. "And my gun."

"Good. I'll follow you to the B&B and we can get a game plan in order. I'll need to know more about the case." Meaning Poppy was going to have to volunteer some personal information. She was included in Cora's victimology, whether or not she wanted to be.

The fact that he wanted to know more about her burrowed under his skin like a splinter.

Poppy clearly had a soft side.

Desiring to see it was dangerous.

Chapter 2

Gray Creek Manor was a large yellow country house nestled into a wooded property framed by a white picket fence. Lights decked the wraparound porch, and poinsettias dotted the steps leading up to the front door, where a large wreath with a red velvet bow hung in the center. The Christmas tree, with twinkling colored lights, beckoned them inside for peace, joy and warmth. All the things Rhett had been missing out on each year by declining to go home for the holidays.

The door was unlocked and Rhett frowned. B&B or not, leaving the door unlocked, especially at this time of night, seemed foolish and left the home vulnerable, even if there were a few houses sprinkled along the road. He motioned Poppy to enter first, then he stepped in to the swirling scents of vanilla and cinnamon, reminding him of Mom's homemade snickerdoodles—his favorite. Shuffling of shoes along the hardwood met his ears before a tall, lithe woman in her late thirties or early forties appeared. Must be Delilah Cordray, the owner. He expected her to be older and, for some odd reason, plumper.

"You must be Agent Wallace. So nice to meet you. I'm Delilah." She shook his hand. "I'll show you to your room." She paused at Poppy's condition, but Poppy waved her off and offered little information. Delilah took the hint that it wasn't her business. "Do you need anything else? Your room suffice?"

"Yes, thank you," Poppy said as they followed her up the wooden stairs.

"I put you next door to Poppy. You both have private baths. Breakfast is served from seven to eight."

Rhett switched on the light when they got to his room. A large four-poster bed, hutch, dresser and writing desk with a small antique chair graced the room. Two Christmas throw pillows had been placed on the bed and a picture of the nativity hung above the headboard. "It looks great. Thanks."

"I'll leave you two alone. There's apple cider, hot chocolate and coffee in large thermal carafes down in the dining room, along with cups, condiments and tins of cookies. Help yourself." She brushed a hair—considerably longer than Poppy's and fiery red—behind her ear and left the room.

He set his travel bag against the wall by an antique rocking chair and turned to Poppy. "Apple cider sounds pretty good." An invitation to discuss the case, or whatever might be on her mind concerning Cora.

Poppy nodded. "I'll change and meet you downstairs."

Poppy's hair was matted with blood and her clothing was dirty. "Do you need to see a doctor?"

"No. I'm fine."

Rhett didn't argue and headed downstairs to help himself to the sweets.

In the dining room, drinks and desserts covered two old, weathered buffets that lined the back wall. One long skinny table held thermal carafes of drinks, and tiny cards with pretty writing labeled what each container held. He poured a cup of cider and lifted the lid of one of the Christmas tins. Snickerdoodles. Jackpot! By the time he'd eaten two of them and washed them down with the tart and sweet cider, Poppy entered the dining room with an accusing eye. Busted dead to rights in the cookie tin.

"I love these things."

"Me too." She grinned. "I already snarfed down two when I arrived earlier." She motioned with her head to the living room on the other side of the entryway. "It's more comfortable in there."

Rhett followed her. Poppy sat in the chair near the lit Christmas tree and he took the matching one opposite her. A table with books and a lamp put space between them, but he caught her freshly showered scent and her hair was damp. She had changed to comfortable clothing, black yoga pants and a zip-up hoodie.

He bit into his third snickerdoodle. He'd never admit it, but these might be better than Mom's. "How you feeling?" he asked.

"I'm miffed. Some jerk tried to kill me tonight. Also, I'm a little sore from being jostled and I have a headache. But I took a few ibuprofens before I came down." She shrugged as if it was no biggie, but Rhett saw through the tough exterior and false bravado. The attack earlier had rattled Poppy, and the evidence that she was still shaken was in the tremor in her hands as she squeezed her insulated paper cup.

"I called the local sheriff—Rudy Pritchard—before I came downstairs to let him know what transpired, and to persuade him to recognize that regular drive-bys aren't enough now. Someone needs to be put on duty the remainder of the night. Who cares about overtime! If Cora's killer lurked because convicting evidence could be found, then he might return." She sipped her hot chocolate and yawned.

"We can talk in the morning, Poppy, if you need to sleep." Though she might need to stay awake a little longer if she had a concussion. "I'm assuming if you truly needed a hospital, you'd go because you're sensible enough to determine that and follow through, right?" He cocked his head, and she rolled her eyes.

"I don't need to be babysat, Rhett."

Debatable.

She dodged his gaze and studied the twinkling lights on the Christmas tree. "Cora loved white lights. I think the pulsing of the colored lights bothered her. She had epilepsy."

Rhett leaned forward, resting his elbows on his knees. "I'm sorry. I imagine that could be scary at times."

"She was a champ. The golden girl. Kind and friendly. She wanted to be a scientist. I bought her a kiddie scientist kit one year for Christmas. It was just slime and test tubes." Her rich alto laugh at the memory sang in his ears, drawing a warm sensation in his gut. Rarely did Poppy laugh—a chuckle here and there, maybe, but that was it. "She was a straight and narrow kind of girl."

"Then why did she sneak out of the house?" Rhett had gone through the case file earlier when Colt sent it to him. But nothing in it gave him much more insight into Cora than adjectives describing how good and honest she was. He needed to know more. If she was normally a rule follower except for this one time—then whatever caused her to break the rule was the key to this case.

Poppy's posture stiffened, and she toyed with the sleeve of her sweater. "I don't know," she murmured.

Rhett wasn't buying it. What was she holding back? "Were you two close?" He laid his cookie on the napkin.

She nodded.

"Then why don't you know?" Pressing a colleague—especially one as tough as Poppy—wasn't his idea of fun, but in order to move forward in the investigation he had no other choice. It wasn't like she was volunteering pertinent information. "Was she acting secretive before that night? Anything happen that you can remember? She sneaked out of the house. Your parents had no idea and were shocked. But if you were close…"

Steely eyes met his. "We argued two days before she vanished. Sisters argue."

"Did you argue over the reason why you were grounded?" The file noted Poppy had been grounded that weekend, but nothing in the notes stated why. It might be important.

"It's irrelevant to the case," she said and balled the edge of her sleeve in her fist.

Rhett wasn't buying that either. "Poppy, you know good and well that everything is relevant to a case, even events and conversations that appear irrelevant."

She licked her bottom lip and cleared her throat. "I was grounded for having marijuana in my nightstand drawer. We argued over the pot. Happy? I never said I was the model teenager." She glared at him as if awaiting judgment to fall with a heavy thud. Rhett hadn't been a model teenager either. He'd been a risk-taking wild card—like Poppy now. She'd receive no judgment from him.

"Happy about you having drugs? No. Happy you're being open about the events that led up to Cora's disappearance, yes." Could the marijuana and the argument over it be connected to Cora's murder? Did Poppy not think so? Being an emotionally invested family member might be blurring her investigative instincts. "What do you know about Cora's friends?" According to the files, she had been heavily involved in her youth group and science club at the high school. Detectives had interviewed her closest friends and all of the students, as well as the science club teacher, Solomon Simms. But nothing led them further in the investigation, thus running it cold.

Poppy's shoulders relaxed when the spotlight shifted to Cora's friends. "Honestly, I didn't know much. I was a senior and had my own circle of friends, but I know she adored Mr. Simms and had a crush on one of the kids in her botany/zoo class—and he was in science club. Dylan Weaverman. I told the detective that then."

Rhett had been waiting for Poppy to bring up this vital fact. Cora had a crush on Dylan. Dylan's parents owned the property that she'd been found on. According to his interview, Dylan didn't know Cora had a crush on him and he liked her—as a friend. But he didn't see her that night, and his older brother, Zack, had been his alibi. "We should start with him, don't you think? Seems like there's more to his story—and his alibi could have been lies by a big brother protecting him."

"I don't know. He wasn't the stereotypieal jock. He was a nice guy and a science geek as well. But I do know she liked him. I found doodles on her notebook and she admitted he was cute and that he might like her too. But he didn't seem to know she liked him." She shrugged. "Teenage girls see what they want. An act of kindness on his part could have easily been misconstrued as romantic interest."

Or maybe Dylan wasn't the nice boy he'd pretended to be. "Now that she's been found on his family's property, he might want to change his tune. He's the only solid link. Who else might know anything? The file was pretty thin." Cora didn't socialize much—probably due to her epilepsy, but if she had meds, then she should have been able to go out and have fun with friends. "Anyone in her youth group stand out?"

"All of her friends were accounted for—on the youth trip. Mom was afraid to send Cora without having a chaperone, and with it being the holiday season, Mom had to work at the store."

"You didn't want to go? Did they not trust you to keep an eye on her?" Rhett asked and inwardly winced as Poppy's mouth hardened. "I'm not saying you were irresponsible because of the weed…"

"I was never careless with Cora. My parents expected me to protect her, and I wanted to. But I didn't want much to do with church back then. Got back into it in my early twenties after my grandma passed. It was her dying wish to see me living for the Lord—her words—and Cora would have wanted me to go."

Poppy attended church with the team, but it didn't sound like she was going because she wanted to. She kept her spiritual life as quiet as her personal life—but they intersected. Faith was deeply personal. "Did Cora want you to attend the youth retreat? Is that what you're holding back, Poppy? Guilt that you should've been on that trip but you were grounded and couldn't go?"

Abruptly standing, Poppy sniffed and grabbed her paper cup. "My parents never grounded us from Jesus. I'd made it clear I wasn't going. Cora knew it and was resigned to the fact. And my parents didn't make me go because they believed if I was resentful about it, I wouldn't keep an eye on Cora—but that's not true. I would have. I did take good care of her because I loved her. And I'm going to bed. My head hurts."

Her heart hurt too. It was there in her angry tone and cold eyes. Rhett knew that pain well. "I didn't mean to—"

"You're doing your job, Rhett." Translation—he was poking a bear. "Good night."

A knock on the front door drew their attention. Rhett frowned. "I thought Delilah didn't have any guests except us."

Poppy peeped out the front window. "It's the sheriff's SUV."

"At midnight? That can't be good." Rhett followed Poppy to the door. Poppy opened it and there stood a hulk of a man with a salt-and-pepper military cut and a short beard. His grim expression matched that of the man next to him in plain clothes—but he wore a belt with a badge and gun. Criminal Investigations Division. Detective.

Sheriff Pritchard looked at Poppy. "Dylan Weaverman is dead."

* * *

Dylan Weaverman had driven his car off the Gray Creek bridge last night some time before eleven, and was discovered by a couple of guys out spotlighting deer.

Poppy slipped on her camel-colored, double-breasted wool coat. She'd chosen thick gray pants and comfortable black boots. She checked her watch. Almost 8:00 a.m. One hour until she had to be at the Weaverman property to comb the well for possible evidence.

Poppy's gut had been in knots since Sheriff Pritchard delivered the news about Dylan Weaverman's death. No way could it be a coincidence—because now they couldn't question him about what might have actually happened seventeen years ago.

A dull ache throbbed across the back of her head, and a small knot had formed, but the nausea and dizziness had dissipated. As she opened the bedroom door, the scent of bacon and blueberry muffins wafted up the stairs, sending her stomach into a growling anticipation. She descended the stairs and found Rhett already in the dining room with a full plate of breakfast casserole, bacon, fruit and grits.

"Morning," he said as she approached. He looked fresh and put together. The man's clothes were consistently wrinkle free. He pulled off his charcoal gray dress pants and a fitted black dress shirt with style. The shirt matched his hair, but his eyes were a shade softer, like dark honey.

"Morning."

Delilah entered from the kitchen wearing a baking apron with reindeer on it. "Agent Holliday, good morning. Agent Wallace told me Rudy and Detective Teague came by last night. Awful news about Dr. Weaverman."

"You knew him?" Poppy asked as she helped herself to the casserole full of eggs, sausage, potatoes and cheese. And was everyone in the town on a first-name basis with the sheriff or was it just Delilah?

"Of course. He ran a vet practice with his brother's wife." Delilah set a fresh pan of cinnamon rolls out and Poppy snagged one, along with a few slices of bacon, but passed on the grits.

"This looks amazing," Poppy said. When Delilah bustled back into the kitchen, Poppy sat across from Rhett and grunted. Sheriff Pritchard wasn't sure what the cause of death was. It hadn't appeared to be a homicide, but he too had a sneaky suspicion foul play might have been at hand—there had been an open container of Jameson on the passenger floorboard. Was Dylan prone to drinking whiskey? The ME should know cause of death by now.

"If Dylan's death was accidental, it's too coincidental. If it was suicide, my first thought is he killed my sister. Couldn't live with it or was afraid of the consequences. He had time to conk me on the head, get away, then kill himself. But why? Why attack me, then kill himself?"

Rhett wiped his mouth with the green linen napkin. "Maybe when you escaped, he felt helpless. You kept him from finding whatever he might have been searching for, and now we're going to discover it. With drive-bys last night, he couldn't risk going back for it. Or he didn't kill her, but knew something, and when her body turned up, he had a change of heart and someone killed him to keep him quiet."

"Which means more than one person was involved in her death if that's the case." Poppy picked at her food, her appetite suddenly gone, but she needed the fuel and forced herself to take a bite.

They finished their breakfast and took Rhett's Maxima to the Weaverman property. Sheriff Pritchard, Detective Teague—who had been with the sheriff last night—and several deputies and forensic people were on the scene.

Rudy Pritchard was in his early forties with eyes the color of dirty ice, a strong jaw covered in a thick dark beard and wide shoulders and biceps. Poppy knew military background when she saw it, and she was seeing it now. He commanded the area with confidence. His sight eventually landed on them and he motioned them over. Rudy was a man who gave orders and was clearly used to having them followed.

As Poppy approached, Detective Brad Teague waved and strode toward them. Based on appearance, he was a former athlete, with kind blue eyes. Poppy had never been one to gravitate to the nice guy, except where Rhett was concerned. He was the man who climbed oak trees to help kids rescue kittens, but just because she was pulled toward him didn't mean she had to allow gravity to do its thing. She'd dug her heels in early on and was standing firm in her spot, which was a safe distance from him.

Rudy Pritchard didn't appear to be the proverbial nice guy, and she caught his interest in her—for a flash, in those calculating eyes—but then it disappeared as quickly as another detective approached. This one was a little younger than Detective Teague, with short-cropped blond hair and a blond stubbly beard to match. He had arms like Gaston from *Beauty and the Beast*.

The sheriff introduced him as Monty Banner and they all made niceties.

"Forensic team dropped into the well three minutes ago," Sheriff Pritchard said. "Lot of trash down there to wade through."

Poppy winced. Cora had been tossed down there too. Garbage. Rhett shifted his body toward her, as if trying to protect her from harsh or hurtful words. The kindness was welcome, but the way it made her feel was not. "Do we have any news from the ME about Dylan Weaverman?"

"Cause of death is blunt force trauma to the head. But the ME can't determine if it's due to nailing his head on the steering wheel—blood's on it—or if it happened prior to the crash." His jaw pulsed and he frowned. She didn't like not knowing concretely whether it was an accident, suicide or homicide.

"I'm going to investigate as if it was a homicide," Brad said. "Like Sheriff said, it's too coincidental. I'd rather waste my time and find out it was accidental or suicide than let a murderer get away with homicide."

Poppy couldn't agree more.

He flipped up the collar on his black wool coat and glanced at the swollen sky. A mix of grays with a blur of sun confirmed a dusting of snow coming before the day's end. She slipped on a pair of black leather gloves.

Bags of evidence—or simply junk—were in the hands of two young men who'd been down in the well. "We got more," one called.

"I'd like to personally go through the muck," Poppy said. "I'd know if something belonged to Cora or was relevant to her."

"You do what you need to, Agent Holliday," Sheriff Pritchard said. "You have our office's full backing. But it'll mostly be on you since we now have Dylan's case to work. If the cases intersect, Detective Teague will keep you apprised."

Small towns. Small law force. Understood.

"Do you have any other information from the ME?" Rhett asked.

Detective Teague sighed, and his breath puffed into the chilly atmosphere. "He was above the legal limit to drive, but due to your sister's case, I'm still going to investigate. Forensics is processing the vehicle. If it was foul play, we'll likely find trace evidence."

Sheriff Pritchard pointed toward the pump house. "We'll get this back to the SO, which is yours as long as you need it." He handed her a business card from his pocket. "Call me if you need anything."

She accepted, catching his subtle but personal invitation. "I'll be sure to do that."

Rhett bristled and excused himself to catch up with the forensic team. Poppy had no romantic interest in Rudy Pritchard, but keeping good lines of communication open was key to getting what she needed to solve Cora's case. Her colleague Mae would have thrown the invitation right back in his face and called it unprofessional. Well Poppy wasn't Mae.

Catching up to Rhett, she surveyed the bags of potential evidence. Cans, bottles and wrappers. Coins. This might be a waste of time. "Let's talk to Dylan's brother, Zack Weaverman. He was in my grade, but I didn't know him well. He'll know more about what kinds of things went down out here over his parents. And he'll likely know more about Dylan's situation. Was he an alcoholic? A social drinker? Was the drink-

ing to numb the guilt over Cora? I have so many unan-
swered questions." Many that might never be answered
now that Dylan was dead.

"And maybe you'll have time to squeeze in a date
while you're here too," Rhett said with quiet force, his
accusing tone grating on Poppy's nerves.

"My personal business isn't any of yours." The au-
dacity of Rhett to even entertain the idea that she would
indulge in personal enjoyment while hunting her sister's
killer was insulting.

"All I'm saying is getting involved with someone
you're working with isn't smart." His cheek twitched.
Leave it to Rhett to be irritated over some unspoken
rule of thumb. No one knew better than Poppy how far
south a romantic relationship mixed with a professional
relationship could spiral. She'd transferred out of the
county due to the mess, but it had worked out for the
best since Poppy had wanted to investigate cold cases
long term. The opening with the Mississippi Bureau of
Investigation came around the time it all went sideways,
and she hadn't looked back.

"Well, I'll be sure to file away that little nugget of
wisdom and remind you of it when you ask me out,"
she barked. *Feel that sarcasm? Good.*

Rhett snorted. "You don't ever have to worry about
that."

"I was being—never mind. And FYI, if you did ever
change your hardheaded mind, my answer would be a
confident no. Not now. Not ever."

"Well, I'll be sure to never give you one of my business cards."

She waved off Mr. Straitlaced and busied herself
with asking the forensic team for information on the

collected debris. After bagging and tagging, professionals filed off the property, leaving the crime scene tape in place as a glaring reminder that tragedy had occurred here.

"Hey," Rhett said as he stood next to her, his hair wind whipped and his nose tinged pink from the cold. But his voice held no ice and his gaze wasn't as chilly. This was their way, though. Bickering—sometimes heatedly—mostly over his strict rule following and his unwanted opinions on how to live by the book. Poppy never took *unnecessary* risks concerning her job. Her personal life was another matter, and it was none of his judgy beeswax.

"Hey," she echoed, no longer angry at him either. "Ready to talk to Zack Weaverman?"

"I got his address from dispatch."

They slid inside his car, the warm seats chasing away the frigid bite. She'd invest in a new car just for these bad boys. Nat King Cole's "The Christmas Song" played quietly as they reached the main highway. "Roasting chestnuts by an open fire would be fantastic right now. Or just an open fire. I can't ever seem to get warm enough in winter. It's a bone-cold kind of chill." She shivered and Rhett pointed his vents in her direction.

"Not me. I love it."

She grunted. Opposites in every way.

"Zack's interview didn't give much information seventeen years ago. Our only hope is he'll spit out something new to aid us now."

Zack Weaverman had admitted his brother and some friends occasionally used the property for hangouts, but he stated that he and Dylan had been at home all night playing video games. His parents had been out Christmas shopping and assumed the kids were in bed when they got home. Neither checked on them. So their video-game-playing alibi wasn't airtight. "You think he will?"

"I don't know. Depends on his involvement, if any. What do we know about the brothers?"

Poppy couldn't say, but siblings kept secrets with each other—and from each other. Zack and Dylan would be no different.

Rhett plugged the address into the GPS. Zack Weaver-man lived on the outskirts of town on another patch of family-owned property. Poppy would like to live out in the country like this with nothing but farmland, pastures and woods as scenery.

Zack's newer brick home was sandwiched by pasture land, with horses grazing. A large white building had a separate drive to the Weaverman Vet Clinic. Beyond it was a large red horse stable. As they turned onto the road leading up to the house, Poppy low-whistled. "This is something out of a movie."

"What does Zack do for a living?" Rhett asked.

"I don't know—"

Pop!

A bullet slammed into the windshield.

Rhett swerved and the car careened through the horse fencing and barreled into the open pasture. Poppy flinched, her heart beating out of her chest. Another bullet connected with the back passenger window, shattering it.

"Get down!" Rhett hollered and hunkered behind the wheel as a third projectile was fired.

Poppy winced and shrieked as a burning sensation bit into the skin on her neck.

"I think I've been hit!"

Chapter 3

Rhett's heart lurched into his throat at Poppy's frantic declaration.

He had to get them to safety but there was nothing but open space, making them prime targets. Blood trickled down her neck.

Another bullet blasted into the back of the car, then another.

As the shooter's intentions registered, Rhett's stomach plummeted. He was aiming for the gas tank, leaving them no choice but to exit the vehicle!

"Poppy, can you move?"

"Yeah. I don't think it was an actual bullet, but a speck of glass from the window." She had her gun in one hand and her other on the door handle, fingers trembling and fear causing her voice to quaver. "We have no covering."

God was their covering.

Quickly, he surveyed the pasture and the large round bales. "Let's aim for the closest haystack and hope for the best."

Poppy nodded, then bolted, Rhett right behind her, keeping low. Another round of shots rang out, then a sudden rush of heat propelled him forward, throwing him several feet before he landed with a teeth-rattling smack.

Poppy! Where was Poppy?

Debris from his exploding car went up in a blaze. Smoke covered the sky, and the smell of burning rubber and scorched metal singed his nose. About five feet away, Poppy lay in a crumpled heap. The taste of gasoline and soot coated his tongue, and his body protested his crawling movement toward her. His brain turned fuzzy as the reality of what Poppy's unmoving body might mean hit him.

"Poppy!" he cried, his throat raspy and raw. Finally reaching her, he lay over her to shield her from further debris and brushed hair from her filthy face, which was stained with blood. "Poppy," he said again as he felt for a pulse, relieved when he registered one. His heart rate increased, knowing she could be severely injured. He caressed her cheek and whispered her name again as he laid his brow on hers, thanking God she was at least alive.

A painful moan passed through her lips.

"Talk to me, Poppy."

She raised a weak hand and rested it on his cheek, the most tender she'd ever been with him. And it shifted places he didn't realize were even inside him. "Get off me," she muttered.

Her words finally registered and he actually laughed.

He should have known she wasn't being emotional. But it had done something to him, which he couldn't deny—but he was going to do his best. "We have to get out of here," he said. "Can you move?"

"If you get off me," she said through a faint grin.

Right. He removed his protective weight from her but remained shielding her just in case. Suddenly, she bolted upright, fear in her eyes—probably the reality of what had happened and the still-present danger. "Was it a bomb?"

"No. Strategic bullet to the gas tank."

The whir of a four-wheeler or motorcycle sounded, and a red blur headed for them. In the distance, the screech of a siren signaled that the police and ambulance had been notified.

Poppy rubbed her lower back and grimaced. "This is turning out to be the second-worst lead-up to a holiday I've ever experienced." Poppy was known to crack jokes during intense situations—it was her defense mechanism. The worst would be Cora's death. "Are you hurt?"

"Not fatally." He'd be sore for days, but nothing was broken. A man in a heavy work jacket approached on the red ATV and hopped off, first aid kit in hand. "Zack Weaverman. I own this land and called the ambulance. Are you two okay?" He knelt and did a double take. "Poppy Holliday?"

"Hey, Zack. Nice to see you again."

"You always make your entrances this grand?" he asked with a lopsided grin.

"Oh, just at Christmas."

An ambulance parked on the edge of the road and paramedics hustled over. First responders rolled onto the scene, and Rhett explained what had happened.

"You're reopening the investigation of your sister's disappearance?" Zack asked Poppy after she was tended and had declined a trip to the hospital.

"If you haven't heard," she said and rotated her right shoulder, wincing, "she's been found. In the bottom of your well."

His face told the tale. He'd heard and wasn't too happy about it.

"Any idea how she ended up there?"

Zack ran his hands through his sandy brown hair and shook his head. "Dylan wasn't out there that night. He had a ton of homework and he wasn't banking on an athletic scholarship so he made sure to keep his grades up, then we played video games until around midnight. And if you haven't heard, we lost him last night. So I don't appreciate you implying he was involved in your sister's death and sullying his good reputation and character."

Rhett had a feeling it might go down like this. "We're not implying anything, Mr. Weaverman." Rhett held out his hand and introduced himself, hoping to gain some ground they'd lost with Poppy's implied accusations. "We had hoped Dylan might have been able to tell us something he may have forgotten or didn't find important at the time. I'm sorry for your loss and hate to infringe on your time of grieving, but Cora's family is grieving, as well. And they want to know what happened to their daughter as much as you want to know what happened to Dylan."

"I do know what happened. He drank too much—per usual—and drove himself off a bridge. I tried to get him help for years, to no avail." Zack's angry expression relaxed. "Brad's investigating but he's going to see that it wasn't murder. It was an accident—or possibly suicide."

"Had he been depressed or given you reason to believe he was suicidal?" Rhett asked.

Zack sighed. "Come on, let's go up to the house and talk. I'll make coffee. Told my wife not to come down in case it was dangerous. I'll text her, have her pick us up."

Filthy and sore, they agreed. Investigating came before comfort and cleanliness. Glancing back, he sighed. Guess they'd be using Poppy's car.

As if reading his thoughts, she shrugged. "Well, if they blow up my car, I can use the insurance money to upgrade to a vehicle with seat warmers."

Rhett snorted as a white pickup truck barreled down the winding driveway. A woman with long blond hair and a concerned expression pulled up. "Everyone okay?" she asked out the driver's window.

"This is my wife, Natalie. Her vet practice is behind the house." Zack motioned them inside the truck.

Poppy studied the woman in the driver's seat. "Natalie Carpenter?"

She held up her ring finger. "It's Weaverman now. I thought that was you but I wasn't sure. Your hair's shorter and you look a little worse for the wear. No offense."

"That'll happen when you've been shot at and blown up." She got inside the truck and Rhett climbed in beside her. "I didn't realize you married Dylan's older brother." They hadn't done a workup yet on each individual initially interviewed.

"Ten years ago, come Valentine's Day," she said as she turned the truck around and aimed back toward her house. "I heard they found Cora, or who they believed to be her."

"I'm sure it is. DNA should be back soon enough."

It was nice to have not only one but two of the people they needed to interview in the same place. Natalie had been in Cora's science class and the science club. She'd stated that on the night Cora went missing, she'd been at the local library studying until nine and then was at home in bed by ten. Her parents had backed up her story, but they went to bed around the same time. If she'd sneaked out like Cora had, they'd be none the wiser.

"I'm sorry. I can't imagine how you've felt all these years," Natalie said and pulled up at her home. "Come on inside. If you want to wash your face and hands, feel free to use the mudroom," she said as they entered a large room with triple sinks and a walk-in shower. "We use this for our dogs when they get filthy, which is often. I'll be in the kitchen. Right through this door."

She left them to make themselves somewhat presentable. Poppy stood at the mirror and groaned. "Wow. I didn't think I could look this terrible."

Rhett ran his hands under the water, washing away the grime, but the smell of smoke clung to his clothing, hair and skin. "Do you think it's weird that she's working and Zack is home today? No family here. It's like Dylan didn't pass away."

Poppy splashed water on her face, rinsing away the soap and grime. "People grieve differently." She dried her face and hands and shrugged. "Good enough."

Rhett followed suit, then they entered the large farmhouse-style kitchen. From paint to cabinets to furniture, everything was white and gray. The smell of coffee brewing was like a welcome mat to his nose.

Once they were all at the table with coffee in hand, Poppy opened up the discussion. "Tell us about Dylan in the days leading up to his death. Anything that might be warning signs of depression? Drinking?" Coming at them with suicide before homicide was smart.

Zack raked a hand through his hair. "Dylan suffered from depression."

"Always or recently?"

Zack shared a look with Natalie. "Truthfully, I think it hit him after Cora died. At least that's when it became noticeable. They were friends, you know. My parents sent him to counseling and I think it helped. He went on to college and vet school."

Rhett sipped the strong brew. "He shared a practice with you?" he asked Natalie, noticing Zack's jaw tick. Interesting.

"We attended school together and when I opened the clinic, I asked him to come on board." She glanced at Zack. "It helped us keep an eye on his drinking. He's fought the liquid battle a long time."

"It would be plausible, then, to have open liquor in his vehicle?"

She nodded. Zack looked away. "I've had to haul him out of ditches before."

Natalie clasped her husband's hand. "Zack's tried to get him help. Staged an intervention. It's gotten heated, but you can't help people who don't want help. The past two weeks, Dylan had barely even been at work."

A bender?

"Better that way," Zack mumbled.

"Dylan has come in drunk and there's been issues. No animals died or anything, but he got into it with a patient for letting her dog rip stitches out after a spay." She frowned. "It lost us business and that wasn't the first time."

So, there was turmoil between the family and the business.

"Is there anyone at all who might want to hurt him?" Poppy asked. "It's too much of a coincidence that on the night they find Cora's remains, on your family property, Dylan dies and now I can't talk to him."

Rhett had witnessed Poppy using less tact before.

Zack worked his jaw. "No one would have wanted Dylan dead. I think his drinking, the open bottle and his depression make it obvious. He was friends with Cora. The news more than likely sent him to the bottle. It was an accident…or a suicide due to depression and the inebriation."

Poppy's mouth pursed and she drummed her thumbs on the table. This line of questioning was hitting walls. He could see her wheels turning. "What do you know about marijuana being sold to freshmen back in the day? Anyone have the hookup?"

Rhett wasn't expecting it to go down this path. If Poppy had been into pot in school—been caught with it—then wouldn't she already know this? Could the drugs found in her nightstand connect to Cora?

"Kids smoked weed," Natalie said. "They always seemed to have it. No one ever asked. Why?" She rubbed her thumb along her wrist and glanced at her husband. Rhett would bank on the fact that Natalie was at this moment lying. Which meant it had to link to Cora. Otherwise, she easily could have coughed up a name with no fear of repercussions. Poppy didn't care about dealers. She cared about catching Cora's killer.

"No reason," Poppy said. She'd picked up on it too and was keeping this info close to her chest. Hopefully, she'd at least clue him in. "We'll be interviewing everyone again, doing a much more thorough investigation. Could you tell us if Ian Kirkwood, Savannah Steadman and Maya Marx still live in the area?"

Natalie and Zack exchanged a puzzled expression with one another. Zack cleared his throat. "Uh…did you not know that Savannah Steadman is married to Detective Teague?"

Brad Teague. The detective investigating Dylan Weaverman's murder.

"No," Poppy said casually. "The other two?"

"Ian Kirkwood has been back several years. Went into the army after high school. Now owns Kirkwood Equipment—farm equipment—and Maya actually works part-time for me answering phones. She also does medical coding from home," Natalie offered.

Looked like the gang stayed close over the years. Could be small-town friendships. Could be something else.

Over two hours had ticked by since Natalie Carpenter-Weaverman gave her and Rhett a ride back to the Gray Creek Sheriff's Office, where she now sat in a hard plastic chair sipping coffee that looked and tasted like tar. But she didn't care. An hour ago she'd received confirmation that the remains they'd found were Cora's. It was official.

She'd called Mom and Dad with the news and Dad had made her promise to find whoever did it and see justice served; Mom said if anyone could, it was Poppy. What Poppy had craved to hear from them both was that they loved her and no matter what, it would all be well.

In a flash she'd gone from being responsible for Cora's well-being to finding her killer. Poppy had every intention of doing that, but the added pressure only compounded an already sore heart.

She was glad Rhett had to deal with the insurance company and was briefing Colt on the investigation. She'd needed the time alone. Her phone rang.

Tackitt.

She answered her oldest brother's call. "Hey, Tack."

"I talked to Dad. How you holding up, kiddo?"

She wasn't a kiddo but that was Tack. "Working the case. Isn't that what we cold case agents do—or Texas Rangers in your case?"

"Yep. It's what we do. You need me up there to help…or be there with you?" His baritone voice softened and tears burned the backs of her eyes. She'd gotten Cora into this mess, and she'd work to right that wrong. "No, Rhett is here and you'd get in his way. I get in his way." She laughed. Rhett was all about systematic investigating. Tasks. To-do lists. Tack was too much like Poppy—on it like a grizzly, not letting up until it was finished.

"He's the straitlaced dude, right?" Tack asked.

"Yeah. His car blew up today so he's learning flexibility." Being abducted had been terrifying, but being blown into the air from searing heat was competing for the most frightful event of the past few days. Even now, her body ached and throbbed, and that was with the ibuprofen she'd taken thirty minutes ago.

"Say that again," his sharp tone cut in.

Way to slip up. Poppy gave him the lowdown.

Tack was silent, then he quietly growled. "Watch your back and be safe. Sounds like whoever—singular or plural—was behind Cora's death wants you off the case and out of the picture."

Poppy agreed, and it sent shivers down her spine, but she wasn't going to back down or let Tack know how terrified she truly felt. "I know. I'm being careful and safe. Besides, this is good news. It tells us the perpetrator is near and likely ingrained in Gray Creek's community. I don't have to go to the ends of the earth tracking him. Or them." Poppy's gut warned her that the small science club clique knew more, and that included Savannah Steadman-Teague. Wife of a detective or not—she would receive no special treatment if it came to light that she had anything to do with Cora's death.

Tack grunted. "Offer still stands. Otherwise, I'm dealing with an unsolved homicide that's driving me nuts."

"The female migrant worker on that ranch?"

"Rosa Velasquez. She's personal to me now. Anyway, call if you're in a jam."

"And you'll come riding in with your white horse and hat and Ranger badge?"

He chuckled, then his tone sobered. "I'll come as your big brother who loves you and wants you to stop blaming yourself for Cora's death."

She swallowed the hard knot in her throat. "Got work to do." Crying over the line would do about as much good as wishing someone would hold her and soothe her pain. None. Time to toughen up. She said her goodbyes and hung up as Rhett waltzed in with the cardboard box under one arm, pushing a rolling whiteboard with his other. Cora had been reduced to a case file number, a picture on a murder board.

"You good?" Rhett asked as he set the box on the table and studied her.

"Yep. Talked to my oldest brother—Tack. I told him we had the case under control."

"That we do." But his eyes held a measure of skepticism. The next two hours, they pored over the case file, reading up on the past interviews and making notes on the whiteboard while conjecturing on Dylan's method of death.

Finally, Rhett asked the question Poppy had been expecting since she'd talked to Natalie. "Okay, let's get it out there. Why did you ask Natalie Weaverman about pot? What are you not telling me? I can't help you if you don't let me."

Poppy sighed. This secret was one of her regrets, to go along with so many others. "It's true that I was grounded the night Cora sneaked out and disappeared."

"Because you'd been caught with a bag of weed." He rolled his hand in the air, signaling her to get to the point faster.

She frowned, but continued. "Right, but it wasn't mine. I'd found it in Cora's backpack two days prior. Talk about stunned. She said she was holding it for a friend who had been caught with it before. She refused to give me a name, but Cora's friends didn't do any kind of drugs."

"You believe it? That it was someone else's?"

"Yes."

Rhett leaned forward, his corded forearms on the table and exposed, causing a second of distraction as she wondered how it would feel to be swept into those powerful arms and comforted.

It was official. She was cracking up.

"You covered for her."

She wished she hadn't. Then Cora would have been

grounded and might not have risked more trouble by sneaking out. She'd always been tenderhearted. All Dad had to say was he was disappointed and she'd crumble. But those words had rarely been stated to her. Cora never did disappoint.

That was Poppy's role.

She nodded. Poppy had needed to cover for her. Because it had been Poppy's snide comments and outburst that had driven her to it.

You never take chances because you're afraid to have fun. You hide behind the epilepsy. I'll never be able to say I didn't do what I wanted. But you'll always be a scaredy-cat. A daddy's girl. So quit lecturing me on the way I live my life. At least I have one.

Cora had cried, but Poppy had refused to take the words back, even if she hadn't meant them. She would regret that argument until the day she died. She never expected or hoped that Cora would take her terrible advice. But she had.

And she'd died.

It should have been Poppy.

"Let's see if we can trace the weed. Small towns. Somebody knows who dealt it and where to get it. If we can identify the seller, he or she might be able to tell us who purchased it and had Cora hold it for safe-keeping." He made a note on the whiteboard. "You said you got into trouble in high school. Where did you get your marijuana from?"

Poppy sighed. "Once we moved to Gray Creek and I started spending time with Grandma, I stopped smoking it. I did drink a little and mostly did things to make my parents mad like break curfew, smoke cigarettes, talk back and date hoodlums—their words."

Rhett grinned. "Poppy Holliday talking back? I don't believe it."

His teasing tone coaxed a smile and provided a sense of comfort she desperately needed, but didn't want— not from Rhett. She was too afraid of the many tangles it would create.

"I know, right?" she joked.

His smirk sent a dip into her belly. She cleared her throat and redirected her thoughts to the case. "What about Ian? His alibi is weak."

Rhett sifted through the pages and grunted in his typical fashion when he didn't care for something. "At *Christmas with the Kranks*. Alone. And he'd conveniently thrown away his ticket stub."

"Did the detective investigating at the time pass a photo to movie employees to try to verify?" Poppy asked.

"Nothing here noting it. No point trying to now. No one is going to remember if Ian Kirkwood saw a movie alone seventeen years ago."

True. "I want to start with him."

Sheriff Pritchard entered the room. "How are things going?"

"Like a turtle in a NASCAR race," Poppy offered with a grin.

He chuckled, then quickly sobered. "I have the medical report on Cora." He held it up. "There were several fractures perimortem. Arms. Collarbone. Ankle."

Poppy nodded. "She had epilepsy and hurt herself occasionally during seizures."

"I see. That's tough, having so many struggles to hurdle." Sheriff Pritchard sat beside Poppy. "The good news is there aren't any other fractures or breaks perimortem. There are some indicating she broke bones falling into the well, but she was already gone."

Poppy clenched her teeth and forced back tears. "Then we officially know it's homicide. The Weavermans stated they always kept the well covered. Cora didn't die and toss herself down."

"I agree." He handed her the file and softened his voice. "If you need anything…"

He gently rubbed her shoulder, then left them.

Rhett sat quietly. Waiting. She needed his patience, but it also scraped against tender places she'd thought she'd toughened up over the years. She slowly opened the report.

Skull fracture, broken ribs, broken neck… She guessed it was a mercy that Cora hadn't endured the pain and fear of plummeting down a dark, dank well. But her manner of death was inconclusive. If she'd been shot, stabbed or even hit over the head, there would likely be marks on the bones indicating so. Cora could have been suffocated, asphyxiated…even poisoned! Panic hit her gut and blood drained from her head.

"Hey…hey…" Rhett jumped up as if he instinctively knew what was going on inside her—the terrible scenarios invading her mind. He gently laid the papers in her hand on the table and hauled her to her feet.

Now she no longer wondered what it would feel like to have him draw her into his arms of his own accord. Her falling into them on the dark road didn't count.

With her head against his chest, his heart beat strong and fast. One arm secured her against him while his other soothingly stroked the side of her head, careful not to rake over her injury. "Don't allow yourself to go there, to imagine, Poppy. She's at peace now. She was at peace before she ever made it into that well."

God's mercies.

She nodded against him and allowed herself a moment of reveling in his stalwart arms, of feeling protected and completely safe. It was the closest she'd ever been to Rhett besides the night she'd been abducted. Never anything more than a high five or fist bump, or an accidental brush of their fingers passing a case file or cup of coffee.

With her head fitting perfectly in the hollow of his neck, he easily rested his chin on top—an intimate gesture, one she wanted to sink and settle into, but the longer she allowed it, the clearer she understood the consequences. She had no business wanting more, wanting this. She certainly didn't deserve it.

Cora couldn't fall into a man's arms—a man she trusted and could depend on. She couldn't love and be loved, or raise a family and enjoy happiness and a life well lived.

Poppy shouldn't have any of those things either.

Breaking from his embrace, she straightened her shoulders and cleared her throat. "I'm fine. It's all water under the creek."

Rhett gave her a pointed look. "Bridge. Water under the bridge."

He hated her idiom mix-ups and that was precisely why she used them; it kept him annoyed and at bay, which was far better than inching closer to her heart and seeping inside. That was too dangerous. Not an option. "Potato pah-tah-toe." She resumed her tough bravado, emotionally pushing him away, and retrieved the file.

"I want to talk to Ian." Focus on catching Cora's killer. No distractions.

Dread filled her gut as they exited the small interview room. When the killer caught wind that he hadn't thwarted their investigation or scared them away, he'd make sure not to miss his mark next time.

Chapter 4

Rhett eyed Detective Brad Teague as he hunched over his desk, appearing stressed-out and in need of a good cup of coffee and some answers. Rhett had none to offer, and most likely would only add to his stress level.

Rhett leaned closer to Poppy's ear, catching a whiff of her flowery shampoo. "Mrs. Teague isn't a suspect," he reminded her. "She's only being requestioned, so don't go over there guns blazing."

Poppy shot him an irritated scowl. As they approached, Teague glanced up. "Hey, Agents, how can I help you? Or can you help me? I could use some." Hope didn't quite reach his tired blue eyes.

"Nothing new on Dylan's case?" Poppy asked.

"Not yet. We checked the shoe cast you took and compared them to the shoes Dylan was wearing at the time of death, as well as the ones we found in his home.

No match. Waiting on trace evidence results from his car, but that could take weeks."

Just because they didn't find a pair of shoes didn't mean it hadn't been Dylan who'd abducted her, but Rhett wasn't a huge fan of that theory anyway.

Poppy grimaced. "Are you familiar with Cora's case?"

"Briefly, in connection to Dylan."

"We'll need to reinterview Savannah. We wanted to let you know ahead of time."

Rhett studied Brad to see if he'd reveal any indication that he knew his wife had valuable information, but his face showed nothing. "I appreciate that. She'll be happy to." He grinned. "I tried to talk to her but she didn't seem too thrilled to discuss an ex-boyfriend with her husband."

Rhett chuckled.

"Where will we find her later today?" Poppy asked.

"She's the president of the historical society. They hold an office at the Castlewood Mansion—an old Victorian on Crenshaw. Christmas is a big deal with the historical-homes tour." He gave Poppy Savannah's cell phone number. "Best to call and ask her. Her schedule's pretty flexible."

Poppy wanted to comb evidence in case something might give them a lead, then they were going to talk to Ian Kirkwood and Savannah Steadman-Teague.

"We need to find out who sold that marijuana and to whom. I think that may be key," Rhett said as they entered the evidence room.

Bags of debris littered several six-foot tables. Great.

"You might be right." Poppy tossed him a pair of gloves and slipped on a pair herself, then started her search. A million empty beer cans and bottles, along with chip bags. A few scraps of paper. Nothing stood out as they carefully searched for about thirty minutes.

"Hey," Poppy said and held up a thick silver bracelet with decorative engraving. "This might be something. It's not Cora's, but don't you find it odd that it was down in a well with a bunch of trash?"

"Run prints. Maybe something will pop." He studied the bracelet. "Raises a new idea. A girl may have been involved or a witness to whatever happened to your sister."

Poppy snapped a photo of the bracelet using her cell phone camera.

"Someone might recognize it." She pocketed her phone. Removing the gloves, she tossed them in the trash and grabbed her light brown coat, which hung on the back of the metal chair. "Ready to talk to Ian Kirkwood?"

"Yep." He'd already filed a claim with the insurance company. "I guess I'll be hitching rides with you. And we need to get lunch."

"Cheese crackers from the vending machine don't count?" She grinned and followed him to the parking lot. At her car, Rhett paused as a crawly sensation rippled under his skin and kicked up his heart rate a notch. Scanning the parking lot, he found it empty, minus a few deputies strolling inside.

Still, he couldn't shake the eerie feeling of being watched.

"Maybe you like hanging out in the cold, but I prefer warmth." Poppy opened the driver's door then froze, following his line of sight. "Never mind," she mumbled.

"You feel it too?" he asked.

"I do now." After another beat or two they got inside her car. Poppy darted glances in the rearview as they headed west toward Ian Kirkwood's business. "We're being tailed. Black sedan. Two cars back."

Rhett adjusted the side mirror and spotted the car. "Take a left up here."

Poppy nodded and slowed at the stop sign. Kirkwood Equipment was past the sign up ahead on the right, according to her GPS. She turned left down a quiet street in an older subdivision. The car didn't follow. "You sure you were being tailed?" Rhett asked.

"I'm sure." She circled the block.

"Circle again before pulling onto the highway. He may know we caught on and could be waiting somewhere to jump back on us."

Poppy made another pass and when she turned onto the main road, there was no sign of the sedan. At Kirkwood Equipment, she parked in a spot facing the highway—baiting him. Rhett wouldn't have invited the attacker to find them so easily, but Poppy was never one to play it safe.

She held her keys in hand, watching traffic zoom by. After a few moments, she frowned and exited the car, muttering about the biting wind.

Inside, machinery and parts littered every open space. The smell of rubber and oil burned his sinuses as they approached the counter. A guy in need of acne meds and bigger arms to fill out his polo shirtsleeves flashed a toothy grin. "Help ya?" he asked.

Poppy flashed her creds, then secured them back on her belt where she kept her gun and cuffs. "We'd like to speak with Ian Kirkwood. He in?"

The young guy's eyes widened and he nodded. "He's in the back. In his office. I'll show ya."

They followed him to a narrow hallway in the back of the building. He knocked on Kirkwood's door and cracked it open. "Hey, Ian, the police are here to see you." After opening it farther, he motioned Poppy and Rhett inside the spacious office. Rhett took notice of the deer antlers covering one wall, and a gun rack on another. A stuffed turkey sat on top of his black filing cabinets.

Ian Kirkwood was a genuine outdoorsman. He stood an inch or so under Rhett's six-foot-three frame and wore flannel, jeans and hiking boots.

"How can I help you?" he asked as he motioned them to have a seat in the two standard office chairs across from his desk.

"I'm Poppy Holliday—"

"I thought maybe you were but I wasn't sure. Heard you were here investigating. You're with the Mississippi Bureau of Investigation, right?"

"I am." Word traveled fast. She wondered from whom. Poppy introduced Rhett. "We're conducting new interviews, so it's going to seem repetitious. Can you tell us what you were doing the night Cora went missing?"

He rubbed his blond bearded chin and blew a sigh from his nose. "I was at a Christmas movie—by myself. I know it seems odd for a teenager to be at a movie alone, but no one could go with me, and I'm a huge Jamie Lee Curtis fan. I wanted to be there opening weekend." He shrugged. "I saw the nine-o'clock movie, then stayed at my grandma's."

And his grandmother couldn't verify it back then

because he'd said he left before she woke. What teenager woke up before a grandparent? "Could we speak with her?"

Ian's mouth curved downward. "I'm afraid not. She has Alzheimer's and is in the nursing home."

Rhett kept a cool composure but inwardly flinched. It was like this guy had thought everything through. Not that he could plan an Alzheimer's diagnosis, but his alibi was perfectly intact with no way to verify and Rhett wasn't getting a good vibe. Not at all.

"I'm sorry to hear that," Rhett replied.

Poppy leaned forward. "What do you think about Dylan's death?"

Ian cocked his head as if waiting for the punch line. It didn't come. "I think it's tragic. I'm not surprised, though."

"That he was murdered? Who would want to murder him?"

Wide eyes met Poppy's. "Murder? I thought he died from drunk driving. Heard he was found with an open bottle of whiskey."

"Brad Teague is investigating it as a murder."

"Really?" He licked his bottom lip. "Look, Dylan was a great guy but he struggled with depression and used drinking to battle it. No one would want Dylan dead. Even when he was drunk, he was a nice guy."

Was he? Natalie said he'd yelled at customers inside the vet clinic.

"Did you know Cora had a crush on Dylan?" Poppy asked, avoiding Ian's statement.

"I suspected. But Dylan was Savannah's guy and that was that. It never would have gone anywhere. And before you get any weird ideas, Savannah would never have hurt Cora if she found out she'd liked Dylan. She could be a real piece of work at times but she wasn't some deranged killer."

Poppy examined the burly guy until he squirmed, then she squinted and slapped her knee. "Okay, then. We'll get out of your hair." Handing him a business card, she said, "If you remember anything else—even if it seems irrelevant—call me. I'm not leaving any time soon." Her words carried a threat that she was far from done with Ian Kirkwood and his friends.

Mr. Kirkwood raised his right eyebrow and accepted the card. "I appreciate that. And if you're gonna be in town for a while, you should go on the Christmas boat tour." He held up a stack of flyers and handed them each one. "I got roped into helping pass these out for the chamber of commerce."

Rhett glanced at it. Seemed interesting. Poppy folded hers up. "I don't know how much free time I'll have what with an unsolved case and a possible homicide that might connect to it, but thanks." She gave him the Poppy-eye—a hard glare mixed with the sentiment that her target was an absolute idiot. She gave it to Rhett often.

In the parking lot, Rhett held up the flyer. "Dinner cruise. We gotta eat. And lunch is way overdue."

That earned him the Poppy-eye.

Gray Creek's Victorian District made up three blocks of the small downtown. Some of the homes had been turned into inns and B&Bs, some had been restored and were now lived in and a few had become historical museums.

"When does this Christmas home tour start?" Rhett

asked as he slowed down and searched for the Castlewood Mansion. It was two houses down with a sign
hung on the wrought iron fence. What a gorgeous place
to spend the workday. Not that Poppy would prefer it.
But being somewhere pretty for a day or so would be
nice, and the Christmas cruise did sound promising. If
only she was here under different circumstances.

A rich golden home with white ornate trim beckoned them inside. Rhett opened the door for Poppy and
motioned her inside—always the gentleman, the good
guy. Mr. Calm and Professional. Just once she'd like
to see him lose his cool—mostly to razz him about it.
How could this man who worked with the darkest part
of humanity never get worked up over it? He'd never
taken it too far. Never blown up on a suspect he knew
was guilty of a crime. Even her chief had lost his cool
a time or two.

Guess Rhett didn't have the bottled-up anger Poppy
kept corked inside her. Why would he?

She inhaled cloves and cinnamon and a touch of
years gone by. The house had much of the original
wood and ornate crown molding, and the paintings
on the walls were definitely vintage. Heels clicking
along wood sounded, and Savannah Steadman-Teague
appeared from the parlor looking like sunshine on a
cloudy day. Fully put together down to her nail polish
and matching lipstick. No wonder she'd been the "it"
girl in high school. She was the face boys salivated over
and girls envied.

"Poppy," Savannah said with her educated Southern belle drawl. She set her phone on a table against
the wall before smothering Poppy in a genteel embrace
as if they'd been friends in school. Poppy hadn't given

two figs about Savannah. She'd been too busy hanging with the wild side. The side that grated on her military father's nerves and sent her mother into nervous pacing. About the only way to garner either of their attention. Unfortunately.

Poppy released herself from the overly perfumed hug and Savannah set her sights on Rhett, appreciation dancing across her face. Whatever. He was easy on the eyes. Her quick and casual appraisal ended quickly, but even so, Poppy detested the pop of green that had reared its ugly head within her chest.

Rhett's greeting was polite and professional. She didn't need to see if he'd returned his own look of appreciation. He wouldn't. Savannah was married, and Rhett was a noble man.

"Brad told me about Cora. I'm so sorry. Is there anything I can do?"

She meant casseroles or prayer. Poppy didn't necessarily need either of those things. She didn't much ask for the lending of God's ear. She'd long worn out her welcome in that department and had resigned herself to that fact—not made peace, since there was no peace. But the acceptance of a situation didn't always mean peace. More often it meant getting over it or dealing with it the best one could.

"Yes, actually." She introduced Rhett as Agent Wallace, then asked if she could question her again.

Savannah complied and motioned them to follow her to the basement. "We keep our offices down here."

"It's a gorgeous house," Poppy said.

Savannah beamed. "It really is. I feel like I'm always putting final touches on it even throughout the Christmas season. I've always wanted to live in this house. I guess I got some of my dream." She eased into her antique chair and offered them the seats across from her dainty vintage desk.

After smoothing her long golden locks, she tented her hands on the desk. "I honestly don't know any more now than I did then."

"We've found that when we question people a second time, who were children and teenagers the first time, there's always something new, something they see as adults that they didn't think important before." Poppy crossed one leg over her knee in a relaxed position, hoping to put Savannah at ease. "Tell me about Cora from personal experience and hearsay. Both could be important to helping me find a lead."

Savannah echoed what others had said. Cora was kind but they didn't know her well. Savannah was aware of the crush Cora had on Dylan.

"That didn't upset you?"

"If every girl who liked Dylan or wrote his name on her notebook upset me, I'd have been upset every single day. No point getting my feathers ruffled unless Dylan liked one back—which he never did." She said it as if it couldn't even have been a possibility, and with her looks it likely wasn't. Cora may have simply seen what she wanted to, as Poppy first suspected. She had been naive at times, especially concerning boys.

"Do you know who was selling pot to students back then?" Poppy asked.

Savannah studied Poppy as if she was testing her somehow, wondering how much Poppy already knew. Finally, she glanced at the desk, avoiding eye contact. "I'm embarrassed to admit it, but sometimes we used Dylan's property to have parties, and yes, sometimes there was alcohol and marijuana—but not always. The liquor was stolen from our parents' liquor cabinets and refrigerators, but I don't know where the drugs came from. Dylan just had them."

And he was dead. Convenient.

"Could Dylan have given some to Cora?" Poppy asked. "She told me she was keeping it for a friend."

Savannah's eyes widened for a flash before she became calm again. "No. They were in-school-only friends. Nothing outside of class and science club. Unless she specifically asked for it—"

"She didn't. She said she was holding it for a friend."

Savannah tossed her a get-real expression. "I said the same thing when I got caught with cigarettes by my mom in eighth grade. It's the oldest one in the book."

Maybe for some. Of course, Poppy made a point of letting her parents know what she was up to. It had been the only way to gain their undivided attention; otherwise, it was spent on Cora and their concern over her health. Or her older brothers. Dad's time had been limited until he retired from the military, and if Cora wasn't being doted upon, her brothers were receiving all the attention.

Poppy had become emaciated from the lack of emotional nourishment and fed herself with nothing that would truly bring any health to her heart. She craved anything—even rants or lectures from Dad about her behavior. Cries and desperate sighs from her mother. Anything over the silence and invisibility. She blinked away the pain and guilt and refocused.

"Where would kids buy it? Surely, as a popular girl, you'd know secrets like that."

Savannah shrugged. "I don't know. I never cared

how I got it, just that when I wanted it, it was available. I do regret all of that. I'd never want my own children to do the things I did."

"I understand." Poppy wasn't sure Savannah was telling the whole truth, but it was obvious she'd get no more out of the woman about where the drugs came from.

Savannah's phone rang and she held it up and apologized, then excused herself into the hallway.

"What do you think?" Rhett asked.

"What do you think?" she countered.

Rhett smirked. "I find it hard to believe she wouldn't know where the drugs came from given her popularity."

"Same."

Savannah popped her head inside. "I'm sorry but I need to run down to the Roubierre House. There's a problem. Feel free to tour the mansion before you let yourself out. It's really quite beautiful, especially during the holidays. If I think of anything else, I'll be in touch."

With that, Savannah disappeared, the sound of her heels on the floor quickly receding.

Poppy sighed, then leaned over Savannah's desk, perusing the items on it.

"Don't even think about it, Poppy."

"What?" she asked innocently. "I'm simply looking at what is out in the open, and if something catches my eye...well, I can't help it."

"You're searching for clues or something that might help you with the case. If she was a diabolical killer, she wouldn't leave pertinent information on the desk or even hidden in her office, then be dumb enough to leave us alone with our curious minds."

Poppy turned up her nose, but Rhett had a point. Probably nothing here anyway. "I've never toured this house, but I always wondered what it looked like inside."

Rhett motioned with his chin toward the door. "Want to take her up on the offer? We have time and we need a chance to decide our next move."

Rhett's answer surprised her. "You don't seem like the Victorian-age admirer."

He smirked and a dimple creased his clean-shaven cheek. "I appreciate exquisite craftsmanship." He held her eye, and her insides squirmed while an emotional red flag was raised. *Warning. Warning.* Rhett wasn't one to communicate in subtext, but this sure felt like it. Or she was being an idiot because maybe she wanted a compliment from him.

"Like Savannah Teague?"

"That woman is nothing short of shallow. When her undeniable beauty fades, there'll be nothing of any substance left."

"Ah, so you're a looks-don't-matter kind of guy." Bunk. She wasn't buying it.

"No. I'm quite a fan of physical beauty, but if there's no substance beneath it, then why waste the time?" He shrugged a shoulder and raised an eyebrow. "What about you?"

"I happen to prefer the shallow end of the pool. I don't need depth to have a good time." Depth meant revealing truths and being vulnerable. No, thank you.

He moved into her personal space, and she refrained from backing up an inch. "I'm not talking about a good time. I'm talking about a lifetime. And you can play the shallow game all day long, Poppy, but I know when it comes down to the wire, you're too intelligent and deep to want someone without any substance."

Her insides pooled and she swallowed hard. How would he know this about her? Stupid observing behavior. And if he said she had depth, did that mean she was some kind of candidate for a lifetime with him? Uh…no, thank you to that too. "You don't know me at all," she murmured.

"I think maybe I do." He held her gaze, then sighed. "I'm gonna go check this place out." He left her with her thoughts, fears and something warm glowing around the outer shell of her heart.

Great. Just what she needed. To be even more attracted to the straitlaced man. She mentally stomped her foot and purposely went the opposite direction to explore the house alone.

Thick evergreen boughs draped the spiraling staircase, permeating the house with a fresh pine scent. Savannah had class and style when it came to decorations, and she'd kept it in theme with the early 1900s—elegant and charming. And yet even in all the warmth of the holidays, something cold and hollow gave Poppy the shivers.

Edging down the dark hall on the third floor, she spotted an old wooden elevator that must have been installed after the home was crafted, yet it was vintage in its own right. A typed notice was framed next to it, making tourists aware that it was not working and they shouldn't touch.

Poppy's rebellious nature itched at those words and she opened the accordion-style door and peered down into nothingness. One step inside was a doozy since the elevator cart was missing. She could see all the way down to the first floor.

Hairs on the back of her neck stood at attention, and

she whirled around to see a masked figure. Before she had a chance to react, he shoved her backward.

Fear lurched into her throat as she lost balance, knowing she was in real trouble. Flailing her arms, she reached out for stability and found none.

A scream burst through her lungs as she plummeted through darkness to certain death.

Chapter 5

Rhett poked around, searching for the secret drawer in the old Biedermeier secretary in the third-floor library. His grandmother had owned one and shared that the craftsman put hidden compartments in all his furniture and not a single secretary was the same. That was the first time a mystery had piqued Rhett's interest. Maybe that's what drove his curiosity concerning Poppy; the woman was like a Biedermeier—unique and hiding all sorts of things about herself in secret compartments. She was a woman of grit and substance, a woman who could be studied for years, and a man would never tire of uncovering all she had to offer.

But she was also impulsive and unpredictable. For those two reasons alone, he neglected to pick up his emotional shovel. The buried treasure within Poppy Holliday would continue to be an unsolved mystery.

A goose-bump-raising shriek broke him from his thoughts and he instantly drew his weapon as he raced toward the sound of Poppy's screams—though he'd never heard her cry out in fear, he couldn't mistake her voice.

He streaked like a bullet down the large hall to an old wooden elevator where the cries had originated. He glanced down, and his heart galloped into his throat as Poppy hung by a thin rope—possibly connected to an old pulley. "Hold on, Poppy!" He quickly inventoried the elevator shaft. The rope appeared old and thread-bare. He wasn't sure what it connected to or why it was there, but using it to raise Poppy was his only shot. At three floors up, she could die if she plummeted to the hardwood floors below. She'd already fallen several feet—not quite a full floor.

"I'm going to pull this rope!" he hollered. *Lord, help me.*

"It's not steady. I can feel it giving. I—I don't have much time and there's nothing else to grab on to!"

Her frantic words sent another uptick in his pulse and sweat beaded on his forehead. How had she fallen? He holstered his gun, grabbed on to the rope and began hoisting her up, using his core and arms, the rope burning his skin as it slid through his palms, but he re-gripped and pulled with all the grit and power he had and with prayer for divine strength.

Poppy wasn't exactly petite in stature with her lean and toned muscles. When it came to fitness, she was no joke. "This would be much easier," he said through his straining, "if you were flabby." Muscle weighed more than fat.

"You can shove snickerdoodles down my throat later," she said with a little more calmness in her tone, but underneath was terror. She knew the outcome if the rope snapped. Arms burning and shaking from strain, he slowly inched backward, digging in his heels, as he lifted her up toward him, perspiration dotting his upper lip and prayer going nonstop internally.

The rope held as Poppy slowly rose to meet him. Just a few more feet. He thought he heard a delicate whimper, but slow and steady was the only way. Yanking might break the delicate rope. "I've almost got you now, Poppy. You're doing great."

"Stop trying to talk me down," she barked. Fear and helplessness had made her vulnerable and her barking was nothing more than a defense mechanism to hang on to her pride, as if that was what mattered at the moment.

"Ah, you give such good gratitude. It's pure satisfaction," he growled under his breath and then he heard it. The straining of the old, decaying pulley.

He locked eyes with Poppy. It was like staring at his brother in the freezing waters. Wild. Terrified. Desperate.

Biceps on fire, Rhett forced a new resolve. "You're going nowhere. Hold—"

The rope snapped between Poppy's grip and Rhett's. Poppy's mouth flew open, but no words or sounds escaped. Like lightning, Rhett threw himself over, using his feet to keep him secure, and caught her fingers as the rope spiraled to the floor below.

After securing a tighter grip, he hauled her up and out of the shaft, tripping over the pile of cord on the floor, and crashed onto his back. Poppy toppled with him and landed heavily on his chest, but she was alive.

He closed his eyes and wrapped his arms around her, thankful she wasn't at the bottom of the elevator shaft, dead or bruised and broken. They lay like that a moment, stunned, silent and grateful. "You okay?" he finally said.

Poppy rose up and nodded, her eyes wet. "Thank you." She glanced down at his hands, bloody and burned from the rope. Grasping them carefully, she stroked the red marks. "Rhett," she choked out. "If you hadn't been here...on the same floor... I was pushed. By a man. The same one who abducted me, I think. Same build."

Rhett sat up. "You saw him?"

She told him how she felt his presence and turned in time to be shoved. He hadn't heard anyone running down the stairs, but then, he'd been laser focused on Poppy and her distress.

"How did he know we were here?" Had they been followed? No one knew their schedule. Unless Savannah had called or texted someone when she was out in the hallway.

"I don't know. But I imagine he's long gone now." She smoothed her hair. "I could stand to freshen up and plot the demise of whoever did this. He's seriously messed with the wrong woman. I wanted him for Cora, and now I want him for me too."

Double trouble. But why come after Poppy with such vengeance? Killing her would only add to the perpetrator's trouble. Did the killer think Poppy knew something that could expose him? If so, she'd have already said so. Unless she didn't realize she had incriminating knowledge or evidence. The only thing she'd kept close to the vest was the argument with Cora. Could it link to the culprit?

Glancing at her disheveled state and aftershock, he knew now was not the time to push. A break to freshen up sounded good. He needed to deal with his own emotions—like the ones that wanted to reach out and connect in a personal way. Protecting her in order to save her life should have been his only reason for hanging on to that rope, but he was afraid that there had been more in his resolve to save her. Something he wouldn't attempt to explore. A few minutes alone to recalibrate was in order.

Back at the B&B, Poppy turned off the engine and rested her head against the seat. "I need you to know that I can't fail in catching this guy, which means I'm going to take risks you aren't comfortable with. I don't know what they are as of now, but you need to know if they come, I'm going to take them." She continued to stare into space and raised her hand. "I won't skirt the law—I don't want anything kicked out on a technicality. But I know how you are." She turned to him. "Are you going to hinder or help?"

Desperation laced her voice and pulsed in her hazel eyes with the need to bring this killer to justice—as if her future depended on it.

The word *fail* knocked into him with a thump. Did she think she'd failed Cora? Rhett understood that line of thinking. He'd failed Keith by standing there watching in horror as the icy waters drained his life. He'd give anything to hear his laugh and be the subject of his razzing again. To feel his scalp burning as he received a brotherly noogie through Keith's knuckles.

Would he hinder or help?

"It depends on your definitions of help and hinder. Will I let you put yourself in unnecessary danger? No, Poppy. I won't do that. I almost lost you—our team, I mean, almost lost you, and I can't lie and say I wasn't afraid. I was."

Poppy nodded, but determination hardened her jaw. "And you have to understand I'm at peace with the fact that it might cost me my life to identify and catch her killer. I didn't want to die earlier because it wouldn't have brought any justice. So before you throw that in my face, it's not the same."

She didn't know what she was saying. "Hasn't your family already lost enough? Do you want to do to them all over again what it did when your sister died?"

A dejected smile came and went from her face. "My family would rather have justice and a killer behind bars. I'm going to give them that no matter what."

Rhett didn't believe her family would be okay with Poppy dying in order to put a murderer in prison, but he couldn't deny feeling, at times, that his family would have been better off if it had been Rhett underwater and not Keith.

If he was in Poppy's shoes, what would he do? He'd stay in control. Take measured steps. Practice patience as he investigated. Recklessness and impulsivity would bring disaster. He was living proof of that.

"I have no intention of being a hindrance, but I have no intention of letting you succumb to destruction in the process either. Emotion isn't going to lead this investigation. A sound mind is. You need a breather."

She opened the driver's door and a rush of wintry air swirled around them. The sky was growing grayer by the hour and the air was wet. Snow was in the forecast this evening. She closed the door without a reply and worry burrowed into Rhett's gut.

How was he going to protect some vigilante who didn't care if she lived or died? And if he attempted to hinder her, by her definition, and she shut him out, then how would he keep her safe?

Poppy sat on the edge of the bed and hung her head, breathing deep. She'd almost died, and would have if Rhett hadn't rescued her in time. She owed him. But not enough to cave to his idea of how the investigation should go. She meant every word she'd said in the car.

But the fear of literally dangling by a thread overwhelmed her here in the privacy of her room and she allowed herself to cry for a few moments before refocusing. If she caught Cora's killer, then she could give her family peace, and maybe feel some herself by knowing she'd worked to right a wrong she was responsible for. It wouldn't bring Cora back. It wouldn't change the trajectory of her life—catching a killer didn't make up for Poppy's mistakes. It wouldn't make up for the argument that led to Cora's death, nor would it remove the black stain of guilt.

But it would give her family closure, and they deserved that at the very least.

She dried her eyes and ran a brush through her hair, then straightened the black V-neck sweater she'd changed into along with a pair of dark skinny jeans and black boots before heading downstairs to meet Rhett by the fire in the living room. He was chatting with Delilah as if nothing had happened, as if Poppy hadn't almost plunged to her death. As if he hadn't ignored his own physical pain in order to save her. Three times in a matter of days, she'd been in his arms. Three times of feeling safe and a sense of belonging, as if he was her personal and private space to run to and would always be open and welcome for her—something she'd never felt before.

Sadly, there hadn't been any space left in Mom and Dad's arms for Poppy. The ache of loneliness and sense of being unloved had moved her to jealousy, and then the shame of feeling envious over someone who struggled with a condition. She'd wondered as a kid why she hadn't been born with an ailment; she'd thought if she had, then Mom and Dad would have loved her as much too.

Poppy, you're strong and healthy. Look after your sister.

But who had looked after her?

Rhett turned as if feeling her presence in the room, and his smile made a direct impact on her emotional cocoon, unraveling the strands that had entombed everything she didn't deserve to feel or hope to embrace. He'd changed into fresh khaki pants and an olive green dress shirt that enhanced his dark good looks.

Delilah beamed, compassion in her eyes, along with a hint of sadness—Poppy was good at recognizing sadness in someone's eyes, since she saw it each day in her own. "Agent Wallace told me what happened at the Castlewood Mansion. That's terrifying. I doctored his hands for him. Do you need anything?"

A tiny sliver of jealousy heated her skin. Why did it matter if another woman had tended to Rhett's wounds? Poppy wasn't a nursemaid. She was a cold case agent. She didn't heal wounds; she took down wound inflictors.

"I'm right as rain." She lifted her chin. "Ready to get back to why we're here."

Delilah clasped her hands. "Well, good to hear. I'll leave you two." She exited the living room and scuttled down the hall.

"You're Mr. Friendly," Poppy said with more bite than she intended. Delilah Cordray was a perfectly nice and attractive woman.

"And you're Miss Frowny." He raised his eyebrows to get his point across.

"I have reason to frown." She paused and glanced at his hands again. "Let me see your hands." Just to be sure they were taken care of. He held them up and she inspected them, then held them in hers, knowing good and well she only wanted an excuse to touch him. They were red and scratched but clean. "They hurt?"

He didn't answer and she peered up into his eyes. Many men were eye level with her, and it was kind of nice to have to look up, but the intensity in his gaze unsettled her.

"No," he murmured. "Tender to the touch but not painful. Not anymore."

She choked down the boulder of emotion in her throat. "Good."

"You hungry?" he asked.

"You trying to fatten me up? Seems I recall you complaining that I wasn't flabby enough while hanging on the precipice of death." She hit him with a stern eye, but she made sure to inflect joking in her tone.

"Did I?" He feigned forgetfulness. "I don't recall."

"Taking a play from most suspects' books now? I'm disappointed." She tsked through a snicker. "Yeah. I could eat."

"I was thinking we could take that Christmas boat tour. Would you want to do that?"

She frowned again. "You asking me out on a date?" She needed to turn this swelling moment full of awareness and feelings around and quickly. "I thought we already talked about that."

He only stared at her, searching her eyes with his. Man, he had gorgeous eyes dotted with flecks of warm gold. "No," he breathed, "I'd never do that."

Well. Good. But her stomach sank.

"Thought we could get out on the water—in the fresh air. Change of scenery. Gain some new perspective." He cocked his head and a sliver of dark hair fell over his right eye. It was all she could do not to slide it out of the way.

Instead she grabbed her coat she'd left on the coat rack by the door and slid into it. "Fine, but then we're right back to the investigation."

"Okay, Poppy." He might as well have said "As you wish" like Westley from *The Princess Bride*. He was being far too agreeable.

Inside the car they discussed his insurance company and what he planned to do about a new car, then where they planned to attend church this coming Sunday. She'd gone to Faith Assembly when she'd lived here as a teenager. "I guess we can go back there." Though attending church only reminded her of her sins, and that God was disappointed in her. Still, she went for Cora and Grandma.

"Alright." Ugh. He'd been all about her and what she wanted to discuss, where she wanted to go for the last fifteen minutes. What happened to the man who rarely conversed about personal things and consistently disagreed and bickered with her? This was entirely too unlike him, and it needed to be nipped in the bud.

"Why aren't you arguing with me?"

"About where to worship? Hmm... I don't know. Could it be that I have no idea where to attend church in this town and you do, so I'm fine with that?" The annoyance returned to his voice, which was far easier to work with.

"Well, when you put it like that. Don't feel sorry for or pity me. I mean it." His grace and compassion were pointless; she was getting exactly what she deserved—reaping what she'd sown. She did not need any of his kindness.

Even if deep down…she wanted it.

"Why should I feel sorry for you?" he asked.

"Why do you ask so many questions?" she countered to summon up a superficial answer that might satisfy him.

"Why do you evade so many?"

"Fine. Because I've been abducted and attacked repeatedly."

He tossed her a nice-try expression. "That possibility comes with the job. Why would I feel sorry for something you willingly knew might happen ahead of time?"

Her secrets, shame and guilt were her own. She wasn't coughing up the truth for him or anybody. "What are you, a head doctor now?"

"Do you need one?"

Anger rose to the surface of her tongue. "That's it. I'm done talking altogether."

His amused smirk only fueled her agitated fire.

"I highly doubt that," he muttered under his breath.

"Has anyone ever told you how annoying you are?" Usually it took less than this to get under his skin and irritate him. What was going on?

"You, every single day. And I thought you were done talking."

"Besides me. And I am."

"I don't see a lot of people." He shrugged and pointed ahead. "Don't miss your turn."

"Don't tell me what to do!" But she was about to miss the turn. Jerking the wheel at the last second, she thrust him against the door and he grabbed the handle above it to brace himself and chuckled under his breath.

"Wouldn't dream of it," he said.

She huffed and whipped into the riverfront parking lot. Colored lights lit up the dock, and the boat was a sight to see. Like a floating Christmas tree decked with garland, thousands of multicolored lights twinkled and wreaths had been spaced out along the railings on both decks of the massive sternwheeler boat. Suddenly, her sour mood dissipated in the awe of the grand display.

"You think they're gonna serve fish?" Rhett asked flatly.

Poppy looked at him and laughed. "Likely."

After securing their tickets—which Rhett paid for, then refused her money—they went aboard the boat, taking in the gorgeous scenery. Poppy nestled her scarf closer to her neck and secured her gloves on her hands. The wind off the river was colder than on land, and the smell of earth and fish hit her senses, along with hints of rosemary and garlic coming from the dining room.

Inside, black-and-white-checkered floors gleamed and tables for two were draped in black tablecloths. Gold hurricane lamps with white candles aglow made for romantic centerpieces. The upper dining deck had been wrapped in white lights too. The atmosphere was elegant, warm and intimate.

Rhett held her chair for her, and she bit back a remark about this not being a date. He'd never pulled her chair out before. Granted, they'd each bought one another coffees, but this was completely different. Felt all too much like a date. While she did a fair share of dating, she couldn't say any of the men were gentlemen, and that made them easy to toss aside when the feeling of companionship slipped away, leaving her empty.

Their menus lay on the table and she laughed when she read that pan-seared fish was one of the choices. She picked steak medium, and Rhett ordered his medium well. Lively conversation and laughter permeated the room. No one appeared to have a care in the world, but then she doubted anyone else had been targeted for murder or was attempting to solve a decades-old cold case.

"Have you ever been on a cruise?" Rhett asked as she surveyed the boat. The engine started and the huge paddles churned in the water, propelling them into motion down the Mississippi River.

"No. I've never been one for confinement in a big floating box for more than a few hours. Kinda creeps me out." She sipped her drink and let her taut muscles relax. For the next two hours she wouldn't be running for her life, and she planned to take advantage of the safety—for now. Because when she hit land, she wouldn't be able to let her guard down. Not like this moment. So she'd savor it. From the atmosphere to the food to the company.

"I went on a cruise the holiday after my brother passed. My parents wanted to change up tradition— start a new one. Truth is, I think they were hoping to float away from everything familiar, like presents under the tree and the open space on the mantel where Keith's stocking used to hang. The corn pudding that no one ate, but she continued to cook because Keith loved it."

Poppy related to Rhett and it connected them whether or not she liked it. "And what are your thoughts on cruises? Yay or nay?"

"I don't know. I haven't been on one since that first year. They did something different each Christmas until grandkids came along. Now it's the same old tradition."

"Minus the corn pudding?"

He paused midsip and smirked. "Minus the corn pudding." He folded his napkin and placed his water on it to absorb the condensation while her glass made rings on the tablecloth. "I probably didn't give it a fair shake. It seemed wrong having a good time on the water knowing Keith had drowned. I might be willing to try it again now. Maybe."

Before Poppy could respond, their server brought sizzling filets mignons, loaded baked potatoes and sides of asparagus smothered in hollandaise sauce.

They made small talk, which revealed more personal sides of each other. Poppy found she enjoyed the conversation. No pressure about how the night was supposed to end. Rhett was honorable. And hilarious. He'd made sarcastic and witty quips in the past, but clearly, he'd been holding back—keeping it professional at work, and they never did after-hours things just the two of them. Until now. Was this a date without them admitting it?

No. He'd never ask her out—even told her so—and she'd let him know she'd never accept if he did. But it felt like two people on a date—one that was far more committed than the kinds Poppy went on.

As the cruise ended with a round of Christmas carols accompanied by the piano on the upper level, they exited the boat. Poppy felt lighter than she had in days. Happier. Even amid the circumstances, which made no sense.

But how long would this feeling last until the guilt reached in and plucked it out with the reminder that it was Cora who should be here and happy?

Chapter 6

Rhett didn't mind not having a rental. Poppy was a good driver when she wasn't in a foul mood. What he did mind was how he'd felt tonight when Poppy had finally lowered her gruff guard. He hadn't quite put his finger on why she kept one up; it was a piece of the mysterious puzzle that was Poppy, and he itched to put it in place. But when it had dropped, she'd freely talked about her childhood and teenage years and Cora's death. He discovered her favorite thing to do was beat her brothers at anything. That he could see one hundred percent.

They'd discussed foods, travel and how they'd been drawn into working cold cases. Rhett wanted to help provide closure for families who hadn't yet received it. He wanted peace for them, and when he could provide it, on occasion, it brought him peace as well. He had gone a little more in depth about Keith's death, but had refrained from admitting that he was to blame. Some things he simply couldn't talk about. Couldn't admit his greatest mistake and failure.

They hadn't discussed the case, but he didn't regret it. A stretch of downtime and a good meal would provide them rest and help them to think clearer come morning.

Maya Marx was left on the list to interview, though she'd probably repeat the same old story like everyone else. Could no one come up with one new thing? That was odd. Generally, after several years, people typically remembered something new or shared something they had kept hidden before, especially if they'd been teenagers and thought their parents might discipline them.

As they walked from the car to the B&B, Rhett noticed Poppy shivering. The temperature had dropped several degrees in the past two hours. And she hated the cold.

"I hate the cold," she said through chattering teeth and he chuckled.

"I know," he murmured. "Let's get you inside before you turn into a Popsicle."

Poppy's teeth chattered in reply and she stepped inside. Rhett closed the door behind them and sighed as the B&B's cozy warmth embraced him. Delilah sat with a steaming mug by the crackling fire. She glanced up with tired eyes. "I put some hot water in the carafe if you want hot chocolate or tea. Both are available."

Peppermint teased his senses and he thanked her, then helped himself to the peppermint hot chocolate. Poppy passed on the hot chocolate and dug into a tin of cookies. Guess the chocolate cake she'd chosen for dessert wasn't enough. He hadn't taken Poppy to have a sweet tooth.

Shuffling along the hall floor drew his attention, and a woman with Down syndrome entered the dining room wearing a pink robe with matching slippers; a little stuffed gray bunny was tucked under her arm. As she caught his eye, she beamed.

"I like hot chocolate too. Delilah said I can have some."

Rhett motioned her toward the carafe. "Well, come and help yourself. I'm Rhett."

"I'm Elizabeth. Delilah calls me Beth. She's my sister. Do you have a sister?"

Rhett nodded. "I do. She's a younger sister."

"I'm a younger sister too." She retrieved an insulated cup and lifted the nozzle to release the hot water. She turned to Poppy. "You're pretty."

Poppy's cheeks reddened and shock hit Rhett's system. He'd never seen her blush. Warmth brightened her eyes and turned her completely radiant. Elizabeth was wrong. Poppy wasn't pretty—she was stunning. "Thank you. So are you. I always wanted red hair."

"You have black hair. And pretty eyes."

"Thank you. You have pretty eyes too," she returned. "I like your bunny." Elizabeth must carry it everywhere; it was old and worn.

"My mom gave me this for Christmas. Did your mom give you a bunny?"

Poppy's smiled faltered. "No," she said, "but she gave me a little brown owl. I called him Mr. Hootie and he went everywhere I went—even to first grade every single day in my backpack."

Rhett tried to picture Poppy as a little girl toting around a stuffed animal. It wasn't easy, not looking at the strong, confident woman before him now.

Mr. Hootie. Rhett smirked. She was clever even then. "Do you still have Mr. Hootie?"

Poppy's bottom lip dipped south. "No. I'm afraid I don't."

Elizabeth laid her hand on Poppy's shoulder and stared into her eyes. "You don't have to be afraid. Jesus loves you, and He will take care of you like He takes care of me and Delilah. You'll find what you lost. He'll help you."

Poppy's eyes filled with moisture and she quickly blinked it away.

"Can I hug you?" Elizabeth asked. "Delilah says it's polite to ask first because not everyone wants a hug."

Throat bobbing, Poppy nodded. "I would definitely like a hug."

Elizabeth set her cup and bunny on the dining table and confidently wrapped her arms around Poppy. Poppy's arms embraced her softly, then tightened. The scene moved him and he fought the emotion burning the backs of his eyes. Poppy sniffed, then released her.

"Thank you," she said through a broken voice. "That was precisely what I needed."

Elizabeth flashed another toothy grin and nodded with satisfaction. "Delilah says that our hugs are God's arms around the people we hold. 'Cause we can't see Him."

Poppy inhaled through her nose as she rubbed her lips together. "Well, it's been a while since God hugged me. So thank you again." She laid her hand on her chest. "I'm going to sit by the fire."

"I see you've met Beth," Delilah said as she entered the room, then looked at Poppy. "Not much fire left, Agent Holliday. I need to bring some firewood inside."

"I can get it," Rhett said. No point sending her out in the cold when he was capable—and besides, Poppy could use a minute to herself. "I'll make sure it's out before turning in."

Delilah's face lit with gratitude and she took Beth's hand. "Thank you. Come on, hon. Let's go to bed now."

"Nice meeting you," Rhett said as Delilah and her sister padded down the hall to their private living quarters. Poppy sat on the hearth near the embers of a dying fire. Her bottom lip quivered and her eyes were squeezed shut. She looked like she might fall apart any minute. "I'd ask if you're doing okay but I know you'll just hiss or bark."

"And all this time I thought you didn't know me." She pulled the arms of her sweater over her hands and rubbed them on her thighs, but smirked, then sobered as she shook her head. "I'm not okay."

Shock split his chest. Was she going to actually open up?

"I could use a fire," she said instead. Maybe it was for the best. If she allowed him into her pain and heartache, he'd only want to stick around to fix it. He couldn't invest in her personally—not when she was a wild card. Mere hours ago, she'd declared if she died in the line of fire due to reckless behavior, then so be it. The thought still roiled his gut.

"Alright. Hang tight. I'll bring in firewood." After slinging on his leather jacket and shoving his hands into his gloves, he proceeded outside. Snow had dusted the brittle grass, leaving it sparkly. His breath plumed and swirled into the heavy night sky.

Poppy's car's interior light blinked on and a black shadowed figure clambered out from the passenger side.

Rhett's pulse spiked. "Hey!" he hollered, drawing his weapon and heading straight for the vehicle. "Stop!"

The man raised a gun and Rhett dived to the ground as gunfire cracked. Rolling his way toward the holly bush by the mailbox, Rhett dodged another bullet and crouched behind the prickly shrub. He fired back. Listened. Footsteps crunched along the ground.

The front door opened and Poppy came running, gun in hand. "You good?" she hollered and ran past him, picking up speed as she chased the shooter across the street. She hadn't even tried to shield herself, just ran headlong into danger—like she said she would.

Rhett growled and tore after; she needed backup.

"He's getting away!" she screamed and jumped a four-foot picket fence into someone's yard. A light inside clicked on. Poppy'd have the whole town awake in no time at this rate.

Rhett caught up with her as they chased the figure through another yard. He bounded onto a picnic table and over a wooden privacy fence. Poppy didn't miss a beat, mimicking his moves, and Rhett sprinted over with her. As Rhett touched ground, the attacker turned and fired another round. Rhett tackled Poppy and tumbled with her behind a huge sweet gum tree. The woman had no sense to take cover on her own!

Another projectile tore into the bark; new lights blinked on.

Rhett held Poppy in place with quiet force. "He's waiting for you. He wants you to chase." A dog barked in the distance. "Don't be stupid."

"Let me go!" she growled as she struggled in his grip. Poppy was strong and putting up a good fight, but at the end of the day Rhett was stronger and held her against him. "He's getting away! I told you not to interfere."

"You aren't any good to Cora dead. Where's the justice in that?"

After a moment, her body relaxed in his arms and her breathing slowed. "He can't run forever, Poppy. We'll get him. But we have to be around with beating hearts to do it."

Poppy wriggled free and leaned her head against the tree. "I know. I'm sick to death of him having the upper hand."

He understood. "He broke into your car. What do you think he was looking for?"

"Who's out there?" a deep voice boomed. "I called the sheriff."

Rhett raised his hands. "I'm Agent Wallace and this is my partner, Agent Holliday. We're with the MBI, chasing a suspect. I can show you my credentials."

He and Poppy eased out and showed their badges to the sleepy-eyed man with mussed hair. He lowered his shotgun as blue lights flashed down the street.

By the time they filled out their report and returned to the B&B, neither of them cared one iota about a fire. They went straight to their rooms, where Rhett tossed and turned, unable to sleep. Someone had pilfered through Poppy's car for a reason. Did he think she had case files or some kind of incriminating evidence on hand?

A more sinister thought crossed his mind and he jumped up and raced outside in his T-shirt and sweats. Turning on his cell phone flashlight, he poked around and felt along underneath the driver's side and jiggled the interior lights. These days it wasn't hard to plant a bug. Then the killer would keep the upper hand.

Rhett pulled the lever on the glove box and instantly heard the click.

Not a bug.

With his blood turning to ice, he kicked open the passenger door, gearing up for his quick exit. He removed his hand and bolted, but it wasn't fast enough.

A burst of exploding heat thrust him three feet in the air, tossing him into a tree like a rag doll.

Poppy stared at the ceiling, the down comforter up to her chin and Beth Cordray's hug on her mind.

God's hug.

If God's hug could have been tangible, Poppy had surely felt it in the arms of Delilah's precious sister. The warmth from that embrace had seeped into hollow, cold spaces until it stretched into her soul, thawing it and coaxing it back to life. All the strength within her had been used to keep from falling to a puddle in front of everyone.

Was God hugging her? Why would He want to? She'd let Him down even before Cora's death. Surely, He was holding her charges against her. Each one was vivid in her mind, with the word *guilty* next to them.

She had just closed her eyes when a sonic boom shook the house and a flash of light appeared in the window. Poppy flew from the bed, her heart skidding into her throat as she snatched her gun, then raced downstairs in her tank top, pajama pants and bare feet. Delilah was rushing toward the living room with a crying Beth clinging to her.

Poppy froze for an instant, taking in the sight. The

front windows had been shattered into glass shards, and the roof of the front porch had caved in. Pieces of shingles were scattered on the living room floor with splintered wood.

"Get her out of the house! Call 911. Now!" Poppy ordered. "Rhett!" No way he slept through that sound. Gawking outside without getting too close to the debris in her bare feet, she saw that her car was up in flames and parts had rained like a meteor shower. She raced out the back door and around the side of the house to the front yard. The fallen porch roof was now being licked by flames from blazing fragments.

If Rhett hadn't come out of his room... He hadn't been in his room.

Fear gripped her by its icy claws. "Rhett!" she called again as she scanned the yard and what was left of her vehicle. A crumpled heap near the oak tree caught her attention.

No. No, please, God, no!

She bounded across the lawn, dodging debris—stings pierced the soles of her feet, but she pressed forward until she reached Rhett and dropped to her knees. Scrapes, soot and blood stained his face. Poppy checked for a pulse. Found one. Shrill sirens rang nearby. "Rhett, can you hear me?"

He shifted, groaned, then his eyes fluttered open.

"It's okay. I'm here." She hastily examined him for further injury and broken bones. He coughed and sputtered, then winced and groaned again.

"I think I'm okay." He shuffled and winced as he shifted into an upright position.

Poppy touched the side of his face. "You're bleeding. What were you doing out here?"

He covered her hand that she hadn't withdrawn from his dirt-stained cheek. "I couldn't sleep and I thought the attacker might not have been searching for something to remove, but to add."

"A bomb? You went bomb checking!" She huffed. He hadn't woken her. "Talk about me going off half-cocked. I don't recall you ever being on a bomb squad."

Rhett chuckled through the pain as first responders pulled onto the edge of the road, away from the clutter of car parts. "Well, in my defense, I wasn't searching for a bomb. I was looking for a bug. They're easy to install, and if the killer wanted to keep up with what we know about the case, that would be a way without tailing us. We've been careful since our little trip to Ian Kirkwood's business."

"Well, you got more than you bargained for. Next time, come get me."

"Only if you return the favor. Watching someone you—you work with run into danger isn't quite so easy, is it?"

"I didn't even get to watch you run." She'd only seen the aftermath and a limp heap by a tree.

"I look pretty good doin' it."

She snickered. "You look like death warmed over right now."

He grinned through the pain. "You give the best compliments."

"Right?" Their lighthearted banter, which was defusing the tense situation, got cut short as Sheriff Pritchard approached with paramedics. Good. She didn't want to ponder what Rhett had intended to say before his careful wording. And she didn't want to think about how she'd felt seeing him lying there—thinking he might be dead.

"I guess he went for bombing over bugging—maybe he's not as smart as you're giving him credit for." She carefully rustled his thick hair and glanced up at Sheriff Pritchard, who was already shrugging out of his thick sheriff's jacket.

He knelt and draped it around her bare arms, the smell of his cologne—something rugged but expensive—clinging to it. "I'm glad you're only cold." He turned to Rhett. "You look worse for the wear, Agent."

"So I've been told. With less subtlety." He glanced at the warm, insulated coat wrapped around Poppy. An eyebrow rose but he didn't remark.

Paramedics examined and treated Rhett, asking a million questions.

Delilah and Beth stood with two deputies as firefighters doused the collapsed porch roof that had caught on fire. Thankfully, they'd gotten to it in time and the actual home hadn't gone up in flames.

Poppy raced toward them, the cuts stinging the soles of her feet. She hugged Beth, held tight and stroked her fiery red hair. "Are you hurt?"

"I was scared."

"I know. Me too, but there's nothing to be afraid of now." Except that wasn't wholly true.

If the bomb had been planted in the house or had reached farther... Poppy's bones turned to lava as a surge of protectiveness for Beth kicked into high gear. "Do you have your bunny?"

She held it up. "I always have my bunny."

"Good. Give him a big hug. He was scared too. He needs you to keep him safe. Can you do that, Beth?"

She nodded. Delilah rubbed her shoulder and mouthed a thank-you to Poppy.

"I'm sorry we've brought trouble." Poppy glanced at Beth, not wanting to go into detail and add to her fears. She was unsure about the damage to the house. No windows. A disaster in the living room. Because of her, Beth and Delilah might not be able to spend Christmas at home.

"No need to apologize. No one could have known." As Sheriff Pritchard approached, she blushed. "Rudy."

He offered a tender and possibly apologetic smile. "Delilah. You and Beth okay?"

She nodded and he patted Beth's cheek. "You sure did a good job protecting that bunny, Beth. You're very brave."

Maybe the sheriff wasn't quite a wild card, as Poppy had originally assumed. He held a tender side, but it didn't have the same effect on her as Rhett's gentleness did. "Well," she said, "I'm going to check on my partner again."

The paramedics left and Rhett stood with a bandage on the left side of his temple. A hole had been ripped in the right knee of his sweatpants. He pointed to the charred remains of her car. "We're now two for two in cars blowing up."

"And I thought that only happened in action movies. Guess we either walk or get a rental—if anyone will loan us one."

"I'll take out the insurance."

"I'm not sure it'll be enough," she teased as she leaned into Rhett, nudging him with her shoulder.

He shrugged. "I never liked your car anyway. The seats are uncomfortable and your speakers are staticky."

Poppy caught his smirk and her belly corkscrewed.

"I at least have a valid excuse for buying a new car—with seat warmers."

He tugged on the fleece collar of Rudy's coat. "Maybe you could keep this. Seems pretty warm, and he doesn't mind parting with it." His voice held a questioning tone and a slight tick of jealousy. Or was she reading too much into it?

Poppy didn't think there was more to the sheriff's kind gesture, but even if there had been, she wasn't into him. But she was freezing. Her toes were numb.

As if reading her thoughts, Rhett glanced down. "Poppy, you're gonna get frostbite. Go get some shoes before you impale your foot on metal or lose a toe."

She didn't argue and found the fire chief to make sure it was safe to go inside. Thankfully, the bomber hadn't had any intention of blowing up anything more than the car and whoever was inside. The house might smell like smoke for a few days but the structure was sound, and once the porch was rebuilt, the mess cleaned and windows fixed, it would be as if nothing had exploded.

Inside, she doctored her feet with a first aid kit Delilah had provided. They would be sore and tender for a few days, but she could wear thicker socks for extra cushion.

Needing a few minutes to process, she plunked onto the bed and fell backward, exhausted. She was a roller coaster of emotions. Rhett had nearly died. He should have known better than to go out there alone. He was smarter than that. So why did he? Why be impulsive when he always chose the safe route? No wonder he got his dander up when Poppy did things like this. She was irritated, angry, frightened and frantic. But she was also thankful and grateful he was still alive.

A knock sounded. "Can I come in?" Rhett asked. Poppy sat up and scooted to the edge of the bed, then granted him permission. "How are your feet?"

"Sore."

He sat beside her. "Detective Teague is here and that other detective. I can't remember his name."

"Monty Banner."

"Right." He perused her room. "Where's the sheriff's coat?"

And the team called her the bulldog. "I gave it to Delilah to return to him."

"I see."

She wasn't sure he did. "You scared me." There, she said it, though uncertain why. It kind of bubbled out without permission, but it was the truth. "I mean, I've been afraid. A killer keeps coming after me. I'd be remiss not to admit some fear. But my need to solve Cora's murder is greater. But tonight..." That wasn't a different kind of fear. The kind she'd only felt once before, when Cora never came home. And while she wasn't ready to discuss the root of it, she wanted him to know that... Well, she wasn't sure what she wanted him to know.

"I'm sorry," he murmured as his shoulder brushed hers. He'd changed into clean sweats and a Vols sweatshirt. She'd only come to know he loved the Volunteers when they'd worked the football corruption case last fall. There was so much she didn't know about Rhett and wanted to, but wouldn't inquire. "I'm not sure what I was thinking."

"Neither am I. You always consider long and hard before going into something. If you had given it more thought, the idea it could have been a bomb would have crossed your mind and the Rhett I know would have called a bomb squad to check. That wasn't like you." Maybe that's what unsettled her—he was out of the ordinary. Predictable Rhett was easy to maneuver around and never crossed lines. Now, what lines might he cross? And how would she keep up her guard if he wasn't the consistent and constant Rhett?

"I know," he breathed and arrested her with his eyes, searching as if she would have the reasons for his impulsive decision. "I... You scare me, Poppy."

Was that his answer to his reckless decision? He'd done it for her or because of her? What was his meaning? If she didn't look away, she might find the answer in his eyes and she dared not ask for fear he'd clarify—and they could not go beyond colleagues who sometimes got along because then there'd be no going back and it would end disastrously. And end it would. She sabotaged her relationships—if they could even be called that. Rhett was no typical guy. He didn't deserve to be hurt, and she would hurt him. Then where would that leave them professionally?

If only her heart and her head would get on the same stupid page! "It's probably best that way," she whispered. If he was scared of her, he'd steer clear of her and then she wouldn't have to worry about making a gargantuan mistake.

"Maybe." He brushed a bang from her eye, sending her pulse into a frenzied skitter. "Probably."

"You're not a risk taker." Except tonight he had been. Her stomach dipped.

"No," he breathed as his head slowly descended toward her lips. "No, I'm not."

Guess he couldn't get his head and heart on the same page either.

As his lips touched hers, a knock jerked them from the crackling moment, saving them from going to a place they couldn't get back from. And still she regretted the interruption. "Come in," Poppy said through a choked voice and stood up, giving her some distance from Rhett and his inviting lips.

Detective Monty Banner opened the door, looming in the door frame. He clearly spent his free time at the gym—he was attractive, with the right amount of stubble and swagger. "Sorry to interrupt, but I need to ask y'all a few questions."

"Where's Detective Teague?" Rhett asked.

"Questioning Delilah and neighbors." He perched on an old ladder-back chair, the seat creaking at the strain of his weight. "Sheriff called in a construction company to secure the breached area. Everyone can remain in the home. So let's move on to more-pressing things. Like what happened."

Rhett explained what transpired prior to the explosion and Poppy picked up from there, since Rhett had been knocked unconscious.

Monty wrote it all on his legal pad. "Bomb appears homemade. Any online tutorial could guide someone. We found the front of an egg timer. Nothing too complicated. But I worked for the Memphis Police Department bomb unit for six years. Thought coming back home would mean never seeing a bomb again. Surprise." His laugh was deep and amusing, and there was ironic humor in his eyes. "That's all I need for now. Get some shut-eye. Sheriff put a unit on the house, especially since there's civilians inside."

Monty closed the door behind them, leaving an awk-wardness hovering over them. The moment for a kiss was gone, but the shocking knowledge they'd almost let it happen remained, and quite frankly, Poppy didn't have it in her to discuss it. "I think we should consider finding somewhere else to stay so as not to put anyone in further danger."

Rhett ran a hand through his hair. "Where? We'd have to find something to rent that was private. Know of any place?"

"There's a campground with cabins a few miles south of the Weaverman property. I can check availability. If Beth and Delilah are harmed because of me... I'd never forgive myself." She wouldn't be responsible for any more deaths.

Rhett stood. "I understand. But we have to be pre-pared that we might not find anywhere else. We'll take more precautions." He scratched the back of his neck. "Should we...uh...talk about—"

"Nothing to talk about. It was a highly emotional mo-ment. That's all. It could have been Detective Banner or Sheriff Pritchard. I may have kissed either of them given the circumstances."

The last thing she wanted to discuss was her feel-ings—her extremely conflicted feelings—and as she made eye contact, the pain she'd intended to inflict hit its mark. It was there in the flash of hurt and the tick in his jaw.

"But *I* wouldn't have kissed just anyone."

"That sounds like a personal problem and talking about it to me is unnecessary. Work out your own feel-ings on your own time." It crushed her to speak such icy words, but she had a wall to rebuild, so she trained her line of sight right above his eyes for fear if she gazed into that warmth and gentleness, she'd desperately want to be pursued and loved by a good, honest man. He'd see her false bravado and maybe even glimpse her emotional struggle concerning her feelings for him, and it would be over for them both.

Rhett squared his shoulders and inhaled sharply through his nose. "I was going to say that even if a kernel of something was there fueling that moment, I'm sorry. I don't date colleagues and I especially don't date loose cannons. But I won't pretend that I'm not attracted to you. You're a beautiful, smart woman—most of the time you're smart." He actually smirked. "And that was obviously what led the charge thanks to heightened emotions that come with near-death experiences. You're right on that account. So that's that. You're free to run off now and kiss any man that crosses your path."

He didn't slam the door. Didn't raise his voice.

She didn't want to kiss anyone except him. And he didn't see her as anything other than an intelligent but pretty face. No, he didn't want her and her loose-cannon ways.

Chapter 7

Rhett stared at the collected bomb debris from Saturday night. Detective Teague's canvassing had gotten zero answers. All they had were suspects, blown-up vehicles and sore bodies. Everyone felt the frustration. Now he sipped lukewarm coffee made by a deputy who didn't know when to stop with the scooping. A spoon could stand up straight in this stuff.

Typical Monday at the sheriff's office. Slow but rushed. It was only 10:00 a.m. but it felt like five o'clock.

Yesterday after church and lunch, Poppy had called the campground to check on a vacant cabin for the rest of their stay. Rhett wasn't keen on spending the remainder of the investigation in that kind of close proximity with her. Alone. No buffers. No barriers. Not because he'd kiss her again, but after their terse conversation Saturday night, he needed space to get his head back in the game and on track. Poppy had been right—it wasn't like him to allow emotions to guide his decisions. He never made quick or impulsive ones. But Poppy had a pull on him, which was terrifying.

He hadn't meant to hurt her feelings—if he even had—when he'd declared he'd never date a loose cannon like her, but she'd drawn first blood when she'd admitted she would have kissed any man who had been sitting there beside her. He wished those words wouldn't have cut, but they had, and his ego took a nice hit too.

Better that it worked out the way it did anyway. Had she admitted there was something there and made a move to finish what they'd started before Detective Banner had become the proverbial bell, it would have meant even greater turmoil for Rhett. He could only hope there would be no vacant cabins and he wouldn't have to suffer being confined with Poppy. She'd left a message and surely the campground manager would call by today.

Poppy entered the evidence room scowling. Dressed in black pants and a black-and-white-striped dress shirt that fit trim at her slender waist, she held a cup of a coffee. "The coffee is rank, I know."

"It's not the coffee—though you're right. We're stuck at the B&B. No cabins available."

A slight breath of relief escaped his lungs and created some space in his chest. He didn't want to put anyone at risk either, but they were on high alert now and would take more precautions. Plus, Delilah had insisted they stay. The woman had a lot of class and grace.

"The bright side is, our rental has seat warmers and that makes me happy." She sipped her sludge.

She'd been going on about that since yesterday when they picked a midsize sedan. "You update the chief yet?"

That garnered a grin. "Colt asked if we blew up each other's cars. Me to be spiteful and you to retaliate." Her grin morphed into the Poppy-eye. "I told him you'd never do something so unpredictable or loose-cannon-like."

Okay, so that statement had affected her. "I wasn't trying to insult you."

"I know. I am both of those things." She shrugged as if it simply was what it was. "Maya Marx. Let's go talk to her. She's at the vet clinic today."

"You want to drive or me?"

"Feel free." She tossed him the keys.

Weaverman Vet Clinic wasn't all that busy. Pet dander and stringent floor cleaner tickled and burned Rhett's nose. A Yellow Lab sat by his owner quietly while a Yorkie in a huge pink bow yapped away while her owner ignored the shrill barks.

A woman wearing scrubs, with frizzy hair and lips that revealed many years of smoking, eyed him and Poppy. He showed her his credentials and explained why they were there.

"Maya is actually on a fifteen-minute break. Follow me." She led them through a door to a large room with kennels and steel tables. Dogs barked and whined. Poor pups. Rhett did a double-take as a huge turtle poked its head from its shell.

Maya Marx stood in the break room, the side door open to the outside while she engaged in a tense conversation with Detective Monty Banner. Well, that was interesting. Rhett cleared his throat and Maya swung her attention to them. She was short and petite with a severe blond ponytail and rich brown eyes.

Detective Banner's cheeks reddened. "Agents," he said and introduced them to Maya, then made a quick exit. What were they discussing? She wasn't a suspect in the attempts on their lives, but she did connect to the cold case, which connected to Rhett's and Poppy's lives being threatened. She'd been in Cora's science class and club, and she had been BFFs with Savannah Steadman-Teague and Natalie Carpenter-Weaverman. And ran with Dylan and Ian.

"How can I help you?" She closed the heavy metal door and a whiff of stale cigarettes reached his nostrils. Cheap cigarettes lay by a box of doughnuts.

Poppy shoved her hands into her coat pockets. "You and Detective Banner seeing each other?"

"For a few months, but I hardly think that's why you're here." She sat in the plastic chair and laid a hand over her pack of cigarettes.

"You're right. We're interviewing past friends, club members and classmates of Cora's, seeing if any new information comes to light. Can you go over that night for us again? And don't leave out the fact that Dylan had a crush on Cora. One of our earlier interviews happened to remember that piece of information after all these years."

Rhett kept a straight face at Poppy's stretch. It wasn't illegal to bend the truth, and Poppy was bending it pretty far. No one had veered outside of their old story, but if Maya thought one of them had, she might offer up information she'd have otherwise withheld. Rhett was never a fan of this tactic, and Poppy knew it.

Maya toyed with the plastic cigarette packaging. "I knew Cora liked Dylan. And yes, Dylan was into her. I saw them passing notes in science club a few times and he carried her books to the next class—but it wasn't going to go anywhere."

And it worked.

"Because of Savannah?" Poppy asked.

"Because it was a crush, and Dylan was ultimately devoted to Savannah. Savannah would never have harmed Cora."

"What about Ian Kirkwood?" Rhett asked. "Could he have killed someone?"

She frowned. "Doubtful."

"His alibi is lame. Movies alone? Does that sound like something he would have done?" Rhett asked, hoping for any scent to hunt.

Maya's cheeks reddened. "No. I doubt he'd have gone to a movie alone, but he was a major Jamie Lee Curtis fan."

"Who was dealing pot back then? I know about the marijuana Cora had too."

Maya snorted. "You want the dealer? Easy enough. Linden Saddler. He was generally at the Pet Company off Highway 10. He owns the place now. We're his vet for animals that get sick at the store."

Another connection Natalie was keeping close. Now they might be getting somewhere. "He ever sell to you?"

"No. I never bought drugs." She didn't say she never did them.

They thanked her for her time and within fifteen minutes pulled into the Pet Company parking lot.

"Let's hope this guy remembers who he dealt to back then, but if he's continued to sell over the years, he'll likely not talk." Rhett unbuckled his seat belt.

"I don't care what he's doing now because at the moment he's our only lead." Poppy slammed the car door and flipped up the collar on her coat. The snow and sleet had let up, but the slate sky was growing heavier by the hour. Snow would fall again tonight.

Inside, animals rattled cages, puppies barked and Rhett frowned. "I'm not a fan of puppy mills. And most pet stores get their animals from them and then jack up the price. That ought to be a crime."

Poppy smirked. "I didn't realize you were such an animal activist." Birds squawked and chirped. A whole row of mice and hamsters ran in hamster wheels. Poppy turned her nose up. "Though I do agree."

Now Rhett chuckled but didn't say anything. A teenager with more acne than hair on his head noticed them and waved. "If you need any help, let me know."

"We're looking for Mr. Saddler. He in?"

"Yes, ma'am. I'll go get him." The guy rushed through the aisles and to the back of the store. A few moments passed and a muscular man with eighties hairband hair and a rock T-shirt came tagging along behind the teenager.

"I'm Linden Saddler. Can I help you?" He kept his eyes on Poppy. Like the teenager. Like most of the male species. Rhett never faulted them for it; he was clearly a sucker too.

"I'm Agent Holliday and this is Agent Wallace. We're investigating the murder of Cora Holliday—yes, she's a relation."

"I heard about that. Sorry for your loss. We can talk in my office. Follow me back."

His office looked more like a boy's bedroom full of posters from bands who had fallen from their prime.

"I love eighties rock."

"I wouldn't have guessed," Poppy teased and Saddler responded with a fat grin. "Look, I'm gonna be straight up with you. I'm not interested in what you might do on the side. Nor am I interested in bringing any charges against you for the past—unless you murdered my sister—so you can be candid with me."

"I didn't kill anyone. Can't get any more candid than that." He tented his fingers on his messy desk.

"Then let's keep rolling with that. Tell me who you sold pot to back then. Cora had a bag and said she was holding it for a friend. I think that friend might have had something to do with her death. It's at the very least a lead for me. You say you're sorry for my loss? Help me find the killer. If it wasn't you, then you have nothing to lose and everything to gain—my gratitude for one." She left it hanging as if there might be more reward for him.

He leaned his head back against his chair. "I don't sell drugs anymore. I did sell weed on the side and used it to save up to buy this place."

"You ever deal to Dylan Weaverman, Ian Kirkwood, Savannah Steadman, Maya Marx or Natalie Carpenter?"

"I sold to all of them except Maya."

"Did you sell to any of them the week or so before Cora went missing? It would have been the week before Thanksgiving," Poppy said.

It was a long shot but who knew. Maybe he kept a record or had a keen mind.

Linden tossed his hands in the air. "That was a long time ago. What I can tell you is that if your sister was on the bad side of mean girl Savannah Steadman and her loyal sidekicks, then if one of them gave her drugs it wasn't to befriend her but to get her in trouble. And if your sister did somehow manage to wiggle her way into their circle, then she was as catty as they were."

Poppy glanced at Rhett, then back to Linden. "Cora

wasn't popular. Her only friends were in youth group. She didn't have a mean bone in her body."

"Then she was a target or being used. Those chicks were ruthless. I seen 'em in action at parties out at the W. That's what they all called the Weaverman property back then."

"Did you go out there the night Cora went missing?"

"Nah." He tapped his pen on the desk. "No party. I'd have heard if there was. Besides, if there had been a big shindig, someone would have seen something and come forward, don't you think?"

"Maybe. Except if a bunch of kids were out there drinking and doing drugs, they'd want to keep it quiet for fear of getting in trouble by parents." She tapped her index finger on her bottom lip. "You remember any of these other girls that were bullied by this mean-girl group? Now that they're older, they might be willing to share their stories, give me some insight. Enjoy a little payback."

He chuckled. "Unless they bought weed from me, I don't know names. Sorry."

"If you remember, call me." She handed him her card and they started for the door.

"Wait. Yes, I do. Her brother went off to the military and moved back home not too long ago. Works for the sheriff now. Detective or something."

"Monty Banner?"

"Banner. Yeah, that's it."

Poppy's eyebrows rose. She must be thinking what Rhett was. Why would Monty Banner be dating a girl who had bullied his sister in high school? And did it have anything to do with not divulging the information to them?

* * *

Poppy plopped into the rental car seat, her mind buzzing with the new information and where it could lead—if anywhere. "I don't remember anything about those girls being bullies. But then, I didn't pay much attention to what didn't personally affect me. I did, however, look out for Cora and she never once said anyone was messing with her." She rubbed her temples. "What if Linden was trying to throw suspicion on anyone but himself?" If Cora had taken her terrible advice, purchased marijuana from Linden then regretted it, if Linden had caught wind she might rat him out, he may have killed her.

"We can continue to look into him. See if he has any priors. In the meantime, let's run down this lead." She called Sheriff Pritchard, put him on speaker and relayed the new update. "Can you tell us where we might find Banner's sister?"

"Candy. Works part-time at the library and she's a photographer."

"Thanks. And if you wouldn't let Monty know, that would be great."

"Won't say a word. But Monty is a stand-up guy. A war hero."

"Either way." She hurriedly ended the call. "Let's try the library first."

The small library was across town, behind the courthouse. The square was in full swing with shoppers. The scent of grilled beef wafted on the air and Poppy's stomach rumbled. It had been a few hours since she'd choked down a stale doughnut and lukewarm coffee.

The railings on the concrete stairs leading to the library were lined with garland and silver bells. Bright green wreaths with red velvet bows graced the glass doors. Inside the library foyer, they were met with a colorfully lit Christmas tree made from books and stacked canned goods nearby for a Christmas food drive. Red and green paper lanterns hung from the ceiling tiles, and red and green lights draped the tops of the bookshelves.

"You go see if you can find Candy Banner, and I'm going to see if the reference section carries old yearbooks. Maybe we can peruse the annuals. Pictures say a thousand words or something like that, right? You can find out a lot about social life from a high school yearbook," Rhett said.

Poppy didn't disagree; they were running out of options. "Have at it." She strolled to the information desk and was greeted by an older woman wearing a Mrs. Claus costume.

"Can I help you?" she asked.

"I'm looking for Candy Banner. Is she in today?"

"I'm afraid not. She's working at Santa's Village as a photographer. She takes the loveliest pictures. She only works here part-time."

"Thanks for your time." She hurried back to the reference section to see Rhett's mile-wide grin.

"What are you doing? Dare I ask?" Poppy asked.

"Research," he mused.

Poppy caught the headline. "Why are you in the seniors' section when you know good and well..." Realization dawned. "Hey! Get out of my senior section."

Rhett low-whistled. "You look nothing like this now."

"Well, times have changed." Back then her hair had hung past her shoulders, and she'd been more lithe than lean muscled due to running but no weight training. And her eye liner was more pronounced. Lips cherry red. It was kind of her thing. He closed the book and grinned at her with smug satisfaction.

"What?" she huffed.

"Nothing. I like you better now."

She rolled her eyes. "Candy Banner works as a photographer and is taking photos at Santa's Village."

"Ah. I noticed when I was doing real research she was on the yearbook staff. Guess her love of the camera stuck with her. Also, there were several members of the science club with Mr. Simms. I think we need to talk to him. Teachers have knowledge about cliques and such. We could ask him about Savannah and her mean-girl crew."

True. He'd only been questioned on whether he knew who might have not liked Cora or if she'd ever mentioned boyfriends or wanting to run away—which had been a joke—but that was the only path the detectives at that time had to walk down.

"Miss Poppy!"

Poppy turned and Beth beamed as she stood with her bunny under her arm and a children's book in her hand. Delilah waved.

"Hi, Beth," Poppy said, thankful for the distraction. She didn't want to rehash her high school days or photos with Rhett any further. She returned Delilah's wave.

"I've been to story time," Beth said with pure delight shining in her eyes. Her hair was pulled back in two green barrettes. She was sunshine in a dark place. Everything good about the world.

"You have? What story did you listen to?" Poppy asked.

"*Runaway Bunny.* It's about a bunny that wants to run away, but his mommy tells him if he runs away she will run after him. We shouldn't run away. We should be who we are."

Poppy grinned, unfamiliar with the storybook. "You're right. You should never run away." If only she'd told Cora that instead of telling her to go. To run to trouble—and ultimately to her death. Instead of telling her to be who she was meant to be, Poppy had persuaded her to be someone else. Someone rebellious disguised as adventurous, out of sheer jealousy and a thirst to have her parents' praise, for once, instead of Cora receiving it. "You're exactly who you're supposed to be, Beth."

Was Poppy? Hadn't she been running since Cora's death—even before?

She couldn't seem to get within two feet of this woman before she wanted to break down. It was as if Beth's purity reflected how filthy Poppy was inside. She wanted to run away. Be someone she wasn't.

"You are too, Poppy," Beth said. "God doesn't make mistakes." She leaned in close. "But people do. I spilled my tea on the carpet this morning. It ran all over and I was scared it would stain the pretty floor, but it didn't. Delilah has special cleaner and I think God uses special cleaner to fix our mistakes." A million-watt smile warmed her face like sunshine. "Have you ever spilled your tea, Poppy?"

She was going to lose it and have a mental breakdown right here in the middle of Gray Creek Library. Her throat grew tight and the backs of her eyes burned like raging fire. She hadn't spilled tea, but she'd made plenty of stains on the carpet of her life and had been trying to scrub them clean ever since. But no matter how much good she did—how many cases she solved and closed—it never removed the stains.

No, she had no special cleaner of her own.

Come now, and let us reason together, saith the Lord: though your sins be as scarlet, they shall be as white as snow; though they be red like crimson, they shall be as wool.

A verse she hadn't thought of in forever struck her heart like a penetrating sword, cutting deep. Was the Lord giving her hope that she could be stain free even after all she'd done? After how far she'd run? How mad she had been at Him? She could remember the insulting words she'd hurled at Him over the years. Could even that be forgiven and cleansed?

"Not tea," she whispered because that was all she had. "But I've made messes. Lots of messes."

"You want to read a book with me?" she asked.

"Oh honey," Delilah interjected, "Agent Holliday has a lot of work to do. She solves cases like Chase in *Paw Patrol*."

"'Chase is on the case!'" Beth cheered. "Do you solve your cases like Chase?"

Poppy had no clue who Chase was, or even what *Paw Patrol* was.

"Agent Poppy," Rhett interjected, "solves more cases than the rest of her team. She's very good and crazy smart."

Poppy's insides slid further into a pile of goo. "I think I have a few minutes to read a story with you." She looked at Rhett and his eyes shone with compassion and something she couldn't quite put her finger on. He gave her a nod and she put her arm around Beth. "What book would you like to read?"

"We can find a Chase-on-the-case book!"

"Sounds perfect."

Poppy spent the next thirty minutes reading books with Beth and talking about how fun it was to live in a B&B and meet new friends each day. Her life was an adventure. Poppy glanced across the library where Rhett sat talking with Delilah. Both had been tasked with the responsibility of caring for their younger sister with some challenges. Poppy had failed. Delilah was thriving with a wonderful business.

Rhett answered his phone and slipped away, then re-entered the library and caught her attention.

Poppy took Beth's hand. "I'm afraid I have to go. Poppy is on the case!"

Beth laughed and walked with her to Delilah and Rhett. He pulled Poppy aside. "I called Mr. Simms. He's out of town and won't return until later tomorrow, but said he'd be happy to talk with us. So I called the former assistant principal—the head principal at that time passed away—and according to her, Savannah, Maya and Natalie terrorized girls who, quote, unquote, got in their way or were rumored to have flirted with or expressed interest in Dylan."

"Like Cora."

"She gave me two names she knew for sure of girls who had been victimized. They had reported them numerous times. Melissa Mann and Candy Banner."

"Who called you? I saw you get up and leave."

"Oh, that was my mom asking about the case and if it would be wrapped up in time for me to come for Christmas." Torment and sadness darkened his usually warm eyes. She knew that feeling well.

"Maybe you should go. Fly in for Christmas Day. I'll be fine."

"Killer's gonna take Christmas off, you think?"

"If he has any kind of family, I do. And all our suspects have roots here. But who knows. Either way, they clearly miss you."

Her parents had stopped asking if she'd come years ago. They had gone from asking if she would be coming to assuming she wouldn't.

"I know they do. It's just…" His jaw pulsed and he searched her eyes as if wrestling with what he wanted to say next. Finally he blew a heavy breath, and the intensity and turmoil in his eyes disappeared. "And anyway, you'll be alone on Christmas if I leave."

Another wave of mental anguish enveloped her. "I'm alone every Christmas, Rhett. I'm no fun either."

"Well, that's a given," he teased. "I'm not saying I want to spend Christmas with you for any other reason than I know the minute I'm gone you'll do something stupid. Like sneak down chimneys of suspects in a Santa costume to pilfer through their homes for what will surely become inadmissible evidence."

Poppy chuckled. "I could even bug the bows and eat the cookies. I do love cookies."

"And if you do find incriminating evidence, I don't need you hijacking the killer in your Santa sack to take back to the North Pole for torturing—I mean questioning. No, in your case I mean torture." Amusement brought his bereaved eyes back to life.

"You're real proud of your little metaphor, aren't you? And I'd never take him to the North Pole. It's too cold. I hate the cold."

"Which you make known hourly." He rolled his eyes.

"It's not a metaphor. It's a—I don't know—a story within a story." He nodded with satisfaction. "And, yes, I am proud."

"Well, speaking of Santa, let's head to his village and talk to Candy Banner. See how naughty Savannah and her minions were."

"Christmas is coming early," Rhett quipped, rubbing his hands together.

Rhett never horsed around like this or humored her ridiculousness. She was seeing a side to him she liked even more—one that was playful and goofy and not so staunch—and therefore it must end, though it was terribly amusing. "Okay, enough with this. It's getting annoying even for me." She paused. "I think it's a play on words."

"Idiom? Which you never get right."

"Hmm…" If he only knew.

They said their goodbyes to Delilah and Beth and rushed out into the frosty air. "I hope this village is indoors." Poppy shivered. "I really do hate the cold." She bent forward fighting the wind as a brand-new shiver raked over her spine.

"Talk about getting annoying," he muttered.

She ignored him and scanned the charming downtown square. Nothing about this moment was charming. No matter how decorated the boutiques and shops were, or how nice the laughter of people shopping on late lunch breaks was.

Something sinister lurked on the currents of the wintery gales. Invisible eyes on Poppy and Rhett could be felt.

"I got a bad feeling, Wallace," Poppy murmured. "Really bad."

Chapter 8

Santa's Village was located inside a small brick activity center with concrete flooring and heat, which was all Poppy cared about. "Holly Jolly Christmas" played in the background as shoppers perused homemade Christmas crafts, candles and goodies. Poppy paused on the boiled peanuts. She hadn't had those since she was a kid. Rhett pointed to the concessions.

"We can make a purchase on our way to talk to Candy Banner."

"Nah. They smell good, though." The crowd was entirely too large for a Monday afternoon. Didn't people work? Her stomach rumbled. "Okay, we do have to eat lunch. And just so you know, if someone is selling turkey legs, it's on."

"Like Donkey Kong." Rhett chuckled as Poppy stepped up to the counter and ordered a warm bag of boiled peanuts. Cajun style. Perfection. She shared a few with him.

"Where's the photos with Santa?"

"Follow the mothers dragging dressed-up, screaming children and we'll be sure to find it." She popped a peanut, shell and all, into her mouth and felt the kick of cayenne. "I need a Coke."

He agreed and bobbed and weaved past the booth stacked with monogrammed stockings. They maneuvered through the large rectangular building until they reached a big sleigh with reindeer and women in elf costumes handing out suckers to children who were in line to tell Santa what they wanted for Christmas. Babies bawled while moms giggled.

Candy stood behind the camera while a young blonde girl shook a jingly toy at a toddler who was having none of it. "You couldn't pay me enough to do this job," Poppy muttered.

"Agreed," Rhett said and snagged a handful of peanuts.

In between kiddos, Poppy approached Candy. The woman was petite. Pretty green eyes. "Candy Banner?"

"Yes."

Poppy made introductions and asked if they could have a moment to speak. "If you give me these next five in line, I'll put a sign out for a break. We could use one." She did appear a little frazzled.

"Sure. We'll look around." Poppy went on the search for a vendor to buy a drink from, and after that they bumped into Delilah and Beth again.

"Are you getting your picture made with Santa?" Beth asked.

"She should," Rhett offered through a chuckle.

"No, we're on a case." Poppy winked at Beth.

"We're going on a train ride next. The Polar Express." Beth beamed and Delilah chuckled.

"It's our annual day to shop and go on the train ride. We wait until Christmas Eve for photos with Santa. The ride is actually pretty fun. They serve cookies and hot chocolate. Only lasts about an hour—a few miles forward then backward. But it's decorated festively and the music gets you in the Christmas spirit."

"You should come!" Beth said. "You get a ticket!"

It was hard to tell this woman no. In so many ways she reminded Poppy of Cora. Kind and trusting and full of wonder and life. The pull to go was strong, but they had so much work to do. People to talk to. Like Candy.

"Well, we'll see." That was the best she could offer. They headed back to Santa's workshop and waited while the last child had his picture made, then Candy yanked off the green elf hat and raked a hand through her hair.

"There's an open food area around back. We can grab a table if that's okay."

They followed her to an area that had been sectioned off with velvet red cording and found a picnic table near the corner. Poppy explained why they were in town.

"I knew Cora," Candy said. "We had algebra together and she helped me out a lot. She was good at math. Me? Not so much."

Poppy sipped her can of Coke. "Did you know Cora had a crush on Dylan Weaverman?"

Candy nodded. "I saw the doodles in the back of her notebook. I warned her that was a bad move."

"Because of Savannah and her entourage of mean girls?" Poppy asked while Rhett sat quietly listening and letting her take the lead.

"They could be spiteful, petty and vindictive." Candy's eyes narrowed.

"We heard you were a target."

Candy groaned. "My freshman year I dropped my backpack and Dylan helped me pick up all the junk and books that had spilled. I thanked him and Savannah saw it all. She spread a vicious rumor about me being pregnant and not knowing who the father was. It was humiliating. She told me if I ever looked at Dylan again, she'd do far worse. She also trashed my car and scratched ugly words into it with her keys—though I couldn't prove it was her or her friends, I know it was."

All for Dylan's kindness. "Did she think you liked him?"

"Anyone who made eye contact with Dylan was obviously in love with him. She did all sorts of mean things to girls over him. And her minions went right along with her. They were her eagle eyes. I don't know what Dylan saw in her. Maybe he was afraid to dump her for fear she'd ruin his life. She had the power to do it."

"And what about now? Are they still mean girls?" Poppy asked.

A kid raced by with a huge corn dog in his hand and his mother chased him down, hollering for him to stop.

"They're still friends but I think they grew out of it. Brad changed Savannah. She was less mean after they started dating. I was shocked when he moved here and she and Dylan were over. I mean, who goes to all that vindictive trouble only to break up a year later?" She sighed. "I'm glad, though. Girls were free from her evil plans."

Maybe it was all water under the bridge then with

Maya. But Poppy still wanted to know. "And what about Maya?"

"And my brother? She apologized for her part in my humiliation. I let it go. It could have been worse, I guess. They've only been dating about three months. I don't see it lasting. Maya is a serial dater, if you know what I mean. I'm more worried about Monty. She's gonna break his heart."

Rhett leaned forward. "Did Savannah know that Cora and Dylan had a crush on each other? What would Savannah do about that back then?"

"If Savannah knew Cora liked Dylan, it would be on, and if it was true that Dylan liked Cora..." Her eyes said it all. Savannah might have done something irreversible. "But the thing is, Savannah usually kept her hands clean and had her girls do the dirty work."

Poppy shared a silent exchange with Rhett.

"Thank you for your time." Poppy stood, and she and Rhett threw away their trash and moved through the hustle and bustle.

"You know, we could take an hour-long train ride," Rhett said. "I can tell you really have a connection with Beth." Mr. Observant hadn't missed that, but it was obvious. And true. "She's really a sweet woman. And I've never been on a train."

"Neither have I." She shrugged.

"We have no leads until we talk to Mr. Simms tomorrow. We could approach Savannah again but she'd likely admit to being mean but not doing anything nefarious to Cora. Let's see what Simms says first. Go from there."

He was right. They had no other leads at the moment and might not have anything more if Simms couldn't give them any insight or new information. They could only hope the lab would find trace evidence on the bomb particles and the debris found in the well. And they still had that bracelet. It could have belonged to any of the girls. Or someone else entirely. Once they had Simms's interview done, she'd go back to the women about their pasts, the bracelet and hopefully new details gained from Simms. She could not fail her family and Cora.

They met up with the Cordray sisters and then followed them to the train station. In line, Delilah leaned over. "It's more crowded at night and the lights are festive, but Beth prefers the daylight trip. I'm glad we can do this. She'd been disappointed when I told her we would be traveling and unable to attend. We rarely travel during the holidays."

"Were you going to visit family?"

"My aunt in Georgia. But she ended up going to California to her brother-in-law's. Our dad passed last year and Mom died three years ago in a car accident."

"I'm sorry."

"Thank you. I've always known Beth would be mine to care for."

Beth was explaining how to paint a rainbow to Rhett, who had given her his undivided attention.

He really was a wonderful man.

She tried not to let the tender moment take root. She refocused on Delilah. "Still, your parents' deaths must have been traumatic for you both."

"It was. Beth was my saving grace. She was grieving, but mostly she wanted to light up my life and comfort me. She is a comfort." She grinned as Beth prattled on with Rhett.

"Was it hard for you? Growing up with Beth?"

Delilah's laugh was wistful. "At times. I felt neglected. She took up a lot of Mom and Dad's attention. But it was hard to be angry at her."

Poppy had been mad at Cora so many times. Jealous of her.

"But there were times I was bitterly jealous. Now, she's all I have and I love her dearly. She's a joy to all our guests too. She's special and precious." Delilah wiped a tear. "I worry about what will happen if something happens to me. I pray God keeps me going so I can tend to her."

"She is special. I've enjoyed being around her." That was about all Poppy could say. What would happen to Beth if her sister tragically died? The thought concerned her. It would be too easy for her to be taken advantage of.

They received their tickets and entered a train car. White lights and pine garland draped the windows. Little Christmas trees were anchored to each table, and Santa's helpers came through delivering sugar cookies and hot chocolate in red and green insulated cups. The soundtrack from *The Polar Express* played in the background, and the engineer came through and greeted everyone. He was dressed like the engineer from the movie.

The whistle blew then they were off down the tracks. They sang Christmas carols and enjoyed the wooded scenery on either side of the train. Snow flurries swirled against the dusky sky then dusted the trees and grass. Kids clapped and stuck their noses against the windows. Some of them had probably never witnessed real snow.

Cora would have loved a Christmas train ride.

"I'm going to find a restroom," Poppy said and exited the car, moving into the next one. A helper told her there was a bathroom at the end of the carriage. She thanked her and maneuvered to the car next to the caboose.

She paused before entering the ladies' room. The hairs on her neck prickled, but the car was empty. She entered and splashed water on her face. She hadn't wanted to ruin anyone's enjoyment but Cora weighed heavily on her mind and she had needed a moment. Once she toweled off her face, she exited the ladies' room.

That same creepy feeling came over her again. She started back toward her car but a man burst out from under one of the tables, charging her and shoving her to the floor as she reached for her gun. He caught what she was doing, and they struggled for the weapon; he batted her hand against the floor and she lost it.

Poppy screamed, hoping someone might hear her, but the odds were slim with the loud music and even louder children. They were several empty cars away from people. But she tried anyway and fought and clawed. If she could tear away his ski mask…identify him…

His gloved hands wrapped around her throat and squeezed. The pressure was unbearable, burning. Fighting to free her leg, she kneed him, then scrambled up but there was nowhere to go. He blocked her path to freedom. Her gun was across the floor behind him. The only way out of this alive was to fight her way out.

She braced herself as he shoved her against the train car door. She punched him in the side, connected with ribs and heard him grunt. He wasn't getting out of this unscathed no matter how it went down for her. Poppy would leave a distinguishing mark and Rhett would observe it. It was his superpower. Her attacker's body pressed against hers, pinning her legs, and she head-butted him—her own brain seeming to rattle around from the force.

He growled and released the door handle, shoving it open.

Frigid wind knocked her off balance and she grabbed the handicap rails and braced her feet against each side of the threshold to keep from tumbling out. The roar of the engine was deafening.

In a battle of tangled limbs, Poppy fought to stay inside as the assailant used all his force to shove her out.

The door to the car opened, drawing their attention, and Poppy froze. No! Beth entered with her little bunny. Poppy's lungs turned to iron.

"Hi, Poppy."

The attacker paused as if unsure what to do. Poppy couldn't push past him, couldn't do anything without Beth becoming collateral damage.

Poppy had no other options. Beth would not lose her life by being in the wrong place at the wrong time.

Poppy grabbed the attacker's coat collar, then let her foot go, startling him as she took him off the side of the train with her.

Rhett finished off his hot chocolate as Delilah discussed her plans for opening another B&B with a friend in the next county. Suddenly Beth rushed into the car, tears streaming down her cheeks.

"Honey, what's wrong?" Delilah asked. "Could you not find the bathroom?"

"Poppy jumped off the train."

Rhett went on high alert. "What?"

"She jumped off the train with a man in a mask."

Rhett bolted, his blood racing wildly as he raced to the bathrooms. How had a killer gotten on the train? How would he have even known he'd have a chance to attack Poppy? So many questions peppered his mind. At the back car, the door was open.

The train wasn't moving incredibly fast, but enough to cause broken bones or other injuries. Had he shoved her off the train? Beth said she jumped. If she jumped off after the killer…

Rhett scanned the woods for any sign of her or the masked attacker, his heart hammering against his ribs.

Poppy was out there with a murderer. Possibly injured and vulnerable. He was wasting time standing here. Without weighing consequences or the danger, he leaped out of the train, landing on the hard, cold ground and jarring his teeth. His head thudded on impact, and his hip took the brunt. He rolled several times and ended up on his back, the breath knocked from his lungs.

Forcing himself to stand on wobbly legs, he pushed forward and in the direction she might have fallen.

Panic and terror pumped his feet faster. He surveyed the woods, hoping to catch a glimpse of her, when a gunshot rang out and his blood curdled.

"Poppy!" he bellowed and pushed even harder, faster.

In the distance, he spotted her darting into the tree line. Rhett fired into the woods, opposite Poppy as not to hit her, but hoping to scare the attacker from shooting again.

Praise the Lord. She was upright and alive.

"Poppy!" he hollered again. No more shots were fired. The attacker was likely jetting through the woods. Rhett found her a few feet inside the thick covering of trees, bent over at the waist panting. Red marks colored her neck; dirt and scratches covered her cheeks. Her pants and sweater were torn. Rhett closed the distance between them and took her by the shoulders, unsure if he wanted to kiss her or shake her for scaring him half to death—or both.

"Did you—did you jump off a train for me?" she asked.

Heat climbed up his neck. "I guess I did." Without any real thought too. No calculating risks. Just taking a dangerous one. He was going to have to chew on the reason why he would do something that cowboy-like. "Are you hurt?"

"I'm gonna have severe bruises. He came out of nowhere. He must have gotten on the train and tucked himself into an empty car hoping for a chance to get me alone, but that was a long shot."

"It's a desperate move on his part. We're getting close somehow—maybe by following the drugs. There was no guarantee he'd get you or me alone. Unless he was already on the ride and used it as an opportunity."

"And he happens to keep a ski mask in his pocket?" She raked a hand through her tangled hair. "Who carries those?"

"Anyone. Hunters? He shot off through the woods like a man who knew them well." Rhett brushed some dirt from her cheek. Another impulsive move. They were becoming one too many. "Did you jump off to catch him?"

Poppy caressed her cheek as if she could still feel his touch. "No." She told him about Beth interrupting and how her only choice was to jump and take him with her. Now he didn't want to shake her. Just kiss her. She was selfless. Brave. Willing to sacrifice herself. She laughed. "He may have been my saving grace. I landed on him and he took the brunt of the fall."

Rhett balled his hands at his side to keep from drawing her into his arms. No more impulsive decisions today. "Once you landed, what happened?"

"I bounced off him and rolled, knocking my breath from me. I sat up and he was still catching his breath. I took off running and he shot at me. Then you fired and sent him farther into the woods. He got away. Again," she said with force. "But he's got to be wounded too. Bruised. Battered. Scratches. Something. That may be to our benefit."

Definitely. "Do you need a doctor?"

"No. But I'm gonna need a bottle of aspirin and a few ice packs." She rubbed her lower back. "You?"

"I'm feeling it. You know, I used to leap off the couch, pretending it was a train and I was catching robbers. Never really thought I'd actually do it in real life. Doesn't quite feel like jumping onto a pile of pillows."

Poppy snickered. "Sure, it does. If the pillows are made of concrete." She surveyed the area. "Now we get to work out the sore muscles by hoofing it back to town. You think when the train comes back through it'll stop for us?"

They followed the tracks that led back to the station. "Doubtful." After a few moments of silence Rhett spoke up. "That was a brave thing you did to protect Beth. I'm proud of you. Don't get me wrong—you scared me half to death. Beth came back crying saying you'd jumped off the train with a man in a mask and... Well, I'm proud of you, Doc." He winked and she laughed.

"I'm no daisy."

Rhett chuckled and it hurt his sides as she referred back to their favorite Western film. Wyatt Earp. Doc Holliday. No, she was not a wimp. She was tough and brave—which he admired, but what had driven her to jump off a train to protect Beth wasn't her tough side; it was the deeply tender and caring side that she often tried to hide. The side he had seen more of in the past few days than in the few years of their working relationship. And he wasn't sure what to do with that.

His physical attraction toward her was no big deal. Plenty of women were attractive, but it wasn't simply physical, and that presented a problem.

Because he feared his dive off that moving train was motivated by far more than backing up his colleague.

The train passed them, moving slowly enough for him to catch a glimpse of a worried Delilah looking out the window. "You have Delilah's number?"

"No. Just the number to the B&B. Do you think she tried to get the engineer to stop?"

Rhett shrugged as the caboose passed them by. "Too bad we can't jump back on like we jumped off."

She snort-laughed and grabbed her side. "I don't think I can hop a puddle let alone a train, Wallace. Slow and stealthy is about all I got in me."

It had only been a matter of time before she messed up an idiom again. But he found he wasn't as annoyed as before… It was…no. He was not going to think of it as endearing. "Steady. It's slow and steady."

"Whatever, Wallace," she quipped with her usual amount of indifference and snarl. But that ship had sailed. Her gruffness and sharp teeth were nothing more than a façade covering up the real Poppy Holliday— the woman who was willing to sacrifice herself for the people she cared about, and there was no mistaking that Poppy had grown to care for Beth in the short amount of time she'd known her. There was no bite along with that bark. It was nothing more than a defense mechanism.

But why use defenses against him?

"I'm just saying."

Finally, they made it to the train station, where they found Delilah and Beth frantically talking to the manager. Beth spotted Poppy and squealed, and Delilah visibly relaxed. They came running and Beth wrapped her arms around Poppy. "I prayed for you, Poppy."

"Thank you, hon. I needed it."

Delilah hugged them too. "We told the train employees what happened, but they wouldn't stop even when they found the door open. I was terrified and trying to get them to go back out there and look for you. What on earth happened?"

Poppy glanced at Beth. "Beth, you want to go get a Coke?" She and Beth left Rhett with Delilah so he could explain without terrifying her sister or causing her anxiety.

"I need to call the sheriff."

"Rudy would want to know for sure."

Rhett raised his eyebrows. He'd noticed Delilah was on a first-name basis with him the night of the explosion, and he was familiar with Beth too. "You two close?"

Delilah's cheeks flushed. "It's complicated. His wife left him and took their daughter. We…had some things in common, but we both knew if there was a chance to reconcile, he needed to take it, and there might be. We're friends."

Then why the interest in Poppy? Because it was hard

not to be attracted to her, or maybe Rhett had misinterpreted his appreciation and kind gestures because... because he'd been jealous.

How ridiculous could Rhett be?

Poppy and Beth returned with drinks. She gave Rhett a bottle of water. Hers was over half-empty already. After leaving the train station, Poppy had called the sheriff to let him know what had transpired and that they were coming into the SO now to give statements.

"After statements, I want a soft bed and several hours of sleep."

"Best idea all day," she said. "Tomorrow we'll start fresh with Solomon Simms."

Surely, they'd get a few hours of uninterrupted sleep. But the way their days were going, that might not be possible. Not when a killer had been thrust from a train and had almost been taken out by the one woman he was targeting. He'd be furious and even more determined.

And that meant Rhett wouldn't be sleeping.

Not when his number-one priority was keeping Poppy safe.

Chapter 9

Poppy woke up the next morning aching and sore. A hot shower had helped with the tight muscles, and pain medication had taken off the edge, but her head still ached and she was in a crummy mood.

Rhett hadn't been a peach to be around either. They'd tested each other's nerves over breakfast and he'd answered most of her questions in grunts as they drove to the sheriff's office, but he'd used actual words with Sheriff Pritchard, Detective Teague and Detective Banner during an update and briefing about the attacks and the news that Dylan's death was being ruled an accident due to drunk driving.

Poppy noted they should push harder, and that maybe Detective Teague wasn't doing his best since his wife could be involved.

That had gone over about as well as feeding steak

to a toothless baby. Teague had choked on it and spit it out. Maybe Poppy had been harsh and overly critical due to the pain and the fact that they were no further in the case than she'd been before. All she had to show for her investigative efforts were dozens of bruises, aches and pains.

Sheriff Pritchard had reminded her she wasn't here to investigate Dylan's death or play judge over teenagers' past behavior.

But if Savannah's behavior was directly linked to Cora's murder, then it had to be followed. If Dylan had hurt Cora, or if Savannah had—with intent or accidentally—Teague wasn't the one Poppy wanted on the case. But neither was Monty Banner. Because Savannah wasn't the only mean girl. Poppy had to look at Maya Marx and Natalie Carpenter-Weaverman and Ian Kirkwood. Any one of them, or all of them, could have harmed Cora.

And there was still Dylan Weaverman himself. He could have been overcome with guilt and taken his life for a part he'd played in Cora's death. Or he could have been killed because he wanted to go to the authorities about Cora when her body was found. The timeline was too close, and she wasn't buying that his death was an accident—though he had been drinking enough to be drunk. Anyone who knew him knew he had an alcohol problem, which meant someone could have used that to his or her advantage.

Somehow.

She pinched the bridge of her nose and paced the small room they'd been using as a work space. They'd come in around ten and it was nearing noon now. Simms would be back in town soon. She was champing at the bit to talk to him.

If Solomon Simms had heard plans to harm or even humiliate Cora and done nothing about it, he'd rue the day he sat on his hands.

She couldn't wait around and do nothing, and Dylan's death was still gnawing at her.

She grabbed her phone off the table and called his older brother, Zack. He answered on the third ring. "Agent Holliday. How are you today?"

News had spread fast about what she and Rhett had gone through yesterday, and of course their cars blowing up had been the talk of the town. "I'm alive and that's about all I can say so far. I wanted to talk to you about your brother again."

"Sure." A door clicked and the background grew quiet. "I'm helping out my wife today and the animals don't know how to stay silent during a phone call."

Poppy waited for him to get settled.

"Sheriff Pritchard told me they ruled Dylan's death accidental. Is there something new in the case?"

"I'm struggling with the fact his accident happened the same night that the remains of my sister were found on your property. And what was he doing out that time of night?"

"He was drinking, Agent. I doubt we'll know the answer to that."

"What if he was going out to the property? Looking for something? Or what if he was there because he felt bad about something that happened in the past?"

"You think my little brother killed your sister and was out there drunk, looking for incriminating evidence? He'd have fallen down that well too."

"I never said anything about looking for evidence down a well."

"Wouldn't that be the obvious place?"

Poppy's gut roiled. "Do you know anything about that night, Zack? Maybe he got drunk. Did something he'd never have done sober. Maybe he told you. We found a bracelet in that well. Know anyone who might have worn a silver bracelet? Let me send you a photo." She put him on speaker and sent the photo of the evidence.

"I don't know anything. My brother didn't do any…" He trailed off as the text came through and the line went silent for a few beats. "I don't recognize that bracelet."

"Maybe Dylan would. Maybe he knew it would be found and decided to come forward. Maybe the owner of that bracelet silenced him before he could and planned to take her chances of it never being linked to her." It could have belonged to any of the mean girls. And Natalie Carpenter-Weaverman had a lot to lose. A husband, a vet practice…her freedom. She and the whole gang she kept close tabs on would lose a lot. No one got a chance to snag that piece of jewelry—if that was what the killer was out there doing that night. Ian Kirkwood. Zack Weaverman himself. Or someone else who had been involved that night they didn't know about.

"Or maybe it fell down there another time. At another party. Prior to your sister's death."

"Maybe. But someone is going to recognize it. Show it to Natalie. See if she does. She was tight with Dylan then and leading up to his death. She went to those parties. She knew Cora. That's all I'm saying."

"The next time you have something to say, you can do it with our lawyers present." He hung up. Rhett entered the room. His eyes looked tired, with dark half moons underneath. A sudden urge to hug and soothe him overcame her, and before she could talk herself out of it, she was on her feet and twining her arms around his back with her head tucked under his chin. His muscles tensed against hers as if he'd been expecting a foe rather than a friend, but then he relaxed and his hands rested lightly on her upper back.

"I'm sorry for all that's happened, Rhett. I didn't want any of this for you." Most of the night she'd been awake picturing him leaping off the train to rescue her and poking at the idea that there had been more to the risk than saving a colleague in danger, but she didn't attempt to explore the idea further out of sheer terror.

Yet here she was hugging him, feeling that same sense of safety and the security of hope and home fill her. "I mean, I told you I'd take every measure to find who killed Cora. I never expected you to."

"You were in trouble. What other option did I have?"

He could have pulled rank and had the train stopped. Or called the sheriff. Or both.

Jumping off the train was reckless. Impulsive. It went against the grain of who Rhett was.

"You had options," she murmured.

Rhett's chin rested on her head. "The only option was getting to you."

Like the mom in *Runaway Bunny*. Pursuing the little bunny because he belonged to her. Chasing him down. Being exactly what he needed in every situation.

A verse that her mother always spoke over them before bedtime swept across her heart.

Fear not, for I have redeemed thee; I have called thee by thy name; thou art Mine.

Thou art Mine. Pursued. Loved. Redeemed. A statement of belonging. A statement that should bring peace to a fearful, searching heart. In Rhett's arms, at least right now, she felt like she might belong.

One thing was for sure: she felt no fear in this moment.

Confess your faults one to another, and pray one for another, that ye may be healed.

She hadn't thought of these Scriptures in years, and they rushed into her memory now like a warm flood, as if they'd never left her heart. Would confession do her heart good? Bring healing? Poppy was like a sweater being eaten by moths. Gaping holes destroying what was once lovely and useful.

Withdrawing from Rhett, she gazed into his eyes. "It's my fault Cora is dead. I've never told anyone that. I was jealous of her sickness—it's horrible, I know. I wished I could be ill because then I'd have my parents' attention and unconditional love. I wouldn't have to be responsible for someone else. Others would tend to and take care of me. What kind of person is jealous over their sister's suffering? Delilah finds it a joy to care for Beth."

Rhett already thought she was a piece of work. How much more judgment could he unleash?

Tears filled her eyes and held, refusing to fall. "I was livid that she was everything good and I had to act like a fool to gain one scrap of attention. And that's what I did, Rhett. I acted foolishly and it never worked. But I kept doing it and expecting the same result—love from my parents. That's the very definition of insanity."

A hot tear slipped out of her eye, and Rhett caught it with his fingertip while his fingers remained cradling her cheek. "You were a girl with a girl's mind. You loved your sister. I know you did. Love is complicated."

Love was complicated. "I did—I do love her. But..." She touched his fingers, and her stomach fluttered. "I've never been in love...while I'm confessing."

He held her gaze and swallowed, his Adam's apple bobbing. "Neither have I."

But a truth whispered to her heart and she shut it out before it formed into words and could take root. She hadn't meant to go down this road, but her tongue had a mind of its own. She reeled back to where the topic of confession was supposed to be. On Cora. Not Poppy's heart. "I told Cora she never allowed herself to live and be free. That at least I was living my life and would have no regrets." She shook her head. "But I have so many of them. My accusations and that argument caused Cora to take chances she normally wouldn't. She looked up to me. Loved me. I drove her to hold that pot for a friend. And it was my words that fueled her to sneak out of the house that night. To go live a life of no regrets."

Torment flashed in Rhett's eyes and he pursed his lips. "Poppy, you are not to blame for her death."

"Except that I am. And now you know why I have to knock down every door and walk into every situation to bring her justice. But I don't expect you to do that too. You can't be jumping trains, Rhett. Not for me. I can't have any more deaths on my hands. I have enough blood there already."

If anyone could relate to Poppy's guilt, it was Rhett. But his situation had been much different. Poppy couldn't be blamed for choices Cora made over an argument, but Rhett had known the ice was dangerous—that's why it had been a dare. His action forced Keith's hand. If he'd have only turned down the dare.

But he hadn't.

And Poppy was right. He'd had other options concerning her safety after she jumped off the train, but he'd done what would get to her fastest—he'd leaped. Looking into her eyes in this moment, he wanted to take another leap.

But he wouldn't.

"Let me worry about my decisions. They are mine alone. We're a team. We have each other's backs. That's the job." He could keep telling himself that, but underneath the surface he knew it had become something more, something he continued to fight tooth and nail. He wasn't sure if he had enough strength to keep it up, but he'd have to muster it from deep down. He wanted predictable. Safe. Structured. Didn't want to get involved with someone he worked with for fear they wouldn't last, and then there would be too many complications.

Love was complicated. No...he wasn't going to admit to that emotion. He'd lose the battle if he let that word linger in his brain and on his tongue. Hearing her confession hadn't helped in the fight; it had only served to connect him even more deeply. He'd harbored the same thoughts and feelings, but Poppy had bared it all—to him alone. Her choice to share it with him revealed her level of trust and vulnerability.

He didn't owe her his own confession. Shouldn't reveal it for fear of what his own vulnerability might do, but he leaped anyway out of a compelling need for her to know how much he did understand her, how much he could identify.

"Poppy, I understand you more than you realize. I have a confession of my own that I've never told anyone either. You know my brother died. And that he drowned. But I get how you feel, because Keith's death actually was my fault." Saying those words out loud released some pent-up agony, especially when he saw compassion and not criticism in Poppy's eyes. No one could understand his sorrow like she did. He preceded to finish the sordid tale.

"That's why I don't go home at Christmas. When the ice cracked, my insides did too. I should've plunged in after him. I didn't. I stood in shock while he drowned. You'd think it'd be loud, you know? But it's deathly silent. After the initial struggle...it goes so quiet."

Poppy wiped her eyes and squeezed him until he felt completely safe, completely accepted even after sharing his darkest shame. He clung to her and buried his face in her hair, enjoying this freedom of being fully known yet still welcomed into an embrace.

"You make so much more sense now, Rhett. Why you calculate everything. Are overly cautious."

Exactly. The very reasons he couldn't be with her, and yet here he was hanging on to her like a lifeline. "This is why I know you're not to blame for Cora's death. You got in a typical sibling argument. Cora made her choice."

She pulled away and poked a finger in his chest. "And you were a boy taking a boy's dare. You panicked and the current took him under the ice, but if you had jumped in you'd have died."

And yet he'd jumped for her.

The door opened, jarring the moment, jarring his thoughts. Poppy stepped away and Detective Banner raised his eyebrows. That was twice he'd found them in what could appear an intimate moment. In its own way, it was the most intimate moment he'd ever shared with anyone—and he'd shared it with her.

Now what was he supposed to do?

"Solomon Simms is here. Said you had called and wanted to talk him. Got in to town a few minutes early and was in the neighborhood. He's in interview room one." He paused and batted a glance between them. "Y'all need another minute?"

"No," Poppy said. She had already snatched up her legal pad and pen and was striding to the door.

Rhett followed her into the interview room, where a man who looked more like a coach than a science teacher sat with a small cup of coffee. He was dressed in jeans and a button-down shirt with a gray cardigan over it. His buzzed hair was silvery blond.

"Mr. Simms," Poppy said. "Thank you for coming in of your own accord. I appreciate that."

Because he'd come in on his own, or because it cut short what had been happening between them?

"I want to help. I liked Cora. She was bright and an all-around sweet girl." Mr. Simms leaned forward, his arms on the table.

Poppy sat across from him. "I never had the privilege of taking one of your classes."

How old was this guy? He couldn't be but maybe a decade or so older than Poppy, putting him in his late twenties or early thirties back when they were in high school. No wonder the kids loved him. He wouldn't have been much more than one himself then.

"What can you tell us about the science club members, specifically Natalie Carpenter, Dylan Weaverman, Ian Kirkwood, Maya Marx and Savannah Steadman?"

"You think one of them had something to do with Cora's death?" Skepticism drew a line across his brow.

"Maybe."

Simms said he didn't believe any of them were capable of murder, and he wasn't aware of drugs being sold. However, he'd been fairly certain that Dylan liked Cora. "He tried to be her lab partner before Natalie could claim him as her own. I think she had an ulterior motive."

"Keeping Cora and Dylan apart?"

Mr. Simms leaned back in his chair. "Yes, but I don't think it was at Savannah's request. I suspected Natalie had a secret crush on Dylan herself."

This changed the game altogether. "After Savannah and Dylan broke up the following year, who did Natalie date? Surely you have an idea."

"I wouldn't say they dated, but Dylan and Natalie became inseparable. Even through college and up until she married Zack." Simms rubbed his chin and smirked. "I guess she ended up with the second-best brother."

Poppy held out her phone. "You recognize this bracelet?"

He studied the photo. "I can't say that I do. Sorry."

Poppy leaned forward. "Do you think Dylan would have hurt Cora?"

"No way. Dylan was a great kid. I'm not real sure what he was doing with Savannah Steadman. The best thing that happened to him, in my opinion, was Savannah meeting Brad Teague. I think things changed—she changed."

"Do you think if something went down with Cora involving Savannah and her cronies, he would have known?"

Dylan's death could have easily been over Cora. They needed some solid evidence. Rhett studied Mr. Simms's wheels turning. "I don't think so. But I don't really know."

They saw him out and Poppy rubbed her temples. "We may have been going at this all wrong. If Natalie had a secret crush on Dylan and knew he liked Cora—she may have had as much reason to get rid of her as Savannah had. She could have done something to my sister with the false pretense she was helping Savannah. All the while setting her own sights on him." She huffed. "Dylan is the key to this thing. My gut says so. Those girls and Ian Kirkwood are hiding the truth."

"What if Natalie was never over Dylan? What if they had a thing and his drinking was guilt over an affair all these years later, and not Cora's death? What if Zack found out and used the opportunity to kill him?"

"And the web thickens."

Rhett chuckled. "No. The *plot thickens*. The web is tangled. 'Oh, what a tangled web we weave.'"

"Either way," she said and lifted a shoulder. "We need to go back to all of them with this new information."

"I understand, but her husband needs some courtesy. She's more of a suspect now."

"That's fair."

Detective Teague's pen hung from his teeth as he clacked away on his computer. A mound of files sat beside him, along with a cup of coffee. He glanced up and spoke without removing the pen from between his teeth. "Agents."

"Detective," Poppy said, keeping her voice soft and friendly. "We need to inform you that our investigation is leading to your wife, as well as her friends, due to some ill-behaved-girl stuff involving Cora. We're going to have to pursue that lead."

He removed the pen from his lips and frowned. "You think Savannah may have knowledge of what happened to your sister?"

Knowledge…bloody hands…

"I don't know. Not until we talk to her again, but we felt you should know. I'm not sure if you're aware of Savannah's reputation in high school—"

"That she could be cruel to other girls?" His face softened. "Yeah. I know. She came from a home that looked happy on the outside, but inside was a rotten mess. Kind of like her as a teenager. She regrets the things she did back then and has even made amends to some of the girls she hurt. But she wouldn't physically hurt anyone, let alone murder them."

Poppy nodded as if she was in complete agreement with the detective. "I'm sorry about her childhood. Hurt people…hurt people. I know that well. But we do need to talk to her again, along with her closest girlfriends at that time, and it won't be as gentle, I'm afraid. Someone in that circle of friends—maybe all of them—is lying."

He paused and worked his jaw, but then he nodded. "I appreciate the heads-up."

Detective Banner breezed inside with a plastic bag that smelled amazing. Rhett was starving. He set it on Teague's desk. "What's going on here?"

Teague sighed. "Their investigation is leading them to Savannah—and Maya."

Monty Banner paused, then picked up his carton of chicken and dumplings and stabbed one with his fork. "Is that why you were at the clinic the other day? You think Maya was involved with your sister's death?"

"I don't know. But that's the only trail we have right now. So we're gonna hunt and sniff out what we can." She nodded toward the food. "Where'd you get that? It looks amazing."

"It is," Monty said with a grin. "Little Evergreen Café. Over by the Christmas Tree Farm. On Hull Road."

After a few more minutes of chitchat, they left the sheriff's office for lunch at the café.

Inside the tiny but cozy establishment decorated with all sizes of artificial pine trees, rustic tin, burlap and red trucks, Rhett guided her to a small table by the window, giving them a gorgeous view of the tree farm across the road. They scanned the brown paper menus in silence, then placed their orders for chicken and dumplings, green beans and corn muffins, along with sweet tea.

Poppy seemed deep in thought, staring off at the trees. "We never had a real Christmas tree," she said as the server brought their big glasses of honey-brown tea. One sip proved it was as sweet as it was big.

"We did. I personally haven't put up a tree in years. My sister bought me one of those little trees with fiber-optic lights. It sits on my breakfast bar. That's about as decorative as I get. Christmas doesn't have the same excitement since Keith died." There wasn't much festivity left.

"You know," she said, "we might not be big on Christmas anymore but you know who is? Delilah and Beth.

And you know what we ruined? Their Christmas tree. She said she was going to buy a pre-lit artificial when she had a chance now that the porch and windows are fixed, but we could always go next door and cut down some Christmas cheer. Besides, I could use some cheer right now. I'm feeling extremely noncheery."

He tossed the wadded-up straw paper at her nose. "Poppy, sometimes you have great ideas. Not always. But sometimes."

It had been ages since he'd gone out in the cold, smelled the pine and picked out a Christmas tree. He and Keith had always agreed on the same one.

Poppy ignored his teasing and drank her tea until their food arrived and they dug into their delicious lunch, barely speaking while they devoured it. After paying, they left the warm atmosphere of the hometown café for the gusty wind and pewter skies.

At the Christmas Tree Farm, they were told they could have their pick delivered. Which was a good thing since they didn't have a truck. Neither of them even owned a car right now.

The gales picked up and icy wind raced down the neck of his sweater but he didn't mind; his blood had been racing hot for days. The farm was void of customers and they had the pick of the litter.

"I like that one," Rhett said, pointing toward a medium-sized one. "Not too full. Not Charlie Brown pitiful either."

"Yeah. That's a pretty one." She nodded in satisfaction. "Tonight might actually be fun. I could use some—"

A shot rang out and the tree branches near Poppy's head exploded.

Chapter 10

Rhett grabbed Poppy around her waist and tossed her to the ground, shielding her with his body. "I don't know how far away the shots are coming from," he said through a strained whisper.

"I don't want to stick around to find out." Adrenaline jolted her system, sending her pulse spiking to dangerous levels.

"Me neither." Rhett drew his weapon and Poppy followed suit, hunching and keeping close to the branches for cover as they sprinted down the rows of trees.

Another projectile was fired and Poppy felt the sting and burn. "I've been grazed!" She grabbed her shoulder. Rhett halted but she motioned him to keep moving. "I'm fine. Let's change direction." Attempting to sound in control proved difficult. Fear propelled her forward as they pushed between the trees instead of running down the smooth paths between them.

Blindly running, they had no clue what was on the other side of the tree farm. Likely more woods, and the shooter had an advantage—he was probably local. Poppy hadn't lived here long enough to know all the trails, woods and back roads.

"Where are we going?" she asked as Rhett led the charge, as if he knew exactly where they were headed.

"Away."

If the situation wasn't life-threatening, she'd have laughed. Away. Good call.

Another shot sounded and instinctively she ducked. The shooter was close enough to get the shots off but far enough back they couldn't see him. Zigging and zagging, they maneuvered out of the trees and to a back road.

They could run down the pavement and hope for a car or take their chances in the woods. Neither option was great. "I don't know what to do!" Poppy declared.

"Woods. We're open targets and he's using a rifle. No way he can see us without a scope. We have a better chance of finding a hiding spot." Rhett motioned to keep running. Poppy pulled out her phone and saw she had a signal. She called 911.

"911. What's your emergency?"

"This is MBI Agent Poppy Holliday. My partner and I are being pursued by a gunman north of the Evergreen. Dispatch units immediately. We are in the woods behind the farm. About a quarter of a mile in." She hung up and pocketed her phone as she leaped over a large dead tree trunk that had fallen.

"Maybe sirens will call him off."

Another shot was fired.

"Up ahead. See that dead hollow tree? We're going in it."

"But he might see us!"

"The bullet would have made a closer connection if he could see us. For now, he's flying blind too. But not for long." Rhett tugged her to the huge fallen tree and she crawled inside the earthy, mushy trunk. The smell of dead animals and rotten leaves thumped her gag reflex. Rhett wiggled in next to her and they lay on their sides, literally nose to nose.

"Be still," he whispered and she caught the hint of mint on his breath, felt his chest rising and falling against hers. Their hands touched. She didn't bother attempting to shift away—there was nowhere to go, and there was nothing romantic about this situation.

Leaves and twigs crunched and snapped, the sounds coming closer. Poppy held her breath. If the killer had any inkling of their location, they might as well be in a coffin as their death was guaranteed.

Another wave of panic washed over her, inducing uncontrollable shudders. Rhett intertwined his fingers with hers, the warmth steadying her. "It's okay," he soothed through a whisper as his forehead pressed into hers, another reassuring and comforting gesture.

Was it okay? No. Nothing was certain. Rhett had to be going bonkers. He thrived on structure, plans and routine. If ever life was chaotic and out of control, it was now. Being stuffed in a tree trunk was a far cry from his carefully crafted life—all due to one teenage slipup. She didn't fault him for Keith's death. But his circumstances were nothing like Poppy's.

A thud on the tree trunk sent Poppy's blood whooshing in her ears.

The killer was standing on them! Did he know it? Was this his cruel way of clueing them in on the fact they were cornered? Poppy squeezed Rhett's hand tighter.

Heavy boots scraped across the tree trunk, and small specks of wood shook loose from above, dusting their heads. Poppy's nose burned and tickled. No. Now was not the time to sneeze. She wiggled her nose, working the sneeze away.

If she could finagle her gun into her hand, she could start shooting; this definitely qualified as a life-threatening situation, but Poppy wanted Cora's killer to rot in a cell, and a dead man couldn't give up anyone else's part in Cora's death. She didn't believe whoever was after her now had acted alone then.

One was already dead and unable to talk.

The trunk shook and footfalls crunched along the ground again, growing fainter with each step until silence loomed.

Rhett's body relaxed against hers. "I think we're in the clear."

The gunman must have used the trunk to gain a better view. "I'm scared to find out."

"Do you wanna lay inside this dead tree all day?" he murmured.

"Kinda...no."

They'd released pent-up breaths, but not their intertwined fingers, and neither was making any effort to let go. But a killer was on the loose and Poppy couldn't hang out in a tree k-i-s-s-i-n-g all day. She broke the hold.

"I'll go first. Cover me." Rhett shimmied his way out of the trunk and Poppy moved quickly to gain a

clear view and watch his back. They stood listening
and watching. Waiting.

When it felt secure, they trudged back toward the
Christmas Tree Farm. "How did he know where we
were? We're not even using the same cars."

"No. No, he blew those up." Rhett sighed. "Ian Kirkwood is military. He'd have the skills to follow, scope us
and hunt us—not to mention he loves hunting in gen-
eral. He knows this town, these woods. But we can't
prove anything. I wish there was a way to get him to
confess."

"He doesn't know we don't have proof. We could
work that in our favor." Fudging the truth wasn't off
the table. Police did it often. Rhett wasn't a fan, though.

He didn't reply. Maybe he was becoming as desperate as Poppy.

"I don't know," he finally said. "This is going to
sound crazy given our situation presently and especially
coming from me, but I think we should still buy a tree
for the Cordrays. I know we should head straight to Ian
Kirkwood's and we still have to talk to Savannah—but
I'll be honest... I need a minute after all that. I'm sorry.
I know this is about Cora—"

"Okay." Poppy understood and agreed. Almost every
day—and sometimes twice a day—they'd been targets
and their bodies were shot. Literally. It was fogging their
minds. One night off wouldn't kill them—she hoped.

Poppy's phone buzzed in her pocket. Her brother.
"Hey, Tack."

"Hey," he said in his baritone voice. "Wanted to see
where you were on the case and let you know that I'm
taking off for a while. My case will be there when I get
back. You gonna come home for Christmas?"

"No. I can't. Besides, they don't really want me there anyway."

"Not true."

Tack was the golden boy. He had no idea what it felt like to be the black sheep.

"We're making some headway."

"Yeah?"

She explained her theory and reluctantly told him about the attacks, the second blown-up car and the graze on her arm, which burned like crazy. "But we're handling it."

Radio silence hung in the air before Tack sighed heavily, clearly unhappy with the turn of events and the fact that his little sister had become a target. "I can be there by nightfall."

"No." She had made the mess and would clean it up by bringing justice and closure. "Rhett and I are being careful."

Rhett's eyebrow twitched north and she grinned. Caution hadn't actually kept them from danger. Sounded good, though. "We're watching our backs." As the killer shot at them. "Go home for the holidays, Tack. If I need you, I'll call you."

"Bunk. But okay."

"I'm serious. See you soon." She hung up. "He's overprotective and competitive. He probably wants to prove he can solve this case before I can."

"Or he wants one sister safe, and justice for his other sister." Rhett hopped a log.

"Do you always have to be so reasonable?" she griped.

"Do you always have to jump to the worst conclusion?" he countered.

"Whatever," she muttered as the tree farm came into view. "Bah humbug."

Tousling her hair, he chuckled. "This was originally your idea."

"I know. And you said it was a good one." She tromped toward the front of the farm to give an employee the number of the tree they'd chosen.

"Doubtful you'll hear that again." He waved over an attendant. "Ready to make a family happy?"

Chapter 11

Tuesday slipped into Wednesday and then into Thursday. Rhett's mom had called one last time, and while he hated to decline, he simply couldn't bear being there even though he longed for his family during the holidays.

The case had stalled when Savannah Steadman-Teague conveniently slipped off for a couple of days to Tupelo for a Christmas flea market. But they'd sent the photo of the bracelet and she claimed she didn't know who it belonged to. The same claim Natalie and Maya had both made.

Tomorrow was Christmas Eve, and Gray Creek residents were in full swing gearing up for the annual Christmas Eve parade. The excitement sizzled in the atmosphere and tugged on his heart. Tuesday night, he and Poppy had brought the tree back to the B&B.

Beth had been hyperexcited about it and Delilah had been grateful. She managed to bring down some older ornaments and they had played Christmas music and decorated the tree together. Poppy had even sung along—a little off-key—to Christmas songs and had brought him hot chocolate then razzed him about putting ornaments of the same color too close together. And she called him a control freak.

She and Beth had chosen a star over an angel to top the tree. Poppy had really taken to Beth.

And sadly, Rhett had really taken to Poppy.

Now Rhett stood on the newly built front porch at the B&B waiting on Poppy to come down and start the day. Decorating the tree had been medicine for their foggy minds and tired bodies. He'd woken early feeling ready to tackle the day—the coffee and snickerdoodles for breakfast hadn't hurt either. His body ached and he was still sore, but his brain was all in and he was in a guns-blazing mood. Poppy deserved closure and peace. Deserved to fight the war inside her and win. It was a battle that he couldn't tag in on, but he could aid her on the investigative battlefield.

"You're gonna catch your death out here while staring into nothing." Poppy held a to-go cup of coffee, the steam pluming into the morning haze. "You must be in deep thought. Didn't even flinch when I walked out the front door." She cocked her head and shot him a quick grin—those were coming easier to her now. Her bangs hung thick across her brow, hiding her eyebrows but framing those gorgeous hazel eyes accented with long lashes. She wore a green turtleneck sweater and a pair of sleek black pants. She buttoned her coat and shivered. "I—"

"Hate the cold," they said in unison and she hooted.

"How'd you know?" she teased. "So what are you out here thinking?"

Nothing he wanted to reveal. "I'm thinking no one we talk to again is going to come forward. And we have no reason to make them." They had no concrete evidence. Only speculation.

"Because it's all we have. We've spent more time trying to save our bacon than finding leads."

Rhett pushed off the railing and motioned Poppy to take the porch steps first. "The last couple of nights have been quiet." They'd run into Ian Kirkwood the other night eating dinner, and while he didn't appear to have any noticeable marks or a limp, he wasn't being ruled out as a suspect. He also hadn't been thrilled to see them and he hadn't recognized the bracelet.

The interior of the car was colder than the outdoors.

"I'd really like those seat warmers to kick in about now," Poppy said and slid her coffee into the cup holder by the console. She whipped out black leather gloves and slipped her slender fingers inside. "PS. I'm not really thrilled about returning to the Castlewood Mansion after nearly dying there."

He wasn't either, but that's where Savannah's office was located. He pulled onto the main road and headed for downtown.

"I was thinking about buying Beth a Christmas gift while we're on the Square. She's attached to the bunny but maybe she'd like a new dress for it. I don't know. And I feel like I owe Delilah something better than a sausage-and-cheese gift set. I hate those things."

Rhett snorted. "I kinda like 'em."

Poppy sipped her coffee. "You would. Well, I'll find something. See it and know it's right."

"The agency is already paying for the damage on her home."

Poppy groaned. "Nothing says Merry Christmas like a reimbursement check to pay for home repairs thanks to a killer trying to blow us to kingdom come. Let's also send them a congratulatory card for not ending up as collateral damage. Well done, Cordrays, you lived." She ended it with a fisted victory pump.

Rhett slowed down when he hit the main strip. "Done yet?"

"A thank-you card for not kicking us out?"

He frowned, but she was amusing. So that's what extra sleep did to her. Raised her snark game. Great.

Stopping at the stop sign, he frowned. It was a madhouse out today with crowded sidewalks and last-minute shoppers. Pushing through throngs of people for a Christmas gift that she would know when she saw it was not on his list of ways to have fun. It meant endless stores and endless lines. He'd almost rather be shot again. Definitely would rather jump off a train.

"Why can't you know what you want before you shop?"

She slurped her coffee. "Seeing is believing."

"What does that mean in the shopping context?" he asked, slightly irritated.

"I have no idea. Sounded good."

"No. It didn't."

She arched an eyebrow. "What bee flew up your tailpipe this morning?"

He ignored her and huffed. Well, if they were stuck shopping, and were going to be at the B&B for Christmas, then Poppy ought to have something to open on Christmas morning. Didn't seem right for her to wake up without a gift. He didn't go home over the holidays, but Mom always mailed his presents. He'd never bought Poppy a gift before, but then they'd never spent a Christmas together.

And…and, well, against his better judgment he simply wanted to. "I'm gonna pass on shopping. Not that I don't want to buy them anything. I'll give you some cash."

"Way to do your part," she said with a slight snarl. "You're such a guy."

He turned up the holiday music. "I'm not insulted by that, you know."

She answered with a huff and silence. "I will take your cash, though."

He laughed and parked in front of the historic home that had nearly taken Poppy's life only days earlier. Poppy hesitated with her hand on the door handle.

"We'll stick to the first floor," he said, hoping his teasing hit its mark.

She pointed at him. "You better believe that." Inside, Savannah met them in the foyer. "Come on in my office. I won't offer for you to take a tour again. I'm mortified that someone would harm you, and here in my work space." She laid a hand on her chest and Rhett heard Poppy mutter under her breath.

"I'm sure."

They sat in Savannah's office. Déjà vu.

"I'm gonna cut to the chase. I've been abducted, choked, shot and chased. I'm over bedside manner," Poppy stated. "I know you smoked pot. I know you bought it from Linden Saddler. I know you were a real piece of work in high school."

Savannah opened her mouth as if to protest, but Poppy held up a hand and cut her off before she began. "I don't care that you've changed. Made amends. Decorate homes now or shop at flea markets. I don't care that your husband is a detective. I'm interested in your behavior in high school—whether or not you're proud of it—and I want to know why you lied about Dylan not having a crush on Cora when I have more than one credible witness stating that he did. I've had victims of your public humiliation schemes spill, so come clean."

Poppy leaned across the desk and gave Savannah the look that made grown men cry. She was the bulldog on the team. "Because so help me if you don't, I will make your mean-girl self look like Barbie. See, I'm pretty adept at getting my way too."

A flash of the mean girl shot through Savanah's eyes but she quickly composed that hot temper. No. Savannah Steadman-Teague did not like Poppy's threats. If only she was wise enough to know that they weren't threats at all. Poppy was proclaiming promises. Ones she would absolutely follow through on. The woman could terrify a person with a cold look, and he found it rather impressive.

Savannah clearly calculated and weighed her options, then she tossed her long blond hair behind her shoulder. "I don't think you need to go that far. I didn't tell you about my behavior in high school because it's irrelevant to your case. I didn't have anything to do with Cora's death. And mostly I'm ashamed of the behavior. So I don't usually go touting my former ways."

Poppy continued to stare. "Tell me about the pot. How did Cora get it?"

Savannah toyed with an ink pen, then sighed. "I could tell you who gave it to her but it would still be irrelevant."

Rhett scooted closer to Poppy in case she decided to come across the table at Savannah's evasiveness. "What would be relevant?" Rhett asked.

"Who gave the marijuana to Linden."

Poppy balled her hand into a fist. "I'm not interested in drug suppliers."

Savannah squirmed. "I think you should be. The pot was Maya's. But she didn't purchase it, and that may be relevant."

"How so?" Poppy asked.

Savannah rapidly blinked and heaved a sigh. "Maya was seeing the supplier on the down low. But she wasn't the only girl being supplied—if you get my drift."

"I'd rather get a solid statement. Who supplied the drugs and why is it relevant?"

Savannah leaned forward. "Mr. Simms. And it's important because he was known to take interest in some of the girls and that included pot if they wanted it—for free."

Poppy's face paled and she stared at Savannah wide-eyed. Linden Saddler had said that Maya never bought drugs. He knew she'd been getting them for free from his supplier. "Are you saying Mr. Simms—the science teacher and club sponsor—was having inappropriate relationships with students? With Cora?"

"I'm saying he had a thing with Maya, and he appeared to have an interest in Cora too, according to

Maya. She was jealous. Simms was *her* older man. She thought it was actually going to go somewhere."

Poppy stood. "If I find out you're lying…"

"I'm not. I never thought Mr. Simms hurt Cora. If I did, I would have told. But the thing is Dylan said he saw something. Mr. Simms kept Cora after class the Friday she disappeared. He didn't overhear anything, but when Cora came out of class she was upset."

"And you didn't think this was pertinent back then or when we were here days ago?" Poppy said, her voice raised.

"Back then I didn't think at all. Because I didn't care. And I didn't say anything days ago because I didn't think about it until you brought up the pot. I don't know if it was nefarious. He may have propositioned Cora and that upset her, or it could have been about her grades. Or anything. I don't know."

Mr. Simms. Drug distributor who was taking advantage of students—and had possibly been involved in Cora's death.

Poppy blew through the front door of the Victorian house, and the blast of wintry air did nothing to cool the blazing fire raging through her. She was no Doc Holliday. She was Wyatt Earp and this law dog was coming for Solomon Simms. With a vengeance.

Rhett caught up with her down the sidewalk. "Poppy…" he warned.

"If he so much as laid one finger on my sister, Rhett…" She couldn't even voice her thoughts. So many emotions.

He caught her arm at the car and forced her to face him. "Then we will bring him down. He will never see the light of day again. But we have to do it by the book so he goes away. One mistake and we're done. Look me in the eye and tell me you'll go by the book. This isn't a standoff at high noon. It's measured steps. Due process. Getting it right."

He was right. One hundred percent, but she didn't want to take measured steps. She wanted to barrel in there, guns blazing and aim and fire. And she'd lose. Lose everything she wanted to bring to her family and to Cora. To herself.

Thankful for Rhett, she stepped into his space and touched his cheek. "I know. You're spot on." Laying her hand against his cheek brought her complete solace and opened up some breathing room. Having a constant, reliable person on her side was a good thing.

Maybe if she brought justice to Cora she could allow herself one good thing.

Maybe.

He covered her hand with his, soft and warm, and lowered their laced fingers to his chest. "I want you to know that I'm writing this down. Poppy Holliday told me I was right."

She laughed. This was no laughing matter but she needed it, and he seemed to not only know it, but to anticipate her needs and follow through to provide for her. It was bittersweet. "Write down anything you want. But you have no witnesses."

"Way to ruin the moment." His lips twitched and she had a mind to peck those lips, but she refrained. Now wasn't the time. It likely would never be the right time.

"Let's go find Simms."

"Oh, you better believe it." He released her hand and hurried to the driver's side. "I'm going to take the

lead with him, Poppy. I need you to restrain yourself.
We also have to consider the possibility that Maya was
jealous that Simms paid attention to Cora. She knew
Dylan had been too. Maybe she thought she would take
care of Cora coming after her man and Savannah's. And
we're still looking at Natalie."

"As if Cora would give Mr. Simms the time of day
or respond to his proposition if there was one."

"No, but Maya may not have known that and she'd
been trained by the best mean girl around." He sighed.
"Restraint. Okay?"

That wasn't going to be easy. But again, he was right.
"Fine," she said testily but he grinned, figuring out her
gruff annoyance with him was all an act. Did he know
it always had been?

By the time they drove into Solomon Simms's mod-
est subdivision, Poppy was champing at the bit. Simms's
car was under the carport. Good.

"Pop, I mean it. Rapport. That's what we need. Less
aggression. If you can't do that, then you need to stay
in the car."

Rhett knew when to be soft and tender and when to
call her on her wayward ways. She hated it and needed it
all at the same time. No one had ever been so…knowing
of her. Words teetered on the tip of her tongue. Words
she'd never spoken to a man who wasn't her brother. A
tidal wave of panic crashed over her.

"What's wrong?" he asked. She couldn't hide anything from Mr. Observant. His knowledge of her only
intensified her fear.

"Nothing," she choked out. "I'll be on my best behavior."

"That's not reassuring. Your best behavior is dismal." He grinned. "Yeah, I said dismal."

She had to get out of this car right now. Right this second, or she was going to throw herself into his arms and say and do something that she might or might *not* regret. Either way it was wrong. "I'll be cool as a cube," she said, intending to frustrate him with another annoying idiom.

But instead he reached out and ran his fingers under her bangs, sliding them from her eyes. "It's cucumber, Agent Holliday," he murmured. "Cool as a cucumber, and we're in this together." He nodded once softly, then removed his touch. She wasn't warm; she was burning. All the way to her bones, and ready to profess thoughts she had no business even flirting with.

Did he have her number on the confusing phrases? How? She was losing every defense she knew to throw out.

He opened the car door and she followed him to the long gray porch. He rang the doorbell and a dog barked. Solomon Simms opened the door and a little Westie barked like a menacing giant. The man didn't deserve such a cute puppy. A stray thought went through her mind that when he went to prison, she'd rescue the dog.

"Agents." He opened the door, motioned them inside and then quieted his yapper by scooping it up. "Come in."

His house was tidy and decorated in masculine tones. Nothing fancy. But nothing that revealed he was a creeper. People were adept at keeping secrets. Rhett gave her the stern eye and stepped forward as Simms motioned for them to sit on the love seat. He sat across from them on the recliner. She noticed, at a closer look, dark purple circles under his eyes and he seemed a little peeved. His dog curled up in his lap.

"Are you feeling okay, Mr. Simms?" Rhett asked. Always polite. Garnering trust.

"So why are you here today?" he asked, evasively. Everyone loved evading their questions. Whatever. His personal health was none of their business.

"It's come to our attention that you had an illegal affair with Maya Marx while she was in high school. It's also come to our attention you grew pot and distributed it through Linden Saddler. So can you clear some stuff up for us?" Rhett asked.

He shifted uncomfortably in his chair.

"Did you have untoward intentions regarding my sister?" Poppy softly asked.

Simms inhaled deeply and stroked his little companion. "Any interest I expressed in Cora was for her impressive scientific mind. She could have received a full academic scholarship. Been something great."

Poppy choked back tears. Cora would never have that chance now. "Maya? The marijuana?"

He looked at his dog as he spoke. "I was twenty-seven at that time. No excuse for my relationship with Maya Marx, but she was the only one I had any kind of personal relationship with. It wasn't *girls*, plural. Only Maya."

"Did Maya think you had a personal interest in Cora?" Rhett asked and leaned forward on his knees. "It's possible that she hurt Cora."

Simms swallowed hard. "I guess it really doesn't matter now."

"What doesn't?" Poppy asked.

"The secrets. The years of secrets and lies." His voice

was distant. Regretful even. "I loved Maya. She was seventeen—older than the rest but held back due to some earlier problems in school. But that is neither here nor there concerning Cora. Maya came to me the night Cora died. Hysterical. Banging on my door around 1:00 a.m. Babbling incoherently. It was a mistake. It wasn't supposed to happen."

Poppy's gut knotted. "What wasn't supposed to happen?"

Simms looked her in the eye and slowly shook his head. "After I got her calmed down, she told me that Savannah found out Dylan was going to break up with her to ask out Cora. Savannah had concocted some elaborate plan to derail it. She befriended Cora and gained her trust by asking her to hold the bag of weed. It wasn't Maya's. I would know. I gave it to Linden specifically for Savannah."

He was admitting to growing and selling pot. "Are you still dealing?"

"No. I sold it back then to help pay off student loans only. That's why I picked Linden to help. He wanted to save for a business. We weren't in it to build a drug empire."

Oh, well then, it must be okay to sell drugs if the reason was noble. Poppy refrained from an eye roll.

"Now I only grow it for medicinal purposes. I'm dying of cancer. I was in Atlanta for treatment. It's terminal. Treatment slows it but won't put me into remission."

Now he wanted to come clean because he was dying and had nothing to lose. But what about all those years ago when they grieved? When they were awake, sick, wondering if she'd been kidnapped and trafficked somewhere without her meds? Poppy clenched her teeth and balled her fists until her nails bit into her flesh.

"Please continue," Rhett said, his jaw tick showing his own depth of restraint.

"Once she gathered Cora's trust, she made a plan with Ian Kirkwood."

Guess he wasn't at the movies alone after all.

"She invited Cora out that night to a little get-to-gether at the Weaverman property. Told her that Ian would pick her up and bring her. Which I assume he did. She was there."

That's why she sneaked out. To meet a boy her parents didn't know. A boy they didn't know wasn't allowed to drive them anywhere, and Poppy had known that Cora liked Dylan and would question why another boy was picking her up and where she was going.

"The plan—" he paused and closed his eyes a moment "—was to make it appear like Cora was into Ian when Dylan arrived by seeing them together in the back seat of Ian's car."

Poppy fumed. "What did he do to her?"

"It wasn't like that. He was only going to make it look like they were kissing in the back seat, but Savannah knew that Cora would never do that."

"Did she force her?"

"No. She took a sedative from her mother that was only supposed to make Cora groggy or even sleep a bit. That way they could plant her in the back seat and make it appear that way. When Dylan saw that Cora wasn't into him like he was into her, then he wouldn't want Cora."

There were some holes in the plot, but teenagers rarely thought things out. Cora could have told Dylan later that she didn't remember or that she was drugged, and knowing Savannah and her friends, Dylan would have known something was up. He could have beaten it out of Ian unless Ian had something to gain by Dylan not liking Cora. Maybe Cora for himself. Or Savannah might have had something on Ian and still did today. Maybe he'd gone into the military to escape this sordid night.

"But whatever they gave her resulted in a seizure and she died." Simms had the decency to look at the floor and pause.

Poppy clamped the inside of her bottom lip to keep from falling into a puddle on the floor.

"I don't think they knew she had a condition, and they certainly wouldn't have thought the sleeping pill could cause an adverse reaction due to the meds she may have been on. I surmised that's what happened and that her death was accidental."

"It was malicious," Poppy hissed. "Over a stupid boy." More than anything, she wanted to run off to a corner and break down and cry for her sister's life that was cut short. But she had a job to do, so she pulled herself together as much as she could. "Finish what you know."

"They panicked. Dylan wanted to go to the police, but Ian, Natalie and Savannah talked him out of it. They... Well, you know where they put her. But Natalie or Savannah or both of them—I don't know really— lost a piece of jewelry in the well and freaked out."

That explained the bracelet. Everyone was lying about who it belonged to. May be why Zack paused so long when Poppy had texted the photo to him. He'd recognized it as his wife's.

"Ian told them no one was going to look down there ever. So they left, but it wrecked Maya."

Poppy gritted her teeth so she wouldn't say anything about Maya at least being alive while Cora was not.

"I'm so sorry," he said.

"You're sorry? You kept the secret because not only did you grow and distribute the marijuana, but you were having an illegal relationship with Maya and needed to protect yourself." Her disgust couldn't be hidden and she didn't care.

Rhett stood. "We'll have to confirm all this with Maya. She'll probably go to prison."

Simms nodded. "I suppose I might be going too."

Except he was terminal and it didn't matter to him. He was already a dead man walking.

"Do you know if Dylan tried to come clean at all over the years?" Rhett asked.

"Maya said on the anniversary of her death he would go out to the Weaverman property. Sometimes she met him there. Sometimes he was alone and he talked a few times of turning them in, but he was in a practice with Natalie and she was married to his brother."

Nice reason to make him keep his trap shut, and to keep tabs on him through the shared practice. Savannah had married a cop and it could ruin his career if he found out—and Savannah's. Ian would lose his business.

But then they'd found her body. Dylan must have either wanted to come forward and one of them killed him, or he couldn't handle the repercussions and committed suicide—or maybe he did drink himself into a stupor and died driving out there or trying to drive to the sheriff's office. Unless someone confessed or the trace evidence came back with something solid, they may never know.

Why would Savannah give up Simms and Maya tonight knowing it would connect back to her and her part in all this? "Does anyone know you're terminal?"

"No. I just found out myself."

Savannah must have been banking on Simms keeping his secrets and lies and his mouth shut. She didn't know he had nothing to lose by telling the truth anymore. Now that it had backfired, she still had the upper hand. All they had to do was call Simms a liar; his reason for it wouldn't matter. All they needed for a hung jury was a reasonable doubt, and if they kept their alibis and stuck to the same story, they'd get off scot-free.

"We'll see ourselves out."

Rhett stayed silent until they were inside the car. "He's going to give Maya a heads-up—you know that."

"Let's hope Maya wants to talk too. Clear her conscience."

Chapter 12

As much as Poppy wanted to make a beeline for Maya Marx, she was at the clinic. Having Natalie nearby wouldn't play in their favor. They needed her alone and uninfluenced by another accessory to the crime. But they could talk to Ian Kirkwood again. Shake him up. Shake something loose. He had a lot to lose, so she wasn't banking on honesty—especially if he was the one trying to shut her down permanently.

Rhett agreed and they kept what they knew to themselves. Courtesy toward Detective Teague was one thing, but letting him know that it had grown to this magnitude meant he could wreck their investigation if he tipped off Savannah that Simms was terminal and had spilled the beans. They needed to play each of these people off the others. Simms's condition and what they'd been told had to stay quiet for now. If the suspects didn't know the confession came from him, they'd assume it came from someone in their clique, and they might turn on each other for a better deal.

But Rhett hated playing dirty.

"I played nice. I restrained myself," Poppy said. "Now it's time to play it my way. We have the upper hand. We can play these guys off one another. We only need one of them to corroborate what Simms said."

"I had a feeling you'd say that." He nodded. "Take the lead, Bulldog. Close this case."

They pulled into the parking lot at Ian Kirkwood's place of business and went inside only to find they'd just missed him. They were told he had to run out for a few errands and said he'd be back in an hour or two.

Or the phone tree had already begun to shake and he was running.

"Now what?" Poppy asked as they marched back to the car and got inside.

"We tip them off if we meet up with Maya and Natalie together. So let's do this," Rhett said. "Let's do nothing for a minute. You need to process—not as an investigator but a family member who's had a bomb dropped."

"Bad choice of words, Wallace." Poppy smirked, knowing once again Rhett was right. Her mind was a whirlwind of thoughts all jumbled with her emotions. She needed to sort them out and make sense of them, and she needed to call Tack. It wasn't time to share this information with her parents. They needed more proof, but Simms had no reason to lie. But Tack was also a Texas Ranger working unsolved homicides, and he needed to hear the story going down.

"My bad. Okay, how about we go get some lunch,

then you can do that shopping and take some time alone at the B&B wrapping gifts."

Poppy rubbed her hands along her thighs. "And what are you going to do while I shop?"

"Anything else. Probably catch Colt up on the case." He backed out of Kirkwood's parking lot. Maybe their heads-up could play to their advantage after all. They'd panic and someone would come forward, admit it and embellish what had happened. Beg for a deal. Identify the bracelet. All they needed was one to tell the truth, or even half truths. They could work that against them too.

They chose a little sandwich shop for lunch and ordered club sandwiches and tomato-basil soup. Poppy didn't realize how hungry she was until she tasted the tangy tomatoes. But her mind was a whirlpool of thoughts. If Savannah gave Cora the sedative, then she was going down for manslaughter and she could get all the others on accessory-after-the-fact. But what about Dylan?

"I know what you're thinking. Best way to get every last one of them." He picked a piece of bacon from his sandwich and took a bite.

"I am." Talking in this little but crowded establishment wasn't an option. "Every last one of them." She echoed his words and finished her soup.

After lunch and splitting a huge pecan brownie, they left the cozy warmth of the café for the blustery temperature outdoors. Snow flurries swirled and a toddler was catching them on her tongue. "I'm going into the doll shop three stores down. Let's meet over there at that cart selling warm drinks in two hours."

He nodded and she weaved through the crowd. Killers were out there and Cora was dead, and she was shopping for a little outfit for Beth's bunny. Seemed off kilter, but also the right thing. Should she be taking a simple pleasure in buying a gift? At one time she wouldn't have even thought about it.

She'd wanted her life to be miserable to prove to Cora how sorry she was. Something had shaken loose, though. And Poppy had a sick feeling she knew what it was. Something she didn't want to happen, had never intended to happen.

After purchasing a pair of pink-and-blue pajamas with little hearts for Beth's bunny, she found a boutique and bought a matching pink gown with one big heart on the front for Beth. Then she found a holiday candle made from soy for Delilah.

There was still time before she had to meet up with Rhett, so she perused all the shops and found a perfect present for him. After all, they would be spending Christmas together. Unless they could get confessions beforehand, and then she'd be spending Christmas alone. She could still leave him with a gift if that happened. He'd be spending Christmas alone too.

She bought him a little plaque that said I Am Silently Correcting Your Grammar. Maybe she'd mark out "Grammar" and add "Idioms." Chuckling, she laid the plaque on the counter and paid for it, then tucked it in the bag with all her other presents.

After meeting up with Rhett, they headed back to the B&B. She borrowed scissors and tape from Delilah and went upstairs to her room to wrap presents and call Tack. He answered on the first ring.

"You okay?" he asked.

"Yes. We have a lead. I feel it in my gut this is it, but we need some confessions." She rolled out the red-and-green Christmas paper she'd purchased. When was the last time she bought a Christmas gift? She cut along the faint lines and cradled the cell phone between her neck and ear.

"Don't beat it out of them," he teased.

Poppy laughed. "No, that's what you'd do, you rough-neck cowboy." She cut along the marked lines. "No worries. Rhett won't let me knock anybody around."

"How's he holding up?"

"Ever the Superman." And ever the Clark Kent too. "He's an excellent agent and he's got a backbone. He's no daisy."

Tack chuckled. "I hear something in that voice of yours. Little more than admiration, Pops. Y'all got something goin'?"

Did they? No. But was there something there? For her? Yes. But she was working on that. "We're colleagues and you know how things worked out with Liam."

"I know he was a jerk who thought the world revolved around him and he was a strong-armer. I've met Wallace. He's a good egg, Pops. Be good for you."

"Yeah, well, I got enough protein in my diet. No matter, I wouldn't be good for him. Besides, he's made it clear that I'm not his type and he'd never ask me out." She was too much of a wild card. Well, he was too much of a stiff shirt. Or stuffed shirt. Whatever.

"So there is something there. Poppy, listen to me. Don't let love slip away if you can hold on to it. Okay? I'm not always the mushy guy—"

"You are the furthest thing from mush unless punching me to show love counts," she teased, but Tack was what people called a man's man. There was nothing flowing through his veins but hot blood and testosterone.

"Yeah, well…maybe that's my cross to bear. It's not yours," he said with power in his voice. "Do you hear me? You don't need to carry an unnecessary burden. Cora wouldn't want you to be miserable because she's gone. That kid forgave anyone for anything. Even that time I accidentally threw her from my handle bars when a dog ran out in front of us. I felt terrible when she broke her arm because of it. She'd broken enough bones from seizures. I could barely look her in the eye, but when I made it to her bedside she wrapped her good arm around me and told me it wasn't my fault. And her death isn't yours."

"What if it is, though? What if we argued and she sneaked out due to something I said? And I couldn't follow her because I was grounded for taking the blame for pot that wasn't mine."

"If that's what happened, I'd say it's still not your fault. She knew right from wrong and made her choice. Don't you think it's time to forgive yourself? She's not in pain. She's in a way better place than us. No more seizures. Would I rather have her here? Yes, but that's purely selfish. I promise she's not angry anymore because you yelled at her and told her she ought to be rebellious for once in her life. And if what's keepin' you from a decent relationship and finding happiness is that you think you don't deserve it, you're wrong. Get over it. Don't create more regrets."

His words were far from soft or eloquent, but that wasn't Tack's approach. And the way he put it made sense. Cora wasn't angry or bitter or regretful. She was pain free, sorrow free and feeling nothing but joy in the presence of God. "I appreciate the pep talk. Truly. But I don't date colleagues."

"You haven't dated the right colleague. If this guy puts up with your hard head and malarkey, then maybe there's more there. Not many would put up with your smart mouth and bossy attitude." His voice held love and teasing.

"Yeah, yeah. Hey, I heard Chelsey was in Texas for a few days. You seen her?"

"Why are you bringing her up in the context of dating?"

She wasn't. Well…maybe she was. "I'm not."

"Mmm…she's fine. I've seen her a few times." The clipped tone meant he wasn't saying any more and she needed to drop it.

"I have to go. We're going to Maya's to get confirmation about Simms. Hopefully."

"She might crack. Go the route of easing her conscience. Doing the right thing. That might work better than strong-arming her."

She huffed. "Yes, Mr. Texas Ranger. Give my love to the fam." She hung up before he could tell her she ought to fly home for Christmas.

After tucking her gifts under the bed, she knocked on Rhett's bedroom door. He opened it with his jacket over his arm. "Ready?"

"Yep."

She followed him downstairs. The house was quiet except for Christmas music playing in the private living space for Delilah and Beth. "I got their presents wrapped," Poppy said as she slipped on her coat and they stepped out into the snow. It was sticking. A few pieces of grass poked through but the way the snow was coming down all fat and flaky, it would be a nice and unusual white Christmas.

Snow was beautiful. Too bad it had to be cold.

"Delilah said that if we can't leave, we're welcome to have dinner on both Christmas Eve and Christmas with her and Beth. It's just them. No immediate family."

That was sad. At least Poppy had family, even though she rarely saw them under the circumstances.

Maya's little brick craftsman sat farther back from the road in a rural area of Gray Creek. Her car was in the drive and a truck was parked behind it. The light was on inside. Good sign.

They parked and climbed the gray concrete steps to the wide porch. A meager Christmas tree twinkled with multicolored lights, and Christmas music played. Not exactly the atmosphere Poppy expected for a woman who'd been given a heads-up that the cops were on to her. Maybe she hadn't been warned by Simms.

Rhett knocked and got no answer. He rang the doorbell then knocked louder. Nothing.

"I'll go around back," Poppy said. She hopped down the porch stairs and rounded the side of the house as a figure came barreling out of the back. "Stop!" Poppy hollered and drew her weapon, trying to get a good look at his face, but he was running away from her. Brown hair. Same build as her own attacker. "Rhett!"

The man kept running and Poppy pursued as Rhett caught up. "Who is it?"

"Not sure."

"I'll keep chase. You go find Maya. He's running for a reason."

Poppy pivoted and raced back to the house, going through the screened-in porch into the kitchen.

Maya lay on the kitchen floor.
Dead.

Rhett pursued the man through the woods. He was sick of running in and out of woods. He hoped the next case would be in the city. Full of traffic and not a tree in sight.

Sirens wailed in the distance. Poppy had called the police and probably an ambulance. Was Maya alive?

He closed in on the killer and tackled him to the ground. "You have the right to remain silent," he said, grabbing his cuffs from his belt and sliding the bracelets on his bloody wrists, then patting him down before rolling him over.

Ian Kirkwood.

"I didn't do it."

"No? Just decided to get bloody, then take a jog through the woods?" He finished Mirandizing him and hauled him to his feet. "Didn't do what, by the way?"

"I didn't stab Maya." He shifted under Rhett's hold on his jacket collar. "I'm not going to run again."

"No, you definitely are not." Rhett let go but pointed his gun on him. "Why run at all?"

"Because when I saw you and Agent Holliday get out of the car I knew you'd think I'd done it. I panicked."

Likely story. This bunch had been lying through their teeth since the beginning. Nothing out of his mouth was believable.

"I need to get this blood off my hands, man!"

"I imagine you have more than one person's blood on your hands." As they approached the house, an ambulance, sheriff's marked units and both Detectives Banner and Teague were on the scene.

Monty came racing toward Ian, and Rhett jumped in front to block the blow the detective was about to deal. "Hey. Hey."

Teague held Monty off. "Don't be stupid, Banner. We got him. He'll pay."

"For what?" Ian hollered. "I didn't kill her."

Teague raised a skeptical eyebrow. "Innocent men don't run." He tugged and pulled Monty away, assuring him of justice. But Rhett knew justice wasn't always served. Not in this life.

Poppy stepped outside, the wind blowing her hair like something out of a movie. The hot tough detective in her blue latex gloves and a chip on her shoulder. His heart thundered and he reminded himself this was a crime scene. She had him spinning out of control, though, and it was terrifying.

She met up with him and turned her hard expression to Ian. "I'll see you at the sheriff's office."

Rhett shoved him in the back of Detective Teague's unmarked car and slammed the door, then went inside to the scene. CSI were photographing and processing the house, as well as Ian's truck.

Poppy knelt by Maya's body. "No sign of a struggle. Coffee was freshly brewed and enough for more than one person. Two mugs were out. One on the table and one unused. She thought her attacker had come as friend not foe. If they got into an argument over Cora or the latest news Simms gave us, then I think there would have been a struggle of some kind. A piece of furniture tossed. My guess is he got up to fix his coffee and grabbed the knife from the block, and it was done before she had a chance to register she was being attacked. It was quick and efficient."

Rhett's stomach roiled. Maya may have taken part in Cora's alleged accidental death but she didn't deserve to be butchered. "Like a hunter or a skilled soldier. Quick cut. Ian hunts, was in the military, and he had blood all over his hands."

Poppy sighed, long and tired. "Let's see if we can get him to talk without a lawyer. You do it. I'll botch it. I'm too..." She burst up and out the door so fast it made his head spin.

He found her alone under a huge tree by the side of the house, eyes closed and head upward. Snow dotted her long lashes.

"We're going to get to the truth, Poppy. We're close."

"I feel like I'm fighting a losing battle. I don't have Dylan's story or Maya's. I have whatever fabrication Ian, Natalie and Savannah are going to give me."

He crossed to the tree and grasped her shoulders. She opened her eyes, blinking away the tiny drops of snow. "Ian is picking them off one by one. The women will be scared. They'll want to talk."

"And say what? Ian did it all. Simms is lying. We have no proof now. The key players are all dead."

Rhett framed her pink cheeks, cold from the temperature. "I know. I know." She melted against him, and seemed to find rest in his embrace. It brought satisfaction and a tremor of anxiety. He liked being her soft place to land. Liked that she trusted him to be a shelter. A safe haven. Without thinking it through carefully, he drew her even closer, cocooning her and resting his head on hers. "I'm sorry you're going through this. I wish there was something more I could do."

Poppy raised her head, and her nose brushed his. Her lips were so close. Pulse spiking and heat chasing away the chill, he peered into her eyes and saw the questions, hope and sincerity. Pure. Intense.

Deliberately he eased down until his lips touched hers. Soft and sweet. It ignited a fire clear to his toes, and he tested the waters to see if she was as willing as she appeared. Her arms slipped around his waist, her hands resting on his back. She stole his breath and infused him with such power, all in one tender kiss.

Poppy was as strong in her kiss as she was in her job. As unpredictable and full of surprises as she was in life. It was like getting a taste of something delicious and craving more.

Finally, she broke away and left his heart gaping open wide. Left his mind scrambled and dazed, and yet he'd never felt more grounded. More in control.

"I wasn't expecting that," she said through a ragged breath.

"I guess I'm not as predictable as you thought." Or as he thought. He licked his bottom lip and breathed deep to bring down his heart rate. He wasn't expecting that either—not the emotion. Not the connection.

She grinned. "I suppose not." Then her grin faltered and she blew out a heavy breath.

"Just another emotional moment?" he asked, worried she'd say yes but also concerned she'd say no. That's what she'd claimed in her room when they'd almost kissed before. That she'd have kissed anyone. But she wasn't kissing anyone.

She'd been in Rhett's arms just a second ago.

Panic replaced her calm expression. "I don't know. You said yourself—"

"I said a lot of things." But he didn't know either.

"Like you don't date colleagues. Just kiss them,

then?" she asked in a lighter tone, then sobered. "I dated a colleague back when I worked for the SO in Desoto County and it ended badly. The truth is, Rhett, all my relationships end badly. And I didn't care. Not even a little. But if we—if it—I'd care," she whispered. "I'd care more than a little. So… I can't think about that right now. I'm sorry."

He nodded. At least she wasn't being brutal or throwing up her biting defense mechanism. She was being purely honest and he respected that because he wasn't sure either. He had strict rules. Control. Structure. Could he toss all that out for the way she made him feel? Was it just about the way she made him feel? He had things to sort out too. "I understand. The timing is bad right now."

"It might not ever be better, Rhett. I don't know if we'd work."

He wasn't sure they would either, but as partners on the job, they worked. "Maybe not."

"Probably not."

The blow was suffocating. But Poppy was thinking clearer than he was. "You're right."

She snickered but it was full of disappointment. "I can't believe it. You say I'm right and no one is here to witness it." Motioning with her head toward the house, she said, "We have a job to do."

He followed her to the car and drove to the sheriff's office with little conversation. There wasn't much to say.

Inside the SO, Detective Teague and Sheriff Pritchard were interviewing Ian Kirkwood over the murder of Maya Marx. Detective Banner stood in the room with the two-way mirror, a scowl on his face. "He's not copping to it, but he admits picking up the knife in shock. Said she was dead when he got there. I don't believe him."

Neither did Rhett, but how did one force the hand of a killer who knew how to keep a secret and take out those who could tell a different tale?

Poppy frowned and left the room, then knocked on the interview room door. Sheriff Pritchard rose and opened it, then he motioned Detective Teague out and Poppy entered. Rhett followed her inside.

"I didn't kill Cora. I didn't kill Maya," Ian recited as if he'd been practicing the words.

"Why were you at Maya's?"

"I told them and I'll tell you. I went by there because my dog has allergies and she had grabbed me some Apoquel—for dog allergies. But when I got there, she was dead. I freaked out. I checked for a pulse and tried compressions but she was gone. Yes, I picked up the knife. I wasn't thinking."

"Did you see anyone on the road passing you? She hadn't been dead long when you arrived," Poppy said as if she believed him.

"No."

"Did you know that she and Solomon Simms were having an illegal affair when you were in high school?"

His face blanched. "Yes. I knew. But not back then. I found out later, when she was about twenty and they were dating. They've been on and off again all these years. Does he even know? They were together the last couple of days."

Had Maya gone to Atlanta with Simms for his treatment? Rhett turned and looked toward the mirror. Did

Monty know that Maya was with Simms? And if so...
was that second cup of coffee his?

"Did she say where they were?"

Ian must have caught on that Monty was on the other
side of the window listening. He glanced at the window
and sighed. "Bed and breakfast to celebrate his recent
remission. He had cancer. Maya told me—he doesn't
know I know. But he's in remission now and that was
the celebration."

They couldn't call to see if he'd been in Atlanta's
cancer center or call a doctor because of HIPPA. Why
would Simms lie about terminal cancer? Why give up
Maya and her friends if he was going to live and they
were together?

Unless she'd told him it was over.

Could Simms be playing them all somehow? And
why? What was his end game?

Chapter 13

Poppy sat at the dining room table at the B&B drinking coffee and overcome with exhaustion. It was Christmas Eve and they'd worked most of the day. Ian Kirkwood never admitted to killing Maya but wouldn't take a polygraph. Probably because of all the other things he'd done.

Solomon Simms had been given the news about Maya and he'd actually cried. He denied Ian's claims, but the fact he wouldn't let them see his medical records to prove it one way or the other left an unsettled feeling in her gut. So many lies. So many deceptions going on with so many people. The truth had long been blurred, and Poppy wasn't sure what to believe. Simms didn't look frail but he didn't exactly look well either.

The investigation of Maya's homicide wasn't in their hands, so they hadn't been able to interview Detective

Monty Banner. He had motive, if she'd been seeing Simms in secret. Detective Teague was conducting that end of things, and he wasn't at all thrilled that his wife was in the middle of this. After her tough talk with Savannah, Teague had been less courteous. That was fair. Poppy had all but called his wife a liar and all-around vile person.

They'd just finished Christmas Eve dinner, and Delilah wouldn't let either of them help with the cleanup. Instead they'd sat at the table and played Candyland with Beth, drank coffee and ate too much pecan pie. Now Beth had gone to lie down and Rhett excused himself to call his sister.

It was almost time for the Gray Creek Christmas Eve parade. The town was all abuzz about it, and Beth had talked nonstop about eating popcorn and drinking hot chocolate while watching the floats come down Main Street and having her picture taken with Santa. The thought of one more bite or swig of sugar roiled Poppy's stomach, and she had no clue what she would ask Santa for if she accompanied Beth for pictures. She'd probably ask him to point her to the killer and help her solve Cora's case. Too bad Santa had no real ability to grant wishes or requests.

She wasn't sure God would answer her prayers either. It had been so long since she'd even prayed to Him. But she offered up a silent request anyway. Expected silence in return.

Which reminded her of yesterday's kiss. She and Rhett had been silent about that, but every time she thought of it, which was often, her belly dipped and her heart fluttered. She'd never once in her life been kissed the way Rhett kissed her.

The thought of it tingled her lips and kicked her heart rate up a notch. She ran her teeth along her bottom lip as if to try and scrape away the sensation. It hadn't even been so much about the way he kissed. It had felt like he'd humbled himself in it, to serve her and reveal beautiful truths about herself.

She was worth his time, devotion and effort.

She was cherished. Respected. Treasured.

How was it possible that she'd felt safe and secure in his kiss when it had been anything but safe, unencumbered by structure? Led by instinct. He'd tasted like adventure, the uncertainty thrilling. He'd revealed he was much more than routine and rules. He was unpredictable and audacious. Strong and secure. Trustworthy. Wild but careful with his kiss.

In that unhurried moment, she'd been content and felt real joy for the first time since Cora died, but it had also petrified her. She made a mess out of relationships and one with Rhett would be no different. Then she'd lose what little of him she held.

Tack's words had been rolling around her heart. Cora was happy now. Free.

She would want Poppy to be free of her guilt and shame and agony.

"What are you dreaming about?" Beth asked and sat next to her.

"I'm dreaming about wishes. Have you ever made a wish?" she asked.

Beth nodded. She was beautiful in her green-and-red sweater and black leggings. She laid her bunny on the table. In the morning, she'd have new pajamas for her sweet bunny. Or maybe Poppy would give them to her before bed so they could both wear their pajamas to sleep.

"I make birthday wishes every year, and I tell Santa my wish. I'm going to tell him my Christmas wish tonight too."

Delilah and Beth had invited her and Rhett to the Christmas Eve parade. Poppy glanced out the window. It had been snowing since yesterday morning and they now had three whole inches, which was like Snowmageddon in the South. It would be a beautiful night for a lit-up parade of Christmas floats. Maybe she would try to enjoy it. "What are you asking him for?"

"It's a surprise."

Poppy smiled. "Okay."

Rhett came downstairs, and Poppy's head went fuzzy. She couldn't deny the effect he had on her. He was dressed in trendy jeans and a red-and-black Buffalo-check shirt with a gray cardigan over it. The man was made for a magazine cover.

"I'm ready for the parade. What about you, Beth?" he asked. Poppy loved the way his eyes lit up and warmed when he was near Beth. Was there any part of Rhett that wasn't admirable?

Delilah entered the dining room with Beth's coat and they set off for the parade. The streets were already lined with families eager to get a good view of the floats and easy access to the candy that would be tossed to the sides of the street. Christmas music played from the speakers and Santa's Village was in full swing, gearing up for eager children giving last-minute wishes and parents hoping for last-minute photos.

Other than the murders, Gray Creek was a wonderful place to live and raise a family.

"Who wants popcorn?" Rhett asked and Poppy groaned. She didn't have room for anything else, even if she could smell the buttery deliciousness from here.

"Me," Beth said.

"I'll be back in a minute," he said.

"Doubtful. Have you seen the line?" It was wrapped around the center of the square. No one should want popcorn that bad.

He winked and she tried to fight the gooey feeling. "I'll be here waiting, saving your spot." About five minutes after Rhett left, her phone rang.

She didn't recognize the number. "Hello?" She covered one ear with her hand and pressed the phone harder to her other.

"Agent Holliday, it's Detective Teague."

"Hey. Do you have something?"

A long sigh filtered through the line. "Against my better judgment, my wife wants to talk to you. She's withheld information," he said and his irritation and disappointment filtered through the line. "I knew something was off with her since the body was discovered, but she wouldn't say a word."

"Until now?" Now that people in her inner circle were dropping like flies and Ian had been caught fleeing the scene. "She wants to make some kind of deal to rat out Ian, doesn't she?" It was only a matter of time before they began turning on one another out of fear and panic and self-preservation.

"She knows only the DA can offer a deal. She also knows what went down that night and it doesn't involve her, Natalie, Maya or Dylan. It doesn't even involve Ian, though he wasn't at the movies that night. He was with

Savannah—" his voice broke "—but it does involve Solomon Simms."

These people deserved some kind of trophy for their ability to lie and hide the truth.

"Just...go easy on her, please? She's... I love her."

"If she tells the truth and she wasn't involved, then I'll do what I can and put in a good word to the DA. That's all I can promise. Fair?"

"Yeah. Yeah, that's fair."

"Where can I find her?" She didn't particularly want to go back to the historical home. That place wigged her out now.

"Santa's Village. I'm the stupid Santa this year. We rotate. We can meet after. I'd like to be with her when you talk."

She might lose her nerve by then. "Let's meet now..." She blinked as she spotted Simms. What was he doing slinking around toward the back of the businesses? "Detective, I just spotted Solomon Simms. He's on the north side of Main Street beside the candle store. Talks will have to wait."

"He's dangerous, Agent. If you plan to do what I think, take Agent Wallace."

"Yeah," she mumbled, then hung up. Where was he going? She excused herself from Delilah. She wasn't going to confront but simply follow him, and she had no time to wait on Rhett. She'd lose Simms. Rhett knew she planned to take necessary risks. This was one.

It wasn't like she was some TV sleuth with no business tracking a villain. She was a trained agent with a gun on her hip, and she wasn't an idiot.

She stealthily moved through the crowd as Solomon Simms maneuvered toward the cobblestone street behind the shops. Was he dealing marijuana? Something even more nefarious? Keeping a safe distance, Poppy tracked him as he darted down the cobbled street by the shop. Cars were parked in every available space due to the parade; Christmas music rang out loud and the crowd was cheering even louder as colorful Christmas floats inched down the street with riders waving and tossing candy.

Simms ducked behind the building. Poppy waited a beat and moved in. She would catch this guy dead to rights, but when she turned the corner he was gone. Poof! Vanished.

She frowned and scanned the vacant street. Where could he have gotten to in such a hurry? Creeping along, she checked between cars. Gun in hand, she moved behind a tree. A scraping noise drew her attention but before she could investigate, something sharp pinched her neck and rough hands wrangled her behind the Dumpster.

Instantly her limbs turned to jelly and her insides became liquid, her muscles relaxing then numbing. Slowly but quickly. She was no longer able to grasp her gun, and it fell to the ground. She couldn't even wiggle her toes!

Panic gripped her as the realization dawned that she'd been injected with a paralyzing agent. Even blinking was becoming more difficult to manage.

"Is my job here done? I'm not into killing people."

Simms! He popped out from behind the car he'd been crouching behind. He'd lured her on purpose. Knew she'd see him and follow, giving the man who was now holding her a chance to get the drop on her with the drug. "I fed her the story about being terminally ill.

Now, we had a bargain—don't forget to uphold your end. Don't you cross me," he warned the man who held Poppy captive.

He'd lied! Of course he had. They had all been lying through their teeth.

She was dragged farther, could feel the softness of her captor's coat, but her head wouldn't turn for her to see his face, and he hadn't spoken so she couldn't identify the voice. Horror filled her and she tried to cry out, to scream, but her lips wouldn't even move! Her throat had been paralyzed. A frenzy started inside and she wanted to claw out of her skin, burst away, but she was at this man's mercy. Simms walked away, leaving her in her captor's clutches.

"By now, you're probably wondering what's happening to you?"

That voice. She knew that voice!

"You've been drugged with succinylcholine. You probably don't know what that is. It's a neuromuscular blocking agent. Should be used in conjunction with anesthesia and a ventilating machine, but that's unnecessary for you. This is about keeping you from destroying everything I've worked for."

How had she done that?

"My mom was murdered when I was fourteen and my brother was eight. My dad became obsessed with finding the killer to the point of neglect. We had to live with my grandmother if we wanted to eat or have running water and heat. You have that same look in your eye. I heard you that night at the Weaverman property, talking about how you'd invade every nook and turn over every rock. I knew it. I knew you had to be stopped. Where other cops might give up searching, obsession would drive you on, and eventually you'd figure out what happened and destroy my life."

Poppy fought to make her muscles move, but there were only twitches and they were slowly dissipating.

"You've given me no choice." Something slid across the snow, as if he was dragging something. "By now you've realized you can hear and see and feel pain, but you can't move or talk or scream. Before too long, your lungs will be paralyzed, and you'll asphyxiate. I'd estimate you have an hour at most, maybe more, seeing you're rather muscular."

One hour and she would be dead.

"Then they'll find your body…or maybe not. Maybe you'll end up where your sister did and this time, they'll seal the top of the well since it's so dangerous. Be best. No one will even know you're down there. They've already done their search. No point going back."

He leaned down and his beard scraped against her cheek, his expensive cologne gagging her. His minty breath might as well have been a foul stench. "I guess time will tell."

Rhett inched through the line and listened as excited children chattered about Christmas gifts and which floats they were most excited to see. A parent reminded her children of the real meaning of Christmas and that Jesus was the biggest and greatest gift.

The kids agreed but didn't seem to believe it quite like their mother.

Had Rhett? Since Keith died, Christmas had changed for him. The joy was lost. The excitement and thrill of what it meant had vanished. Keith's death had inadvertently become the magnification of the holiday.

As "O Holy Night" played from the speakers, echoing words of the wondrous night of joy and hope, the lyrics struck him hard and in a way they hadn't before. He'd heard this carol—sung it even—half a dozen times this year at least, but as he listened to it now while a young mother tried to teach her children where the greatest hope and joy came from, the song reminded him of his lost hope and stolen joy. It had drowned that night in the icy waters. Grief snuffed out any thrill or excitement, and Rhett had buried the true meaning of Christmas.

It wasn't about toys, tradition or even loss.

It was about a loving God sending His Son to a lost and joyless world to rescue them.

A Keith-sized hole would always be inside him, but Jesus still saved even if He hadn't physically saved Keith that night. Keith was in heaven with Him.

Jesus still filled people with hope and joy. Rhett hadn't wanted to be filled with either of those. He'd assumed that living with the void was simply the way it was. What he deserved.

But Christmas was still a time to celebrate truth.

Rhett had changed after tragedy altered his life. What happened that holy night had not.

The backs of his eyes burned.

"Mama, I love Jesus, but I love my toys too," the little boy said and nudged his sister to respond.

She frowned at her brother, then broke out in a cheesy grin, revealing two gaps where her top front teeth should be. "Jesus is big in my heart. And a puppy will be little in my arms!"

Their mother grinned, fully amused and proud and slightly exasperated.

Was his mother proud? Rhett never showed up to celebrate the birth of Christ or that Jesus was the giver of life. He was too busy mourning and magnifying death.

The little girl turned and looked up at him. "Do you know the reason for the season, mister?"

Rhett's eyes continued to burn, but he nodded. "I do. I really do."

"And what are you asking Santa for? Can big people ask Santa for gifts?"

He glanced at their mom, who rolled her eyes. He'd help her out. "I guess. But Jesus is the greater gift giver, so I ask Him."

The woman laid a hand on her chest and mouthed, "Thank you." He gave her a nod and they stepped up and placed their orders. By the time he grabbed his popcorn and two Cokes, the parade was in full swing.

"Where's Poppy?" he asked Delilah as he approached and handed her popcorn and a drink.

"She slipped off about ten, maybe fifteen minutes ago. She got a phone call then bolted toward the candle shop."

He handed Beth the other popcorn and drink. "I'll be back. If you see her, call me." Since the train incident, she had both their numbers now. He slipped through the crowd, calling Poppy's phone. Voice mail. Irritation replaced the tender feeling that had been inside him only seconds ago. How many times did he tell her not to go off half-cocked? The past couple of days she'd acquiesced to his warnings and let him take the lead. She was proving she could follow orders and be methodical and cautious.

Rhett should have known it wouldn't last, and now his heart jackhammered against his ribs. In this crazy crowd, with all the noise and hoopla, it wouldn't be difficult to make off with someone and no one notice. Everybody's attention was on Main Street. Why didn't she call him and tell him where she was going?

Because she was impulsive and hardheaded. That was the crux of why he'd pushed against being drawn to her, but it had backfired regardless of his efforts. Poppy had slipped right past his carefully constructed walls and gotten the jump on him.

He approached the candle store, but it was closed for the parade. He checked the door to be sure. Locked. She hadn't gone inside, then. Snagging the toe of his shoe on the cobblestone, he grimaced but hurried behind the building. Nothing but parked vehicles and a Dumpster.

He called her phone again and the shrill timbre sounded nearby. Blood pooled in his brain, leaving him lightheaded. Following the rings, he found her phone behind the big Dumpster. He pocketed it and surveyed his surroundings.

She would never leave her phone on purpose.

With shaking hands, he called Sheriff Pritchard. Voice mail again. Would no one answer their phone today? Yet he knew the sheriff might be working crowd control and couldn't hear his phone.

He tried again. No answer. Frustration burned his gut.

He attempted Detective Teague, who answered on the second ring. "Agent Wallace. Please tell me you're with Agent Holliday."

Rhett's stomach sank. "No. Why?"

Teague relayed his phone call with her earlier and that she'd postponed the conversation to tail Solomon Simms.

"I'm afraid she's been taken."

"Have you called Rudy?"

"He's not answering—that's why I called you."

"He's technically not on duty today but I saw him here earlier. Try again. Look, I'm Santa for today, or I'd help you search. Call Detective Banner." He gave him Monty's cell phone number. "He's around here too with his sister somewhere."

He wanted to call in the National Guard. "If you see anything at all, call me." As he raced down sidewalks behind buildings, he prayed he would find her. He tried Monty's cell phone. Voice mail. Then he continued to call Sheriff Pritchard to no avail.

Why wouldn't he pick up his phone?

Chapter 14

Poppy's body was being jostled as her captor and soon-to-be killer carried her concealed body.

"You know, Poppy," he said, "I'm not a bad man. I'm really not. I'm in a Santa suit! I'm a family man. I guess you know that was your partner on the phone. He's looking for you. I'm sure he'll be broken up about it when he can't find you. He's a nice guy and good agent. I feel bad for him."

Poppy couldn't ask Brad Teague all the questions she wanted to, like was Savannah in on it with him? Who killed Cora? How deep in was his wife?

"The truth is I had no idea about Cora or what happened that night. All of that went down before I moved to Gray Creek."

Poppy's body jostled and bumped against his back as he toted her in the Santa sack meant to hold gifts for children. Nope, just a dying woman in here.

"Rudy called me about a body in a well and I went out to the scene. When I got home and told Savannah what we'd found, she freaked out and confessed. I knew she'd done some spiteful things in school, but I had no idea she'd plotted to turn Dylan's affections away from your sister. But when she told me she'd dropped her ring down the well when they threw your sister down, I knew I could lose my family—it was Savannah who crushed the pill and put it in Cora's soft drink. I went out there to retrieve it but you were there. Already ruining everything."

He greeted people by name and ho-ho-ho-ed, laughing with citizens as if he weren't hauling a paralyzed woman over his shoulder. Several pillows covered her, rounding out the bag. No one would realize a body was inside. Poppy couldn't even cry—her tear ducts wouldn't work, but she felt the burning sensation of her dry eyes. Blinking was becoming more difficult.

"I was going to kill you, then go back for the ring, but that plan got messed up too," he growled. A door slammed shut. He must be inside the center now. "Man, this suit is hot and you're no lightweight."

It was becoming harder to breathe.

"When I got home that night, with the bad news that the ring was still in the well and you were here to reopen the case, I found Dylan in my front hall, dead. He'd heard the news and wanted to come forward. He wanted all of them to confess. She's a wife and a mother now. No longer that girl. She panicked and hit him. So I had to fix that situation too, but it was worth it because Savannah saved me all those years ago. I had no one after my mom died. I was so lost. Until Savannah found me."

Water ran from a faucet. They must be in a bathroom. The smell of his expensive cologne wafted into the bag. He must be freshening up. Carrying a woman who weighed a good 130 pounds wasn't a cakewalk. The beard she'd felt must have been his Santa beard, and the down of his coat the Santa costume.

"When we pulled up evidence, I saw the ring and pocketed it. I didn't know about a bracelet or I'd have taken that too."

What was Teague's endgame? To use Simms and frame him? Frame Ian? She was going to die without giving her family closure and peace. She'd never have the chance to admit out loud that she was in love with Rhett and probably had been for a long time without allowing herself to realize it. He'd blame himself for losing her, for her death, even though it was no more his fault than Keith's death had been.

She'd made the impulsive decision to follow Simms instead of waiting on Rhett or even calling him for fear he'd tell her to wait, and then Simms would have given her the slip. They'd timed it that way, she suddenly realized. Waited for the mild-mannered, cool-headed agent to leave and then appear before the hotheaded, impulsive agent. Teague knew she'd follow. Wouldn't wait.

"Okay, it's showtime. I hate the way this is going down. I'm not a killer by nature. But you have to go with me into Santa's Village. If I'm not there, your partner will put it together. He's smart. You aren't nearly as bright, but it's the obsession driving you. I knew you'd take the bait when you saw Simms."

Teague was a smart man himself. Inserted himself when needed and backed away at other times. Knew how to play them all.

She was lifted and hauled over his shoulder again.

Voices grew louder, then kids cheered and hollered, "Santa!" while clapping. Teague let out his best Santa laugh, and she had to admit it was the best she'd ever heard. She was lowered to the floor, and he nudged her with his foot. What kind of monster was going to allow kids on his lap while his victim slowly died at his feet?

Breathing was increasingly difficult; only shallow pants came as her lungs began to slowly paralyze. Panic kicked in another round and she couldn't even shiver or shake, though she was more terrified than she'd ever been in her life.

"Well, hello there, Beth!"

"You know my name, Santa?"

Beth! Beth was having her picture made with a killer and would never know that Poppy was in the picture with her—only hidden. At least a piece of Poppy would always be with her. She'd quickly become attached to the sweet lady.

"What do you want for Christmas? What's your wish?" he asked with way more of a jolly attitude than a killer should possess.

"My wish this year isn't for me. Is that okay, Santa?"

"Oh yes. Giving is much better than receiving."

Poppy wanted to puke.

"My wish then is for my new friend Poppy."

Me? Poppy's heart sank. No point wasting her wish on a dead woman, but it deeply touched her that Beth would think of her.

"Oh?" Brad asked, and his boot nudged her again. If she had use of her muscles...

"Yes. I wish she wouldn't be sad anymore, and that she would feel God's hugs. 'Cause He loves her and He wants her to have Christmas joy again."

If Poppy could cry, she'd be a sobbing mess. Well, she could give Beth a last wish too, but not to Santa, who wasn't real. But to God. If she prayed. It had been so long since she really talked to God, trusted Him. She'd been going through the motions for the benefit of loved ones, but not for herself.

And since Cora died, Poppy had no peace. No joy.

Along the way she'd stopped allowing herself to feel God's hugs, because she didn't believe He'd want to hug her anymore, and with every rebellious choice she made she assumed He loved her less and less to go along with the initial disappointment in her for her part in Cora's death.

But Beth was right.

God loved her.

He came because He loved. He died because He loved. And He was coming back because He loved.

But Poppy hadn't loved herself.

God, forgive me. I've wasted so much time believing my own lies. Other people's lies. I'm loved. No matter what I said. What I did. No matter how many times I was jealous of a sister who had a medical problem... I'm loved. By You.

Here in this bag, with her breath leaving her body, silently screaming for oxygen, she felt peace wash over her.

Felt the invisible hug of Jesus Christ warm her heart, which was well on its way to stilling.

The last words she'd hear were those of Beth Cordray. As if God wanted her to hear them now. To know them now. That she wasn't alone in this velvet bag.

God was with her. He knew precisely where she was. He knew exactly what she was going through. And whether she lived or died, He was with her and not abandoning her and He never had.

Cora... I'll see you soon, sis...

Rhett raced toward Santa's Village. He needed backup, and Santa would have to take a break and help him search. Poppy's life was at stake! He pushed through people and spotted Rudy Pritchard. "Hey!" he hollered and waved until he got his attention. Running over, he was ready to punch the guy for not answering his phone. "Never heard of picking up your phone, you jerk?"

Rudy scowled and glanced down.

Rhett noticed a little girl about seven or eight holding Rudy's hand. A little girl with Down syndrome. That explained his kindness and gentleness with Beth the night of the explosion.

"I'll ask you to watch your tone, Agent. I'm off duty and with my daughter."

Blinking, Rhett pulled his frantic self together. "Hello," he said to the little girl, then addressed the sheriff. "I'm sorry. It's Poppy. I found her phone. She's missing. He's got her. Solomon Simms. Teague said Solomon was dangerous and responsible for Cora's death."

Rudy frowned and looked down at his daughter.

"We need to pull Teague off Santa duty."

Rudy knelt in front of his daughter and cradled her face. "I have to go help find a lost lady. Can you stay here with Miss Shelley?"

She nodded and hugged him. Rhett recognized the woman standing with the sheriff from the popcorn stand. Her two kids were grabbing candy at the street's edge. "Hello again."

"Hello," he managed. Poppy was the only thing on his mind and time was running out. They left the crowd and sprinted toward Santa's Village.

"We'll find her," Rudy said.

They entered Santa's Village. On his lap Teague had a little boy in a cowboy hat who didn't seem thrilled to be there. He was squirming while Teague tried to calm him. Rhett caught his eye and waved. The boy slid from Teague's lap and tripped over Santa's sack, opening the mouth.

If Rhett wasn't in a state of panic, he'd have laughed at the ridiculous display as Teague scrambled to close the sack, but something caught Rhett's eye. He stepped forward, then began moving closer to Teague, who glanced up and paused, catching his eye again.

Green the color of Poppy's sweater poked through a pillow's edge in the sack. Rhett turned and hollered, "It's Brad!"

Brad hurdled over the velvet bag and shot out back, Rudy hot on his tail.

Kids cried and parents murmured. Sliding to the floor, Rhett peered into the bag, using discretion to keep the children from being traumatized further. Santa had fled the building.

Poppy lay in a heap, staring at him with wide, lifeless eyes.

No. No. No.

"Clear out! We...we have an emergency with the reindeer. Everybody out!" Adults caught on and rushed their children from the building.

Paramedics arrived, running toward him. Rudy must have radioed them.

With trembling hands, Rhett carefully withdrew Poppy from the red velvet Santa sack and cradled her lifeless body, feeling for a pulse but he couldn't find one. "No, you can't be gone. You can't leave me without a fight or a single snide remark, Poppy Holliday." He laid his forehead against hers, his heart breaking in small pieces. "I love you. I don't care that we're colleagues. Because it wouldn't have ended badly. It wouldn't have ended at all."

He'd been so stupid to hold back out of fear. Now a greater fear had come true. He laid her out to begin compressions. To attempt to revive her. Anything. He'd do anything.

He'd give up structure and order. Take a risk, take a chance. But it was too late.

God, please revive her. Give us another chance.

"Sir, let us through," a paramedic said. Pushing Rhett aside, they knelt and went to work on her.

Moisture filled his eyes as he stared into Poppy's unblinking eyes. "Please, please bring her back. I love that woman. I can't lose her. Please help her."

The woman working on her frowned, then grew wide-eyed. "She's not dead. I've seen this before," she said to the other paramedic. "Rape case two years ago in Oxford. She's not dead—she's paralyzed. I need a line! We're gonna lose her."

Everything happened so fast and in slow motion.

Poppy was alive. Alive!

For now.

Rhett walked into Poppy's hospital room. The doctors had been able to save her and bring her out of paralysis. Rhett had called their unit chief, Colt, and the team. Then he'd called her brother Tack. Poppy's cell phone password had been easy to figure out—Cora's birthday.

Rudy had caught Brad and had him, Solomon Simms, Savannah Steadman-Teague, Natalie Carpenter-Weaverman and Ian Kirkwood in custody. Brad had run, thinking he could get to Savannah and his family and get out of the country.

Savannah had no choice but to admit she'd accidentally killed Cora because Ian and Natalie were now talking and hoping for plea deals.

"You can see her now," a nurse said.

It was after midnight. Officially Christmas. Rhett tiptoed inside and stood at the foot of Poppy's bed. She was pale and asleep. But alive.

Her eyes fluttered open as if she sensed his presence. She took his fingers in her weak hand and squeezed. "Did you get him?"

"We got him," he whispered. "Natalie and Ian said it went down like Solomon Simms told us. Maya was seeing him and she did go to him that night and confess. The death was an accident and they panicked. It was Savannah who came up with the idea to throw Cora down the well, then they made a pact to never speak of it again, but Dylan balked. They finally talked him into it, but it took a toll on him."

"Savannah killed Dylan, and Brad made it look like an accident or suicide—doubtful he cared which. They can spray luminol for blood evidence in Savannah's foyer. He told me what he did. He was going to put me in that well, Rhett."

He kissed her hand. "No one is going to hurt you now, Poppy."

She closed her eyes and nodded. "They're being charged?"

"Savannah for manslaughter and murder in the second degree—for Dylan. She knew what Brad was up to. She admitted to calling him in the hall at the mansion and leaving on purpose to give herself an alibi when he showed up and shoved you down the broken elevator shaft. She was in on the frame-up."

Poppy squeezed her eyes shut. "And the others?"

"Ian and Natalie are being charged as accessories to murder. Brad is being charged for attempted murder and murdering Maya, along with tampering with evidence and anything else the DA can get him on. Zack admitted to lying about Dylan's alibi. He wasn't sure what Dylan had been a part of, but he believed Dylan when he insisted he had nothing to do with Cora's death. And he hadn't." He'd been tortured internally all these years with a horrible secret. "Zack has suspected Natalie and Dylan of an affair over the years, even though they'd denied it the few times he'd asked. It wasn't until after you showed him the photo of the bracelet he knew what had bonded them so tightly—they were keeping each other held together by a thin thread over Cora's murder. But he kept silent to protect Natalie."

"What about Solomon Simms? Is he terminally ill or not?"

"No. He did have cancer and he is in remission. He and Maya still see each other sometimes—even if she was seeing Monty. I guess her confession to him, and the fact he'd taken advantage of her so young, created a twisted bond between them."

"He's still actively growing and distributing marijuana. I heard him say it."

"I think Brad and Savannah wanted to pin every-thing on Simms and get Ian and Natalie to go along with it, which I think they would have. But according to Simms, Brad was pinning the murders on Ian. I believe Brad lied to Simms and had plans to make it look like he killed Cora and had an interest in her. She refused the advances and threatened to tell. But Maya wouldn't go along with that because she still loved Simms. So Teague killed her and told Simms that Ian did it. It worked out nicely for Teague that Ian had shown up for animal meds, really sold it to Simms. He thought he was helping Teague set up Ian Kirkwood, but actually they were setting up Simms. It might have worked too."

"And to think, if it hadn't been for a bratty kid ac-cidentally knocking open the Santa sack..." Poppy's eyes closed and her head rolled to the side, but a smile graced her gorgeous face.

Rhett softly kissed her forehead. They had more to talk about.

Much more.

Once she rested.

"Merry Christmas, Poppy," he whispered.

Chapter 15

Poppy had been released from the hospital a little after noon. This would be another Christmas she'd never forget. The year Santa abducted and tried to murder her. She'd walked into the B&B and been stunned by the full house of people. Her whole family had flown in—Mom, Dad, all of her brothers. Tack had shaken his head and congratulated her for not being careful and watching her back like he'd told her to, but wrapped her up in a big bear hug.

And Rhett's family was there too. He looked like his dad. He was going to age nicely.

Even her cold case unit had flown in from the mountains and the islands. Colt and Georgia. Mae and Cash. She couldn't believe they'd cut their honeymoon short for her, but she was thankful and moved. Poppy had never been hugged and loved on so much in her life, and there was no doubt that God was in every single arm that embraced her.

When she had a moment alone with her parents, she confessed the argument, her jealousies and her shame. She admitted how unloved she'd felt, and for the first time in her life, she saw her military father cry. She hadn't even witnessed it when Cora died—though he surely had shed tears in private.

Her parents had always loved her, but confessed too that although sometimes Poppy and the boys took the backburner, they never loved Cora more, nor did they ever blame Poppy. But in Poppy's own guilt and shame, she'd misinterpreted their grief. Saw what she wanted based on the lies she believed about herself and assumed her parents thought the same.

Delilah had been thrilled to have her home brimming with company, and she had plenty of room for everyone. Mom and Rhett's mother helped Delilah prepare the meal and they'd all eaten together. Family. Togetherness. Everything Christmas should be, but hadn't been in many years.

But even if Poppy had been alone, she wasn't truly alone.

She and Rhett hadn't had a chance to talk in private but it appeared he'd had some kind of reunion with his own family, and his mother had hugged her in a way that made her wonder exactly what Rhett had told her about Poppy.

Needing a minute to breathe—now that she actually could—she'd come upstairs to her room. She retrieved Rhett's gift from under the bed. Beth had loved her presents and had made Poppy a pinecone wreath as a gift, but Beth was Poppy's best Christmas gift. She'd been the bridge back to her faith. It was Poppy who had to cross it, but it might still be burned to ash if not for the precious woman with more wisdom and pure joy than anyone she'd ever met.

A light knock sounded. "Come in."

Rhett opened the door and slipped inside, closing it behind him. "How you feeling?" he asked.

"Better. Overwhelmed. Alive." In so many ways.

"You look amazing. It couldn't have been an easy haul for Teague with you in that sack. I know how heavy you are." He winked and she laughed.

"Rhett the stiff shirt, tossing out jokes."

"I know you know it's stuffed shirt."

"I do." She stood and closed the distance between them. "I know a lot of things." Like the fact he'd told her he loved her when he pulled her from that bag. Would he tell her again? Strange how it took her being forced to be still to listen, and what she heard in those moments was the best thing she'd ever heard.

"I know you do." He sighed. "I got you something." He handed her a wrapped present from behind his back. "Open it."

She grinned and ripped off the paper and held up a T-shirt that read I Do What I Want. I Say What I Want. Get over It. Laughing, she held it up to her.

"It felt appropriate at the time I saw it."

"I made some bad decisions doing what I want. I'm sorry for not calling you first. For not taking the measured steps you tried to drill into me." She loved the shirt but… "I'm not sure I'm this person anymore." She grabbed his gift from the bed. "I got you something too."

He cocked his head with a skeptical expression, but

opened the wooden sign that said he was silently correcting her grammar. She'd marked out "Grammar" and written *"Idioms"* in a permanent marker. Rhett laughed and shook his head. "So true." He studied the plaque then looked at Poppy. "After Keith died, I was afraid to take chances—any chance that might have a negative consequence. Got into a routine. I'm not sure I'm this man anymore." He held up the plaque.

"What do we do about that?" Poppy asked.

He laid the present on the edge of the bed and framed her face. "I love you, Poppy. I think I have for a really long time. And I know you know this because the doctor told me you were paralyzed but in full control of your faculties." He grinned.

"I do. And it gave me hope and a reason to fight to live. Because I love you too, and I think I have for a really long time."

He brushed his thumb across her cheek. "Good. 'Cause I plan to be here for the long haul." He drew her into his arms. She loved this place best. Against him, warm and secure.

"If you make a joke about how much I weigh—"

He cut her off with a kiss that proved every word he said and sealed it with a promise for forever. Partnership in every way.

"Merry Christmas," he whispered against her lips. "I'll get you a much more elaborate gift next Christmas."

Poppy pecked his lips. "If you're referring to a ring, Valentine's is coming up sooner."

He laughed. "I think you could still wear the shirt and get away with it." He kissed her again and trailed his lips along her jaw to her ear. "But I agree about Valentine's," he breathed.

Poppy hadn't been this happy, this full of joy and faith in a long time.

She glanced up and knew Cora would be happy for her.

* * * * *